Praise for

NIGHT OF THE BEAR

"A stimulating and captivating read, gently seasoned with the fault lines of military and political egos."

—Major General Harold A. Cross, retired USAF

"This book passes the author test—you can't wait to read the next page, the next chapter. These two authors, both with backgrounds as fighter pilots, understand aviation, military affairs, national security, espionage, and the current international political setting. When you pick up *Night of the Bear*, you will want to keep reading until the last sentence."

—Major General Don Shepperd, retired USAF, former CNN military analyst and coauthor of *Bury Us Upside Down: The Misty Pilots and the Secret Battle for the Ho Chi Minh Trail*

"These two authors really nailed it with the central character in this novel. The story grabbed me within the first ten pages, and I could hardly set it down."

—Bob Holliker, former USAF T-38 instructor pilot and creator of the YouTube channel *Three's In*

"This book makes you wonder what really goes on behind the scenes in our government. I loved the cat-and-mouse scenarios between the Bears, F-15s, and Russian fighter crews."

—Master Sergeant Johnny Gressett, retired USAF, author of *Tumbletite: The Misadventures of a Mississippi Flyboy*

"With their large literary gifts, these two aviation wizards have constructed a clockwork plot that is intricate, fast-moving, lucid, and stuffed with accurate second-by-second portrayals of war-fighting air crews and military aircraft in action. The writing is crisp. The tension is electric. This is a fantastic book and a great read!"

—Richard Scott Sacks, author of *Drinking from the Stream*

"Wow! Well written and so true to life. *Night of the Bear* is one of many plausible WWIII scenarios our enemy could easily conjure up to take down the United States of America. Cockrell and Hess introduce their readers to one of those scenarios. You'll be riveted throughout as you discover how the plan unfolds and whether it will be accomplished. Though fiction, this story could always become reality!"

—Tod Gohl, USAF Desert Storm veteran and author of *Saving America's Citizens*

"If you like military-themed thrillers, then this book is for you. Fast-paced and hard to put down, *Night of the Bear* is a suspenseful page-turner with an overwhelming sense of authenticity thanks to the decades of experience both authors have flying frontline combat aircraft. Ride along as you learn about the world of military technology and the people who man it."

—Bob Lutz, former Marine Corps fighter pilot and retired Vice-Chairman of General Motors

"Hold on tight. *Night of the Bear* takes you on a tense, wild ride through international terrorism, political skulduggery, and gripping scenes of realistic air combat, with themes and events seemingly plucked right out of today's news."

—Buck Wyndham, author of *Hogs in the Sand*

Night of the Bear
by Alan Cockrell and Richard Hess

© Copyright 2025 Alan Cockrell and Richard Hess

ISBN 979-8-88824-628-3

All rights reserved. No part of this publication may be reproduced, stored in a retrieval system, or transmitted in any form or by any means—electronic, mechanical, photocopy, recording, or any other—except for brief quotations in printed reviews, without the prior written permission of the author.

This is a work of fiction. All the characters in this book are fictitious, and any resemblance to actual persons, living or dead, is purely coincidental. The names, incidents, dialogue, and opinions expressed are products of the author's imagination and are not to be construed as real.

Published by

◀ köehlerbooks™

3705 Shore Drive
Virginia Beach, VA 23455
800-435-4811
www.koehlerbooks.com

NIGHT
OF THE
BEAR

ALAN COCKRELL AND **RICHARD HESS**

VIRGINIA BEACH
CAPE CHARLES

In memory of Captain David DeRamus
Brother, Friend, Visionary, Inspirer
And a talented virtuoso at the controls of an F-106

CHAPTER ONE

LABOR DAY
LONG ISLAND SOUND

"Ilya, are you sure you told him the correct location and he knows the name of the boat?" asked Viktor Darginsky as he scanned the crowded waterway with binoculars.

"Patience, comrade," replied the other Russian agent. "He knows it's the *Natasha*, and I told him we'd be anchored just south of Plum Island. He'll be along presently. Why don't you make like Americans and 'soak up a few rays'? It'll be your last chance before winter, you know. Wait! I bet that's Lucifer coming there."

"You mean in that big cruiser?"

"No, there to the left, in the blue speed boat."

Darginsky trained the binoculars on the approaching vessel. He immediately recognized the three Code Y agents. Alexei was driving the boat and Mikhail was looking back at him with his own binoculars. The figure lounging in the back of the boat was Lucifer. "That's them. Let's get the ladder down and the anchor up. I think we're better off staying on the move."

In a matter of minutes, the *Natasha* was underway, cruising slowly toward Gardiners Island with the speedboat in tow. When they'd reached the island, the Code Y agents boarded the *Natasha*, and the five men greeted each other. After fifteen minutes of light conversation, Darginsky suggested that he and Lucifer, the man's classified name, go below where they could talk privately.

"It's been a long time," Darginsky said, smiling at his protégé across the mahogany table. "I must say I'm impressed with your accomplishments."

"I hope when you read our plan, you'll call us geniuses."

Darginsky studied his agent's face. "You said it was a plan for victory?"

"Yes, Viktor. We have a short window of opportunity to achieve total victory over the United States with only four rather small nuclear weapons and one air-to-air missile. But we must hurry. We have less than five months to get it set up."

"That sounds awfully ambitious," said Darginsky, showing his doubts. "How much damage does our side sustain?"

"None."

"And when those four weapons go off, why are we not obliterated by a return strike?"

"Because, Victor, how do you know who to swing at when you don't know who sucker-punched you?"

Darginsky's respect for his most important agent in America was total. If Lucifer said it could be done, more than likely it could be. He would read the plan, but he still had his doubts.

"What's required to deliver these weapons?"

"Two manned bombers, carrying two cruise missiles each, and a single fighter."

"And with so small a force, we will totally conquer the mightiest military on the planet?"

"Totally."

Darginsky noted his agent's grinning expression. "I assume you brought a copy of the plan with you."

"Certainly." He laid a leather-bound book on the table. "That's why I requested this face-to-face meeting. It's too important to risk using the usual channels."

Darginsky noticed that Lucifer had been carrying the Holy Bible when he boarded the *Natasha*, but he just assumed it was part of the agent's undercover identity. "I'm sorry, I don't—"

The agent laughed out loud. "Like many Americans, I carry a

Bible all the time, so having it wouldn't arouse any suspicions. The plan is embedded in the Book of Revelations, the last book of the Bible. Fittingly, that's where you can read about Armageddon."

"I'll read your plan. And if I think it's worth it, I'll do my best to get it to our esteemed leader. I assume the plan has a name?"

"Of course," he responded, his blue eyes alight with amusement. "It's called 'LUCIFER/INBLUE.'"

"Hmm," Darginsky murmured, pondering the ominous sound of the operation's name. "It may take a while, so be patient. As you know, our leader has some problems at home and—"

"Viktor!" Lucifer interrupted. "We don't have a while. This opportunity might not come around again. They're politically weak. Trust me on this."

Darginsky studied Lucifer's astonishingly blue eyes. "I don't have to trust you on that score, Chatman, I know," said Darginsky, using the man's real name and rising to follow him topside. "It's my job to watch them."

Chatman offered his hand in farewell to his mentor. "I know all about our leader's troubles, and all the shit he's gotten us into. But he has a way out now, and I'm confident he'll see it that way."

"Bobby, you know he is unpredictable. I must be one hundred percent sure of this plan or it could cost me my career—or worse. I cannot promise you I will risk it. But I'll read it, and I'll call you if I have questions."

Chatman smiled. "I know you will. We'll be standing by. God be with you, Brother Gabriel."

"And with you, Brother Lucifer," replied Darginsky, sharing in the humor.

The *Natasha* slowed to a stop to allow the three agents to reboard their speedboat. Just before Alex gunned their vessel away, Darginsky's curiosity got the best of him. "Say, Brother Chatman, you said two bombers and a fighter. I assume we're talking supersonic Backfire or Blackjack bombers?"

"No, Viktor. Two Tu-95 bombers, H-models. NATO calls it the Bear. You'll understand when you read the plan. Your boys can decide which fighter, but I would suggest the new two-seat Su-57. Read the plan. You'll understand why I recommend using these aircraft."

With a roar the speedboat was gone.

"Ilya, how long has the Tu-95 bomber been around?" asked Darginsky.

Ilya laughed as he eased the *Natasha*'s throttles forward. "Oh, about seventy years!"

"Take it slow back to Glen Cove," said Darginsky as he watched the other boat disappear. "I have some reading to do."

SEPTEMBER 11
BARNES AIR NATIONAL GUARD BASE
WESTFIELD, MASSACHUSETTS

"Last Chance Inspection"—an ominous-sounding term. Technicians at the end of the runway checked for leaks and tire condition. The pilots kept their hands in sight as technicians worked underneath the jets. It wasn't unusual to be sent back to the ramp from Last Chance for repairs. But it was the last thing Captain Mark "Suds" Matthews wanted. He had a score to settle and today his F-15 Eagle was the weapon of choice.

Matthews was number four in Shark 20, a flight of four Eagles. After takeoff they would split into two-ship elements. The mission called for a simulated point defense against high-speed bombers. After the intercept exercise would come the good stuff: "2v2" air combat training engagements, an old-fashioned dogfight with jets that could accelerate vertically and weapons that could kill from beyond visual range.

Matthews was flying with his best friend, Captain Tom Rushton, the squadron's Top Gun. The other two-ship element was led by Major Richard Robertson, a last-minute change. Matthews smiled, thinking of Robertson being dragged, bitching and moaning, from his desk.

Robertson had transferred in from a nearby C-130 unit. It was unusual for a cargo pilot to transition to fighters, but Robertson had pulled the right strings, and now he had wangled a full-time position as well. He was a marginal performer, in Matthews's opinion, and to make matters worse, Robertson wrote his annual performance evaluations. He'd already given Matthews a downgraded evaluation for Professional Qualities. The downgrade virtually assured that Matthews would be passed over for major.

All four jets cleared Last Chance, entered the runway, and stopped in the classic fingertip formation. Then came the transmission from the tower that Mark Matthews lived for. "Shark two-zero flight, the wind is one-one-zero at five, change to departure frequency, cleared for takeoff."

Robertson gave the visual signal for the engine run-up. "Shark two-zero is cleared to go, two-zero flight, channel four, go."

Each pilot responded in quick sequence.

"Two!"

"Three."

"Four."

Matthews set the power at 80 percent, scanned the gauges of the two giant fan-jets, and swished the stick, checking that the flight controls were free and clear. Robertson and his wingman lit their afterburners and released brakes together. Fifteen seconds later Rushton raised his head, paused, then dropped his chin to signal brake release. Each pilot selected afterburner and the two Eagles surged ahead. At 120 knots, they rotated to the takeoff attitude. Half a minute later they were passing a thousand feet, accelerating through 250 knots, with the gear and flaps up.

Soon all four aircraft were formed up and accelerating toward the warning area off the coast of Portsmouth, New Hampshire.

After the comparatively routine intercept drills were finished, Matthews's adrenaline surged as they set up for the dogfight. "Shark two-zero flight," called Chamber Control, the military controller. "You have targets northeast for fifty-two miles. Two bogies, line abreast, two-mile split, estimate medium altitude."

This, mused Matthews, *is what it's all about.*

"Push it up," said Rushton, as he pointed Matthews out to a tactical spread and rolled out on a heading pointing directly at their simulated enemy.

Inside of two minutes Matthews caught sight of both bandits. Simulating a radar missile shot, he called out, "Fox-1 on the eastern F-15."

The other F-15 was dead ahead for four miles. There'd just be time for a heat-seeker shot. He commanded the missile to "look" straight ahead. The computer immediately generated a circle on his heads-up display which showed the field of view of the infrared seeker head. He heard the tone in his headset, quickly punched the track mode, and thumbed the pickle button. "Fox-2 on the F-15 headed east!"

"Chamber Control, we can knock it off and take another setup," called Robertson, sounding frustrated.

They all stopped maneuvering and set up for another engagement. For the second engagement they would meet Robertson's flight head-on again, but this time they would go vertical, confident Robertson didn't have the savvy to counter with his own vertical maneuver.

Sighting Robertson and his wingman, Rushton and Matthews surged into the vertical, then rolled inverted. They now had a panoramic view of the world in the tops of their canopies with their adversaries far below.

"Fox-1 on the F-15 heading zero-four-five," said Rushton. "Closing to guns." From his vantage point above, Rushton had a perfect setup to slice down to Robertson's wingman's exposed six o'clock position.

"GUNS, GUNS, GUNS on the F-15 in the hard left turn passing heading three-four-zero," said Rushton as he simulated hosing Robertson's inexperienced wingman. "I'm off-target high and to the right. The leader's all yours, Suds."

Matthews rolled his Eagle to the outside of Robertson's turn, dissipating some of his energy, stabilizing a mile back. With "Guns" selected, his radar quickly achieved a lock-on.

Robertson was making the rookie mistake of hard-turning left and right, each reversal allowing Matthews to get a little closer, but he was careful not to get inside the five-hundred-foot minimum range restriction.

"GUNS, GUNS, GUNS on the F-15 passing heading zero-nine-zero!" He then pulled up hard, rolling up and over Robertson.

The debriefing went as Matthews expected. Robertson had an excuse for everything. Their gun camera film verified all the kills, including the last pass with the aiming pipper centered on Robertson's helmet.

"I'm thinking about reporting you to the commander for that last pass," said Robertson tersely. "You were inside minimum range."

"Now, Major," replied Rushton in his cool Texas drawl, "you can see the range marker on the pipper. It clearly shows Captain Matthews was at exactly five hundred feet when he took the shot."

Robertson glared at Matthews then barked, "Captain Matthews, you need to grow up," as he stormed out of the briefing room. Matthews hated the condescending way that Robertson avoided using his call sign.

Shortly after Matthews joined the squadron, a Friday afternoon beer call was announced. All the pilots mustered around a three-foot-long glass tube with a ball-shaped bottom. One of the flight commanders filled the vessel with cheap beer, then passed it around, refilling it after each attempt, the objective being to down the "yard of beer" in one breathless swallow. Matthews, being a new guy, wanted to establish his turf. He upended it and gulped until his face turned red, his peers urging him on as he raised the glass higher. With only inches of beer remaining, the golden liquid rushed from the ball-shaped bottom to his waiting lips and exploded all over his face, covering his upper body in froth. His squadron mates let out thunderous howls. A call sign ceremony was held, and "Suds" walked out that night carrying a name that would go proudly with him for the rest of his career.

Matthews remembered that Major Robertson didn't participate in the call sign ceremony.

Rushton walked with Matthews to the parking lot. "Suds, you're one of the best sticks in the squadron . . . right behind me." He grinned. "But you've got to play the game. Give Robertson whatever he wants. Being passed over is not worth it. You'll never see that pension."

"Screw the pension," mumbled Matthews.

With a resigned look, Rushton nodded. "Okay, knucklehead. Have it your way."

Matthews sat at the squadron picnic table and watched Rushton leave. After a few minutes of brooding, he pulled out his phone and tapped her picture.

"Agent McCormick here."

He held his nose to disguise his voice. "Miss McCormick? Please hold for the world's greatest fighter pilot."

He heard a sigh. "The world's greatest? Hmm. I don't understand. My phone says it's Mark Matthews calling."

"Oh, you just flamed me. Got a minute?"

"Surely I can spare a minute for the greatest."

"I just got out of a briefing with Robertson."

"Oh no."

"Yeah. This creep's getting to me, Dare. I swear he's going to give me another downgraded performance report. This asshole won't rest until I'm passed over for major." He let out a heavy sigh. "I gotta get out of here for a while."

"Like where?"

"I'll volunteer for alert pad duty down at Eglin Air Force Base in Florida. Tom wants to go too. Maybe you can come down. The rotation is twenty-four hours on, twenty-four off. We can log some beach time."

"I don't know. Since they moved me into counterterrorism, I've gotten insanely busy."

"What's going on?"

He had been dating her for a few months and had become accustomed to enduring her silence before answering questions related to her job. Finally, she replied. "Come down here Friday and we'll go to the Crab Cab. It's my turn to buy. But don't expect me to tell you anything."

"I'll take that deal! See you then."

CHAPTER TWO

**SEPTEMBER 15
THE KREMLIN
MOSCOW, RUSSIA**

American Affairs Division Chief Viktor Darginsky, SVR, stepped into the lobby outside the office of the president of the Russian Federation. The two guards who escorted him up from the Kremlin's entrance nodded toward the attractive receptionist and left. The woman asked him to sit and offered tea. He politely refused.

Before sitting he stepped to a mirror and straightened his uniform. The forceful searching of his person by the guards bordered on brutality—a symptom of the callous morass his country had sunk into. But then, Viktor himself had come up through the merciless Foreign Intelligence Service, or SVR, ranks. He had no grounds to grumble.

He fidgeted—an alien emotional state for the seasoned agent. He reflected on his years of service with the KGB, the Soviet Union's primary security agency, and its successor, the SVR. He had been a fair and evenhanded man, he thought, and a ruthless one when the situation called for harshness, in the interest of the Motherland, of course. He had no regrets, but his past haunted him. Whatever his former punitive excesses were, they paled in comparison with the man he was about to visit.

It wasn't their first meeting. He remembered past meetings with Kozlov, always in a group. Kozlov, a former KGB operative himself, had risen to become the leader of the Russian Federation. A difficult man to read, poker-faced and intimidating, Kozlov made it risky to counter him with a different idea.

What Darginsky was about to do was possibly the biggest risk of his career, the success or failure of which might largely depend on the man's mood. Darginsky's friends in the Kremlin told him about the president's mood changes, which had become more frequent in recent months.

As he waited, he pondered Kozlov's mounting problems. News coming in from the wars Kozlov had started were increasingly pessimistic. The nation's military resources were dangerously low. Even his allies, North Korea, Iran, and China, had gotten stingy with their arms support. Compounding Kozlov's problem, his conscription order had caused open protests among a population that was already disgruntled with the harsh economic sanctions imposed on them because of the wars. And then there were the mysterious deaths of certain political opponents. Darginsky wondered if a Stalinist-style purge was in the offing.

No doubt Nikolai Kozlov was in trouble. His impending downfall, Darginsky figured, could result in one of two unacceptable outcomes. The most probable successors to Kozlov were not men Darginsky wanted to see in control of the country. They would be no better, possibly worse, and would be the beginning of yet another long run of dreadful leadership that pinned the Russian people to their hopeless past.

The other possible outcome was even worse. A cornered and hopeless Kozlov might start World War III. Indeed, he had recently told an interviewer that if Russia went down, why should he care about the rest of the world? Darginsky tried unsuccessfully to relax before meeting with the man who could end the human race in one single fit of rage.

In his briefcase Darginsky hoped he had a way out for the president—a third option. His challenge was to get Kozlov to see the plan's potential, the salvation of himself and Russia, and the sheer ingenuity of what the agent Lucifer, who was not a military man, had presented to him on the boat in New York.

The receptionist glanced at her clock and picked up her phone. "Sir, Colonel Darginsky is here . . . Darginsky . . . of the SVR. He is on the day's schedule." With a look of exasperation, she got up and opened the door to the president's office. Darginsky stepped in behind her but saw no one in the room. As he followed her to a side door, she told him with a sardonic smirk, "You're in luck, Colonel. He is in one of his better moods this morning." When she pulled the side door open, he heard the pounding of feet and heavy grunting. She motioned him in and closed the door, leaving him alone with a treadmill-pounding, profusely sweating, heavily breathing Nikolai Kozlov.

The racket of the pounding feet caused Darginsky to momentarily lose his train of thought. The room was dim, save for a red light directly over his head. He strained to make out the figure pounding the treadmill in front of him.

"What do you want?"

The question was so terse Darginsky wanted to turn and leave. "I have a plan to eliminate the American threat to our Motherland."

"Get out!" Kozlov yelled without looking at him. "Do you know how many fucking idiots come in here with a cockeyed plan to start World War III?"

Darginsky had practiced a rational spiel that should have worked well in the comfort of a conference room. But what he had walked into called for a different approach—a risky one. He took a deep breath. "Lucifer sent me."

Kozlov abruptly stopped the treadmill and leaned into the handlebars. He stared aside at Darginsky. "The TV preacher?"

"Yes, sir."

"What has he ever done for us?"

"Sir, he has devoted his entire career to getting the ear of the president of the United States, and he has done it."

Kozlov became visibly impatient. "And how does that help me?"

"Mr. President, he has developed an ingenious plan to defeat the US with just four nuclear-tipped cruise missiles, launched," he paused for effect, "from within the US's own borders. They won't even see them coming."

Kozlov continued to lean on the treadmill's handlebars, catching his breath. He eyed Darginsky menacingly. "We shoot four and they retaliate with a thousand? You talk nonsense. Your preacher man is a moron."

Darginsky pulled the plan out of his briefcase. "Sir . . . please read it. You'll see why they will not retaliate." He smiled.

Kozlov stepped off the treadmill and took the package, staring at the title, LUCIFER/INBLUE. He looked up at Darginsky. "If this wastes my time, I'll have you shot."

Darginsky felt the threat was not an empty one. He tried to smile again. "Sir, this plan will be the salvation of Russia—and of your administration."

SEPTEMBER 16
OLATHE, KANSAS

As Keith Anderson made his way along the slick, rainy highway from the Center to his home, he brooded about how lonely he was. There was no one to go home to except his beloved dog, Lucy. He'd hoped the transfer to the FAA's Kansas City Air Route Traffic Control Center would have marked a new beginning in his life, but so far, that hadn't materialized.

As he entered his second year with the FAA, he felt like a man who had the world by the tail. At only twenty-six years old, he was a fully qualified air traffic controller with a reputation for being among the best.

An hour later, with his Scottish terrier full of Purina and resting her head at his feet, he opened his laptop. "Okay, Lucy, let's look into KC CONNEXIONS."

Keith had heard good things about the local social media platform, one that men often used to meet other men. It had been difficult meeting people since he'd moved to the area, and he was intrigued. He went to the website and clicked on the "Sign Up" page.

Keith found meeting people online to be impersonal, but it beat the cliquish atmosphere of the Kansas City bar scene.

"What do you think, Lucy, should we make a profile of our own tonight?" The dog licked her front paws once then closed her eyes. "I agree. I think we should." He uploaded a few photos of himself, and then began typing his bio, under a pseudonym, which was common for the platform.

> Hi everybody. I'm new to the KC area and hoping to make some new friends. I'm a white male, age 26, 5'10", and 145 pounds. I have black hair and brown eyes. I'm an air traffic controller. My interests, outside of my job, include good books, good music, and good movies. I enjoy an occasional night out, but I prefer quiet evenings at home. I'd like to meet other men with similar interests—I'm open to both friendship and more serious romantic relationships. DM me!
>
> Scope Dope

OCTOBER 1
THE PRESIDENTIAL RANCH OUTSIDE OF MOSCOW

"Your papers?"

"Here they are," answered the limo driver.

The voices woke up Viktor Darginsky, slumping in the back seat. He rubbed his eyes and watched the driver present his pass to the gate guard. The last few days had taken a toll on him, and now he grabbed every chance he got to rest. The guard motioned the car through.

They passed a massive log cabin dacha. Darginsky marveled at the impressive lodge. He watched it slide by and wondered where he was being taken. Soon a horse stable came into view and the limo stopped.

"This is where they told me to take you, sir," the driver said.

"Very well," responded Darginsky. "I don't know how long I'll be." He gathered his briefcase and overcoat and got out.

A man greeted Darginsky and escorted him to a paddock. "Do you ride, comrade?" the assistant asked.

Darginsky answered while a security guard searched him for weapons. "It's been a while." He looked at the man. "Am I about to ride now?"

The aide laughed. "Don't worry. The president selected a nice gentle Tennessee walker for you."

"Lovely," lamented an unenthusiastic Darginsky.

The aide assisted Darginsky in mounting up and offered to take the briefcase, which Darginsky refused. The aide then found a lanyard and attached the case to the back of the saddle. He led the horse by the reins to the gate. "There he is now," the aide remarked. "I'll leave you with him. Good luck, comrade."

In the distance Darginsky saw a galloping horse coming toward him, turf flying behind the beating hooves. He noticed heavily armed riders with the president, on both sides and bringing up the rear. A couple of them were carrying shoulder-launched antiaircraft missiles. Nikolai Kozlov reined up beside Darginsky, his muscular Belgian stallion's gaping nostrils blowing fog into the crisp air.

"Do you like horses, Comrade Darginsky?" asked the smiling Russian leader.

"I'm not used to them, sir. But I will do my best."

Kozlov gestured to Darginsky's mount. "You will like that girl." They trotted together for some minutes before Kozlov spoke. "I've been reading the packet you left me. I have some questions."

"Certainly," Darginsky responded, a bit on edge at Kozlov's sober manner. Then Kozlov smiled.

"Have you discovered, as the new American president claimed, that Satan is living in our embassy building in Washington?" Kozlov asked, laughing.

Might there be a human inside the president after all? Darginsky wondered.

"No," he answered. "Satan lives in North Carolina."

"Tell me about him."

Darginsky quickly gathered his thoughts. "Our Code Y agents operate in the deepest of cover in foreign nations—"

"Dammit, man! I know what a Code Y agent is. I want to know about this man. I want to know if he can be trusted. Tell me his background."

Darginsky nervously swallowed. "His Russian name was Leonid Ivanovich Chetverikov. He was three years old when his mother died from pneumonia. The elder Chetverikov was a career officer and doctor in the Russian Army and spent a lot of time deployed.

"Leonid was a smart child who joined the Young Pioneers at age eight. He worshipped his father, according to his file. Consequently, the news of his father's death in Afghanistan was a tremendous blow. An American Stinger missile fired by a mujahideen rebel struck the medivac helicopter he was in. That kindled in the boy a burning hatred for America that only got worse. Chetverikov's brother, his only sibling, was killed in Syria by an American A-10. You might say his hatred for the Americans doubled.

"He became an expert at writing and speaking English. During a Komsomol summer camp paramilitary exercise that involved a mock interrogation, a visiting SVR officer noticed how convincing Chetverikov was while playing the role of the American CIA agent conducting the interrogation. After learning of his desire to serve his country in some capacity that would allow him to avenge his father's and brother's deaths, the SVR officer recommended Chetverikov for consideration as a Code Y agent."

Darginsky paused as they entered a long narrow horse path lined with evergreens. Kozlov glanced at him expectantly.

Darginsky continued. "The young man soon became known among his peers for his total dedication to the triumph of Russia over America. He became a student in everything American. His personnel files are overflowing with praise. Words like 'excellent candidate,' 'highly motivated,' and 'quick learner.' When his training was over, they gave him the name 'Boris Chatoff,' the real Boris Chatoff having been killed in a military training accident. They gave him a fake family and infiltrated him into the US."

Darginsky paused again to organize his thoughts. Much of the information was in the LUCIFER/INBLUE packet, but apparently Kozlov had not read it thoroughly.

"With the assistance of our people the family immigrated to America, but after two years, according to the plan, the family announced they wanted to return to Russia." He glanced at Kozlov, who seemed fascinated. "Now here's the ingenious part. The boy became enamored with religion and refused to leave with his fake parents and family. He fought to remain behind in America to practice his newfound religion. Honestly, sir, I don't think this could have turned out better if we had planned it."

Kozlov halted his horse. "What do you mean?"

"It was before I was assigned to my present post, but I know the expectation was that he would use his engineering degree to work his way into sensitive American military research. But he had a different idea. Religious organizations and leaders in America joined in his fight to stay in America, and Chatoff prevailed. The whole damn plan was so ingenious. He brushed the engineering degree aside and went to divinity school and—"

"What?" Kozlov interrupted.

"Where they train religious men. Preachers, priests, and such."

Kozlov nodded and started his horse back up the trail, increasing the pace to a trot.

"We were concerned," Darginsky continued in an unsteady voice, his butt hammering against the saddle, "that he would abandon his mission and pursue a bona fide career in religion. But he stayed loyal to us, and we watched as he worked his way into the Washington inner circle, where he knew he could do more good for Russia than in an American aircraft or missile factory. Along the way he changed his name to one that sounded more American, earned his pilot license, and even became qualified in small business jets. And, the 'icing on the cake' as the Americans say, he made a fortune raising money from the American faithful to support his ministry." He grinned at Kozlov. "He pays his own way. Doesn't cost us anything!"

"Hmph. We'll see just how valuable your preacher really is—because I haven't seen anything yet," Kozlov grunted as they cantered along the path.

"Sir, he has used his charisma to work his way right into the White House. I am amazed. A man with the intellect and intuition to achieve *that* is a man to be trusted."

The president had heard enough. He halted and faced Darginsky. "How many people know about this plan?"

"Comrade President, on this side of the Atlantic, only you. In our office in the New York consulate, two of my analysts helped me evaluate the plan. Finally, there is the agent Lucifer and two individuals whose names are Alexei Marecek and Mikhail Gerchick. They are the other Code Y agents who work with Lucifer in the US. No one else knows."

"Let's keep it that way for now," ordered Kozlov as he spurred his horse. "Did Lucifer create this plan himself?"

"Sir, as much as I wish I could take credit for such an ingenious plan, I must admit that Lucifer and his associates created it. He's an extremely intelligent individual. And our two friends working with him are tops in their respective fields. They are also licensed pilots—Marecek flew with Russian Naval Aviation—and they both regularly fly his personal jet around the United States carrying out the business of his religious empire. So, they understand how the airspace system of the United States operates. They have no doubt that once our aircraft are inside US airspace, they can go wherever they like."

"How can that be?" Kozlov asked. "Won't they be able to detect our aircraft coming in from the south?"

"An excellent question, sir. The radar they use is concentrated over the land portions of their border with Mexico. Their air defense radars are the same air traffic control radars that are optimized for high-flying commercial aircraft. They do have some capability to search over the Gulf of Mexico, but their ability to see aircraft low over the water is limited. Plus, they've assumed for decades an attack would never come from the south, so they're not looking for us. About the only things that try to sneak in over the Gulf of Mexico are drug-running aircraft, but most of that illegal product arrives by ship or airline cargo these days.

"Besides, as you know," Darginsky added, "our Bear bombers operating out of Cuba on electronic intelligence missions have verified that US capability to detect intruder aircraft along its southern coasts is marginal."

"So, you're confident the technical side of LUCIFER/INBLUE is feasible?" asked Kozlov. "Even the part that calls for refueling our Su-57 on the ground in the US?"

"Absolutely, sir. The technical side of the plan will be the easy part. We can get the planes in, get them to their targets, and get them out, undetected. The tricky part is convincing the American people they've been the victims of another mass terrorist attack, and that we had nothing to do with the nuclear destruction of their nation's capital and three other cities, which also eliminates all upper-level command and control of their strategic weapons. It's critical that we maintain the deception during the several days of confusion that will certainly follow."

Kozlov rode along silently.

"Once we have successfully moved our Kh-102s to Cuba and Venezuela and have parked all of our missile-carrying submarines off their coasts, we can use the agent Lucifer, and some of our friends in the US media, to convince American citizens that they'll have no choice but to submit, and they will have no high-level authority to tell them otherwise."

"I am convinced of the feasibility of that part of the plan," Kozlov said. "The Americans are fools. They believe anything their Facebook and Twitter tells them. Now tell me more about this plan to involve the fucking Chechens."

"Sir, you are aware that we experimentally built some very small nuclear weapons in the 1970s, ones that could be carried in a backpack?"

Kozlov reined in his horse. "Do you think I'm an idiot? Of course I know this."

"Sorry, sir, just reminding you. We still have them, although we're not sure they would detonate after so long a time in storage. I am not a nuclear expert, but I think they're museum pieces more than anything."

Kozlov nodded. "So, in the lead-up to the attack, we tell the Americans the Chechens have stolen the backpack bombs and sold them to terrorists?"

"Yes, sir. We even give them photographs so they know what to look for."

"Make sure the story is that they stole them when that idiot Yeltsin was running the country, understand?"

"Absolutely, sir."

"So, which terrorists?"

"The Houthis in Yemen. They have vowed to attack the United States. They fall right into our plan. We launch a disinformation campaign alleging the Houthis moved the bombs through Iran and are planning to smuggle them into the US. The American Navy is stretched so thin it will be very believable."

Kozlov reined back his horse again. "I want to make something absolutely clear. Those devices are not to leave our inventory."

"They will not, sir."

"Now, what if our deception fails, could we still back out of LUCIFER?"

"Yes, sir. You can back out at any point up to the launch of the first cruise missile."

"All right. You say you are ready to execute the false-flag story about the missing bombs?"

Darginsky smiled. "Yes, sir. Meanwhile, Lucifer is ready to start setting up the operation in America."

"Why Tu-95 bombers? We have newer aircraft."

Darginsky knew that question was answered in the mission package. He wondered again if Kozlov hadn't thoroughly read it. "Range is the primary consideration," replied Darginsky, "but, the Americans are accustomed to seeing Tu-95s all over the world. Two Bears in Venezuela might raise an eyebrow, but two Tu-160s would set off an alarm. President Phillips is weak, but he will not be able to ignore his generals if they start making a fuss over supersonic Russian bombers operating nearby, sir."

Darginsky glanced at Kozlov, hoping to receive some sort of look of understanding. When he didn't, he continued. "The planned target date is January 31, and the optimum time over target for the weapon is between 2030 and 2230, Eastern Standard Time. At that time the president of the United States will be delivering his annual State of the Union message to the assembled members of his government."

Kozlov suddenly reared his horse. "The stolen bomb story is approved. Report to me when it is successfully delivered to the Americans. I will advise you of my intentions for the rest of the operation at that time." He spurred the stallion and left Darginsky sitting on his horse, completely puzzled over the president's abrupt departure. Obviously, there would be no invitation to warm up in front of the fireplace in the presidential dacha.

CHAPTER THREE

OCTOBER 8
WASHINGTON, DC

It was midmorning on a cold, cloudy day. Reverend Bobby Chatman sat in the traffic jam that never abated around Ronald Reagan Washington National Airport. It was the closest airport to the White House, which was his destination.

Ever since the swearing in of his friend, and brother in the faith, Andrew Phillips, Chatman had been spending a lot of time here as an adviser to the new president. Chatman had to land at Reagan Airport and deal with well-wishers in the lobby who recognized him from his *Free World Gospel Hour* television program. Then came the dreaded fight through traffic.

As they inched along, he pondered his rise in the preposterous scheme of American politics. Despite his notoriety, Bobby Chatman lived a very private personal life, and he liked it that way. He lived on a farm in the North Carolina foothills and regularly flew the Cessna Citation jet that the ministry owned from his private airstrip in North Carolina to a second country home in southern Mississippi, then to his ranch in Kansas. However, the Citation was usually flown by Alex Marsh or Michael Gerson, who each served as a combination pilot, chauffeur, and bodyguard.

Chatman's popularity had attracted politicians who wanted his endorsement, which led him to the three-term Kansas senator Andrew Phillips. The senator prevailed in the presidential primaries and faced the former vice president, James Bailey. Phillips edged Bailey by a slim margin and was sworn in with Bobby Chatman delivering a stirring inaugural prayer.

Chatman began shuttling back and forth from North Carolina and had even taped editions of his *Free World Gospel Hour* from the White House press room. Chatman knew the importance of maintaining and cultivating a close relationship with Phillips, so he tolerated the frequent visits to DC. But this traffic!

"I'm sorry, Bobby, but you might be late for this morning's meeting," said the driver, Alex Marsh.

"No sweat," said the television evangelist confidently. "They won't start without me."

Bobby Chatman arrived ten minutes late. He walked quickly so he could join Phillips at the joint meeting of key cabinet members and congressional representatives. Phillips held Chatman's counsel in high regard when developing domestic policy.

The reverend was surprised when he entered the Cabinet Room and found two members of the Joint Chiefs of Staff and the secretary of state present. "Ah, Bobby, glad you could make it," said an obviously harried Andrew Phillips. "I'm afraid some foreign policy problems have popped up. I'll wrap it up with these gentlemen and get on with the original agenda as soon as possible."

Chatman took the hint that he needed to exit the room. "Of course, Andrew. I understand," he replied, smiling. "I'll wait in the chapel."

"I'm sorry," Phillips consoled. "I'll come get you when all the classified stuff is over." The president then put out his hand to Chatman. "Pray for us, Bobby!"

"I will, Andrew."

An hour later a presidential aide came to fetch him. Chatman waited in the hallway across from the Cabinet Room for several minutes before a grim-faced marine opened the door. The secretary of state and the two members of the Joint Chiefs of Staff filed out of the room without so much as a nod in Chatman's direction. President Phillips then stepped out and motioned Chatman to follow him. When they were out of earshot of anyone, an exasperated Phillips described the meeting to his friend.

"Bobby, sometimes I think the devil himself is working against us. Other times I think we are living in the days before Armageddon."

"Hey, Andrew, relax," soothed Chatman. "I spent the past forty-five minutes in prayer on your behalf. What's all the excitement about?"

"They aren't sure yet, but independent intelligence sources are all reporting that some old Soviet 'suitcase' nuclear weapons were stolen from Russia by the Chechens and sold to the Houthis in Yemen. We're trying to verify the whole thing. Several terrorist leaders are privately bragging that Washington will soon be blown off the map."

"Hmm. What do the Russians say about this?"

"They haven't said anything yet. Before we contact them, we want to learn as much as we can from our sources."

Chatman smiled. "You know, Andrew, they will stay silent as long as silence benefits them. They're probably hoping you don't know about the theft. Why don't you press them?"

Phillips pondered the question, then nodded. "You have a point, my friend."

"Did the meeting result in a plan of action?" Chatman asked.

"No. I insisted we need time for prayer and reflection. In the meantime, we're trying to verify if the bombs are in unfriendly hands."

Chatman maintained his composure. "I have a suggestion, if you don't mind my opinion."

"Sure, Bobby, you know I cherish your advice on all matters."

"I think the Russians are just as interested as we are about keeping nuclear weapons out of the hands of terrorists. Who knows, opening dialogue with them could lead to a new era of cooperation and world peace."

The president's smile grew as his eyes widened. He grabbed Chatman's arms. "Bobby, God sent you to me for a reason. Thank you, brother. Those Pentagon shirts will balk at this, but I'm going to pitch it to them."

Bobby Chatman made it through the afternoon meeting with the president and key members of Congress. Heading back to his limo, he smiled, smugly satisfied with his performance.

The late evening drive to Reagan Airport was peaceful in light traffic, but Alex noticed that his boss seemed preoccupied. "How did your meeting with Phillips go today?" he asked, hoping to learn what was bothering the boss. Alex Marsh, who had worked with Chatman for three years, was surprised at the TV minister's reaction. Chatman started laughing, just a giggle at first, then it became a deep belly laugh, complete with tears.

As he regained control, Chatman leaned over the front seat and whispered, "Alexei, my friend, our work has paid off. You and Mikhail will soon be flying for Red Star Express, and in three months the White House and the capital won't exist."

When Chatman had settled back in the seat, Alex studied the face reflected in the mirror. What surprised him was that even after the hysterical laughter had stopped, the tears remained.

OCTOBER 14
THE NORTH CAROLINA FARM

It had been another long day, but there was one more task to accomplish. Chatman sat down in his office and opened the contacts on his phone, finding the number for Ron Goodman.

"Goodman here," said the expectant voice.

"Good evening, Ron. Bobby Chatman. How are things in the news business?"

"Ah, Chatman, good evening. The term 'news' has taken on a different meaning with your friend Phillips in the White House."

Chatman couldn't help but smile at the sarcasm. "I guess you didn't hear about the stolen nuclear weapons?" The silence on the other end answered Chatman's question.

"Say that again?" Goodman asked.

"I said, 'I guess you didn't hear about the stolen nuclear weapons,'" Chatman repeated. "I was in Washington today, and I caught snatches of conversation about some missing Russian 'suitcase' weapons. They wouldn't tell me about it, but I gather they're very concerned about the terrorist implications. I prayed about it and decided if it's true, the American people have a right to know. I figured you're the best man to tell the people."

Chatman smiled as he heard Goodman, normally so composed, become flustered as he sensed a big scoop.

"Oh, and Ron, please don't list me as your source. I just think the American people have a right to know."

"Oh, sure, Bobby. If it's true, the American people most certainly have a right to know. Thank you for the tip."

When the call ended Chatman laughed out loud. "Oh, Ron, do I have plans for you." Thoroughly satisfied with the day's events, a tired Chatman prepared to turn in. After falling quickly into a deep sleep, the dream came upon him yet again. *"I'll get them, brother!"* he heard himself scream. *"I'll get them!"*

OCTOBER 15
EGLIN AIR FORCE BASE, FLORIDA

It was quiet and dark in the alert barn—just the way Captain Mark "Suds" Matthews liked it. He was into the second twenty-four hours of a two-week TDY alert tour where he lived, ate, and slept only steps away from an armed F-15 Eagle. The pilots sarcastically referred to it as "guarding the country."

Matthews was counting the hours until the changeover when he'd be released for twenty-four hours. Sitting alert wasn't so bad, especially in sunny Florida when it was winter back home in Massachusetts. But he was miserable with whom he'd been paired with.

He and Tom Rushton had looked forward to this TDY, or temporary duty station. Rush had wanted to bring his family down so he could spend time with them when off alert. But that fell apart at the last minute when Rush's dad had a stroke. Matthews became nauseated when he saw Major Richard Robertson's name on the scheduling board as his flight leader.

Sleeping is how Matthews preferred to pass the time. It kept him away from Robertson. He was in a deep sleep when something jolted him fully awake. Was that the horn, or did he dream it? The Klaxon tore into his senses again, an audible trigger that set his body in motion. "Battle stations!" he heard the duty controller at the command post say over the PA. As the Klaxon continued to tear at his ears, he heard feet already running for the door. "Battle stations!"

It took Matthews twenty seconds to step into his flight suit, zip up, and get his boots on, cinching them with the zippers. As he grabbed his flight jacket and ran for alert pad number two, he caught sight of Robertson going into pad number one. *Dammit*, he thought, *that bastard beat me out here.*

At the foot of the cockpit ladder, Matthews wiggled into his survival vest and anti-G suit. Then he scampered up and into the cockpit of his F-15. The alert crew chief followed him up the ladder. *Hurry!* he thought. *Be strapped in and ready if that scramble light turns green.* Matthews slid into the parachute harness, buckled himself into the ejection seat, and slipped his helmet on. As the crew chief scurried down the ladder and removed it, Matthews hooked up his anti-g suit hose and checked all the connections mating him to the "cocked" F-15. He was all set, his eyes focused on the status light on the hangar wall, waiting for it to turn green. He suspected the battle stations call had been triggered by an unknown airborne target somewhere in the Air Defense Identification Zone, or ADIZ, a strip of airspace, in this case, in the Gulf of Mexico.

Matthews sometimes pondered that "guarding the country" would be an exciting duty. But he knew the opposite was true. In the age of intercontinental ballistic missiles, a manned bomber would likely be used only as a standoff cruise missile launch platform, or in a follow-up role after a missile attack.

Almost all the squadrons dedicated to the air defense role were supplied by a handful of Air National Guard units. He was glad his unit's deployed base was in Florida.

Damn! he thought, as the seconds dragged on. *Make up your minds. Let's go!*

It was almost as if the powers that be were tuned into Matthews's mind as two long blasts spewed from the Klaxon. He saw the battle stations light change from yellow to green. It was a scramble.

Matthews's hands moved in a litany he had practiced innumerable times. The drill was relatively simple because as many switches as possible had been preset to the "on" position. Get the engines going, and you'd automatically have their generators online. Then you could power up the rest of the weapons system. He activated the jet fuel starter and felt the fighter come alive as the right engine spooled up.

"Okay," murmured Matthews, "good start on number two. Let's get our position into the inertial navigation system." As his fingers worked the keyboard, he noticed that Robertson's number two engine had just started. *I'm ahead of you, wimp,* he thought, as he keyed in the coordinates for the Eglin alert barn, *and I'll be waiting for you when it's time to taxi.*

He was just getting ready to start the left engine when he heard the command post calling on the radio. "Shark zero-three and zero-four, your scramble has been canceled. Repeat. Your scramble has been canceled. Eglin Command Post is standing by for authentication."

"Well, damn!" he said out loud, as he dug into his left G-suit pocket for the authentication table. It took Matthews less than fifteen minutes to get the F-15 recocked onto five-minute alert status.

A few minutes later he stood in the TV room chatting with his crew chief when Major Robertson walked in. "Did you tell the command post you're back up on five?" asked Robertson.

"Yes, sir," replied Matthews, amused at Robertson's pomposity.

"Fine," Robertson said. "FYI, Captain, the 'unknown' was an Aero Mexico 737 that was running ahead of schedule and somewhat off course." He turned to the crew chief. "If you'll excuse us, Sergeant," he said with an air of dismissal, "we need to debrief."

Matthews couldn't believe his ears. "What's to debrief, Major?" He was smiling, but he felt anger boiling up inside. "The horn went off. I ran to my jet. You ran to yours. We strapped in. The green light came on and we each started an engine. Then they canceled the scramble. We authenticated the cancel, then we shut down our jets. We each set them back up on five, and now we're both in here. Now, what else is there to debrief... sir?"

Robertson's reply stunned Matthews. "Well, I'm not sure that covers it all, Mark. Suppose I get the debriefing guide, and we'll sit down and go through each item just to be sure. Okay?"

As Robertson insisted on going step-by-step through the debriefing guide, Matthews fumed. The next fifteen minutes were a painful recap of an event that, for all practical purposes, never even happened.

"So, are there any questions, Mark?"

There was that snootiness again. Why the hell couldn't he just use his call sign like everyone else?

"No, sir. If you're finished, I'm going to go get some fresh air." Matthews didn't wait for a response as he headed outside.

The cool night air felt good as he walked around the edge of the ramp. This was his favorite time of year in northwest Florida. The days were still warm, but the nights were cool and refreshing. The alert area was located well away from the main ramp, but he could hear plenty of activity across the field. Late night was when a lot of maintenance for the next day's flying was accomplished. The sounds came from the engine test cell where he could hear an F-15 or an F-35 engine go from idle to military power, pause for a second, and then surge into afterburner. Even this far away, the ground shook under his feet. That's how all this got started, he recalled with a smile. The sound of airplanes.

Matthews remembered his Little League coach berating him for standing in center field and watching the passage of any airplane rather than paying attention to what was happening on the ball field. And there were all the model airplanes he built, and the many school projects, all focused on aviation.

He used every penny he earned from his part-time job to take flying lessons. After he had earned his private pilot license, he flew a rented Cessna 152 to see an air show. He was fascinated, getting to see the real versions of all those models he'd built.

The air show was good, featuring aerobatic biplanes and wing walkers. But the military fighters captured him. The Thunderbirds awed him. He remembered, like it was yesterday, the huge grin on his face.

He was a lucky man, Darryl had told him—lucky he had determined at an early age what he wanted to do with his life.

Darryl? He glanced at his watch. *I better get some more sleep*, he thought, as he turned back to the alert barn.

Matthews was startled by the young enlisted security guard who had walked up behind him. "Oh, good evening, Sergeant."

"Good evening, sir. May I ask you a question?"

"Of course," Matthews replied.

"What's it like to fly an F-15, sir?"

Matthews had been asked this question many times. "Well, on takeoff the afterburner kicks you in the back like no race car ever could. As we do our air-to-air dogfighting, it's like you're running along the edge of a huge, steep drop-off, right on the verge of disaster, yet you're in total control. It's the best damn thing I've ever experienced!"

The sergeant laughed openly. "Wow, sir, how do you stand it!" he exclaimed.

Matthews just smiled and looked at his watch. "Geez, it's almost two a.m. I guess I ought to be turning in."

"Say, sir, did you hear about the stolen nuclear weapons?" asked the sergeant.

"What stolen weapons?"

"Well, sir," said the guard, "just before we started talking, I heard over the security net that Ron Goodman was on TV saying that some small nuclear weapons, 'suitcase' bombs he called them, were stolen from Russia—and the rumor is that they've fallen into terrorist hands."

After a few hours of sleep, Matthews walked out of the alert barn into searing sunshine and fumbled for his sunglasses. There she was, leaning against a rental car.

Darryl McCormick was known as "Dare" for her penchant for bucking the system. She despised bureaucracy and the accompanying red tape that wasted everyone's time and delayed their case work. Not unlike himself, that was one of the things he liked most about her.

He remembered the first time they met at a security conference in DC. With a trim build, auburn hair, smooth milky skin, and sea-green eyes, FBI agent Darryl McCormick didn't seem concerned with what people thought about her looks. The best effort she could muster was a few runs of a brush through the shoulder-length mane and a swipe of a subtle shade of vermilion on her lips. FBI agents, male and female, wore drab suits on the job that did nothing to enhance their looks, but to Matthews, the sight of her was a welcome runway swimming out of the fog. He was smitten.

Dare shaded her eyes, looking side to side, as he approached.

"What in the heck are you looking for?" he implored, as he walked up to the car. "It's me!"

"I'm looking for the world's greatest fighter pilot," she retorted. "Have you seen him?"

"Hell, you're lookin' at him, Agent McCormick!" They hugged long and tight, kissed. and got in the car. "Where we going to lunch?" Matthews asked as she headed for the gate. "I'm starving."

"Of course, you always are. The Magnolia Grill," she replied with a smile.

"I like the sound of it."

They found a table and ordered cocktails. Matthews opened the conversation with his disgust with Robertson. She knew about their conflict and nodded pensively.

"What's the matter?" he asked. "You've got a thousand-yard stare."

"Oh," she said, sighing. "My mind's still at the bureau. I'm sorry."

"Bad time to come here, eh?"

"No. I needed it." She paused. "Mark, you remember when we first met?"

"Yeah. Robertson sent me kicking and screaming to that counterterrorism conference in DC. They wanted a representative from the Air Guard there. I detested going, but there was a silver lining in that cloud—you."

She smiled. "Yeah, I felt much the same."

After the drinks came, they placed their lunch orders. "I've never told you this," she continued, "but the bureau took me off an interesting high-level government security case and assigned me to counterterrorism. I think they wanted to ice me somewhere."

"Why's that?"

"Well, you know, I'm a quiet person generally, but I'm a gadfly when I see bullshit happening."

"I know you are. That's what attracted me to you."

Her eyebrows wrinkled in a menace. "It wasn't my stunning good looks?"

"That too. What was this security about?"

She stared out the window for a moment. "Have you heard of Reverend Bobby Chatman?"

"Sure. You can't turn on the TV without seeing him."

"Mark, not many people know this, but he's the president's closest confidant."

"So? Billy Graham was in the same role for a bunch of presidents."

"Mark, this son of a bitch is not a Billy Graham."

Matthews studied her face. "The reverend is a security risk? Why doesn't the Secret Service handle that?"

"Because the president told them to lay off. A friend of mine in the Service tipped me off and I started looking into it. I can give Chatman a pass for being Russian in his youth, but now he has virtually unlimited access to the president. I want to know what the president is telling him. And I want to know what he's telling the president." She paused to order their food, then continued. "The director got wind of it and reassigned me to counterterrorism."

"And the rest is history," Matthews blurted. "Meeting you is the only thing worthwhile that came out of that sym . . . symp . . . whatever you call it—"

"Symposium, knucklehead. It's where people get together to convince each other they're important."

"I know. I was there. Remember?"

"What I remember is, I'm representing the FBI at this thing—that you can't even pronounce—on the mounting terrorist threat—which is legitimate—and I'm trying to be serious, and right across from me is this creepy bastard wearing a blue uniform and undressing me with his beady eyes."

He grinned. "That's me!"

She smiled and rolled her eyes. "Can you be serious for once?"

He motioned out the window. "There's a beautiful beach waiting for us just a mile away and you want to talk seriously? Okay, here's a serious question. I heard the Russians are missing some nuclear weapons and terrorists might have them. Is that true?"

"I can't talk about that."

"Hmm. It sounds to me like another 9/11 is coming."

Her response came after a few seconds of silence. "I don't know, Mark. But I'm worried."

CHAPTER FOUR

NOVEMBER 1
KOLA PENINSULA, RUSSIA

"Kola zero-five is flight level 350 and proceeding direct to Murmansk. Please inform Murmansk that we are a precautionary aircraft with one hydraulic system, prop synchronization, HF radio, and both autopilots and yaw dampers inoperative."

Major Gregori Petrov tweaked the power levers and adjusted the cockpit lights. The November sun had already disappeared in a blaze below the cold arctic horizon of northern Russia at only 1615 hours.

Petrov's entire day had been unpleasant. He'd been scheduled for a six o'clock brief. He tried not to wake Olya or Stefan as he left their small apartment. He had been scraping the frost off the windshield of his Lada while the engine warmed when Stefan, fourteen now, appeared.

"Will you make it to the swim meet tonight, Papa?" Stefan had asked, his teeth chattering in the cold. "This is the All-Murmansk championships."

"I will try, son," Petrov had replied, wrapping the boy in the folds of his uniform greatcoat. "If the flight goes well, I'll be there to watch you win, okay?" He gently pushed the boy toward the door. "Now get back inside before you catch cold."

The boy's face was briefly doubtful, having heard the promises before. "All right, Papa. Do it for me again, okay?"

Petrov smiled. "Yes, Stefan, I will say hello to the sun."

That was their little ritual. Dreary winters in Murmansk were especially tough on Stefan. The one story he never grew tired of hearing was how thrilling it was to burst through the clouds into blue sky and sunshine on top.

Saying "hello to the sun" had become a father-and-son ritual, but Petrov knew the chances of his being back in time to watch Stefan compete were very slim. Shakedown flights almost never went well, and this one had been no exception.

"Kola zero-five, Talagi," came the voice over the radio.

"Go ahead."

"Kola zero-five, Murmansk has been advised of your status. The emergency equipment is standing by. I have a representative from the Tupolev design bureau asking if he can be of assistance."

"Roger. Everything is under control. We will see him at Murmansk in forty-five minutes."

"That must be Kirov," said Captain Vladimir Sheptak, Petrov's copilot, who was currently flying the giant Tu-95 bomber. "If we lose this piece-of-shit airplane, he'll be clearing timber in Siberia."

"So much for 'the grand technological achievement of the workers of Zhukovsky,'" commented Petrov.

The morning had begun with a standard briefing for an operational shakedown flight on an airplane fresh out of the overhaul factory. The meeting had been conducted by technicians from Tupolev, builders of the heavy bomber. The crew had been handpicked for acceptance test flights of the overhauled "H" version of the Tu-95, a model specifically designed to launch Kh-55M cruise missiles.

Today, though, they'd learned the regular briefing with the Tupolev engineers would be cut short to allow for a presentation in the huge hangar at the Murmansk Northeast Air Base.

The presentation commemorated the acceptance of tail number 88015, the four hundredth production Tu-95. Colonel Josef Piekarski, commander of the Bear-H squadron at Murmansk, accepted the bomber from Igor Kirov, director of production at the Tupolev factory. Petrov's crew had stood under the left wing of the bomber while Kirov praised it as "a monument to the grand technological achievement of the workers at Zhukovsky."

Piekarski had then kept them at attention for thirty-two minutes and forty seconds exactly—according to a fuming Sheptak—while he thanked everybody from Lenin to old man Tupolev. Then he had directed Petrov and his crew to proceed "on behalf of the Russian people."

"This plane is a tail-wagging bitch," said Misha Grotsky from the tail gunner's compartment. I'm afraid to use the relief tube and piss all over myself!"

"Sounds like a personal problem related to your shortness, Grotsky," came the reply from the aft crew compartment. "At least you can see outside. We're turning green back here."

"I'm sorry about the tail-wagging," replied Petrov. "But there's nothing we can do about it. I was just thinking about that stupid presentation this morning."

"I thought Piekarski would never shut up," growled Sheptak.

"Gentlemen," said Petrov, putting an end to the conversation, "let's run the descent check."

"Navigator, descent check complete." Lieutenant Arkady Itzkoff, dubbed "Missile Man" by the crew, doubled as a navigator and bombardier/missile launch officer. "We're currently forty-three minutes south of Murmansk, and directly over the fighter base at Talagi. I'm working on the fuel figures. Be advised Murmansk weather is going down. Let's get this pig on the ground!"

The mission plan had been a low altitude, simulated attack profile in which the Tu-95 simulated a B-52. Fighters scrambled to stop the "intruder," and the Tu-95 crew had practiced operating the new electronic countermeasures package as well as the radar system for the twin 20mm cannons in the tail stinger. Next, they simulated a missile launch on the electronic missile range at Vorkuta Sovetsky Air Base just west of the Ural Mountain chain.

"EO, descent check complete."

The EO—short for electronics officer, and "Electron Man" to the crew—was Lieutenant Vitalie Orshansky. He was responsible for the on-board radar and the electronic countermeasures, or ECM system. The on-board radar could function as a search radar, a ground-mapping radar, or a weather radar. The ECM system was an automatic radar jamming system, capable of identifying signals from an attacking fighter, or a surface-to-air missile (SAM) system.

"Tail gunner," Misha Grotsky announced himself, "descent check complete." Grotsky, the only enlisted man on the crew, rode in the glassed-in tail gunner compartment at the rear of the aircraft. Grotsky was chosen not only because of his expertise in the operation of the I-band radar that aimed the twin 20mm cannon, but also because he was small enough to turn around and face forward, seeing both wings, the landing gear nacelles, and the engines, a feat impossible for a larger man. Like enlisted crew members in every air force, Grotsky enjoyed a friendly companionship with his officer crewmates.

"Copilot, descent check complete," said the right-seater.

Captain Vladimir Sheptak had been handpicked to assist Petrov with the flying duties. Short and stocky, Sheptak was a Tu-95 systems expert, having committed the system performance limits to memory, and having a mechanic's feel for how the aircraft's systems worked.

"Zampolit, descent check complete!" a voice exclaimed, unmistakably Orshanky's. "But the desk chair needs oiling." The comment brought a round of laughter over the interphone.

A seat on the cockpit flight deck was reserved for the zampolit, or political officer. However, since the demise of the USSR, a zampolit had become a rare sight aboard Russian bombers. The position was a holdover from Soviet days when crew members were monitored for their party loyalty. Not being trained airmen, the zampolits bore the brunt of many crew member jokes.

"All right," said Petrov, when the laughter died down, "descent check complete. I'm glad we all agree it's been a trying day."

There had been inertial navigation and radar system problems which caused a three-hour delay. They'd lost the number two hydraulic system in the middle of the simulated attack leg. En route to Vorkuta, the prop synchronization system failed, making it difficult to set equal power settings on all four engines. In the ensuing tail-wagging, the autopilot and yaw dampers gave up trying to compensate, so Petrov and Sheptak took turns every thirty minutes hand-flying while the other adjusted the throttles. Now, with fuel lower than expected and weather conditions at Murmansk deteriorating, they were trying to nurse the crippled bomber home.

"Hey, boss, I just got another flicker on the number four engine oil pressure gauge," said Sheptak, reaching around the control wheel and tapping the gauge. The oil pressure gauge on the right outboard engine had been reading a little low all day. Other than a propeller that operated sluggishly, the engine had performed as expected. It was something to add to the list of maintenance write-ups.

"Don't let me forget that pressure gauge during the debriefing, Vladimir," Petrov said. "I'll take it in a few minutes. I want to check on the weather first."

"Try to order something good," replied the copilot as he continued to fight the controls.

"Talagi, Kola zero-five."

"Zero-five, go ahead."

"What's the weather at Talagi?"

"Kola zero-five, the current Talagi weather is indefinite ceiling, sky obscured, one-kilometer visibility in blowing snow." The storm is moving in faster than forecast."

Petrov frowned. "Roger, Talagi, we'll continue to Murmansk."

Petrov's internal caution lights were beginning to come on, and he did not like the way the cards were stacking up. He was facing a night instrument approach, and he would have to do the emergency procedure for lowering his landing gear and flaps because of the number two hydraulic system failure. Considering the weather and his fuel situation, once the gear was down, he was committed to

Murmansk. He hated being backed into that corner.

"Do you have those fuel figures yet, Arkady?"

"Yes, sir," said Itzkoff from the navigator's compartment. "Forty-one minutes to the air base, and we should begin the approach with fifty-five hundred kilograms of fuel. We can miss one approach, fly a close-in pattern with the gear hanging, and still be on the ground with two thousand kilograms."

Itzkoff's fuel figures erased any doubts. There would not be time for screwing around at Murmansk. Petrov planned to delay the descent as long as possible, then take it down at idle power, and hopefully not have to push the power levers up until final approach. That was the most fuel-efficient way to descend.

Petrov turned to his copilot. "I'm planning to take it just prior to the descent." He then keyed the interphone and spoke to the rest of the crew. "Gentlemen, I want you to stow your personal gear and get set for a precautionary landing. We're in a race with the fuel gauges and the weather."

Petrov took control from Sheptak. "Vladimir, I have it. Tell Murmansk we're starting our descent."

As Petrov retarded the power levers toward idle, there was a "whump," and the cockpit filled with the smell of hot oil. The giant airplane yawed hard to the left and started to roll over on its back. Fighting desperately for control, Petrov stood hard on the right rudder and cranked the control wheel to the right stop.

"We have a runaway prop on number four!" shouted Sheptak. "Oil pressure's dropping rapidly!"

"Feather number four!" Petrov barked as he slammed the power levers up on the two left-wing engines to stop the rolling motion. "Do it while there's still oil pressure!"

Sheptak grabbed the number four prop control lever, lifted it over the detent and into the feather range. "Number four prop feathered!"

Nothing happened.

"Vladimir, emergency feather number four!"

Sheptak lifted the cover on the switch that was supposed to electrically feather the eight blades of the number four propellers, rotating them parallel to the direction of flight, thus reducing wind resistance. The airplane shook violently as the prop mechanism, operating at full power with no oil going to it, started to self-destruct.

Sheptak shouted, "No emergency feather on number four propeller! I think we've lost it, sir!" The sickening metal-on-metal screeching filled the air.

"Vladimir, shut down number four engine and manually close that bleed valve. I can barely breathe in here. Arkady, get on the radio to Murmansk. Tell them we have a runaway prop on number four. Give them a position and estimated time to the base." He paused a moment, fighting to control the airplane. "Arkady, advise them we are now an emergency."

THE STREETS OF MOSCOW

Georgi Kabchefsky spent his working days at the Kuybyshev plant assembling insulated electrical relays. The work was boringly repetitive. The relays were electromechanical and were designed to turn an electrical signal into a mechanical action. Being insulated relays, they were designed to perform in all climatic conditions. But something unusual had happened tonight, and it troubled him as he made his way home.

Thirty minutes before his shift ended, Georgi had run out of insulating material. Since it was a ten-minute walk to the parts depot, and a five-minute verbal hassle to acquire additional sealing material, he decided to assemble the last five relays without the insulation. He knew the relays would pass any quality control test since such tests just checked that it performed its mechanical movement satisfactorily. He also knew there was no specific serial number that could trace a suspect relay back to him. The relays were used in several common applications, usually in the starting system of Russian-built automobiles and trucks, but also in the aerospace and weapons industries.

Like a lot of Russian citizens, Kabchefsky tried to sort truth from lie as he walked from the Metro station to the small one-room flat he shared with his wife, Laryssa. It seemed that everybody was trying to reconcile the government version of events with what they really knew.

When he was young, he watched some boys get ahead in Russian society based on whose father was in government and outranked the other fathers. He had spent most of his boyhood near the back of the line, literally and figuratively, since his father was just a machinist. "The government is lying. There, I've said it out loud," he murmured. "What else are they lying about?"

Now that the Soviet years were long passed, he thought, were they any better? The rise of the oligarchs had ushered in a whole new privileged class. They had billions—upscale apartments, limousines, and dachas. He shook his head as he compared such luxurious living conditions to his own. Yes, it was better than the Soviet years when you had to wait for a one-room apartment with a shared bathroom.

And a car? On his salary it would take Georgi three years to pay for a tiny sedan. Yes, he and his coworkers were better off, but not by much.

He had been sharing what little credible news he could glean from government-filtered internet sources with some of his coworkers. The wars, the shortages, and the riots had been the dominant subject of conversation among his fellow workers. He knew the Americans—and, by proxy, its allies—were boycotting almost all Russian-made products, including crude oil. Georgi knew his nation depended on those exports for hard currency. With the annexation of Crimea as punishment for the Ukraine trying to join the European Union, and the disastrous 'special operation' eight years later, it had been almost impossible to import everything from grain to chocolate.

"I doubt those oligarchs will be going without butter for their bread, and milk to wash it down," Georgi murmured.

As he'd made his way home through the frigid night, he finally felt satisfaction with what he'd done. He regarded himself as honest and reliable, but he chuckled at the thought of some big shot wondering why his fancy Senat was dead as a hammer on some cold winter night. That thought, and the realization that Laryssa was waiting for him in a warm bed, made Georgi laugh out loud as he entered his apartment building.

"Hello, Georgi!" bellowed a coworker in the hallway. "Why are you smiling, my friend?"

"I was just thinking. In this life, it is the little victories that keep one going. Do you know what I mean?"

"Indeed, I do," replied the coworker as they started up the stairs. He reached into the liner of his topcoat and held up a flask of vodka. "Here's to little victories!" he proclaimed as he turned up the flask then handed it to Georgi.

OVER THE KOLA PENINSULA, RUSSIA

"I have it under control now," said Gregori Petrov as he retrimmed the flight controls and adjusted the power levers on the three remaining engines.

"The prop is still in flat pitch," the copilot said. "With no oil it will windmill for a while and eventually seize. We need to get on the ground."

"Major, Murmansk is asking for your intentions," said Itzkoff.

Sweat dripped from Petrov's forehead from the physical exertion of flying the crippled Tu-95. The crew waited expectantly for him to make a decision.

"Gentlemen, we can continue the descent and fly the approach. However, once the gear and flaps are down there'll be no going around. The other option is to proceed to the bailout area and exit the aircraft. Remember, there's a weather system approaching, so you'll probably spend the night outdoors. I am open to suggestions."

Grotsky, from the tail gun compartment, spoke first. "Major, you promised me a hot supper. Let's get this whore on the ground!"

"I'm for that," said Itzkoff.

"Me too," chimed in Orshansky. "I have a date with that blond nurse, and I intend to sleep rolled up in her arms tonight." Everyone laughed, breaking the tension.

"All right, Vladimir," said Petrov. "Tell them we want a descending turn onto a thirty-five kilometer straight-in precision radar approach with their best man on that scope. We'll delay configuring as long as possible."

As Sheptak coordinated with the radar controller, Petrov reviewed everything in his mind. The precision radar controller would talk him down through the dense clouds to the runway. He needed to allow Sheptak enough time to hand pump the landing gear down and emergency-lower the flaps. He had to touch down fast enough to have effective rudder control on rollout. Stopping should be no problem using reverse thrust on the three good engines and normal brakes.

As they entered the clouds at 4,700 meters, Petrov hoped the next thing he would see would be the runway approach lights. The crew remained silent as the two pilots prepared the crippled bomber for emergency landing gear and flap extension.

When Sheptak contacted the final controller, Petrov felt relief wash over him. He recognized the female voice he'd heard many times before and was profoundly glad she was at the console. She'd always delivered him precisely to the landing point. Just hearing her voice settled the pilot.

"Kola zero-five, turn right heading three-one-zero. You are two-five kilometers from touchdown, slightly right of course, well above glide path and correcting."

For the next five minutes her soft but reassuring voice guided every movement of Petrov's hands and feet.

As Sheptak lowered the flaps and landing gear by the alternate methods, which required more time than usual, she continued to talk Petrov toward the safety of the waiting runway—or was it safe? There was ice to be dealt with. *Don't dare relax until you get this beast stopped,* he told himself.

On the fifty-first stroke of the pump handle, Sheptak announced,

"Landing gear down and locked."

Petrov knew they were getting into the fine hairs now. The airspeed was bleeding through 290 kilometers per hour, and as the nose gear came down and locked, Petrov told Sheptak to turn on the landing lights, which made the snowflakes look like sparkling diamonds.

"On course, on glide path, two kilometers from touchdown. Heading three-three-five. Kola zero-five cleared to land."

"Vladimir, call out the runway," said Petrov. "There's going to be a lot of blowing snow."

"On course, on glide path, over the approach lights." They were only sixty meters above the ground now with the airspeed touching 275 kilometers per hour just as Petrov planned. He desperately wanted to hear Sheptak call the runway in sight, but he forced himself to stay on the instruments.

"On course, on glide path, three-three-five heading, at decision height."

They were passing through thirty meters in altitude, and still Sheptak had not called the runway in sight. The rules said that he should execute a missed approach, but a go-around was not an option.

"On course, on glide path, heading three-three-five, over the approach end."

"Centerline lights in sight!" shouted Sheptak.

Petrov looked up and saw the snow-covered runway stretching before him. He retarded the power levers and allowed the airplane to settle. Petrov suspected the braking action was going to be marginal due to the snow. The drag from the dead engine required almost full rudder to keep the airplane on the runway centerline. As he placed the power levers in reverse a cloud of billowing snow enveloped the bomber.

"Two thousand meters remaining, and two hundred kilometers per hour," said Sheptak as Petrov fought to keep the bomber tracking straight on the slick runway and carefully applied the brakes.

"A thousand meters remaining, and one hundred forty kilometers per hour."

The runway end lights were just becoming visible through the cloud of blowing snow when he finally had effective steering and braking control. Almost six hours from the time they'd left it, Major Gregori Petrov finally brought tail number 88015 to a sliding stop on runway thirty-three at Murmansk Northeast.

"Murmansk, Kola zero-five is down. Thanks for your help tonight."

"Roger, zero-five, welcome home. Call the tower on 118.5."

"I am going to marry that woman!" shouted Orshansky.

"Hands off! She's enlisted—she's mine," yelled Grotsky.

The resulting laughter died off as Sheptak contacted the tower.

Petrov taxied the aircraft to the door of the huge hangar and stopped in the same spot it had been parked that morning. He sighed as he shut down the engines.

"Nice job, Major. Thanks for bringing us home."

"It was a nice job, Major, and I would like to release my sphincter muscle, but I'm afraid I would soil myself," said the tail gunner.

"You are a sphincter muscle, Grotsky," said Orshansky.

"Okay, guys," Petrov interrupted, "we still have work to do," though he was feeling the same relief. "Thanks for the compliments."

As they completed the checklist, a maintenance technician buzzed them from outside over the interphone. "Sorry to bother you, sir. Colonel Piekarski is waiting to see Major Petrov."

"Shit," said Petrov. "Can't he wait until we get the paperwork done? You know what needs to go in the logbook, Vladimir. Let me see what the boss wants."

Petrov lowered himself out of the crew hatch and into the winter wind outside, surprised to see a black Senat limousine idling under the bomber's left wing. Piekarski didn't rate a Senat, but as the rear window slid down, it was Piekarski who motioned him over. As the door opened, he was astonished to see that the other occupant was Major General Gustav Chervony, commander of the Long-Range Aviation Branch of the Russian Air Force.

"Greetings, Gregori. My compliments on an outstanding job

tonight," said Piekarski, his eyes big behind his glasses. "Climb in. I think you know General Chervony?"

Petrov had never met his supreme commander. Nevertheless, he took the general's proffered hand. "Good evening, sir. Nice to see you again," he lied.

"Good evening, Major. That was superb flying. I'm glad to see the aircraft of our Long-Range Aviation forces are in such capable hands," replied Chervony. "Do shakedown flights usually cause such trouble?"

"No, sir," Petrov lied again. "Today was just one of those days."

"Well, gentlemen," Chervony began. "I've already discussed the purpose of my visit with Colonel Piekarski. The two of you have been selected for a very special mission, one that is vital to the security of the Homeland, and one directed from the highest levels of our government."

To Petrov's astonishment, the general, who had been speaking in Russian, suddenly switched to English. "I'm directing you to pack a bag, with clothing suitable for a variety of climates, including tropical, and meet me here at zero-six hundred hours tomorrow. I'll personally see you off on the first flight to Moscow, where you will be briefed further. I know you have questions, but the truth is that I know very little more than I've already revealed. So, gentlemen, I will see you in the morning. Good night."

Petrov and Piekarski stepped out of the limo into the night air. He could hardly hide his astonishment. "What is this about, Colonel? Why was he speaking English?"

"You know everything I know, Gregori," replied a jubilant Piekarski. "A message came from Moscow, designated top secret, requesting recommendations for two highly capable pilots from our squadron to lead an important mission. The prime requirement, in addition to flying skills, was a ranking in the upper five percent of their Officer Training School class in advanced English. Naturally, I thought of you and me, so I recommended us for the mission. I guess we'll find out more in Moscow. See you in the morning."

During the maintenance debriefing, Petrov replayed the conversation with Piekarski. Superior flying skills, huh? And Piekarski had recommended himself! Petrov decided not to worry about it until he got to Moscow.

Olya Petrov met her husband at the door of their apartment with a look of profound relief. She had heard the fire trucks screaming toward the runway and her intuition told her another shakedown flight had "experienced some minor difficulties."

"I was worried about you tonight, Gregori," she said, snuggling her petite body into his arms. "The snow was coming down hard and I was afraid you might not make it in."

"We had to make it in," he said, looking into her dark eyes. "It was either land here and cuddle up with you or sleep in a parachute."

Feeling her shudder at the thought of the unspoken third option, he held her close and stroked her black hair. He knew the thought of him dying in an airplane haunted her.

"I'm afraid there's some bad news," he said. "Piekarski and Chervony met the airplane tonight. Josef and I have been selected for some sort of special mission. I have to leave for Moscow first thing in the morning."

"How long will you be gone?"

"They didn't say," he replied. "I don't think they know themselves."

"Well, eat something first, and then you better go tell Stefan," she said. "He's been waiting for you all evening."

He found Stefan dozing on the bed with an algebra textbook on his chest and a first-place ribbon from the swim meet clutched in his hand. The boy stirred as he entered the room. "I won, Papa!" he exclaimed as he snuggled into his father's arms. "I beat the second-place swimmer by ten meters!"

Petrov congratulated the boy and apologized for missing the

meet. He then told him about the mission and the problems they had without revealing too many details. Finally, he told his son that he was going to be gone for a while. As he talked, the boy's eyes began to water, but when his father told him it was a special mission for the Russian people, the boy perked up.

Stefan had been taught in school about his patriotic duty to the Russian homeland. After Petrov said good night, he promised to say hello to the sun during his special mission.

Olya was waiting for him in the bedroom. On the bed stand was a tray with two glasses of wine and a candle. "I didn't know if you remembered," he said, as he stripped off his flight suit and lay down on the bed.

"Of course I remembered," she said with a smile. "Stefan is fourteen, so it was fifteen years ago, on a cold arctic night, just like this one, and we had met each other only a few days before when you came into the clinic to have a cavity filled."

"I was a dashing lieutenant with a new set of wings."

"No, my love," she said, sliding into bed with him, "you were a shy young man, away from home for the first time, and I was a timid young woman."

He smiled and pulled her close.

Later, when they had cuddled together in the warmth of each other's bodies, Petrov lay awake listening to Olya's rhythmic breathing and the sound of the wind howling outside, wondering what this special mission was all about.

CHAPTER FIVE

NOVEMBER 2
MOSCOW

The early winter storm had raged around Murmansk all night. Gregori Petrov had said goodbye to Olya and Stephan, then trudged with his bags through knee-deep snow to General Chervony's car. Chervony's chauffeur had brought along some pastries and coffee, and Petrov had rolled his tired eyes at the cheerful, chatty mood of Josef Piekarski as he sipped his coffee.

At the civil terminal they said goodbye to the general, who counseled that missions like this led to general's stars. After they boarded their flight, Petrov wanted to be left alone, but Piekarski wanted to talk.

"What do you think this is all about?" he asked, leaning close to Petrov.

"I don't know, Josef," replied Petrov. "You're the one who listens to the rumor mill."

"I don't know," Piekarski confided, "but since they want people proficient in English, I figure it's something big."

Petrov laughed. "Come on, Josef. I'm betting it's something so insignificant that it doesn't justify a place on the 'security of the Motherland' rumor mill."

Petrov had first met Josef Piekarski when they were new cadets at the Tambov Higher Military Aviation School for Pilots. Josef did very well at English and academics, but his flying skills were lacking. He took longer to solo than the rest—a difficulty that would have gotten most students washed out. But it made perfect sense to Petrov, since Josef's father was an influential party official.

Petrov couldn't remember how it happened, but he became Piekarski's only friend during his stay at Tambov. He guessed it was because they both had a knack for the mandatory English courses. But Piekarski was one of those guys who needed watching when he had an airplane under his command.

They landed at Domodedovo Airport southwest of Moscow and both pilots were surprised to be met by a grim-faced man who led them to a late-model Aurus. His cohort soon appeared with their baggage, and without another word, they set off on another slippery journey. Petrov was certain their chauffeurs were SVR, and he found it amusing that Piekarski was visibly shaken as evidenced by his silence.

Petrov took note when their driver headed away from the city and into the forests on the metropolitan outskirts. They entered a freshly paved country lane, and finally turned onto a driveway that brought them to a locked gate. A civilian guard, with an AK-47 in his hands, checked their papers and motioned them through the gate.

They stopped in front of the most beautiful dacha Petrov had ever seen. It was constructed completely from cedar. A young SVR agent with a pistol under his left armpit opened the door to the country house "This way, gentlemen," he said, in perfect Americanized English. "I understand your journey has been a tiring one, so perhaps you would like to rest before lunch. Your rooms are at the top of the stairs to the left. We will bring your baggage shortly. Lunch will be served in the main dining room promptly at twelve hundred hours, and your dress uniforms will do. If we can be of any assistance, just let us know."

An hour later Petrov started down the stairs, nurturing a burning curiosity, and realized Piekarski's initial assessment was probably correct. They'd been selected for something big.

Piekarski was already engaged in conversation, in English, with a well-dressed man in civilian attire and two other Air Force pilots. As he walked up, the man in the suit held out his hand.

"You must be Major Petrov. I'm Viktor Darginsky, and this is Major Valentin Ridgik and Major Anton Bachvaroff, both from the Su-57 regiment at Rostov-on-Don."

"Gentlemen," said Petrov, in English, as he shook hands all around.

"I know all of you are curious about why you're here," continued Darginsky. "I promise you will receive a detailed briefing this afternoon. We have an important guest for lunch who should be arriving shortly. While he's here, Russian will be the language of conversation. In the meantime, there's coffee and Swiss pastry on the table. So, please help yourselves."

Petrov noted the restrained atmosphere as they stood around making small talk. Suddenly, the big double doors to the dining room opened. "Gentlemen," Darginsky said, "May I present the president of the Russian Federation, Nikolai Kozlov."

Petrov couldn't believe his eyes as everyone hurriedly set their coffee cups down and popped to attention. Kozlov handed his coat and hat to an aide and walked over to their assembled group. Darginsky made the introductions and Kozlov shook hands with each man. Petrov was last, and as he returned the firm grip of his commander in chief, Darginsky relayed an abbreviated version of the previous evening's shakedown flight. Petrov's face reddened as Darginsky praised him for his skills. He didn't enjoy being singled out in the presence of his peers just for doing his job.

"Gentlemen," Kozlov said, "I'm glad you could make it for lunch today. I'm starving. Let's eat."

Halfway through the meal Petrov realized he was enjoying himself. This surprised him because he had heard that Kozlov had a quick temper and was not someone to trifle with. Petrov learned, during the conversation, that Ridgik and Bachvaroff had flown together—as pilot and weapons system operator—in previous assignments in the

MiG-31. Apparently, they had won every major weapons competition among Russian fighter pilots during the past two years. That didn't surprise Petrov. They had that sniper pilot aura about them. He had no doubt they would be a formidable team in any aerial duel. They were now reunited and assigned to the Su-57, which was curious. He knew the Su-57 was a single-seat aircraft.

The real bombshell was dropped by Kozlov himself when he mentioned that Viktor Darginsky was chief of covert operations, American Branch, SVR. There was no longer any doubt that they had been chosen for something very big.

"Ah, that was delicious," said Kozlov as he rose from the table. "Let's retire to the study for coffee."

They all followed the president, and each poured a cup of coffee before taking chairs around a big table. "Gentlemen, I only have a few important remarks to make, and then I must leave you. You have been selected for a very sensitive mission. You are now working directly for me through Comrade Darginsky."

Well, that clears up one thing, thought Petrov. *I'm now working for the SVR.*

"Your services," continued Kozlov, "will be required for approximately three months. During that time, you are not to communicate for any reason with your military units, your friends, or even your families. If any of you feels that you cannot meet this requirement, now is the time to speak up and return to your units." Kozlov paused, to allow them to think it over. They each nodded their acceptance.

"Everybody is staying?" asked Kozlov. "Good! I want to emphasize that this mission is vital to the security of the Motherland. No matter what its results are, once it is concluded, it is never to be discussed again. Is everybody clear on that?" He paused again. "If we ever hear rumors of this mission or read about it in any press publication, we will hunt down the individual who talked, and that individual will be silenced . . . permanently. Do we understand one another?" The group again indicated their assent. Petrov felt sweat forming on his forehead. This was the Kozlov everyone whispered about. "Very well. But before I go, I'd like to propose a toast."

The men rose. Darginsky brought over a tray on which rode a bottle of Stolichnaya Elit vodka and six crystal glasses. Kozlov himself poured the vodka and passed out the filled glasses. When everybody had a glass, the president raised his and said, "To the Motherland, and to the mission."

"Here, here!" they all replied, then downed the vodka. Petrov had the peculiar feeling he had just sworn a blood oath.

"Comrade Darginsky, they're all yours," said Kozlov. "Keep me updated." The door closed behind him and the lock clicked once again.

"If you take your seats, we'll get started," said Darginsky. "English will be the only language you use with me and among yourselves during your stay here. We want you to become as proficient as possible, especially in Americanized English, so study the videos and materials we will give you.

"As each of you know," he continued, "'Mutual Assured Destruction,' or 'MAD,' the Americans say jokingly, has worked well over recent decades because the two sides have been fairly equal in the balance of power. Recent events, however, lead us to believe it is time to examine some different approaches regarding the deployment of strategic weapons. You have been selected to help us develop those new approaches."

Petrov listened with intensity as Darginsky explained that, except for the American stealth bombers, both sides had de-emphasized the manned bomber as a first-strike weapon, instead using them as a stand-off platform, much like submarines. "The Americans are so convinced of the uselessness of Russian bombers as a penetrating first-strike weapon that they have a minimal air defense system protecting their borders." He added that with cruise missiles there are some new attack scenarios available.

"Now, forget what you've learned in war college—at least for now—and join me in thinking outside the box. We believe we can employ a single Russian long-range fighter, like the Su-57, in concert with only two bombers, and emerge the clear winners without a full-scale nuclear exchange . . . in fact, without a single nuclear weapon being detonated on Russian soil. Think of this as a feasibility study, and you are going to help us verify the feasibility of this option."

Petrov scoffed at the ridiculous notion.

"Sir, I'm confused," said Major Ridgik. "If this is just a 'feasibility study,' why all the secrecy? Why not just do it through usual military channels, instead of through the SVR? I mean, it is going to be an 'on-paper' study, right?"

"Wrong," replied Darginsky. "But a good question. What's the first thing you learned about the psychology of your enemy?"

"Know your enemy, sir," was the immediate answer.

"Right!" agreed Darginsky. "And before we are through, you're going to know a lot about our American enemy. You're going to know how he talks and how he lives because we're going to train you as we do deep-cover agents. You're going to learn how his air defense system functions and how his air traffic control system works because we're going to take some of you to America to fly in it. Then and only then will you be able to tell us about the feasibility of our proposed new doctrine."

Silence fell across the room as each pilot realized what Darginsky had said. "Did you say we're going to America, sir?" asked Piekarski.

"That's the plan for you and Major Petrov," replied Darginsky. "Our Su-57 crew will not train in America but will be deeply involved in the mission planning. The plan could change, of course. In fact, the whole operation could be canceled, but Kozlov is very interested in this study. So, any other questions?"

"I'm stunned," said Ridgik. "I have so many questions I don't know where to start."

The other pilots nodded in agreement.

"You will find all sorts of interesting things to read in the library.

Dinner will be served at eighteen hundred hours. You can get out of those stuffy uniforms. We will let you know when formal attire is required."

Halfway up the stairs Piekarski caught up with Petrov. "I told you it was going to be big," he said, his eyes wide. "Lunch with the president and a trip to America. It doesn't get any bigger than that!"

"Yes, you're right," agreed Petrov. "I'm like the sniper pilot, though. I don't understand why they're going about it this way, and that troubles me."

"Just like Comrade Darginsky said," replied Piekarski, testily, "there is no better way to know your enemy than to live with him, and only the SVR could pull that off. You don't think you could just jet over to America in your uniform, and say, 'I'm here to do a feasibility study for the Russian Air Force involving some new bomber attack plan,' do you?"

"Of course not," said Petrov. "I have every intention of going along with it. A trip to America for whatever reason sounds fine to me."

An hour later as Petrov read *The New York Times*, he noticed that the headline dealt with some small Russian nuclear weapons that had been acquired by a terrorist group, but his English was so rusty he was only able to translate about half the story.

EN ROUTE TO NORTH CAROLINA

Bobby Chatman gazed at a flower-studded field that rose toward a hill. The sun was warm on his face. He could hear the wind rustling through the grass. In the distance a lone figure walked toward the crest. Chatman recognized his brother. He saw the specks on the horizon, descending rapidly. The specks grew larger. He saw that the pair were warplanes as they leveled off just above the crest. His heart pounded as he tried to scream a warning to his brother.

He could tell by their devil's cross shape that they were American

A-10s. Just as they crossed the hill, two green canisters separated from the wing pylons of each airplane and tumbled lazily toward the earth. He watched in horrid fascination as the cluster-bomb canisters split open, releasing hundreds of deadly bomblets. The ensuing explosions rumbled like rolling thunder as they engulfed his brother.

Chatman awoke with a start. He realized Alex had just landed the Citation at the farm outside of Henderson, North Carolina.

"Sorry about the bumpy touchdown," Alex called from the cockpit of the business jet, quickly glancing back at his boss seated in the cabin. "It's a little windy tonight."

"That's okay," he said, remembering the dream. Chatman pulled a folded email printout from his jacket pocket and reread it.

As Alex stopped the Citation in front of the hangar door, Chatman leaned into the cockpit. He handed the message to Alex and Michael.

They each read it and grinned. "It looks like a go-ahead," said Michael.

Chatman nodded. "We have a lot to talk about. You guys put the airplane away. I'll run up to the house and open the safe and meet you back here."

Chatman shivered as he stepped through the hangar's office door fifteen minutes later. "Damn, it's cold tonight. Michael, why don't you put on a pot of coffee, and we'll get started. I want to iron out as many details as possible."

"Sure, Bobby," Michael replied. "Do you mind if we order out for pizza? I like to plan surprise attacks on a full stomach." While Alex ordered pizza and Michael set up the coffee maker, Chatman reviewed the LUCIFER/INBLUE operations plan. He marveled at how lucky he was to have his coworkers. It would have been disastrous if Moscow had sent him clumsy novices.

Alex had come first, as Chatman couldn't do all the flying himself. Later, when Moscow realized the importance of Chatman's work, Michael arrived. He was also a pilot, but his expertise was covert operations.

Even before the Phillips presidency, Chatman had access to a wealth of sensitive information. The Citation had been granted landing privileges at many US military facilities, and Chatman had received low-level classified briefings reserved for congressmen.

When Phillips made his bid for the presidency, Alex and Michael, trained in intelligence gathering, reaped a gold mine of information as they jetted around for Chatman's meetings on Phillips's behalf. In fact, it was because of their numerous operations in the US airspace system that the LUCIFER/INBLUE plan was born.

"Okay, the pizza is on the way," Alex said as he took a seat. "So, tell us, Bobby, what did you hear today?"

"Yes, tell us," Michael prompted, offering Chatman a cup of coffee. "Is Red Star Express a go?"

Chatman studied his cup. "As you know, Phillips already told me there's a rumor that some stolen Russian nuclear weapons were missing somewhere in the Middle East. This morning Darginsky confirmed he's running the stolen weapons story. For now, we are to proceed with our plan."

Each man silently considered the significance of Chatman's words. Alex finally spoke. "So, let's get on with it. What's the next step?"

"You have no doubts about the LUCIFER plan?" Chatman asked, his eyes locked on those of his fellow agents.

No doubts whatsoever," Alex replied.

"And what about you, Mikhail?" Chatman asked, purposely using his Russian name.

"None at all, Leonid," came the reply as Michael's steel-gray eyes met Chatman's blue-eyed gaze head-on. "LUCIFER/INBLUE is why we are here. I believe Kozlov can pull it off. This whole nuclear standoff between Russia and the US will drag on forever until there's an accident or a misunderstanding and the world gets blown up."

"All right, time is of the essence. The ministry will have to function as usual, maintaining a normal schedule, including during Thanksgiving and Christmas."

Both men nodded their agreement. Michael asked, "What's the target date?"

"The State of the Union is scheduled for January 31. So, we have ninety days to set it up."

Alex whistled his surprise. "Time certainly is of the essence."

Chatman continued, "Alex, we need to buy two more Citations. They don't have to be pretty, just in good mechanical shape. We'll be using them to haul canned goods and clothes."

Alex looked perplexed. "Using Citations to carry canned goods and clothes doesn't make sense. Shouldn't we be using bigger planes? What about old 737s? Wouldn't that look more convincing?"

"We don't have time for it," Chatman answered. "It would take months to negotiate leasing contracts and hire crews to fly them. Besides, we don't need strangers so close to the operation."

"And if we're asked why we're not flying bigger planes," Michael mused, "we can say we're proving our concept before we expand."

"Exactly!" Chatman agreed. "Decent avionics are a must, too. We'll be operating across the Gulf of Mexico and the Caribbean. And they need to be Citation X planes, which we're all type-rated on."

"I know who to call," Alex responded.

"Good. Alex, set the whole thing up with the FAA and Customs," Chatman said. "Be sure they think it's a humanitarian effort."

Alex nodded, asking, "Will the bomber pilots be joining us as we proposed in the plan?"

"I don't know yet. Darginsky wasn't specific in the message, but I think we should plan on them being here." Chatman arose and began to pace. "In the meanwhile, Alex, become an expert on Target Route Alpha, the East Coast routing. You'll train one of the bomber pilots for that route."

A knock on the office door interrupted them. Michael reached for his pistol, but Chatman stopped him with a wave of his hand as he moved toward the door. "It's probably the food." Chatman paid the delivery boy. Michael took the pizza box and set it on the coffee table.

Then he started toward the refrigerator for beer.

"Let's limit it to one. I want clear heads while we brainstorm," Chatman cautioned. "Michael, you'll be flying the third Citation on the west target route, or Target Route Bravo, between Bay St. Louis and the Kansas ranch. Like Alex, I want you to become an expert on that route since you'll be training the other bomber pilot. You'll also be involved with Target Route Charlie, the mission profile of the Su-57. The Su-57 poses some special problems due to its fuel capacity. We're going to have to refuel at the Kansas ranch. Since Alex has flown the aircraft, he'll work with you on the procedure. We must plan to do its turnaround in ten minutes."

"Okay," Michael replied.

"As you both know, the Americans keep two planes on alert that carry sophisticated communications equipment and a staff of people, including a general or an admiral. The senior officer on board the plane has the authority to launch nuclear weapons in the absence of orders from the president or any other authority in their chain of command if the people above him are wiped out. One of these planes is an E-4B, a Boeing 747 based at Offutt Air Force Base in Omaha. The other is the Navy's E-6B, a Boeing 707 based at Tinker Air Force Base in Oklahoma City.

"Both those bases are in the interior of the continental United States. There's a reason for that. Taking out those bases would require missiles launched from either ocean or from Russian territory over the North Pole. An attack quick enough to get those planes before they take off is not feasible. We must destroy them by surprise, and simultaneously. This is the most difficult part of the plan."

He noticed Alex frowning. "What are you thinking, Alex?" Chatman asked.

"If one of those planes gets airborne, our Su-57 will have to do its job quickly."

"How will we know if either aircraft gets off the ground before our missiles hit their bases?" Michael asked.

"We'll already know which one is in the air," Alex offered.

"Indeed!" Chatman exclaimed. "Those planes don't always stay on ground-alert status. It's their practice to launch at least one of them during a crisis, but there's at least one other occasion that they automatically launch."

Alex and Michael responded in unison. "The State of the Union address."

Chatman smiled. "Comrades, we need to know which one is in the air during the speech and its route of flight. Any ideas?"

"Yeah," answered Alex. "Their Airborne Command Post most certainly operates on canned flight plan routes which I'm sure are in the FAA's computer."

"How do we find out which of those routes and which plane will fly that night?" asked Chatman.

"Somebody involved in operations at those bases can tell us if we can convince them," said Michael.

Chatman nodded. "We will get Darginsky to find us that person. Then you, Michael, will do the convincing."

"I've got an idea," Alex said. "The Kansas City Air Route Traffic Control Center is responsible for the airspace over both Omaha and Oklahoma City. Let's focus on finding someone in that center."

"Bravo," said Michael. "But if we locate such an individual, how does that help the Su-57?"

Chatman explained, "If we know the location of the plane, the Su-57's navigation package can calculate an intercept and destroy it. Then they'll proceed to the ranch where you'll refuel it. By that time, the four cruise missiles will have destroyed Washington, Norfolk, Omaha, and Oklahoma City, and the United States will be a mass of confusion with no government. And they will think it was all done by terrorists." He smiled. "During the initial confusion, the Sukhoi will fly back to Cuba, and the two bombers will depart US airspace to the south."

"Bobby," Michael interjected, "killing the Airborne Command Post will certainly be interpreted as an attack by a so-called 'peer nation.' No sane person would think terrorists were capable of that."

"You're correct, Michael, but be patient. I'll show you why it won't matter in a minute."

"Yeah, then comes the real challenge," said Alex. "I hope the guys back home handle the aftermath properly, or it's going to be much worse than when the Japanese attacked Pearl Harbor."

"Alex has a point," Michael agreed. "It's going to be the biggest gamble in Russian history."

Chatman nodded. "Let's brew another pot of coffee. But first, do either of you have any questions so far?"

"Are we sure that the missiles can reach their targets without being intercepted?" asked Alex.

"It's a good question," Chatman responded. "But yes, we are. The missiles will be coming in low and fast enough that any air defense would have only seconds to respond. And remember, the missiles will be flying at the same speeds and profiles as regular airplanes but without an operating transponder. The chain of command simply won't be able to act fast enough at any of the target locations."

Michael nodded in agreement as he said, "You haven't mentioned NORAD. What's their role in this and why aren't we taking them out too?"

Alex, the former fighter pilot, provided the answer. "The North American Aerospace Defense Command is defensive only. They cannot pull any nuclear triggers. They mostly track satellites and launch interceptors to chase drug runners or little airplanes that blunder into restricted airspace. NORAD is a shell of what it used to be."

Chatman nodded, "That's right. The worst NORAD can do is detect us coming over the Gulf of Mexico, and that's not going to happen if we split their coverage and stay low. I'm not saying it will be impossible for the Americans to detect them, just that the probability is extremely slim."

"Alex," Michael said, "they've got interceptors on alert in New Orleans!"

Alex agreed. "But their tiny interceptor force exists mostly for anti-terrorist operations. They're afraid of another 9/11 attack. They're not planning on a low-altitude attack from the south."

"What about balloons?" Michael asked.

Alex shook his head. "They're phasing them out. But they're experimenting with untethered balloons that change altitude to take advantage of wind direction. It's still in the test phase, and they don't know when or where these things will be up, but those balloons are designed to survey vehicles on the ground." He looked at his cohorts. "They're too busy spying on themselves." All three men snickered.

"Now, then," Chatman said, "let's talk about the pre-attack and post-attack game plans, which are crucial to the success of LUCIFER/INBLUE. I feel confident about our ability to pull the tiger's tail, and yes, Michael, it's the biggest gamble in history."

Chatman stressed that control of information about the events was the most crucial factor for success. He noted that those measures had already been set in motion with the rumors about the stolen weapons. That, he emphasized, would become a full-fledged international scare with the Houthis threatening to use them. "The Houthis are not in on this plan," he told them, "so they'll deny they're involved, but their track record of anti-US rhetoric won't convince anybody. We want the threat of a nuclear terrorist act to be the focal point of Western intelligence over the next three months. If we keep their attention on events overseas, the Americans will be convinced they can locate the missing weapons before they cross the ocean . . . until they do.

"The Kremlin is cooling down the adversarial rhetoric. Kozlov wants the Americans thinking we're sincere in helping them with this terrorist threat. They will provide some verifiable information to demonstrate their peaceful intentions to the world."

"But, Bobby," Michael asked, "the Americans have been down on Kozlov. Will they take the bait?"

"I think they will," answered Chatman. "They won't have a choice and, knowing Phillips, he'll welcome better relations. It would look good if he ran again. Anyway, the disinformation campaign is Darginsky's job."

Chatman added that he would use his friends in the US media to ensure the nuclear terrorist threat made front-page news leading up to mission night. "The threat of nuclear terrorism will be justification for having Phillips declare that January 31—the day of the State of the Union address—will be a national day of prayer and unity. A lot of Americans will snicker at the idea, but the prayer day plan does a lot of things for us. If Phillips declares it a federal holiday, there will be minimal manning at US military installations, including all radar sites. Our aircraft should be able to slip across the Mississippi coast. There'll be mass confusion during the first few days after the mission. It's essential that we use that confusion to our advantage."

"I've no doubt our guys in Moscow can handle that part of it," said Alex. "Look at what they achieved in the last few US elections. I just hope some trigger-happy American submarine commander doesn't decide to blow Mother Russia off the map."

"Remember," Chatman responded, "that under the US two-person concept no single individual can launch a nuclear weapon. And those missiles are preloaded with the codes. They won't launch until the right code is entered, and the sub commanders must get the codes from a proper presidential authority. Even if they somehow found a way to get around the code protocol, both the commander and the exec have safes with individual keys inside them, and they have to insert those keys in two different keyholes many feet apart and turn them at the same time."

"I see your point," said Michael. "But surely someone in the administration will be sent to some secret bunker."

Chatman smiled. "Have you heard of the 'designated survivor'?"

"Yes," Michael said. "How will we deal with him or her?"

"Last year their designated survivor was the secretary of education." Alex and Michael grunted their amusement. "The year before that," Chatman continued, "it was the secretary of agriculture."

More guffaws were issued by the two agents. "Maybe next time it'll be the assistant dogcatcher!" Alex blurted.

Chatman allowed himself a grin. "But we could be making a mistake assuming the person Phillips selects will be too timid to pull the trigger. There is nothing that requires the president to designate a cabinet member. I'll persuade the president to appoint the honorable Senator Dan Hawkins to be the designee. That would improve Phillips's relations with the opposition party. I think he'll go for it. If Phillips won't cross party lines, then I'll suggest he appoint the secretary of housing and human development. She has a PhD in social work but knows nothing about national defense. She would be highly reluctant to pull the nuclear trigger. But regardless of who is appointed, there will still be the confusion and the strong indications that terrorists are responsible."

"Bobby, why not just have Darginsky arrange to take the designated survivor out on attack night?" Alex asked.

"Because the survivor always has plenty of protection. Taking him out is not feasible. Let's put our confidence in the terrorist deception. Hawkins will fall for it."

"And if he doesn't?" Michael asked.

"Senator Hawkins is a dove of the highest order. He voted against appropriations for the B-21 bomber and the F-35; he voted against nuclear weapons modernization; he has opposed nearly every defense initiative that's come before the Senate."

"He led opposition against supporting Ukraine, didn't he?" Michael added.

"Yes, he did. And he led the Senate delegation to Moscow to meet with our esteemed leader. Comrades, this is the guy we want to take the helm of American government in the aftermath of the attack. If I can't persuade Phillips to appoint him as the designee, I'll see that he is not in Washington on attack night."

"How are you going to do that?" Alex asked.

"We'll see that Senator Hawkins is called away from the capital.

He will then become the sole surviving member of Congress."

Chatman took a moment to reflect on this particular facet of decapitating the US government. Certainly, every aspect was important—the bombers, the Sukhoi, the news media, the threat after the attack—but who survives in the chain of authority would be the most critical element. He knew it was crucial that someone friendly to Russia, and unlikely to order a military retaliation, be the remaining decision-maker.

"Won't it look suspicious?" Alex asked.

"Alex," Michael said, "Did you hear what Bobby just said? It won't matter if it looks suspicious because all the other government lackies will be dead."

Smiling, Chatman continued, "We'll also guarantee our friends in the media miss the Washington speech. We'll need them in the new America."

"Again, how are you going to do that?" Michael asked.

"I'm becoming the greatest friend Ron Goodman ever had."

"No shit?" Michael said, chuckling.

"Now, we have a golden opportunity to ensure certain hard-line generals and politicians don't cause any problems. I will suggest that Phillips invite those individuals to the State of the Union address. Remember, American military capacity for obtaining and analyzing real-time intelligence will be severely curtailed by the nuclear detonations over Washington and Norfolk since the Pentagon will be destroyed and the CIA won't have anyone in power to report to. Meanwhile, Russian missile subs will move toward launch positions off the American coasts and SS-25s will be positioned in Cuba and Venezuela."

"Then comes the threat, which of course is an empty one," observed Michael.

"Yes," agreed Chatman. "Kozlov will announce that Russia was responsible for the attack on the United States, that the US is surrounded by Russian nuclear weaponry, and that further resistance will only result in the needless loss of millions of lives."

"That's why destroying the Airborne Command Post airplanes and their bases is so important," Michael said. "That removes anyone who can order the use of nuclear weapons."

"Exactly," Chatman agreed. "And I believe I can influence Kozlov not to use any more nuclear weapons either."

"Sounds good to me," Alex said. "I'm ready, but I wonder if the American people will be ready."

Chatman considered his response. Having lived in America for decades, he was well aware that its population could be controlled by a sophisticated and purposeful news media. "Again, it's a problem of controlling information about events," he said. "If the media—led by correspondents that we influence—barrage the American people with the notion that joining hands with their Russian brothers is the only available option, then that's the option they will choose. Imagine Ron Goodman refusing to entertain any other option than surrender, and of course, I will trumpet the same opinion to my followers."

"Are we sure some general won't decide to go it alone?" asked Alex.

"We talked about that," Chatman replied. "It can't happen. Alex, put yourself in his shoes. There will have been four nuclear detonations already, and that is no bluff. Plus, anyone who had access to the nuclear codes will be dead. That's why it won't matter when the US government finally figures out this wasn't a terrorist attack. And the claim of an imminent and massive secondary attack will have to be respected."

"I'll start the search for two Citations first thing in the morning," Alex said.

"And I'll be standing by to go to Omaha to meet our informer, whenever they find him," added Michael.

"Great!" Chatman replied. "I'm going to request Darginsky search for our new friend in Omaha." Chatman smiled. "Get some sleep. The next few weeks are going to be very busy."

CHAPTER SIX

NOVEMBER 5
RALEIGH, NORTH CAROLINA

Bobby Chatman sat down behind the desk in the television studio. They were preparing to tape his midweek devotion which would air on the *Free World Gospel Hour.* However, the events of the past few days made it difficult to settle into his pastoral frame of mind.

"Okay," shouted Lily Norman, production director. "Five minutes on the set! We're all set, Brother Chatman. Here's your ending segment to cue the follow-on program."

"Thank you, Lily," he replied, shuffling the paper to the rear of his own notes. "What music are we opening with today?"

She consulted her schedule. "We're opening with 'Power in the Blood,' music only."

"Not bad, Lily," he said thoughtfully. "However, we have some big news which makes me feel 'Onward Christian Soldiers' would be a better opening song. Is it too late to substitute?"

"Oh, no, Brother Chatman," she replied confidently. "We just need to queue up the correct MP3. I'll have the sound room do it right away."

"Thank you so much."

A few minutes later Chatman sat in his study listening to the powerful marching strains of the old hymn. Soon he was sliding into character.

"Ten seconds!" shouted Lily. As the music faded, he was ready to play Bobby Chatman. "And now, from his study at the Free World

Gospel Cathedral in Raleigh, North Carolina, the founder of the *Free World Gospel Hour*," said the announcer, "Reverend Bobby Chatman!"

"Good afternoon, brothers and sisters," he began, wearing a confident smile. "Welcome to our *Free World Gospel Hour*. We believe in keeping you apprised of what's going on in the world, and that's the focus of our Thursday program. If you haven't already done so, I hope you'll consider becoming a Faith Warrior. We'll tell you how you can do that later in the program.

"I reported last Thursday that I would be in Washington for a meeting with our brother, President Andrew Phillips, and some of our friends in Congress, to discuss several pieces of legislation." He went on to summarize his efforts with the president and Congress to limit pornography and to allow student prayer in school.

"I'm sorry to say not all the news from Washington is good. The president has been dealing with the threat of stolen Russian nuclear weapons." He shifted in his chair. "I want to ask you to join with me and pray for the president as he deals with this crisis. Let's bow our heads right now and ask God to guide Andrew Phillips as he leads our nation." He lowered his head in silent prayer.

Chatman lifted his head after thirty seconds and looked directly into the camera. "Now, friends, if you're a regular follower of the *Free World Gospel Hour*, you know I have devoted my life to using the power of prayer to defeat the forces of godless Communism. I am happy to announce a giant step forward in this battle."

He rose from behind the desk and walked over to a large map of the United States with aerial photos of the *Free World Gospel Hour* facilities in North Carolina, Kansas, and Mississippi. An arrow pointed toward South America.

"The real battle against oppression is in Latin America. It's a battle that we must not lose. First Cuba fell under Russian influence, followed by Nicaragua, El Salvador, and most recently Venezuela. Friends, we must defeat godless tyranny in our hemisphere through the love of God!

"God has led us in research aimed at increasing the food supply by developing heartier, heat-tolerant strains of wheat, and increasing the yield of farmed shrimp. We'll soon share this technology with our southern neighbors. But first we need to establish a distribution system. We will use this system to distribute food and clothing as our agricultural program is developed."

Chatman picked up a model of a Cessna Citation business jet. "To do this we're going to set up our own mini airline. We'll use two Cessna Citations, just like this one that we'll reconfigure to carry cargo.

"Fellow believers, nothing has the potential for defeating Russian and Chinese influence in Latin America like this new project. We'll start out small to prove the concept, and later we'll purchase larger jet freighters. With Thanksgiving and Christmas coming up, we'll let you know how you can take part in this initial effort."

He explained how they could be part of this effort by sending in contributions earmarked for fuel for the jets. To show appreciation the ministry would award gifts depending on the level of donations. The gifts ranged from the ministry's official lapel pins to 1/32 scale models of a Citation.

Taking a seat behind the desk again, he said, "We'll defeat them by flying food, clothing, and technological know-how to the people they seek to enslave. From this day forward our 'airline' will be known as Red Star Express. We need your help, and God is counting on you to support His plan by helping us get Red Star Express off the ground."

As the notes to 'Onward Christian Soldiers' struck up again, Chatman's face faded from view and an announcer began instructing viewers on how to support Red Star Express or to become a new Faith Warrior. Chatman relaxed, feeling satisfied with his performance.

Three hours later Bobby Chatman sat in the hangar with Alex and Michael, watching the playback of the morning taping as they ate barbecue ribs and Brunswick stew.

"A nice job," commented Alex. "You told them just enough to get them interested."

"Well, we're off and running," said Chatman. "I want to remind each of you that we must convince the FAA and Customs that we're running a legitimate charitable operation. Any potential problem areas?"

"Things are moving along fine at my end," said Alex. "I already found one Citation and I'm sure another lead will pan out. Also, I'll touch base with the FAA district offices to brief them on our plan. The same goes for Customs."

Chatman nodded his approval. "Any other problems you can think of?" They both shook their heads in the negative. "Okay. Keep me updated."

After jogging up to the house, Chatman walked into his study. He turned on the television, intending to get an update on the day's events. He was surprised to see Ron Goodman in conversation with President Andrew Phillips. They were discussing the missing Russian nuclear weapons and US fears that they had fallen into terrorist hands. To Chatman's delight the president confirmed that Russian intelligence had verified the 'backpack' weapons were sold by the Chechens to the Houthis in Yemen. The Russian ambassador had offered assistance in determining their location and had even provided photographs of the weapons in question. The interview closed with Phillips assuring the nation that no stone would remain unturned until the bombs were located, and the threat of their use eliminated.

"Ah, Comrade Kozlov, you are doing your part," he murmured. He removed the LUCIFER/INBLUE flash drive from his safe and inserted it into the computer. He logged on to Darginsky's secure platform and typed a report on the announcement of the Red Star Express operation.

There, thought Chatman as he shut the computer down and returned the LUCIFER/INBLUE drive to the safe. *I've done all I can. Ninety days until the mission. An eternity one way and the blink of an eye in another.*

MOSCOW

Viktor Darginsky was running late. He was supposed to meet Nikolai Kozlov in the Kremlin in twenty minutes, but the Senat limousine was stuck in a traffic jam. A large truck had overturned after skidding on a patch of black ice.

"We'll be moving shortly, sir," said the driver. "They're towing the truck away now."

"Good," said Darginsky. "Try to hurry. We cannot keep the president waiting."

Darginsky had a lot to think about as they inched along. He logged onto the secure channel with his laptop. After reading the message from Lucifer, he realized time was short to solve some of the problems mentioned. He needed to report to Kozlov on the status of all known problem areas.

Identifying a compromisable American citizen, who would be used to track the US Airborne Command Post's location, was the task that most concerned him. If Kozlov asked, he would say he had the perfect agent working on it, Agent Katarina Feskanich, a modern-day Mata Hari.

As the Senat pulled up to the VIP entrance of the Kremlin, his driver said, "Sorry about the delay."

"No problem," replied Darginsky. "I should be about an hour and will want to return to the dacha afterward."

The Russian leader's secretary met him in the outer office and showed him directly into Kozlov's study. The president motioned for Darginsky to sit.

"I'm sorry I'm late, sir," said Darginsky.

"Just don't make a habit of it," warned Kozlov.

"Yes, sir. I received two messages from Lucifer detailing some problems that I was researching."

Kozlov wasted no time with small talk. "I have had little time to study your plan. I called you here to answer my questions. I received this today at the Security Council meeting from General Gavrilov," he said ominously as he slid a file across the desk.

The report was classified top secret and was a strategic analysis of the current internal situation in Russia with emphasis on the widespread unemployment. The report warned of rioting over lack of food during the winter and that internal revolution within the other Federation nations was a distinct possibility.

"Comrade President, we're already aware of these facts."

"True," grumbled Kozlov, "but what *is* new is the open hostility among the members. They are dividing themselves into factions and Gavrilov is the head of one. He has been popular ever since he returned from Ukraine. To maintain control, I had to reveal some details about our new caper."

Darginsky became alarmed. "What did you tell them?"

"I acknowledged the danger of internal strife this winter. Therefore, I announced massive Federation military exercises to begin on January 15. The presence of battle-ready troops will help control the population. Gavrilov and his faction were argumentative, so I felt a trump card was needed. I told them we were behind the false-flag story, anticipating the Americans might be willing to renegotiate selling us grain and lifting embargoes in return for information about the stolen weapons. I said nothing, of course, about LUCIFER/INBLUE."

Darginsky breathed a sigh of relief. "Did your trump card work?"

"For the moment," replied Kozlov. "I got a standing ovation and Gavrilov left with a scowl on his face. I bought us some time. But something has been bothering me. I was impressed with the group, all except the colonel from the bomber wing, Piekarski. He had the smell of a politician. I have enough of that kind here."

"Yes, sir, I know exactly what you mean. I'm afraid we are victims of our own haste. We sent a message to the bomber wing seeking highly qualified individuals with solid English skills, giving them less than twenty-four hours to report to Moscow. Piekarski, smelling something big, selected himself. According to his records, he is a mediocre pilot but was at the top of his officer training class in English. He is also the son of our minister of agriculture, so—"

"I don't give a fuck whose son he is!" shouted Kozlov.

Darginsky quickly replied, "Sir, his English skills are critical. We will make sure he has a top-notch copilot, and we'll have a spare aircraft commander riding in Piekarski's zampolit seat for the mission."

"You do that," said Kozlov, menacingly. "Now, you said Lucifer had mentioned some problems. What?"

Darginsky outlined the problems Lucifer had detailed. Kozlov smiled at the mention of Agent Feskanich. Darginsky hesitated. "You know her, sir?"

Kozlov slowly nodded, still grinning wolfishly.

Darginsky cleared his throat. Then he outlined his plan for allowing Feskanich to use her expertise in locating an American in the air traffic control center in Kansas City who could be compromised.

Kozlov leaned forward for emphasis, speaking in a threatening tone, "If you fail in finding us an informer—which I doubt you can do with the time we have left—this operation will be immediately canceled and your future will be . . . *uncertain*, shall we say."

Darginsky nodded nervously.

"You're certain our cruise missiles won't be detected once they're launched?"

"Quite certain, sir," replied Darginsky confidently. "The Kh-55s will not have a transponder on board, and they are so small that it's doubtful they'll be detected on air traffic control radar. The filters used on American radar scopes eliminate most of the small raw returns. Our missiles will be at the speed of typical airliners and using normal air traffic routes, so they won't stand out."

Kozlov got up and walked around the desk to face Darginsky. "You're going to personally make sure this stolen weapons story gets pressed to its fullest effectiveness?"

"Absolutely, sir," responded the agent, not sure if he should stand. He decided not to since he was taller than Kozlov.

Kozlov nodded. "Is Major Petrov to be the aircraft commander on the mission to Washington?"

"Yes, sir."

"That will make him responsible for both Washington and Norfolk, while Piekarski is responsible for what?"

"Omaha and Oklahoma City," Darginsky added.

"And Ridgik will be in charge of destroying the Airborne Command Post." Darginsky nodded, and the president continued. "You are to time the launch of the missiles so the Washington missile is launched first. No other weapons are to be activated until confirmation is received that the Washington missile is on its way and the arming sequence is confirmed."

"That's the plan, sir."

Kozlov eyed the agent. "If the Washington weapon indicates any failure, the rest of the mission is to be aborted, and our aircraft are to get the hell out of US airspace. Do you understand?"

"Yes, sir. I must say, I'm impressed with your grasp of the challenges with this plan." He immediately regretted his remark.

Kozlov stared a hole in Darginsky's forehead. "I have enough people trying to flatter me."

Darginsky apologized and squirmed.

Kozlov continued. "I want you to keep me posted on any new problems either here or at Lucifer's end. The next ninety days are going to go quickly. Do not be surprised if this whole thing turns out to be just a feasibility study. You can have my secretary call for your car."

Darginsky rose and started for the door. "Viktor," said Kozlov, "if we do attempt the LUCIFER/INBLUE plan, we must be sure we do not fail."

"We won't, Comrade President," he said as he closed the door behind him, pleased that Kozlov had finally addressed him by his first name, but uneasy with the way he deliberately articulated it.

CHAPTER SEVEN

DECEMBER 8
MOSCOW

The morning was bitter cold as the sun rose low in the winter sky, but it was warm and cozy at the cedar dacha in the forest.

"Well, boys, we've been here for five weeks," said Major Ridgik, trying to lighten things up with his down-home American dialect, cracking them up with his heavy accent. "What do y'all figure is gonna happen?"

"Well, pardner," answered Bachvaroff, his back seater, butchering the dialect even worse than the sniper pilot, "I don't rightly know, but I'm about to jet down to Texas and eat a little barbecue."

It had been an intensive experience—improving their English and learning a new lifestyle—but Gregori Petrov appreciated the Su-57 crew's comic relief.

The double doors to the room opened and Viktor Darginsky entered with a tall dark-haired Russian wearing the uniform and four stripes of an Aeroflot captain.

"Good morning, gentlemen," said Darginsky. "Welcome back to our classroom in the forest. If you will take your seats, we can get started."

Darginsky and the Aeroflot captain unpacked a computer and set up a PowerPoint presentation. They passed out a pamphlet with the Aeroflot logo on the front entitled "Operations in American Airspace."

"Gentlemen, we have a few items to cover before you get back in your cockpits. The feasibility studies you've been chosen for involve penetration of American air defenses during a lowered American-readiness condition."

"A surprise attack!" blurted Ridgik.

Darginsky smiled. "Precisely! We are confident of successfully penetrating America's coastal defense, but we need to discuss what happens once inside the American ADIZ. Today we have Captain Gustav Musuriak with us. As chief pilot in charge of American operations for Aeroflot, he is an expert on the American airspace system. Captain Musuriak is a lieutenant colonel in our Air Force Reserve and an IL-76 pilot, so he understands the challenge you have ahead of you. Learn everything you can from him. The success of this mission, and your own lives, could depend on it."

Petrov raised an eyebrow. This sounded like more than a "feasibility study." Catching Ridgik's eye, he sensed the sniper pilot was bothered by the same notion.

"Good morning," began Musuriak. "I will begin with some comparisons between the airspace systems of the United States and Russia." His first PowerPoint slide showed a lineup of various aircraft types waiting for takeoff that included airliners, a corporate jet, and a Cessna 172. "All of the aircraft shown in this slide are owned either by major airlines or by private individuals. They all have equal access to the US airspace system."

The slide changed to a B-52 in flight, and Musuriak continued. "The only real government-owned aircraft in the United States are those assigned to the military, and some that are operated by civil government agencies. But even they operate either within assigned military training areas or in civil airspace following the same rules as everybody else. There are tens of thousands of aircraft movements within the US every day, and thousands of citizens own their own small airplanes. It is one of the freest airspace systems in the world."

Petrov had a momentary vision of Olya, Stefan, and himself "saying hello to the sun" in their own plane. It was almost too much to comprehend.

"The primary air traffic control radar system in the US is what they call ARSR-4. It was deployed at dozens of locations in the early 1990s and has been continuously upgraded. These radar sites serve a dual purpose of civilian air traffic control and military surveillance. They have a range of two hundred fifty nautical miles—about four hundred sixty kilometers. But unless they are elevated, they have limited capacity to see low-flying targets. Identified air traffic is routed to their air traffic control centers, while unidentified returns are sent directly to their air defense control centers. Currently, the military side is focused on antidrug operations and the possibility of hijacked airliners.

"Now, this will amaze you: with a transponder turned off, many aircraft within US airspace rarely show up on radar. They are not even required to have ADS-B installed if they remain clear of controlled airspace."

"What's their definition of controlled airspace?" Ridgik asked.

"It's the areas around larger cities, big airports, and all airspace between eighteen thousand and sixty thousand feet." Musuriak looked around. "Is everyone familiar with ADS-B?"

All heads nodded.

Petrov recalled that ADS-B was a relatively new technology adopted around the world. It allowed air traffic control to follow aircraft without the use of radar. A supplement to radar, it was dependent on GPS and ground transmitters. In the US, ADS-B was required only in airspace where transponders were required.

Petrov signaled a question. "Our military planes do not have ADS-B. Will that pose a problem?"

"No," Musuriak answered. "Our host tells me they may install such units in your aircraft if time allows. If not, the penalty for not using ADS-B where it is required is a letter from their agency. They could investigate and impose penalties, but that would take weeks." He smiled. "It's safe to say the Americans will not pull your pilot licenses."

After the laughter subsided, Musuriak added, "Remember: once you have crossed into the US undetected, you are assumed to be 'friendly' and can go anywhere you want. You can choose to utilize the air traffic control system or not. Once over the continental land mass, you're dealing with civilian controllers with virtually no training in military operations. They do have contingency plans such as during the September 11, 2001 terrorist attacks. They completely shut down their airspace within minutes—most impressive. Whoever is left . . . becomes—"

"A target," Ridgik blurted.

"Exactly."

Petrov raised his hand. "You said this ARSR has a four-hundred-sixty-kilometer range, with the ability to detect low-running intruders over the water, if the radars are located high enough. Are they?"

"Along the Gulf of Mexico, generally not, although they are built on short towers to get above the clutter," Musuriak answered.

"There's no high ground along the coast that you are going to enter," Darginsky added.

"Suppose they do detect us," Ridgik asked. "What then?"

"Then that data is linked to their air defense command center, who could order the closest alert fighters to investigate," Musuriak responded.

"If that happened, how would we know?" Ridgik added.

"We've given this some thought," Darginsky interjected. "If we placed human resources within visual observation distance of the airports that have alert fighters and they observe a scramble, they would report it to us and we would turn our aircraft around."

"And if the interceptors got close enough to identify us?" Bachvaroff asked.

Darginsky shrugged. "This is the chance we take. This theoretical mission scenario . . ." His eyes cut to Musuriak. ". . . is not without its risks."

"The ability to operate under Visual Flight Rules," Musuriak continued, "gives American pilots tremendous freedom and flexibility. A pilot could conceivably depart an uncontrolled airport on the East

Coast and fly all the way to the West Coast without talking to air traffic control. So do you understand now, Major Ridgik, how airplanes can be ignored in US airspace?"

The sniper pilot nodded. "It's amazing there's no requirement to file a flight plan or to be positively identified."

"Yes, as long as they are not in airspace or weather where it is required. But we're talking about thousands of airplanes flying at any one time. To track so much traffic would require a colossal air traffic control system, or a drastic reduction in freedom of movement. Americans are not ready for the cost of the one, or the restrictions of the other."

"What about altitudes?" asked Petrov. "Do their air traffic control radars have height-finder capability?"

"None," replied Musuriak. "They depend on the Mode C function of your transponder to announce your altitude, and it is against their rules for a pilot to turn Mode C off in controlled airspace where it is required or above ten thousand feet." He went on to explain that turning off the mode C function would only cause an investigation against them, not a fighter scramble. "Now, unless there are further questions, that is all I have. Good luck and good hunting."

"Take a break," said Darginsky. "Lunch in the main dining room in an hour, then I want to see our Su-57 crew in here at thirteen hundred hours, followed by our Bear pilots at thirteen thirty hours."

"A fascinating morning," said Ridgik as the meeting broke up.

Petrov nodded. "Can you believe how easy it is to enter US airspace and fly around at your leisure?"

"And how about owning your own airplane? Can you imagine flying down to the Black Sea anytime you like?"

"No, I cannot," said Petrov, remembering his earlier thoughts.

"I sure hope we have fried chicken for lunch," said Ridgik, smacking his lips. "That's my favorite American food."

Darginsky led a disappointed Ridgik and Bachvaroff into the study after a beef stew lunch. "Have a seat," he said as he closed the door. "Today is the last day you two will train together with Petrov and Piekarski. You both will be moving to the Murom air base just south of Gorky. I am aware you two have been testing the new two-seat Su-57s. Your first task is to get very good using the air refueling system. You must become proficient under all conditions—even lights out, if necessary. The hypothetical mission depends on crossing the Atlantic with no available divert runways.

"While you are burning up all that fuel, you will be working on the second project: getting very good at using the on-board navigation equipment and your expertise in intercept geometry to solve long-range intercept problems. Your primary armament will be the R77M air-to-air missile. We want you to be able to find the target, at night, in all kinds of weather, and with no outside assistance other than a position, course, and speed report on the target."

"I think we can handle that," commented Bachvaroff confidently.

"May I ask what kind of target?" asked Ridgik.

"Assume it's a very large aircraft," replied Darginsky. "There is one other thing. You are going to practice night approaches and landings to a very short runway, only twenty-five hundred meters long by thirty meters wide. You must get very good at getting the '57 down and stopped with minimal approach aids. We will refuel your aircraft with the type available in the US, Jet A. It is of a lesser grade than the TS-1 your Su-57 normally uses. That will result in degraded performance. You will practice your short field operations with Jet A fuel."

"I can feel my asshole puckering up already," said Ridgik, with a grin on his face.

"Yours! How about mine?" laughed Bachvaroff.

"We didn't say it would be easy," said Darginsky with a smile. "I will be in touch regularly. You are to convey any problems only to me. Any questions?"

"Only one," replied Ridgik. "You promised me a trip to America as part of this 'feasibility study.' Is that still part of the plan?"

"Patience, my friend."

"Well, you have my curiosity aroused," said Ridgik.

"Mine too," agreed Bachvaroff.

"Have a good trip, comrades."

The two pilots filed out of the room to find one of the SVR chauffeurs waiting with their bags. They met Petrov and Piekarski in the hallway, and the four of them shook hands.

"Well, wherever you're going, fly safe!" Petrov said in English to his new friend.

"You too," Ridgik replied. "And be checking six for friend and foe alike if you know what I mean," he said in obvious reference to Piekarski. "Maybe we'll be seeing you soon."

"Perhaps," said Petrov, "but I don't know if that's something to look forward to."

"Me neither," confided Ridgik.

After saying goodbye to Ridgik and Bachvaroff, Petrov and Piekarski filed into the study with Darginsky.

As the two bomber pilots took their seats, Darginsky set two briefcases and a laptop computer on the table. "The two of you will be going in a different direction from Majors Ridgik and Bachvaroff. They will be working on some projects here in Russia."

He started a video on the laptop which opened with organ music. Petrov immediately recognized it as some sort of religious hymn.

An announcer welcomed the audience to the *Free World Gospel Hour* and introduced Reverend Bobby Chatman. They sat for half an hour and listened to this Chatman discuss news events and a meeting he had with the president of the United States. The pilots perked up when Chatman began talking about a "mini airline" and announced he was going to name it "Red Star Express." The video was unlike anything Petrov had ever seen before, and from Piekarski's expression, Petrov could tell he had never seen anything like it before either.

"So, what did you think of the Reverend Bobby Chatman, comrades?" Darginsky asked.

Petrov spoke first. "Is he for real? I mean, was that some kind of propaganda?"

"Oh, he is most certainly for real," answered Darginsky, "and his message is one that huge numbers of Americans take very seriously. He is a television evangelist. Most religious Americans are Christians, and he is a very powerful spokesman for them."

"Did he really meet with the president of the United States?" asked Piekarski. "I can't imagine such a person sitting down with President Kozlov and influencing government policy."

"Everything he claimed is true," answered Darginsky. "The current US president, Andrew Phillips, is a strong follower of Chatman. He believes that he is being guided by his God. This has caused problems for nations trying to deal with the United States. It has been especially difficult for us after the recent debacle on the Finnish border. Bobby Chatman is a close confidant of this US president."

"How about the mini airline he talked about?" asked Petrov. "Can a television evangelist do that?"

"Yes," said Darginsky with a smile. "And you can ask him yourself. You see, the Reverend Bobby Chatman is a Russian citizen who's been working in the United States as a deep-cover agent for twenty years, and he currently reports directly to me. You can imagine how important he is since he has direct access to the American president. You'll have the pleasure of meeting him soon." Petrov was shocked, and he could tell Darginsky enjoyed seeing his and Piekarski's expressions.

"Soon?" Petrov asked. "How soon? Is he traveling to Russia?"

Darginsky threw his head back and let loose an uncharacteristic cackle. "No, he is not. You two will be going to the United States and flying as copilots in his new Red Star Express operation. Such an experience will allow you to learn firsthand about the workings of the

American air traffic control system. Now you know why we spent the last five weeks giving you a crash course in American culture."

"You say that Josef and I will be copilots," said Petrov. "Who will we be flying with?"

"A good question," Darginsky said, starting the video again. "This is footage of the inaugural flight of Red Star Express," answered Darginsky. "That is Bobby Chatman, and the two gentlemen who will be leaving the plane next are his regular pilots. Their American names are Alex Marsh and Michael Gerson. They also happen to work for me. When Red Star Express becomes operational, they will each be flying a Citation like the one shown here. The airplane can be flown single-pilot, but in the interest of safety, the two of you will serve as copilots."

"So, Red Star Express is a bogus operation?" asked Piekarski.

"Absolutely," replied Darginsky. "But part of your mission will be to assist Chatman in convincing the American public that it is legitimate until our work there is complete. Now," he continued, "these two briefcases contain the paperwork necessary to make you US citizens—passports, driver's and pilot's licenses, medical records, even credit cards in the names of Gregory Peters and Joseph Pierson. There is a total of fifty thousand American dollars in each of those accounts if you need it. Finally, there is a file on your new identity with details on your personal history, including birthplace, education, and family background. You must know the facts cold. Any questions?"

"Yes," replied Petrov. "Won't our accents attract attention?"

"Absolutely not," Darginsky answered. "America is full of people with foreign accents, even with pilots. There will be no suspicion. Any other questions?" He paused. "No? All right, we are expecting great things from you two."

"Where are we off to today?" asked Piekarski.

"Oh, I'm sorry," replied Darginsky. "You will be traveling to the US via Venezuela. You are scheduled out on the Aeroflot flight this afternoon to Havana, then you will be continuing to Caracas. Your regular Russian Air Force uniform and identification card, and the orders Sergei will be carrying, will suffice for the next couple of days. Sergei is waiting for you in the hall. Have a successful trip, comrades."

After the pilots departed, Darginsky called for his limousine and instructed the driver to take him to an industrial area on the outskirts of Moscow. He directed the driver to park outside the locked gate of a formidable-looking warehouse.

While waiting for his contact to appear, Darginsky thought about Agent Feskanich's report—her office in New York had made no progress in locating a compromisable individual knowledgeable of the Airborne Command Post's movements. He reminded himself such things took time.

His thoughts were interrupted by the arrival of a large truck pulling a nondescript trailer. The driver unlocked the gate, drove through, then backed the trailer up to one of the loading docks.

"Greetings, Eduard," Darginsky said to the man emerging from the passenger side of the cab. "Is everything in order?"

"Yes, sir. Five total with the modifications you specified."

"Excellent!" said Darginsky. "And the warheads?"

"Marked 'inert.'"

"How did the test program go?"

"We tested every channel of the nav receivers for accuracy. We have run each engine three times and have repeatedly tested the launch and arming circuitry. And, as far as any official record is concerned, these birds do not exist."

"And as far as you are concerned, they never existed," advised Darginsky. "Let's get the trailer in the warehouse, and then I'd like to look inside."

Ten minutes later Darginsky was looking at the business ends of twenty Kh-55 "Ganat" cruise missiles. They were all painted with black undersides and dark gray upper surfaces. Other than the word "inert" painted on both the airframes and warhead assemblies, there were no markings except for tiny numbers stenciled at the base of each vertical fin.

"How do you tell the real ones?" asked Darginsky.

"By the tail number. If it ends with the same two-digit number, such as one-one or two-two, then it is a live missile."

"It's amazing, is it not?" Darginsky finally said. "Considering their destructive power, they seem so small."

"Yes, sir. These babies are ten times more powerful than the bomb the Americans dropped on Hiroshima—and look at how much damage it wreaked."

"Can you vary the yields on these warheads?" Darginsky asked.

"Yes, sir. How big a blast do you want?"

"A one-mile radius."

"Easy, sir. I can do it in minutes."

"Can you do it after you arrive with the missiles in Venezuela?" Eduard nodded. "Well, lock them up," said Darginsky as he stepped down from the trailer. I want to thank you for all your help. Are you ready for a little trip to make final tests on the missiles prior to loading them?"

"Any time you desire, sir."

The two shook hands and Darginsky climbed back into his limo. As the lights of Moscow faded from view, he could not stop smiling.

CHAPTER EIGHT

DECEMBER 12
OVER SOUTHERN MISSISSIPPI

Sausage and biscuit: another culinary delicacy that Bobby Chatman loved, especially when prepared by Lulu Mae Turner, the huge lovable lady who ran the kitchen and took care of the house at the farm just outside Bay St. Louis, Mississippi.

"Houston Center, Redex zero-one is climbing through five thousand feet," he transmitted. "I filed an IFR flight plan to Henderson, North Carolina. Clearance on request."

"Roger, Redex zero-one," replied the controller. "Proceed direct to Semmes. I'll have your clearance momentarily."

The clearance to the Semmes VOR, a ground navigation station, indicated that Houston ATC was getting acquainted with the Red Star Express operation. It was that familiarity that would make LUCIFER/INBLUE a success.

"Thank God we have fifty days," he murmured. "We'll need every day of it."

The start-up of Red Star Express had not gone smoothly. One of the Citations they wanted to buy had missing maintenance records. But the airplane problems were minor compared to the bureaucratic obstacles raised by the FAA and the FCC. They initially denied him the three-letter identifier "RDX" to identify his operation, as well as the Redex call signs. But Bobby Chatman, spiritual counselor to the president, had the White House intervene, and on December 1, Red

Star Express made its inaugural flight using Redex 01 as its call sign.

Alex had done well getting US Customs approval. The chief customs inspector was an ardent follower of Chatman's ministry. He pledged maximum cooperation to make return trips from Latin America as painless as possible. Alex was confident they would receive "courtesy customs" so they could land at Bay St. Louis without stopping in New Orleans.

Houston Center interrupted his thoughts with his IFR clearance, which allowed jet aircraft to make use of the high-altitude airspace where their engines were most efficient. *Beautiful!* thought Chatman, as he read back the clearance. *That's exactly Target Route Alpha.*

"Read back correct," said the controller. "Confirm your destination is One Fox Whiskey Golf."

"That's affirmative," replied Chatman. "1FWG" was computer identifier code for the Henderson farm along with "2FWG" for Bay St. Louis and "3FWG" for the Kansas ranch.

As he munched on a sausage and biscuit, he reread Darginsky's last message. The bomber pilots were in Venezuela awaiting transport to the United States. He was surprised Moscow had moved that fast. A dossier outlining the new identities of the two Russian Air Force officers said they had been told they were part of a feasibility study. Alex would fly into Caracas to drop off missionary items and the "American citizens," Peters and Pierson, would fly out with him.

A radio transmission from another plane interrupted his concentration.

"Houston Center, Redex zero-two is with you passing forty-five hundred feet."

Excellent! thought Chatman. Michael was checking in with Houston for his clearance.

Michael read back the clearance, which aligned exactly with Target Route Bravo. An hour and twenty minutes later, Chatman called Atlanta Center and requested a descent and cancelation of his IFR clearance when he got below eighteen thousand feet. He continued along the planned target route to the John H. Kerr Reservoir, a huge body of water also known as Buggs Island Lake, which they had dubbed "Launch Point Alpha." He could see Norfolk on the horizon. Richmond was also visible, as was much of the Chesapeake Bay and the southern end of the Potomac River.

The Norfolk target will be easy, he thought. The final leg of the missile's flight would track down the James River. Its warhead should take out the naval facilities, including the command-and-control facilities for missile-launching submarines. Just beyond Norfolk, Joint Base Langley-Eustis near Hampton, Virginia would be partially damaged. Any naval vessels caught in port would just be icing on the cake.

"Adios, Norfolk," mumbled Chatman sarcastically. "For the DC target, it'll have to be direct to the Richmond VOR, then direct to the Washington VOR, then northbound to ground zero for a primary route," he mused out loud.

After landing at the Henderson farm, Chatman stored all the mission-related materials in his office safe. He then spent a couple of hours taking care of *Free World Gospel Hour* financial matters. Lily Norman showed up in the early afternoon with her television crew to tape his midweek devotion. He displayed the proper spirit of Christmas, but he also made sure Red Star Express got plenty of coverage. They were planning a "sizable airlift" over Christmas.

As soon as they were done taping, he was back in the Citation, flying the cruise missile profiles, verifying the primary and secondary routings.

So far, a most productive day, he thought.

THE WHITE HOUSE

A few hours later, Bobby Chatman's limousine approached the executive mansion. It had been weeks since Chatman had been in Washington. Security in the city was very tight. Each vehicle waiting to enter the White House grounds was being carefully checked.

Chatman was amused at what LUCIFER/INBLUE had wrought. Once inside, he ducked into the men's room.

"Well, look who's here," said Ron Goodman, joining the reverend at the wash basins. "Good to see you again, Brother Chatman."

"Hi, Ron," Chatman replied. "What brings you to the executive mansion today?"

"Oh, business as usual. I guess the president's going to meet with you preachers first, then tell us what God is leading him to do about this terrorist mess. Hey, thank you for that late-night phone call. I really appreciate the scoop."

"No problem, Ron. The Lord does work in mysterious ways sometimes," he said, ignoring Goodman's anti-religious remarks. "By the way, what's the latest? I was amazed at the security today."

"Yeah, it's the tightest I've ever seen. According to my sources, the Houthis are still pissed about our airstrikes during the Israeli-Hamas war. They're threatening to use the four 'backpack' bombs to blow up a few cities and, apparently, the Russians think the threat is real."

"Fascinating," said Chatman, "assuming we trust the Russians. Ron, what do your sources think the chances are of Washington being attacked?"

"Oh, they're concerned," said Goodman. "But moving nuclear weapons, even small ones, into the US undetected will be difficult. They think we'll seize them as they enter the country."

"That's good to hear," said Chatman, enjoying the irony. "Say, it's good to see you, but I've got to run. I'm sure we'll talk again before this whole thing is over."

"Same to you, Brother Chatman," said Goodman. "And if God leads you to call me again, feel free."

"Oh I will, Ron."

A tired Andrew Phillips shook hands with Bobby Chatman in the doorway of the Cabinet Room. He watched the reverend take a seat then he looked over the room-full of ministers. Phillips admitted in his opening remarks that he was frightened by the events of the past few weeks and that he felt powerless to stop the nuclear threat. US intelligence was focusing all available resources. He told the group he believed the weapons had not left the Middle East yet. Russian information seemed to verify that fact.

"Resolve is the key," said Phillips. "I believe you ministers are uniquely equipped to help me demonstrate that resolve. I'm personally asking that you use the upcoming Christmas and New Year celebrations to rally your congregations around stopping this terrorist menace. Now, I'd like to throw the meeting open to discussion of specific game plans for generating the support of the American people."

I don't believe it, thought Chatman. *He's playing the game exactly as I wanted without any prompting.*

They all agreed that now was the time to put away petty differences and stand together as Americans. Chatman sensed he had a unique opportunity now to ensure the ultimate success of LUCIFER/INBLUE.

"Andrew," he said, as all eyes turned in his direction, "I'd like to add a thought for consideration."

"By all means, Bobby," replied a smiling Andrew Phillips. "I was beginning to think you were going to let us plan this whole thing without your input."

"You must not know Bobby Chatman as well as we do," said Reverend Billy Green, a popular Atlanta minister. "He's just been biding his time," he quipped, "and now he'll probably shoot down everything we've suggested."

"You're wrong, Billy," said a smiling Chatman. "Actually, I'm in total agreement with everything we've planned." He paused. "I've been trying to look beyond Christmas and New Year's Eve. We need a plan to keep this on the front burner during the post-holiday psychological lull."

"I'd have to agree with you," said the president. "What's your plan?"

"I was thinking," continued Chatman, "there's only one big national event during January, and that's the State of the Union address, which is scheduled for January 31. I suggest that you consider issuing an executive order declaring January 31 the 'National Day of Prayer and Unity.' You could make it a onetime federal holiday, and it would climax with your address that night."

There was a murmur of excitement as the ministers nodded their heads in agreement with Chatman's idea. Billy Green shouted, "I think it's an excellent idea!"

"I agree!" came a call from the back of the room.

The president held up his hands for order. "I agree, but it's a long time between New Year's Eve and January 31." He consulted his phone calendar. "Congress convenes on January 3. Why don't we wait exactly two weeks and have the State of the Union address on January 17? We'll declare that day, as Bobby suggested, a national day of prayer."

"I have an even better idea," said Billy Green. "Monday, the fifteenth of January, is Martin Luther King Day. Why don't we kill two birds with one stone, have a three-day 'Weekend of Prayer and Unity,' and finish it with the president's State of the Union message?"

"An outstanding idea!" said the president. "January 13 through the fifteenth will be the 'National Weekend of Prayer and Unity,' and I'll deliver the State of the Union on the evening of the fifteenth!"

NO! Chatman wanted to shout.

"Yes!" cheered the group.

"Thank you, Bobby," said the president. "As usual your inputs were outstanding. Now, let's divide into working groups to plan it."

Chatman sat in stunned silence. In the blink of an eye, he'd lost two weeks for setting up LUCIFER/INBLUE. He had exactly thirty-two days until mission night. It was essential that Darginsky be advised immediately.

"... if that's okay with you, Bobby."

Chatman realized the president was talking to him. "I'm sorry, Andrew. I was just mentally going over my January schedule. What did you say?"

"I was hoping that you would work with me on the guest list for State of the Union night," said the president. "It's a unique opportunity to show national unity by inviting all living ex-presidents, some retired generals, and such. I think we can assemble quite a group."

"I couldn't agree more, Andrew," said Chatman, realizing that with adversity had come opportunity.

When the meeting broke up Chatman wanted to call Darginsky, but he ran headlong into Ron Goodman.

"Ah, Chatman," said the reporter, sensing another scoop. "What's all the excitement about?"

"I've only got a second, Ron," replied the TV minister. "Just mark the thirteenth through the fifteenth of January on your calendar as a 'Weekend of National Prayer and Unity,' to be climaxed by the president's State of the Union message to Congress. The plan is to show resolve in the face of a nuclear terrorist threat."

"That's what you guys came up with?" asked a skeptical Goodman.

"Tell you what," said Chatman. "I have a prediction. The National Weekend of Prayer and Unity will be one of the most significant events in our history."

BAY ST. LOUIS FARM

Chatman described the day's events to Michael as they sat around the kitchen table at the Bay St. Louis farm, anxiously awaiting Alex's arrival from Venezuela. It had been a long but productive day for both of them, and they were tired.

"So, now we're looking at January 15 as the target date," said Michael, as Chatman nodded his head. "Shit! That isn't totally out of the question, but there sure are a lot of things to accomplish between now and then."

"You're right," said Chatman, "so let's compare notes on the target route analysis. There's still time for refinement if needed. When the bomber pilots have retired for the night, we'll brief Alex on our conclusions. It's essential to only talk in terms of feasibility around Petrov and Piekarski."

"At this late date, why don't we just go ahead and tell them the whole thing so they can get the maximum amount of training while they're here?"

"Because, Mikhail," replied Chatman patiently, "this is what Kozlov wants.

"We still have time to verify the routing and timing details before we give the package to Darginsky, and we'll have two additional pilots to assist with that. Speaking of them, it's one thirty in the morning. Where the hell are they?"

"Red Star Ops, Redex zero-three."

"Finally!" said Chatman, as he picked up the portable VHF radio. "Good morning Redex zero-three. We read you loud and clear. Are you close?"

"That's affirm," replied a tired-sounding Alex. "We're ten minutes out. Customs gave us courtesy customs tonight, so we didn't have to stop at Moisant."

"Great," said Chatman. "Michael and I are standing by to meet you."

The two put on their coats and walked out into the brisk air to watch Alex's arrival. "You know," said Michael. "Everything we've talked about tonight on both target routes assumes good weather the night of the mission. Considering it'll be January, that might not be a good assumption."

"A good point and one I've also considered," Chatman replied.

"The truth is that decent weather is only critical at the Kansas ranch, so the Su-57 can land to refuel. Worse case, he can fly the instrument approach. If it's solid cloud over Launch Points Alpha and Bravo, the bombers can cancel IFR, turn off their transponders, and adjust their flight profile as necessary to complete the mission.

"We're dealing with a lot of unknowns once those weapons go off, but I suspect any airplane in the air will be on their own within thirty minutes after launch time. We have four weeks to teach our mission pilots all the possibilities."

They could see the landing lights of the Citation long before they could hear its engines as Alex glided onto a long straight-in final. He turned off the runway and stopped in front of the hangar doors. The engines were still spinning down when the cabin door opened and Alex stepped out, followed by his passengers.

"Bobby Chatman and Michael Gerson, I'd like you to meet Joseph Pierson and Gregory Peters," said Alex wearily.

"Gentlemen, it's a pleasure," acknowledged Michael, shaking hands with the new arrivals.

"Josef, Gregori," said Chatman, using the Russian pronunciation. "Welcome to the USA, comrades."

Thirty minutes later, Chatman and his cohorts were at the kitchen table, finishing up some frozen pizza and beer. Their new arrivals then excused themselves for some well-deserved sleep.

"Plan on a late breakfast around ten," said Chatman, "and you won't want to miss it. Lulu Mae Turner is the lady who will prepare all your meals while you're here."

"What do you think?" asked Alex, after the two bomber pilots closed their bedroom doors.

"I'm impressed," replied Chatman. "Their English is fine, and that's important. But I see why Kozlov wants Petrov on Route Alpha.

The colonel is a politician. We'll need to watch him closely."

"Yeah, it was interesting on the trip up," said Alex. "Petrov insisted on helping with the piloting chores just because he loves to fly, while Piekarski rode in back like an executive."

Chatman outlined the events of the day, especially the loss of two weeks of preparations.

"What difference does it make?" Alex asked. "It sounds like events at home will drive us to an earlier mission date anyway."

"Fair enough," agreed Chatman. "I'm going to leave a message for Darginsky and then I'm going to get some sleep. I suggest you two do the same."

Chatman went straight to his office and typed a message for Darginsky.

> *To: Angel Gabriel*
> *From: Lucifer*
> *Subject: Red Star Express*
>
> *Greetings from Mississippi. Good news and bad news. The bad: important speech moved up to 15 January. Feel confident we can be ready. Good news on several fronts. Temporary helpers arrived safely. Bank deposit received. Biggest problem remaining is new friend in Kansas City. Hope to hear solution soon.*

CHAPTER NINE

DECEMBER 14
RUSSIAN CONSULATE
GLEN COVE, NEW YORK

An SVR computer sounded an alert tone. Ilya, the agent on duty, opened the notification. He immediately picked up the telephone and dialed the local number for Agent Feskanich. A youngish male voice answered with a sleepy, "Hello?"

"Is Katarina there?" said Ilya impatiently.

"Yes, she's here," said the boyish voice. "I hear the shower running. I'll get her."

You do that, thought Ilya.

Three minutes later the female agent finally picked up the phone. "*Yes?*" she said impatiently.

"Have you adopted another son, my dear?" he asked sarcastically, in pointed reference to her youngish tastes in the opposite sex.

"Ah, Ilya, don't let your jealousy show so obviously," she mocked. "This better be important."

"We have a bite from Kansas City. I think it's good, but I need your approval."

"Ilya, I trust your judgment implicitly. Make the necessary arrangements and notify the home office. Call me back tomorrow if you have any problems. Okay? Good night!"

Ilya placed a phone call to a local New York City number and left a message for the high-cost hustler who went by the name of Shawn, a person the SVR had previously used in setting up unsuspecting Americans. He then logged onto KC CONNEXIONS and left a DM for "SCOPE DOPE," advising him he would be receiving a phone call from Shawn in response to Keith's post on the message board.

Darginsky's standing orders were to notify him the moment a compromisable American was identified. It was early morning in Moscow time, so Ilya used the secure line to dial Darginsky's office in Moscow.

"Darginsky's office. Go ahead, please," answered the secretary.

"Yes, I'm calling from Glen Cove. Is Colonel Darginsky in?"

"I'm sorry. He's in the field and cannot be reached. He said he'd check in during the day. Whom should I say is calling?"

"Tell him to call Katarina Feskanich at his earliest convenience," said Ilya. "Tell him it's urgent."

KANSAS CITY

"I did a nice job decorating the tree I bought, don't you agree, Lucy?" Keith asked the dog. "If you're a good dog, maybe Santa will bring you a new ball to chew on." The dog yelped her excitement, then stared at the Christmas tree. "I'm going to see what's happening on KC CONNEXIONS."

It had been six weeks since Keith made his profile on KC CONNEXIONS, and he'd been disappointed with the results so far. There'd been a few trashy replies. He'd exchanged direct messages with "Bat Man" before discovering he had a "Robin"—his wife—and two "bat boys" in the nest. He actually talked to "High Flier" on the phone, only to discover he did his flying on chemicals. Keith was hoping that eventually he would find somebody worth meeting.

Keith saw a new DM for "SCOPE DOPE."

Hello, Scope Dope. It sounds like we have some things in common. I'm brand new to KC. Will be attending school next semester. I'm

21, 6'0" tall, and 165 lbs. I have strawberry blond hair and green eyes. My interests are similar to yours. Will arrive in KC after Christmas. You sound like the perfect new friend. Hope to hear back soon. Leave phone number and good time to call.

New Kid in Town (Shawn)

Keith read the message several times before replying that he was looking forward to Shawn's visit.

"Hey, Lucy! Where are you?" called Keith. He found the dog standing guard over the Christmas tree. "I have some good news. We may have a new friend." He picked the dog up and flicked off the Christmas tree lights. "It's time to get some sleep."

The dog waited while Keith went through the usual bedtime routine. "His name is Shawn. He's going to be attending school here next semester, so he doesn't know anybody. He sounds like a nice guy, Lucy."

DECEMBER 21
SAROVA AIRFIELD, RUSSIA

It was a Russian winter night and Viktor Darginsky felt cold and tired. He sat in the tiny flight line shack at the Sarova airfield, 120 kilometers south of Gorky, waiting for the arrival of Majors Ridgik and Bachvaroff. The two pilots were practicing night air refueling and testing the short-field capabilities of the Su-57, NATO reporting name: Felon.

Dammit! Where are they? He paced around the shack, never getting too far from the woodstove that kept out the raw cold of the subarctic night. The helicopter was picking him up in exactly one hour.

"Would you like some hot tea, sir?" asked the young warrant officer who doubled as a radio operator and crew chief. "I don't have any sugar, but it'll help you stay warm while you wait."

"Sure," said Darginsky, as he walked into the cubicle that served as the warrant officer's work area. "That sounds good, and in return for your hospitality, you can have half of my chocolate bar."

The young officer's eyes widened as Darginsky pulled out a full-size Hershey chocolate bar, complete with almonds. Darginsky made a show of removing the wrapper and breaking the bar in two, giving the young soldier the bigger piece.

The young man took tiny bites, savoring its taste. "It's the most delicious chocolate I've ever tasted, even better than the ones we used to be able to buy from Ukraine!"

"It's American," replied Darginsky with a smile as he sipped the strong tea, "and, yes, it's quite good. You still haven't heard from our friends in the Sukhoi?"

"No, sir, not yet," replied the soldier.

Dammit to hell, where are those fighter jocks! I have a meeting with Kozlov in two hours. He stepped quickly outside to scan the night sky, willing the two pilots onto the final approach.

"Can you warm it up a little in here?" said Bachvaroff teasingly from the back seat of the Su-57 as Ridgik maneuvered the fighter into the precontact position. "I'm freezing back here."

"Fuck you!" exclaimed Ridgik. "I'm sweating up here."

"I have the drogue dead ahead for ten meters," said Bachvaroff calmly. "Confirm you have the paddle switch down."

"Paddle switch is down. Keep talking to me, Anton."

"Bring it up . . . that's good! Now ease straight ahead. Five meters . . . three meters . . . two meters . . . good . . . one meter . . . you're in! Release the switch. Good contact."

"I have a green light," replied Ridgik. "Nice job, pardner."

"Kola eight-eight is contact," he said over the intercom connection through the tanker's refueling drogue. The use of exterior lights for the rendezvous, and drogue-enabled intercom between the tanker and receiver aircraft, allowed this choreographed operation to be conducted radio-out.

It was easy from that point on. All they had to do was maintain a steady position on the ghostly outline ahead. The tanker could off-load a thousand kilograms a minute, so all they had to do was stay hooked up for five minutes.

"Kola eight-eight, we show you have your off-load," said the tanker pilot.

"Off-load confirmed," said Ridgik. "Kola eight-eight is disconnect—now." He depressed the paddle switch, retarded the throttles slightly, and allowed the tanker to move ahead. The night sky soon swallowed the lightless IL-78.

Ridgik turned direct to Sarova and checked in with air traffic control.

"Anton, see if you can raise Sarova and tell them we'll be there in twenty minutes."

The cold at Sarova had finally gotten to Viktor Darginsky. He carried in several pieces of firewood to stoke the stove's fire. When the fire was roaring, he dragged one of the chairs over and sat down less than a meter from its glowing side.

The radio crackled. "Sarova, Kola eight-eight."

"It's them, sir!" exclaimed the young warrant officer. "Kola eight-eight, Sarova reads you loud and clear. What's your ETA?"

"Kola eight-eight will be landing in fifteen minutes. Please confirm the approach-zone floodlights are operational, you are set to refuel us, and a visitor is waiting for us."

"Roger, Kola eight-eight, the approach-zone floodlights are on and I'm ready to refuel. Runway two-zero is in use. The winds are light out of the south. The altimeter is 1015 millibars. Your visitor is right here."

"Great!" said Bachvaroff, in English. "Tell him I hope he brought some fried chicken. These two good ole boys are hungry."

The warrant officer's face showed his perplexity at the English transmission. "What did he say?"

"A private joke," Darginsky replied, surprised Bachvaroff would use English while operating in Russian airspace. It fit Bachvaroff's mischievous behavior, which amused Darginsky. "Let me talk to them," he said, taking the microphone. "Since you're running late, I was hoping you could use some of the speed of the Motherland's newest fighter to get here as soon as possible."

"I'll pass that on to the front seat," said Bachvaroff, switching back to Russian.

The young warrant officer began dressing in arctic clothes. "I'd better get that old fuel truck started up, and I need to check on those approach-zone floodlights."

"I wanted to ask you about those," said Darginsky. "Is that an addition to the normal airfield lighting?"

"Yes, sir. When Major Ridgik started doing night landings, he felt he could not see enough as he approached the runway to judge his height. So, we installed floodlights at each end of the runway to illuminate the ground during the final approach. It made all the difference. Wait until you see the major land. He is an artist in that airplane! I'm going outside. Would you mind talking to them if they call back on the radio?"

"No problem," said Darginsky as he made a mental note about the floodlights.

Ten minutes later the young officer stuck his head in the door. "I can see them out on final."

The sound of the fighter's engines grew louder, spooling up and down as Ridgik kept the fighter on the edge of a stall. When the Sukhoi entered the area lit up by the floodlights, Darginsky was surprised how nose-high Ridgik was flying it. He heard the engines spool up one last time as the fighter crossed the runway threshold. He was amazed to see the huge drag chute spilling out before the aircraft's wheels touched the ground. Ridgik held the nose off the ground to help slow down. In a matter of seconds the nosewheel touched down and the fighter stopped a thousand meters from the end of the runway.

"That's the best one yet!" cheered the warrant officer. "I told you he was an artist!"

"Impressive," replied Darginsky.

"Sir, you might want to wait inside until they are shut down. The engines are awfully loud if you don't have ear protection."

"Sounds good. I'll be by the stove."

Darginsky heard Ridgik and Bachvaroff kidding each other as they approached the line shack. The two stepped in wearing their high-altitude flying suits and carrying their helmets.

"Viktor!" greeted Ridgik when he saw Darginsky standing by the woodstove. "I see you found the only warm spot on this airfield." He extended his hand. "It's good to see you. I thought you had forgotten about us!"

"No way!" replied Darginsky. "It's just that every time I called you were flying."

"Just carrying out your orders," noted Ridgik. "We've accomplished quite a lot since we saw you last."

"Yes, I want to hear all about that, but what is he up to?" Darginsky gestured at Bachvaroff, walking around the room with his nose in the air.

"I'm almost certain I can smell it," the back seater said in English with a smile. "Fried chicken. I can smell it."

"I cannot lie," laughed Darginsky, as he pulled out two more Hershey chocolate bars with almonds. "Here's a drumstick for each of you."

"Shit! I was hoping for white meat!" complained Bachvaroff as he took the candy with his left hand and offered his right for a handshake.

"Good to see you, Viktor. Valentin and I have made enough progress to take that trip you promised. You did come here to tell us to pack our bags for our little 'feasibility study' in warmer climes, didn't you?"

Darginsky smiled. "We'll talk about that in a minute. First, I want to hear all about your work the past few weeks."

They talked about the status of the various projects Darginsky had assigned them. They explained the problems they'd encountered and the solutions they'd applied. When they were done, Darginsky was pleased. "My compliments on an outstanding job."

"A critical item seems to be the approach-zone floodlighting system. If we're going to land at night on a runway of Sarova's length, then we're going to need them," replied Ridgik. "The visual cues just aren't good enough without them."

"Very well. Any other critical items?" asked Darginsky. "You're happy with the Su-57's capabilities to complete an intercept given minimal target information? You'd have no qualms doing night air refueling, operating out of Sarova-sized airfields, and using lower-grade fuel?"

The conversation was interrupted by the sounds of a helicopter starting engines outside. "As long as the critical items we've already discussed are taken care of, I have no qualms about operating the Su-57 as you've outlined," replied Ridgik.

"Me neither," said Bachvaroff. "We have a one hundred percent success rate completing intercepts. You tell us the mission; we'll complete it for you."

Darginsky decided it was time to tell them something. "Continue your practice here and then take a week off," Darginsky told them. "After January 5, I want you two and your jet sitting at Murmansk, ready to go to Cuba at a moment's notice. The entire trip will be at night, so adjust your internal schedules. We'll want the right weather along the American East Coast, so they don't realize we're moving a Su-57 to Cuba. They're used to bombers and tankers over the Atlantic, but a Su-57 would cause a stir. I want you on the ground in Cuba by January 12."

"And then what?" asked Ridgik.

"That's all I can tell you for now," said Darginsky. "Just be patient. That helicopter is here for me. I'm on my way to see the president and I'm running late. Keep up the excellent work."

"Thanks for the chocolate," sighed a frustrated Ridgik. "Give our regards to President Kozlov."

"I don't suppose you can tell us where our two bomber-pilot friends might be?" asked Bachvaroff.

"Not a snowball's chance in hell," said Darginsky as he stepped out the door.

THE KREMLIN

Nikolai Kozlov appeared tired as he reviewed a report. Darginsky noticed it as soon as he entered the president's office.

Kozlov peered over his reading glasses. "What do you have?" he asked curtly.

Darginsky sensed Kozlov was pondering his perilous political situation, which apparently had something to do with the report he was reading. He pointed to the document. "There's a solution to that, sir." Kozlov's icy stare made Darginsky swallow. "LUCIFER/INBLUE will change everything."

"If you can pull it off!" barked Kozlov. "Our incompetent generals can't even win a ground war against a bunch of fucking farmers! What makes you think you and your preacher pal can save us?"

The question took Darginsky aback. The president seemed to be wavering in his commitment to the operation. Ignoring the affront and trying not to think about Kozlov's possible mental instability, Darginsky calmly replied, "Sir, I have a status report on LUCIFER/INBLUE if you'd like to hear it."

Kozlov simply flipped both hands toward the agent as an exasperated gesture to continue.

Darginsky spent the next twenty minutes briefing the leader of the Russian Federation on the status of LUCIFER/INBLUE. When he was finished, he waited uneasily while Kozlov stared through him.

"What do you need from me?" Kozlov finally asked.

"Sir, I recommend you approve the LUCIFER/INBLUE plan and allow the pre-positioning of the missiles and aircraft to Cuba and Venezuela. We should tell the American government we have reliable information that the weapons are still in the Middle East. A few days before the mission we can announce the bombs were shipped and they arrived in the US. They will be in crisis mode trying to locate them. It will provide the cover we need so their intelligence resources are not focused on us. Then, when those cruise missiles fly, everybody in the world will believe it was a terrorist act."

CHAPTER TEN

DECEMBER 27
BAY ST. LOUIS, MISSISSIPPI

Birds were singing. Petrov was amazed that he could be awakened on a December morning by birds singing outside his window. In Murmansk the birds disappeared in September and didn't return until May. He'd done the flying with Red Star Express wearing only a shirt, tie, and dress slacks. As he listened to the sounds of a Mississippi morning, the entire experience was hard to believe.

It had been a busy two weeks for Petrov and Piekarski. Petrov was flying exclusively with Alex between the North Carolina facility and the Bay St. Louis farm, while Piekarski and Michael flew between the Kansas ranch and Bay St. Louis.

The landscape across the United States was beautiful. He particularly loved the lakes, huge bodies of water created by man-made dams. Petrov wondered what it would be like to have a home on one of those beautiful lakes.

What he had been taught about American people had been all wrong. One thing he didn't see were faces full of fear. Compared to the day-to-day life of the average Russian, Americans were freer. They were free to make all kinds of choices, and if they disliked things enough, Americans had the greatest freedom of all: they were free to protest or leave.

"Comrades, breakfast is ready," shouted Bobby Chatman from the kitchen of the Bay St. Louis farmhouse. "We're eating buffet-style this morning while Lulu Mae is on vacation."

"You sound joyful this morning, Brother Chatman," said Alex. "One would think you received an important message from heaven."

Michael turned to the two Russian bomber pilots. "In the entire time I've been working with our esteemed comrade, I've never known him to cook a meal for us. He must be pleased with our work."

"Ah, yes," said Chatman. "I am most pleased. Red Star Express is a resounding success. It gives me great pleasure to serve God's soldiers. Sit and enjoy with His blessings."

Petrov had no idea what the others were talking about. The three SVR agents were always talking in circles.

When breakfast was done, Chatman addressed the two bomber pilots. "Gentlemen, I want to talk about why you're here. As Darginsky told you, we're rethinking in terms of strategic planning. What do you think of such a plan's probability of success?"

Piekarski was itching to reply. "I would rate it as a certain success," he said, "assuming someone on the bomber can speak fluent English, and the Tu-95s are properly equipped to operate in US airspace.

"And assuming some other important things as well," noted Petrov, irritated by Piekarski's enthusiasm.

"Like what, Gregori?" asked Chatman, appraising him coolly.

"First of all, it should be done in darkness or in solid cloud. We could be seen and identified, especially by a pilot with a military background."

"I think we all agree," said Chatman, "we're talking about a nighttime-attack scenario. What other assumptions were you referring to?"

"It would have to be during a period of calm relations between the two countries," said Petrov, putting off what he really wanted to say. "If there is any increased military readiness, I have doubts about our bombers' ability to enter US airspace unchallenged. If they had their AWACS"—Airborne Warning and Control System aircraft—"patrolling their ADIZs, for instance, I would rate our chances at near zero."

"Agreed!" said Chatman. "Anything else?"

The bomber pilot stared down a few moments before raising his head and meeting Bobby Chatman's gaze. "Our side had better have a damn good reason. We're talking about World War III. I'm flattered that someone in strategic planning recognizes the first-strike possibilities of the manned bomber with modern cruise missiles, but, once those warheads detonate, we're in danger of a full-scale retaliation."

"Well said, Major," commented Chatman. "But suppose we're able to manipulate world opinion so there'd be serious doubts as to who mounted the attack. Let's say we make it appear to be the work of terrorists, and just when the world is convinced of our innocence, we announce we did it with just four of many nuclear weapons embedded across the United States, and more such weapons are poised to detonate. Now, how would you rate our probability of success?"

"Brilliant!" exclaimed Piekarski. "I'm looking forward to writing up such a war plan."

"And your opinion, Gregori?" asked Chatman.

"I'd say such a plan has possibilities," replied Petrov coolly. "But in all honesty, I hope any Russian leader who implemented such a plan was sure the loss of lives was justified. From what I've seen the last two weeks, I'm not sure that's the case."

"Frankly, I would agree," said Chatman. "But imagine the possibilities of the combined peoples of our two nations joined as one." Chatman was rolling now. "Imagine, being able to raise your grandchildren in a nuclear-free world because Russia took the steps necessary to ensure such a world!"

Petrov was surprised by Chatman's impassioned speech. He decided they were, after all, only discussing a feasibility study. "I agree such a plan has merit," he finally said, "and I'd rate its probability of success as high."

"Outstanding!" cheered Chatman. "We all agree with your assessment!" He paused for a moment. "Here's the game plan for the next couple of weeks. Michael and I will be working on a project in Kansas City. When we return, the two of you will resume flying. We will game some mission scenarios during Red Star Express flights. That should prepare the two of you for writing possible war plans when you return home. By the way, you can plan on leaving the US around January 13 or 14 and be back in Russia a few days after that. Any questions?"

"Yeah, comrade, I have a question," Alex said. "Who's in charge of doing these fucking dishes?"

"You are, of course," said Chatman, "and you better be sure this kitchen stays spotless, or Lulu Mae will have your ass."

EN ROUTE TO KANSAS CITY

"Memphis Center, Redex zero-two is with you at flight level 320," said Michael over the radio as he flew the Citation toward Little Rock.

Chatman slid into the right pilot seat. He looked over at Michael. "Except for Keith Anderson giving us the information regarding Target Route Charlie, we're almost all set up."

"That's good. You have the aircraft," replied Michael. "Let me look at your folder on these two guys one more time." Chatman pulled it out of his briefcase and handed it to Michael.

Opening the folder, Michael found a dossier and a grainy photo of a pleasant-faced man in his mid-twenties who was playing with a black mixed-breed dog. The dossier contained several pages of transcripts of recorded conversations between Keith Anderson and Shawn Cochran, the hustler. The transcripts were a gold mine of information. The dossier on Shawn Thomas Cochran described him as a "sixteen-year-old hustler with the face and body of an older man."

Michael shook his head. In times past, simply being gay was all that was needed to compromise a citizen. The threat of being outed was usually enough to extort what was needed, and as a result, Russia had long before gotten in the habit of targeting gay men. But these days, being outed was less threatening in the US, and they needed to be more creative. Fortunately, having sex with minors was still a crime.

"What are you smiling at, Michael?" Chatman asked.

Michael shrugged. "It's the perfect setup." He studied the photo of Shawn Cochran. "This Cochran guy doesn't look like a male prostitute. No tats, no crazy hair, no wild attire. He's conservative looking, and so is Anderson. We need Keith Anderson to like him so that I get it all on tape."

"So, tell me," Chatman asked, "what's the game plan once we get to KC?"

"We'll keep it simple. Anderson thinks Shawn is coming to town to look at apartments prior to moving here for school next semester. He knows he'll be staying at a hotel. We'll rent a car then get adjoining hotel rooms. I'll set up the video equipment and we'll pick up the hustler when he arrives. They have a date tomorrow night. We'll brief Mr. Cochran on his part. He'll bring Anderson back to the hotel after dinner and we'll get it all on tape. I want to be able to exercise maximum control over Mr. Anderson as early as possible. The fact that we totally invaded his private life will, hopefully, break his will to resist, and make the compromise easy."

"Sounds good," said Chatman. "I think we should rent a third room for my personal use. I'm afraid of being recognized. A little distance from your activities might be a good idea."

KANSAS CITY, MISSOURI

Michael was waiting as the Southwest Airlines Boeing 737 from JFK blocked in. He had no trouble picking out Shawn Cochran in his Yankees jacket and cap, but the real surprise came when Cochran walked up to him and said, "I believe you're waiting for me. I'm Shawn."

"Uh . . . right," said a stunned Michael. "The car's this way."

They were quiet until they'd gotten clear of the terminal and were heading toward the Ramada, where Shawn would be staying.

The hustler finally broke the silence. "Listen," Shawn said, "could you at least give me a name, so I'll know what to call you?"

Michael laughed and relaxed. "Sorry, I'm Michael. Pleased to meet you."

"I'm pleased to meet you too," Shawn replied. "I guess it surprised you when I picked you out of the crowd."

"Yes, it did," admitted Michael.

"Well, you can relax. They showed me your picture before I left JFK. It surprised the hell out of me. Some guy just walked up to me in the men's room, showed me your picture, and said you'd be meeting me in KC. He said time was important, and they couldn't risk any mix-ups. So, this Keith Anderson's pretty important to you guys?"

"Yes, he is," replied Michael, surprised at Shawn's forwardness. "But that's none of your concern. Now, let's talk about tomorrow night—"

"I know," Shawn interrupted. "Convince him to do it with the lights on but down low. I'll put the 'Do Not Disturb' sign out all day tomorrow to prevent nosy maids from discovering the video equipment. Tell me, how does it end once you have us on tape?"

Michael couldn't help shaking his head. "It'll end with a bottle of wine before bed. You'll put a strong sedative in his glass, and when he's groggy, but still able to walk, we'll get him to the car, and I'll take him to his house. Once he's in the car, I'll pay you for your services. Then you can get a good night's sleep and go back to the airport the next day. Any questions?"

"No questions," replied Shawn, "but I have a comment."

"And that is . . ."

"I just hope you aren't going to hurt Keith Anderson. He seems like a nice guy."

They didn't say anything else until they were inside the hotel, and Michael accompanied Shawn into his room. He showed him the technical layout, gave him the bottle of wine and the sedative, and then headed for his own room.

"Okay, all set?" he asked as he opened the adjoining door.

"As far as I'm concerned," replied Shawn. "I don't suppose you'd come over a little later and tuck me in, would you?"

"Not a chance," laughed Michael. "I couldn't afford you even if you were my type—female, that is. Hey, not to worry about Keith Anderson. All we want is information. If he cooperates, he'll live to be very old with no scars. Fair enough?"

"Fair enough," Shawn replied.

"You're on your own from here. Make it good tomorrow night. I'll see you when it's over. Good night!"

CHAPTER ELEVEN

DECEMBER 28
KANSAS CITY, MISSOURI

Keith Anderson knocked on the door of Shawn's hotel room. The door opened to reveal one of the most attractive men Keith had ever seen.

"Hi. You must be Keith," said the smiling face.

"And you must be Shawn," Keith responded. "Welcome to Kansas City. I hope you're hungry. I made a reservation at a great steak restaurant."

"I'm famished! Lead the way," Shawn exclaimed as he grabbed his coat, and they headed out to Keith's car.

After dinner they drove around the Main Street area. The bars were open, but the Thursday night crowd was predictably small. Shawn suggested they return to the hotel and relax with a bottle of wine.

It had certainly been an enjoyable evening, but something about Shawn was bugging Keith. He couldn't quite put his finger on it, but it felt like Shawn was putting on a show.

"You're awfully quiet all of a sudden," Shawn said as they drove back to his hotel.

"I'm sorry. I was just wondering if I should show you more of KC tonight since you're going apartment hunting tomorrow."

"I appreciate that," Shawn said, as he took hold of Keith's right hand. "But why don't we worry about that tomorrow?"

Keith hadn't been with anyone for a long time. In spite of

his reservations, he certainly was attracted to Shawn. He made a snap decision. *What's the harm?* He nodded and smiled. "You're right, Shawn."

When they'd reached the hotel, they rode the elevator up to Shawn's floor. "I've got a bottle of wine cooling in the fridge," Shawn said as they entered the room. "What say we save it for later?" he suggested with a flirtatious smile as they removed their coats.

Two hours after arriving at the room, Shawn got out of bed and went to the refrigerator. "Here we are," he said as he padded back to the bed with two glasses of wine. He handed a glass to Keith and sat down beside him.

Shortly after downing the wine, Keith began to feel lightheaded. He heard Shawn talking, but his voice sounded as if it were coming from the bottom of a well.

"This wine is really strong," Keith mumbled as he lay back down and closed his eyes.

"Don't go to sleep yet, Keith," he heard Shawn say.

He heard another voice in the room now. "Get him dressed and don't let him fall asleep until we get him in the car."

He felt his body being moved. "Okay, Keith, we have to walk to the car," Shawn said. "You can do it. Just hold on to me."

"Where are we going?"

"You're going home."

"Put him in the back seat," Keith heard the new voice say. "Let him lie down. Well done. I'll take it from here."

"Be careful with him," said Michael as he and Chatman removed Keith from the Toyota. Chatman had followed Michael in the rented Chevy to Keith's house. They parked the Celica in Keith's garage so they could move the unconscious air traffic controller out of sight of the neighbors.

"Find the house key on his key ring," Michael commanded.

"How long will he be out?" asked Chatman, as he held up each key to the light filtering in from a streetlight.

"He'd be in dreamland until tomorrow if we let him. But letting him sleep that long is not to our advantage. We want him tired and it to still be dark outside for maximum effectiveness. Hurry up, Bobby."

"I've got it," said Chatman, as he slid the key into the lock. "Okay, let's get him inside. I found the light switch. Watch your eyes."

As the kitchen light came on, they were accosted by the furious barking of a medium-sized black dog. Both men froze in place.

"Okay, it's behind you, but it's moving backward," said Chatman. "I think it's afraid of us. Keep going."

They maneuvered Anderson into the living room with the dog watching their every move. They laid the unconscious controller on the sofa and propped his head up with a pillow. The dog jumped on the sofa at Anderson's feet and began smelling him.

"It's okay," said Michael. "Let her check him out. Try to make friends with it while I set things up." Michael pulled up a chair for his laptop. He inserted a thumb drive that held the video from Shawn's hotel room. "Reverend, I suggest you remain in the shadows. He won't be able to see us. Just let me do the talking. I'll give him the antidote. We'll be able to talk to him in a few minutes."

EARLY MORNING HOURS, DECEMBER 29

"Don't open your eyes yet," Keith heard a voice say as he slowly woke up. "Just lie still."

He felt tired, and his mouth was incredibly dry. "Where am I?" he croaked.

"You're at home, Keith, and you're with friends."

He felt something moving at his feet, then up to his face. His befuddled mind slowly recognized he was being bathed in kisses from his beloved Lucy. "Hello, Lucy," he managed to say.

"You can open your eyes now," said the voice, "but it's going to be very bright."

It took him a few minutes to focus. He realized he was lying on his living room sofa with Lucy by his left cheek, but something was terribly wrong. "Who are you?"

"My name is Michael."

His mind was clearing rapidly. He tried to see the man talking to him, but he was partway across the room. With a bright light shining directly into Keith's eyes, he could only see the man's lower body. "Where's Shawn?"

"Shawn's fine. He'll be leaving town tomorrow. He thanks you for a nice evening. It'd be best if you do not try to contact him. He won't be coming back to Kansas City. Now, Keith, I need to ask you a few questions."

"I don't know you, so get the hell out of my house!"

"Ah, Keith," said Michael gently. "Things aren't that simple, and I can think of several things you need my help with at the moment."

"Like what!" demanded Keith, surprised that his mind had cleared yet his body felt almost paralyzed.

"Like whether you ever move off that sofa or not. You see, I need some information, and you're uniquely qualified to provide it. Shawn laced that glass of wine with a strong drug that causes paralysis. I've given you just enough of the antidote to be able to talk. If you ever want to walk again . . . well, you get the picture."

"What information could I possibly have that you need?" Keith pleaded, scared now. "I'm just an air traffic controller."

"No, Keith, you're much more than that. Just answer a few questions for me."

"I'm listening," he said, oddly curious.

"You're Keith Anderson, an air traffic controller at the Kansas City Air Route Traffic Control Center. Correct?"

"Correct."

"And you control military and civilian aircraft as they move through your sector. Kansas City Center is responsible for aircraft flying in and out of Offutt Air Force Base in Omaha and Tinker Air Force Base in Oklahoma City."

Keith nodded.

"Keith, you have the reputation of being a top-grade controller. You should advance to a supervisory position and eventually have a nice retirement, right?

"I suppose so."

"But there's a problem. You see, having sex with underage people is socially unacceptable, and also illegal in the state of Missouri. You can go to prison for it, and the FAA would fire you if they knew about that scene with Shawn tonight . . . wouldn't they?"

"What do you mean, underage?"

In a calm, fatherly voice, Michael said, "Shawn is only sixteen years old . . . he's just a boy."

"Oh, Jesus! No! You're lying!" he yelled.

Michael stayed quiet while Keith finally calmed down.

"I was there, Keith. Me and my little video camera."

Keith was horrified to see the image of himself and Shawn on Michael's laptop in bed together. The sight of it made him realize Michael was deadly serious.

"I got it all, and I can assure you I won't hesitate to give it to your supervisor and the authorities if you don't cooperate with me."

"How will they know? You have no proof he's underage."

"You think I overlooked that little detail?" Michael pulled up an enlarged picture of Shawn Cochran's student driver's license. "The police will be interested in this, and the video, don't you think?"

"But I still don't know what you want!" he bellowed.

"True," replied Michael. "Calm down. Let me explain. Kansas City Center issues IFR clearances to any aircraft departing Offutt or Tinker Air Force Base, correct?"

"That's correct, but there's very little traffic out of either of those bases. I don't see how I can help."

"What about the 747s, Keith?"

"The 747?" Keith asked, sounding confused.

"The Airborne Command Post, Mr. Anderson. The 747s that are always on alert and sometimes in the air in case of a nuclear attack."

Keith knew exactly which aircraft Michael was talking about—the Airborne National Command Post or 'Doomsday' Plane.

"You know about those aircraft, don't you Keith?"

"Yes."

"Where do they go, Keith? And where do the E-6Bs, the 707s, out of Tinker go?"

"How do I know? They go all over the sky, and they're moving at six hundred miles an hour."

"They're operating on IFR clearances, aren't they? And their flight plan is stored in the Kansas City Center computer, right?"

"Yes, but they change routes all the time."

"Probably with five or six canned flight plans, right Keith?"

"Well, there are ten canned routes for the 747s and six for the 707s. I still don't know what you want from me. We work them while they're in our airspace, then we hand them off to the next control center. What else can I possibly tell you?"

"For starters, you can provide me with the exact flight plans that make up those sixteen canned routes," Michael said quietly. "Just the route designator and the navigation fixes that make up the route."

"That's classified information!" Keith shouted.

Michael laughed out loud. "Yes, Keith, and that's why I'm here. If you value your job and your freedom, you'll give it to me."

"That's all you want?"

"I'll probably need some other stuff later, but the route information will do for starters. You get it in the next forty-eight hours, and I'll be in touch. If it's good information, the video will stay in my possession. If it's not good information, well . . ."

"What if I said fuck you!" Keith yelled, trying to rise from the sofa. The dog began growling at the enemy who remained in the shadows. "What if I refuse to be manipulated?"

"Ah, Keith," said Michael slowly, "I wish you hadn't said that."

Keith could see only the waist and hands of the man threatening him. He saw the right hand reach into the coat and extract a semiautomatic pistol. "Do you see this, Keith?"

Keith knew he'd pushed things too far.

The left hand reached into the coat, removing a four-inch-long metal tube and attaching it to the end of the pistol.

Keith recognized the ominous shape of the silencer. He flinched when the hands pulled the slide back and released it. The snap as it slammed into the receiver was like an explosion.

Keith's heart pounded as Michael raised the pistol. "You asked a question, Keith, and I think it deserves an answer." The gun was still pointed at him. "The answer to your question is simple. Refuse to cooperate with me, for any reason, and you'll die."

Keith never saw the slight movement of the pistol, but he heard the bang. The dog's head exploded from the impact of the bullet. Instantly, he was covered with Lucy's blood and unrecognizable pieces of tissue.

"Jesus, Mikhail," said a strange voice, also from the shadows. "You didn't have to—"

"Shut the fuck up!" Michael thundered.

It took a moment for the impact of what had just happened to register in Keith's mind. When it did, he felt tears coming to his eyes, and he knew he was going to be sick. "Damn you," he managed to say before his stomach emptied itself. "That wasn't necessary," he sobbed between stomach spasms.

"Do we understand each other now?"

Keith dejectedly mumbled, "Yes."

"Good!" said the voice. "Gather the data on those flight plans and I'll be in touch."

"Wait!" pleaded Keith. "What about the antidote?"

"Oh, I was bluffing," replied Michael. "You'll get all your normal body functions back in a couple of hours. Just lie there and relax. You look awful."

He heard footsteps heading for the kitchen. Keith elected to keep his eyes closed, but he could hear the car start, then leave his driveway. As the car drove away, he felt a profound sense of relief as sleep mercifully overtook him.

They didn't speak to each other until they'd checked out of the hotel and headed for the airport. The first rays of dawn were peaking over the southeastern horizon.

"I was hoping to be landing at the ranch about now," said Michael. "I hate staying up all night."

"Me too," growled Chatman.

Michael turned his head to study Chatman's face. The silence was broken only by the rhythmic thumping of the car's tires on the interstate pavement. "So, you can tell Darginsky we're all set with Route Charlie."

"I guess," mumbled Chatman.

"Okay, Bobby, let's talk about it," Michael prompted. "You think I was rough back there, and I'm sorry I cursed at you, but I did what was necessary. We only have two weeks to set this up. Keith Anderson is the only potential candidate we have, so breaking him totally was essential."

"Yes, but playing the video might have served your purpose. Did you see the look on his face when you pulled it up?"

"Did you see the look on his face when I took the gun out of my coat?" Michael countered. "I recall a speech of yours to the effect that a man, or a nation, that's looking down the barrel of a gun sees the available options with crystal clarity. If I had to do it over again, I'd handle it exactly the same way."

"You didn't have to kill the dog," Chatman grumbled. "It was . . . excessive."

Fifteen minutes after arriving at the Citation, they were airborne for the short flight to the Kansas ranch.

"Okay, I didn't have to kill the dog," Michael said, "but you can't argue with success. You know what amazes me?"

"What's that?"

"You're upset about the death of a dog, but on January 15, those cruise missiles are going to kill several million human beings! And you're going to be principally responsible!"

Chatman was silent a minute before answering. "That's different."

"Oh? How so?"

"That's war," Chatman said, refusing to meet the eyes of his compatriot.

"Bullshit!" Michael barked. "That was war this morning. The only difference is that I was willing to pull the trigger and face the consequences. On January 15, Brother Chatman, you'd better be ready to face the consequences. I'm sorry, but it's all war, comrade."

CHAPTER TWELVE

DECEMBER 31
THE WHITE HOUSE

Bobby Chatman was pleased with the evening's events. The nationally televised *Free World Gospel Hour*, with President Andrew Phillips as a guest, had gone well. The appearance of the president had emphasized the nuclear terrorist threat while lending continued credibility to his ministry. Both actions were critical to the success of LUCIFER/INBLUE.

Chatman walked toward the Oval Office for their planned meeting after the broadcast. "Ah, Bobby, come in," said Phillips, frowning. "There's coffee on the desk, if you like."

"You look troubled, Andrew," Chatman said. "What's on your mind?"

"Things aren't going well. Frankly, this entire terrorist thing is maddening! We're doing everything we can to find those bombs, but we're unable to verify the information from Russia, and that scares me to death."

Chatman needed to tread carefully. "Do you suspect the Russians of lying?"

"I'm frankly not sure what to think. As you know, Kozlov is a sly fox."

"Are the rumors true about Kozlov's domestic situation? From what I hear on the news, he is facing big internal problems."

"Essentially," replied the president. "They're hurting for grain, meat, and commodities. The Russian ambassador relayed that Kozlov was hoping for a quid pro quo on oil exports relief, and wheat and corn at most-favored-nation terms."

"Then why would they lie about the bombs?" asked Chatman. "We would discover the lie before they could purchase all the grain they need. So, why pass on bogus intelligence?"

"I know, but they're pros at disinformation and the stakes are too high this time not to take them seriously."

Chatman decided to ask the question that was really on his mind. "So, Andrew, what are you going to do about selling grain to the Russians?"

"I'm glad you asked me that. The teachings of our Lord would seem to say, 'Yes, give it to them.' Is that how you see it, Bobby?"

Chatman was silent a beat before answering. "Andrew, I think Jesus was teaching us to be compassionate on an individual level, not on a geopolitical level."

Chatman could see that Phillips was visibly relieved. "That's what He seems to be leading me to do, and I feel better knowing you agree. The CIA feels we must be ready to exploit these problems."

Chatman was surprised by the direction of the conversation. "I hope you're going to tell me more."

"Russia isn't the only totalitarian nation. China poses a more serious threat to us in the long run. I think it's essential that we see this strategy through so we can focus our attention on Asia."

"Oh, I couldn't agree with you more, Andrew," he said with feigned enthusiasm.

"Pray for us, Bobby," Phillips said as he walked Chatman to the door of the Oval Office.

Chatman felt very satisfied. His meeting with Phillips convinced him the attention of the various US agencies was focused on all the right things. "Only two weeks to go," he murmured as he left the White House. He was now more confident of his plan's success than ever before.

JANUARY 4
MOSCOW

Viktor Darginsky arrived in Moscow carrying a sealed document, at the request of the Russian ambassador, from the president of the United States. The streets of Moscow were quiet. There was a curfew enforced by the Army to control riots. Tanks were in the capital yet again. Staring out the car's window, Darginsky felt a foreboding as his limo whisked him toward the Kremlin. Arriving, he saw soldiers everywhere, but he was cleared through each of the security checkpoints.

Some things had changed since Darginsky's last visit. There was an armed guard at both the outer and inner office doors. Once inside the Kremlin, he noticed the windows were covered by steel shutters. He felt as if he were entering a locked-down fortress. He made his way under watchful eyes through the hallways and into Nikolai Kozlov's lair.

"What do you have?" Kozlov asked curtly as he emerged from the bathroom. The president made no effort to hide the handgun in his shoulder harness.

"The Americans are very concerned about the missing backpack weapons," replied Darginsky. "They are doing everything to locate them and are promoting a unity movement to show national will in the face of international terrorism. That will culminate with President Phillips's State of the Union address on January 15. They have swallowed the entire story."

Kozlov seemed unimpressed. "What about the letter from Phillips? Give it to me."

Darginsky sat in silence while the president read a lengthy message from the US president. The poker-faced Russian leader read the entire letter without so much as a raised eyebrow.

When he had finished reading, Kozlov angrily wadded it and tossed it to Darginsky. "So that is how it will be." He rose from his desk and gestured toward the fireplace. "I can't even have a fucking fire! I told them to plug the chimney." Kozlov pivoted toward Darginsky. "Phillips and his NATO stooges are amateurs. They talk openly about my downfall. Don't they know I'd never allow that to happen? If Russia falls, what do I care about the rest of the *fucking world*?"

Darginsky was too stunned to respond.

"I should have stopped with taking Crimea, but who knew the Ukrainians would fight so hard, or that the West would supply them with so many advanced weapons? Even the Finns fought like demons! I still can't believe how many tanks and aircraft we lost. And who would have thought so many countries would join NATO's sanctions against us?" Kozlov fell silent as he stared at Darginsky. "How dare that pompous bastard talk to me that way? Does he not know who he's dealing with? Can he not see it is in his best interest to sell us the grain we need and drop the sanctions to avoid more bloodshed? They think we are spent. They think we can't rise again. But, next time, we will not make the same mistakes. No half measures. We will use the full might of the Rodina and take what we want. God help anyone who gets in our way!"

Kozlov paused a moment to catch his breath after his tirade. "The American president is a fool," he grumbled. "God is leading the mighty United States of America. Well, we will see about that."

Since his first meeting with Nikolai Kozlov, Darginsky had hoped to establish a friendly rapport with the president. Instead, he had been progressively subjected to the president's fuming tirades, moody lamentations, and heated outbursts. He'd become increasingly uneasy with the thought that Kozlov was unstable and wondered if these traits were a threat to the success of LUCIFER/INBLUE. The mission's success now seemed, to Darginsky, of paramount importance to the prevention of worldwide nuclear war.

Much to Darginsky's relief, Kozlov's demeanor abruptly changed. He sat down at his desk and drank some water. He looked up and gestured with an open hand. "We are eleven days away from the target date for LUCIFER/INBLUE. What's the status?"

Darginsky cleared his throat. "Everything is set, sir. All weapons are in place in Cuba and Venezuela. The Su-57 crew will arrive in Murmansk tomorrow to await the flight to Cuba. They will be escorted by an IL-78 tanker. We need to send two other tankers to Cuba as well. They'll meet the Bear bombers over the Atlantic en route from the Central African Republic to Venezuela and will be over the Atlantic to refuel the bombers after the mission. You need to issue the orders to send the bombers and tankers as part of the current Federation exercise."

Kozlov nodded. "And the bomber pilots . . . where are they?"

"Major Petrov and Colonel Piekarski are still in the US flying with Lucifer's two agents and will rendezvous with their crews and aircraft. Also, Lucifer and I will be working next week to ensure someone friendly to us survives the Washington attack. We're planning for it to be Senator Dan Hawkins from Connecticut, whom you met a year ago when he made his goodwill trip to Moscow. We also want the right media representatives to survive the attack."

"What else do you need from me?" asked a calmer Kozlov.

"Sir, you need to order our submarines to proceed toward their launch points off the US coasts twelve hours prior to commencing the mission. We want them to be in position in case—"

"In case this big, risky fucking plan blows up in our faces!" Kozlov interjected.

Darginsky nodded. "Yes, sir."

"If our little scheme is successful, what makes you think Americans will accept their fate? They all have guns. They'll fight us on the streets."

"This is where Lucifer will be indispensable. He will use his ministry to exert considerable influence toward the same goal. The Americans will have little choice but to accept your terms."

Kozlov nodded but seemed skeptical. "Tell me again, how is your stolen nuclear weapon story going to shield us from a counterattack? Even I know a backpack weapon has far less destructive force than one of our missiles. You really think the Americans won't figure that out?"

"Sir, there will be total chaos for the first few days, and everyone in authority will be dead. By the time we admit to having carried out the attack, all our forces will be in place, and it won't matter."

Kozlov nodded slowly. "All right," he said, reaching into a desk drawer. "As you requested, I have prepared the authorization codes for the mission. I will send a message to the SVR station in Caracas, for your eyes only, sometime during the evening of January 14, using these codes to either give you the green light or cancel the operation."

"Very well, sir."

When they got to the office door the president grabbed Darginsky's arm. "Don't fail!" he growled, boring holes directly into the agent's eyes.

JANUARY 8
KANSAS CITY, MISSOURI

Keith Anderson was beat. A major snowstorm had swept across the plains states, impacting airports from Denver to Chicago. He had come straight home after an exhausting work shift. He stood in his garage, fumbling with the house key when his cell phone rang.

"Hello, Keith," said a voice that sent a shudder down his spine. "I hope I didn't wake you."

"No," he replied, trying to control his fear. "I just got home from work."

"Do you know who this is?"

Keith considered playing dumb, but there was no point. "Sure, Michael. I'm just wondering why you called. I gave you the routing information you asked for, and I know it's current because I verified it with base operations at Offutt and Tinker. So, what's the problem?"

"No problem . . . so far," Michael replied, "but our little project isn't quite finished yet."

Keith felt his stomach knotting up. "What else do you want?"

he asked bluntly. "I told you my knowledge about military matters is very limited, so how can I be of any further help?"

"You'll be infinitely valuable to me over the next week, and then it'll all be over. I need to ask you a few questions. My advice is to answer them honestly."

"I'm listening," Keith replied, angered at the implied threat.

"Suppose I needed to know which route our friend was flying. Could you provide that information?"

"Yes, assuming we had a way to communicate. The routing is stored in the computer."

"Good. Let's assume I also needed to know where he was along that route at any given time. Could you determine that as well?"

"Sure," said Keith. "I just query the computer as to present location."

"Very good. Now, suppose we wanted our friend to fly a particular route. Could you call Offutt or Tinker and suggest that, due to turbulence or weather, they should consider flying a particular route?"

Keith was alarmed with where the conversation was going. Still, calling Offutt or Tinker and "suggesting" a particular routing for the Airborne Command Post due to turbulence wouldn't be difficult to do.

"Keith, are you there?" Michael asked when Keith had been silent for too long.

"Yes, I'm here," replied the controller. "I just needed to think. Such a thing could be done, but since I don't normally work the Omaha or Oklahoma City sector, it would be unusual for me to do it."

"But you could do it," Michael pressed. "If you called base operations, identified yourself as the sector controller, and suggested routing due to severe turbulence, nobody would question it, right?"

Keith knew he had no choice. "Yeah, I could do that," he said, hating himself, but hating the caller even more. "They would follow my recommendation, but I might get some feedback."

"Excellent!" Michael cheered. "Now, since you worked today, I assume you'll also be working a week from today on the night of the fifteenth?"

"That's right," he said, holding his breath for what was coming next. "That'll be a minimum-manning night due to the federal holiday."

"And the usual afternoon takeoff for the Airborne Command Post is at 2200 Zulu, or 1600 local, correct?"

"Yes, that's correct."

"And your normal shift is from 1500 local to 2300 local?"

"Yes. I usually report about 1430 so I can familiarize myself with the weather and equipment outages."

"Could you show up as early as 1400?"

"I suppose."

"Great! Next Monday I want you to report to work by 1400. I want you to check on the filed routing for the Airborne Command Post. If it's any of the northern routes for the 747, then I want you to call base operations at Offutt and suggest that, due to reported severe turbulence, they consider filing one of the southern routes. My personal choice is Route 5. I'll also need to know if the 707 out of Tinker is planning to fly that night and which route. Have you got all that?"

"I have it," replied the controller, hating himself even more.

"What time do you take your first break?"

"Usually three hours into the shift," said Keith, "but it depends on whether there's somebody available to relieve me."

"That's 1800 at the earliest," observed Michael. "Can I call you while you're working?"

"Yes, but if I don't answer my cell phone it means I'm working the console. I won't be able to return the call until I go on break." Keith knew the Airborne Command Post carried a sizable crew, and the thought that he might be endangering their lives haunted him. "You said this will be over in a week," he decided to ask. "Can I count on that?"

"Yes, you can," replied the agent. "I'll have one more task for you that night, so try to monitor the position of the Airborne Command

Post throughout the evening. If anybody asks, tell them your cousin is the copilot. Fair enough?"

"Fair?" Keith repeated sarcastically. "Fuck you."

"Listen, Keith, you're doing fine. Hang in there another week, and you'll be done."

"This better be over on the fifteenth!"

"It will be," said Michael. "Trust me. I'll talk to you then."

As the phone went dead, Keith found himself reliving the awful night when he first encountered Michael. He was afraid of the consequences if he refused to cooperate. The silence of the darkened house reminded him of his beloved Lucy. Cold, heartless bastard!

CHAPTER THIRTEEN

JANUARY 10
GLEN COVE, NEW YORK

A black Peugeot sedan passed through the gates of the old Killenworth Mansion, a forty-nine-room facility in Glen Cove, New York, purchased long ago by the USSR for Soviet diplomatic personnel recreational use. The SVR agent headed northeast to see if he was being followed. The FBI's occasional tail reminded the Russian "diplomats" that Uncle Sam was watching.

Satisfied, the driver made his way south to the Long Island Expressway. He headed east, carefully observing the speed limit. Fifteen minutes later he took the Medford exit and eased to a stop at an all-night Shell station.

Using a burner phone, he listened to the ringing at the other end. The phone was answered on the seventh ring.

"Hello. Ron Goodman here," said a sleepy voice.

"I only have three minutes, so just listen and take notes. The missing backpack nuclear devices are already in the United States. They were originally delivered to Islamic Jihad, who is assisting the Houthis, and hidden in the crude oil tanks of the *Petroleum Princess*—"

"Wait a minute," demanded the CNS reporter. "Islamic Jihad . . . Houthis . . . *Petroleum Princess* . . . go on."

"The *Petroleum Princess* sailed from the Kharg Island oil terminal in Iran on November 20 and arrived in Bremen, Germany, on December 1."

"You're saying the weapons never arrived in Yemen?"

"Correct. That was leaked to throw off the US Navy, who is

searching every ship heading to Yemen. Jihad sympathizers met the ship and removed the weapons, which were sealed in lead containers to avoid detection. The German group transported the material to a private research lab where they were modified. Got it so far?"

"Yeah, I got it. Why were they modified?"

"Let me finish. The four weapons were resealed into lead-lined, stainless steel containers. The containers are the same size and shape as auxiliary fuel tanks which are sold for aftermarket installation on Mercedes-Benz diesel trucks. The weapons were included in a shipment to a Canadian-based Islamic cell under the name of a bogus trucking firm. The fuel tanks departed Bremen for Halifax aboard the *City of Hanover* on December 20 and arrived in Nova Scotia two days after Christmas. Representatives of the bogus trucking company claimed the fuel tanks and installed them on four Mercedes trucks. On January 5, the four trucks crossed into the United States. The weapons are to be detonated with a timing device that is located on the bottom of the tank. That's it."

"Well, that's an interesting story, but how do I know you're telling the truth? And why call me with such crucial information?"

The agent was ready for the question. "I am one of several Yemeni nuclear engineers trained and working in Canada. Like many of my countrymen, I view the United States as the cause of much turmoil in my country. However, my brothers are going too far. The bombs would kill thousands of our own people living in America. I don't think Allah would approve."

"And how do I know your tale is true?"

"Check it out. Check the movements of the ships."

"But it's such detailed information," said Goodman, "especially about the fake auxiliary fuel tanks."

"It's detailed, Mr. Goodman, because I planned the entire operation. My Islamic brothers came to me, and I could not turn them down. They would have killed me. This way, maybe I can prevent the deaths of many innocents."

After talking to Goodman, Ilya dialed a number in Glen Cove.

"Yes?"

"It's done," said Ilya.

"Very good. Did he buy it?"

"He had some questions," Ilya answered carefully, in case the call was being monitored by the FBI, "but considering his personality, I suspect it will be confirmed very soon."

"Excellent! So, you're continuing with your second project?"

"That's correct. I'll contact you when I'm settled in."

Soon the Peugeot was back on the expressway. The SVR agent made his way into Queens, working his way northbound toward the Bronx, and eventually ended up on Interstate 95. He was in no hurry. He had an entire week to prepare for his next assignment. At 0235, Ilya checked into the Marriott on the northwest side of downtown New Haven under the name "Charles Fagan."

Not bad, Ilya thought as he carried his luggage into his room. *Only a few blocks from Yale University, so my movements can be on foot.*

He punched in the number again for the Glen Cove mansion.

"Yes?" asked the same voice after only one ring.

"I'm in position. I'll check with you in a couple of days." He ended the call and got comfortable on the bed. "And tomorrow," he mumbled, "I'll find young Josh Hawkins, college student and the senator's son."

JANUARY 12
MURMANSK AIR BASE COMPLEX, RUSSIA
THE SU-57 CREW

"Let's practice our English between us for the flight, Anton."

"Roger that, ole buddy. But I'm itching like hell, Valentin," said Bachvaroff from the back seat of the Su-57.

"Shut up," came the reply over the interphone. "I don't want to hear it."

"Yeah, but . . ." He let the conversation pause just the right number of beats. "My balls especially itch, and I already need to take a piss!"

"You bastard!" Ridgik replied over the laughter from the back seat.

"Here comes the tanker," observed Bachvaroff. "Thank God he's finally ready to go."

"Yeah, it's going to be a long night."

"Don't forget it's going to be an itchy night, too, but just keep thinking about those Latin women . . . and try not to think about taking a piss."

"Bastard!" Ridgik watched the lumbering tanker approach the end of the runway. "Dammit, can't he taxi any faster?" he growled.

"Patience, comrade," came the reply from the back seat. "He's loaded with fuel that's going to get us to Cuba. If you were riding in a flying fuel tank, would you not taxi slowly?"

"I suppose," said Ridgik testily. "What time did the first flight of tankers get airborne?"

"Exactly one hour and twenty-three minutes ago," replied Bachvaroff. "That was a good plan. Those first two will draw interceptors that will use up their fuel and have to recover for more. That's when we fly by thumbing our nose. Why don't you relax and concentrate on how comfortable you are?"

Comfort was something they could not fathom in the Su-57, hastily modified as it was for the extra cockpit in back, especially when sitting on a hard ejection seat for twelve hours, where the only relief was shifting from cheek to cheek. And the sweaty rubber anti-exposure suits they wore under their flight suits, in case they ejected over water, made them feel as though they were swimming around inside a condom.

"All set, Anton?" asked Ridgik.

"Yes," replied Bachvaroff, serious now. "The radar's set for the in-trail departure with the tanker."

"Thirty seconds should give us safe spacing, and there's enough crosswind to clear his wake turbulence." Ridgik maneuvered the Sukhoi into position behind the left wingtip of the tanker. "I have good heading and attitude indicators, and my ejection seat safety pin is out and stowed."

"Out and stowed," acknowledged Bachvaroff.

They had planned a radio-out departure, not wanting to alert NATO listening bases in Norway that they were coming their way. The tanker flashed its lights. The tower responded with a green light and the tanker started to roll.

Ridgik spooled up the Sukhoi's engines to military power. The Sukhoi quivered from nose to tail, straining against the brakes.

"We have two good engines!" shouted Ridgik. "RPM, temperatures, and pressures are in the green!"

"I'm set!" Bachvaroff yelled back. "Ten seconds . . . three . . . two . . . one . . . go!"

Ridgik released the brakes and the Sukhoi, despite its heavy fuel load, accelerated rapidly. "Here come the burners," he said, easing the throttles into afterburner. "Two good burner lights." They surged ahead. "Airspeed check, two hundred."

"Two hundred back here."

The Su-57 needed 315 kilometers per hour at this weight to lift off. It reached that speed after using one-third of the runway. Ridgik reached for the landing gear handle. "Gear up . . . flaps up. Burners coming out . . . now."

"I have him on the scope dead ahead for five kilometers," said Bachvaroff. "He's starting his turn."

They had studied the route for days and knew they would clear the Norwegian coast by two hundred kilometers, then gradually bend around to the southwest, eventually heading down the middle of the Norwegian Sea, just west of the Faroe Islands, and into the North Atlantic.

"Valentin, we're inside of one kilometer," advised Bachvaroff.

"You might want to kill some overtake."

"I got him," replied Ridgik as he reduced the power, extended the speed brakes, and slid up next to the Midas. "I'll start out on the right wing and change sides every hour so I don't end up with a sore neck. Do you have the radar warning gear powered up in case the Norwegians scramble on us?"

"Powered up and ready," said Bachvaroff.

OVER MONTGOMERY, ALABAMA
CHATMAN'S CITATION

Bobby Chatman was early for his meeting with Darginsky, having decided to get out of Bay St. Louis before the predicted rain and fog arrived. He entered the traffic pattern at the St. Clair County Airport and touched down on runway 04. He turned off the runway and taxied toward the airport's small transient ramp area. A Lear 35 business jet sat among a half dozen smaller planes. Chatman could see Darginsky standing by the Learjet holding a paper bag in each hand. Chatman swung the Citation into the parking spot next to the Learjet, set the brakes, and shut down the engines.

"Hello, Viktor," he said as he opened the door of the Citation to find the Russian agent standing there with a big grin on his face. "It's good to see you!"

"It's good to see you too," said Darginsky. He set the paper bags on the floor of the Citation, then held out his hand to Chatman. "I got here a little early, so I rustled up some barbecue. I hope you're hungry."

"I'm always hungry for barbecue," Chatman said, grinning. "Come aboard. I have some drinks."

"Bobby, we are three days from one of the biggest events in history," said Darginsky when they'd spread the barbecue out on the small table in the rear of the Citation. "Are you ready?"

"We are," replied Chatman between bites of sandwich. "Alex and

Michael tell me both Petrov and Piekarski are set on their respective routes. They've learned all the appropriate procedures and have practiced them with controllers."

"Good, and Piekarski's holding up psychologically?"

"Yes, but oddly enough, it's Petrov who has us concerned."

"Oh? Why's that?"

"There's no doubt Petrov is the better pilot, and the truth is I feel more comfortable with him in command of the Route Alpha airplane, but his time in the US has raised questions in his mind about the loss of life. I think he needs to be reminded of his duty to the Motherland and the oath he took."

"I'll keep that in mind when I brief them Sunday night in Venezuela. Now, tell me the status of Route Charlie."

"Michael says the air traffic controller has already given us the canned routes, and he will suggest a southerly route for turbulence. Michael will call the controller before our friends enter US airspace, verify the routing of the Airborne Command Post, and get its current position. We will then pass the information to the Sukhoi when it is within range of the Kansas ranch."

"Excellent!"

"I'll be back in Bay St. Louis tonight," Chatman continued. "Sunday afternoon I'm flying to Washington to work with the president on the final preparations for the National Day of Prayer and Unity. I'll be there until Monday evening, but I need to disappear prior to the State of the Union address. Plus, Phillips didn't approve making Senator Hawkins the designated survivor, so he'll also be in DC. He said it was a bad idea politically."

"I think I can give you a viable excuse for disappearing," Darginsky said. "I have already hedged against the possibility Phillips would choose another person as the designated survivor. Ilya is in New Haven, Connecticut, keeping the senator's son under surveillance. In the early evening, prior to the mission, the senator's son will be roughed up enough to end up in the hospital. What if a minister friend of yours just happened to be at the hospital when the kid was admitted and called to tell you, with the senator in the capital, about it? You could break the news to the senator and offer to fly him to New Haven."

"Sounds great," said Chatman. "I think he'd jump at the offer."

"Good. Plan on it. Now, what's the story with our reporter friend?"

"I talked with him yesterday. He'll be working the New York anchor desk Monday night. My compliments on the bomb story." Chatman chuckled. "Goodman really ran with it."

Darginsky snickered. "I think it was on the air within two hours of Ilya's call."

"Andrew Phillips and his staff are pulling their hair out," Chatman said.

Darginsky smiled.

"How are things in Moscow, Viktor?" Chatman asked. "Judging from the news, it sounds like things are tough for Kozlov."

"They are," confirmed Darginsky. "When I saw him last, he was locked in his office under guard for his own protection. There have been three recent attempts on his life, all of which were successfully kept out of the media. Moscow is under curfew to prevent riots. I personally saw tanks on some streets."

"What about our people in the Washington embassy? Are we planning to get any of them out prior to Monday night?"

"Some of them are on the list to come out," replied Darginsky, ". . . and some are not. We've quietly asked those on the list to attend a winter party at Glen Cove. They will be invited to stay through Monday night." He rose to leave. "Tomorrow I'm flying to Havana. I'll brief the Su-57 crew on the mission and then fly to Caracas Sunday morning. I'll meet Petrov and Piekarski when they arrive in La Orchila, and I'll conduct the mission brief with them. I plan to be in our Havana embassy Monday night when the fireworks start. I'll monitor the secure radio traffic between our aircraft and issue the abort code if necessary. Bobby, we must be cautious. We cannot allow this operation to be executed in part. All three planes must accomplish their mission at the same time."

"I understand, Viktor."

"I know you do, my friend. After all, you came up with the idea. But this bears repeating. The consequences of failure to coordinate the attack are inconceivably bad. Kozlov must give us a final green light. I'll advise Glen Cove and the agent there will call Alex and Michael with the appropriate code. Do you have any last-minute questions?"

"None," said Chatman. "But I'd like to propose a toast." He opened the plane's bar cabinet, withdrew a bottle of fine vodka, and poured some into two plastic cups. "To the success of LUCIFER/INBLUE, to our leader, Nikolai Kozlov, and to the beginning of a new world order."

"Here, here!" returned Darginsky. "And to a job well done by our finest agent." They touched cups and drank the vodka in one swallow. "Now, I must be going. If any problems develop, let me know." He stepped out of the Citation, turned, and extended his hand. "It's all coming together, Bobby. Good luck."

CHAPTER FOURTEEN

JANUARY 12
OVER THE ATLANTIC, 0321Z
THE SU-57 CREW

They had been intercepted only once so far, and that had been in moderate clouds off the Norwegian coast. Unlike the American F-22, the Su-57 was not stealthy when approached from the rear, and the external fuel tanks increased its radar signature. The Norwegian F-35 fighters had gotten quite close with solid radar lock-on. However, the tanker's refueling drogue operator verified he had not seen any lights.

There had been an attempt by F-15s from RAF Lakenheath in England to run down the IL-78/Sukhoi flight, but as Ridgik had planned, the Eagles scrambled on the tankers an hour in front of them, and they had been on the ground refueling when his own flight went by.

"Aren't you done up there yet?" asked Bachvaroff. "You're making me sick back here."

"Damn this worthless exposure suit!" growled a frustrated Ridgik as he tried to pee in the bottle, fly the jet, and maintain formation with the tanker simultaneously. "The one time I need the autopilot it refuses to work!"

"Sounds like a personal problem," came the reply from the back seat. "You better hurry. I just got the first hit from an F-35 radar. They must be out of Shaw Air Force Base in South Carolina. The tanker will be diving for the clouds again."

"I'm all done," said Ridgik. He slid behind the tanker and into position on the right wing. "Do you still hear the radar?"

"Yep," replied Bachvaroff. "Definitely an APG-81. Hold it . . . make that two F-35s."

Bachvaroff knew American and Russian fifth-generation fighters had never squared off, not even in Syria where they once operated in the same airspace. Both Russian pilots couldn't help but wonder how they'd fare in a one-on-one engagement.

"Where are they, Anton?" Ridgik asked, as he hugged the wingtip of the tanker.

"They're currently at two o'clock. One has just achieved a radar lock. I would guess they are seventy kilometers out."

Bachvaroff resisted the temptation to power up their own radar. The Americans needed to believe that both airplanes were IL-78 tankers.

"Hang on," replied Ridgik. "The tanker pilot is headed for the clouds."

They were in thin cirrus clouds, but the tanker pilot, following Ridgik's instructions, continued the descent until they leveled off in solid cumulus clouds. Both planes bounced together in moderate turbulence.

Ridgik fought to keep the tanker's wingtip light in sight. "Those F-35 pilots are going to have their work cut out for them to get close enough for identification. Their rules say they can't come closer than one nautical mile unless they are in visual conditions."

"They're dead astern now, and close," advised Bachvaroff. "Shit! What the fuck was that?"

"That was lightning," came the reply from the front seat. "The tanker pilot's dragging us through the tops of thunderstorms."

"The Americans have some friends on the way!" Bachvaroff exclaimed. "I'm getting long-range hits from . . . another two F-35s! They're currently at one o'clock. I thought the weather at the American bases was going down and . . . *shit!* Can't you guys be a little smoother?"

"Tighten your harness and quit bitching," came the reply from the front seat. "It's all I can do to keep the tanker in sight!"

They continued in heavy clouds and rain showers. Lightning flashed intermittently, and on one occasion they were pelted with what sounded like ice pellets. The tanker pilot turned left and right to make the interceptors' job as difficult as possible.

"Both F-35s have a lock-on," advised Bachvaroff. "They're at three o'clock now, and . . . wait. The other F-35s just broke lock. Apparently they're leaving."

"And a pleasant good night to them," replied Ridgik. "What I wouldn't give to get into a dogfight with an F-35!"

The ride smoothed out considerably as the clouds thinned, and Ridgik could see the dim outline again of the IL-78 in the gray murk.

"The clouds are thinning out," noted Bachvaroff. "I'm worried those F-35 guys may be able to see us."

"Can you tell where they are?"

"Dead astern and close." Twisting around and looking backward, Bachvaroff grunted. "I see a dim strobe light."

"*Shit!*" yelled Ridgik. A brilliant light suddenly lit the clouds behind the tanker, causing Ridgik to flinch. Then the tanker pilot abruptly chopped his throttles and made a hard descending right turn. Ridgik, squinting against the intense light, awkwardly rolled with the tanker. "What the hell is that!"

"Rear-facing landing lights!" Bachvaroff shouted. "I've never seen them used, but they're designed to blind an interceptor."

"Well, it blinded the hell out of me!"

"He's trying to make the F-35s overshoot," said Bachvaroff. "And—holy shit! Did you see that? The F-35s just passed overhead, afterburner cooking. Damn, that was close!"

"This is getting crazy!" said Ridgik, as the tanker turned off the lights and accelerated.

"Wait! They've both broken lock. I think they're calling it off. I wonder if the first guy was able to ID us?"

"Who knows," said Ridgik.

"Now, could you hold this thing level for a few minutes? It's my turn to pee in the bottle."

JANUARY 12
OVER SOUTHERN IDAHO
ABOARD UNITED AIRLINES

Mark Matthews's mission was simple. There was an F-15 at McChord AFB outside Tacoma, Washington, that was being transferred to his unit in Massachusetts. His squadron commander had offered him the opportunity to go out and pick it up. After putting in his papers to leave the Air National Guard, they'd downgraded him to "proficiency only" status, which meant he was no longer a mission-ready pilot. It was a status usually reserved for staff officers who didn't have time for combat-readiness continuation training.

Before boarding the United flight to Seattle, he had checked in with Dare to let her know he was about to make his final F-15 flight. He told her how depressed he was that his last ride would be a cross-country ferry flight rather than an air-to-air contest.

"Mark, you're supposed to be the 'world's greatest fighter pilot.' Are you sure you're making the right decision?"

"Dare, I love flying the Eagle, but I can't stay, especially not while guys like Richard Robertson get to ride roughshod over us! I need to find something else to do."

"I get it. Just go to McChord, enjoy your time with your friend, and think about it. It's maybe the most important career decision you'll ever make."

An hour into the flight, a flight attendant asked, "What will you be drinking tonight, sir?" after she'd set down a tray with some sort of chicken dish.

He smiled at her and said, "A beer, any beer."

Returning to place a can on his tray, she said with a smile, "Here's your 'any beer.'" He reached into his pocket for his wallet. She leaned in close, whispering so the other passengers wouldn't protest, "You can put your money away. The captain knows you're back here."

"And how did he know that?" Matthews asked, also whispering.

"Oh, he had a little help."

"And how did the little help know who I was?" Matthews asked, enjoying the exchange.

She gestured toward his patch-studded helmet bag sitting on the floor at his feet. "Just a gal's intuition."

"Okay," he replied, nodding. "Please tell him I appreciate that."

A damned fine gesture, thought Matthews. *If I'm ever an airline captain, I'm going to do the same thing.*

Two and a half hours later Matthews was inside the terminal shaking hands with his friend Craig Morton and exchanging hugs with his wife, Sarah. "I hope you've eaten," Craig said. "It's late, so we put the steaks up until tomorrow night."

"Yeah, I ate on the plane," Matthews replied, "but I was really looking forward to some of Sarah's famous apple pie."

"Well, we can still have some of that over coffee when we get home," Sarah said.

When the threesome got to the house, Sarah put on a pot of coffee and cut two generous slices of apple pie for Mark and Craig. They hadn't seen each other since F-15 school, and there was a lot of catching up to do. With fresh coffee and a plate of Sarah's pie in front of him, Matthews told them the story of the gun camera film with the pipper centered on the helmet of Richard Robertson. The laughter died off when he told them about the Officer Performance Report Robertson had written.

"So, do you think this flight Monday will be your last ride in the F-15?" Craig asked.

"I don't know. I'm going to miss flying it. A lot depends on what job I find. Maybe my engineering degree is still worth something."

"Airlines?" Craig asked.

"I'm thinking about it."

"I'm wiped out," Sarah sighed. "I'll see you guys in the morning."

"Oh, wait!" Matthews said. "I met a woman."

"Oh?" Sarah asked.

"She's an FBI agent."

Matthews told them about Dare, and afterward, when the conversation returned to flying, Sarah went to bed.

The two pilots were silent for a few moments after she left the room. Craig finally broke the silence. "Any second thoughts?"

"Sure. I've spent hours wondering if I'm doing the right thing, but it boils down to one truth. I can't stay."

APPROACHING THE CUBAN COAST
THE SU-57

Bachvaroff smiled under his oxygen mask. "Just think, little buddy, this time tomorrow we'll be sunburned, drunk, and enjoying the company of some cute Cuban comrades."

"There are only five things on my mind right now, Anton," came the terse reply. "I want to get on the ground and get out of this fucking suit. Then I want a shower, a decent meal, and a good night's sleep. *Then* getting drunk and getting laid, not necessarily in that order."

"I counted six things. Maybe seven."

"Anton. Reach down and pull those pretty yellow handles, would you, little buddy?"

"No. Not going swimming. You need me to keep you awake, Valentin."

"How far out are we?"

"A little less than two hundred kilometers."

The trip had been long and exhausting, but satisfying. They had proven the feasibility of air-refueling Su-57s and flying them nonstop over a long distance. The sniper pilots knew Americans did that routinely. Their thoughts turned to the remote air base Darginsky had directed for their arrival on the western side of the island.

"How's the fuel?" asked Bachvaroff.

"We're fat," replied Ridgik. We will land with two thousand kilograms."

"Hmm," muttered Bachvaroff. "I'm getting hits from a J-band radar like those on late-model MiG-21s. I guess we're going to have a welcoming committee."

The Felon and the Midas tanker turned on their navigation lights to make themselves easily visible to the Cuban interceptor pilots. Within ten minutes they were being escorted by a pair of old Soviet MiG-21s, with the Cuban flight lead wagging his wings in the moonlight to signal them to follow while his wingman slid in tight to get a good look at the Su-57.

The MiGs led them through the descent and got them established in the traffic pattern at San Julián. The tanker landed first, followed three minutes later by the Sukhoi. They had done it radio-out, using light-gun signals, just as they had at Murmansk. As they were clearing the runway Ridgik noticed a truck with the words "Follow Me" printed in Russian on the back. "I'm opening my canopy."

"Mine's open," came the excited reply. "I can smell the ocean!"

The truck led them past the midfield turnoff where the tanker had gone. "Where is he taking us?" Ridgik muttered. "I have a bad feeling he's taking us to that old alert facility. I can see armed guards everywhere."

"Well, we are the first Su-57 that's ever flown nonstop to Cuba," said Bachvaroff, "and I assume they want to keep that a secret. I bet they will hide this one inside."

The Sukhoi entered the small ramp area, which was enclosed in chain-link fence topped with barbed wire, and a ground crewman directed them toward the hangar. He directed Ridgik to hold the brakes, then a tractor tow bar was connected to the nose gear of the fighter. The ground crewman signaled for engine shutdown, and the Felon's engines whined to a stop. The tractor started pushing the jet backward into the hangar.

"I see AK-47s everywhere. And look to the left. That's an R-77M missile storage crate."

"What's going on?"

"I don't know," replied Ridgik, "but maybe this SVR colonel standing by the ladder can tell us."

It took the two pilots a few minutes to gather their gear and unstrap from their ejection seats.

"Welcome to Cuba," said the colonel, who returned their salutes as they exited the jet. "I'm Colonel Pavel Prokepenko. I was directed by Comrade Viktor Darginsky to see to your needs. If you will follow me, please, I will show you to your quarters. One of the technicians will remove your bags from the baggage pod and bring them shortly."

Walking awkwardly in their survival suits, they followed the colonel across the ramp. After passing through a security checkpoint, they entered a small building, walked to a locked door, and entered a corridor to the top of a stairway that led to an underground bunker.

The colonel opened the door to a large room and stood aside. "This will be your home for the next few days. Your meals will be served here. Sleeping and toilet facilities are through that door. Colonel Darginsky will be here tomorrow evening. Per his orders, you are not to leave the fenced compound. Walks on the ramp are approved, but be sure you notify security on that phone of your intentions. It's a direct line. Do you have cell phones?" The two pilots nodded. "I will need to take them. If you need anything, ask the guards to ring me. I know you need to rest. Consequently, you will not be disturbed for the next twelve hours. A hot meal is on the way. Now, gentlemen, can I answer any questions?"

"Yes," said Ridgik. "Can you tell us why we are being placed under such tight security?"

Prokepenko tried to hide a smile. "Funny you should ask me

that, Major. I was planning to ask you the same question. I guess we will both have to await Colonel Darginsky's arrival. Any other questions . . . none? Very well. Have a nice evening, gentlemen."

"Wait," Bachvaroff called. "One more question. We saw a nice beach on the way in. Can we get over there for a swim?"

"No. You have to stay inside the compound. Sorry."

After the colonel left, a seemingly disappointed Bachvaroff slumped into a chair. "So much for the beach and getting laid."

Ridgik was already stripping out of his flight suit and hated anti-exposure suit. "I'd say things are going to be very interesting when Darginsky arrives. I'm heading for the shower. If our bags aren't here in a few minutes, call security and have them check on them."

Ridgik was luxuriating under the cascading hot water when Bachvaroff stuck his head in the door. "Hey, Valentin, you'd better hurry. Darginsky really took care of us with this food. Guess what he ordered for the main dish?"

"I give up," said the tired pilot.

"Fried chicken," laughed Bachvaroff. "And there's apple pie for dessert!"

"Alcohol?"

"Puerto Rican rum, with a note from Darginsky that says, 'Welcome to Cuba, caballeros!'"

CHAPTER FIFTEEN

SATURDAY, JANUARY 13
TIME TO WEAPONS RELEASE: 61 HR, 25 MIN
GRIFFISS AIR FORCE BASE, NEW YORK

Lieutenant Colonel Pete Pearson was pissed. He'd been scheduled to have the three-day weekend off and had just sat down for breakfast when the phone rang. The caller explained that the officer scheduled for duty was sick, and he, Pearson, was next on the standby list.

Pearson, a senior director at the North American Aerospace Defense Command's Eastern Air Defense Sector, EADS, took his time finishing breakfast and getting dressed. He drove unhurriedly from his home in Utica, New York, to nearby Griffiss Air Force Base, where he worked as a full-time guardsman. Pearson didn't care. He'd been passed over twice for colonel and was only five months from retirement.

"Good morning, sir," said Captain Ronald Kirby, the weapons director who was about to finish his shift. "Sorry about calling you in on short notice."

"No problem," said Pearson, not hiding his disappointment. "So, another boring Friday night?"

"Not exactly, sir. We scrambled four sets of alert birds last night."

"No kidding? What happened?"

"The Russians launched two flights of two airplanes each about an hour and twenty-five minutes apart from the Kilpyavr Air Base in Murmansk. The first flight was routine with normal radio communications that were monitored in Norway. We assumed it was the usual flight of Bears or IL-76 transports to Cuba. We scrambled from Norway and England, then sequentially along our East Coast. The Norwegian F-35s identified the first pair of IL-76s, but it was two tankers, not transports. This first flight was cruising clear of clouds."

"Sounds routine," commented Pearson.

"Yes, sir, but it got interesting with the second flight of two. They launched from Kilpyavr in complete radio silence. The Norwegians closed to within a mile of the second Russian flight, which was cruising in heavy cloud and blacked out. The F-15s at Lakenheath were caught on the ground refueling and were unable to run down the second pair. We managed to get some F-22s out of Langley-Eustis in close. Then we diverted four F-35s out of Shaw from a training sortie, but when they got close, the lead Russian airplane turned on one of those rearward-facing landing lights, and the flight lead abandoned the intercept without a positive ID when he got a collision warning on his radar."

"Sounds like normal Russian fun and games. Using the bright light in the clouds goes back to F-106 days," the old Delta Dart pilot said smiling.

"Yes, sir, but I think the analysis of the F-35 and F-22 radar data is interesting," said Kirby patiently. "The pilots in every other interceptor assumed the aircraft were the same type, so none of them used their radars to analyze the flight."

"Get to the point, Ron."

"Sir, the lead Russian aircraft was another IL-76. His wingman, however, was a Russian fighter. The data indicated it was a Foxhound or a Felon."

"Hmm . . ." mused Pearson, interested now, but not impressed. "Did we ever get a visual identification?"

"No, sir. The alert bases south of Shaw were all down in fog, so we elected not to risk scrambling any other airplanes."

"Did we pick up any radio chatter from the second flight?"

"Only bits and pieces. The interesting thing is they did it all at night and blacked out. The recovery in Cuba was the San Julián Air Base on the west end of the island, not their usual destination outside of Havana. Could they be trying to hide the movement of the fighter?"

"Maybe," said Pearson. "Do we have any satellite photos of a MiG-31 or a Su-57 on the ground in Cuba?"

"Not yet, sir. It's too early. We only got the intel message from Langley-Eustis two hours ago—"

"Just say 'Langley,'" Pearson interrupted. "You know I'm old-school and hate tacking Army names onto our bases."

"I forgot, sir. Sorry."

Pearson scanned through the top secret message. "Well, Ron, we should pass this up the line, but I don't see any reason for priority handling. Everybody in the intelligence business is only interested in one thing right now, and that's finding those Mercedes trucks with the nukes."

"So, you don't want to put a priority tag on it to NORAD?" Kirby pressed, frowning.

"Nah. The only conclusion they'll come to is that the Russians successfully refueled a fighter aircraft en route to Cuba. They can do that on Tuesday morning. Just pass it through normal channels."

TIME TO WEAPONS RELEASE: 58 HR, 21 MIN
SAN JULIÁN AIR BASE, CUBA

"I can't believe it," moaned Bachvaroff dejectedly. "There's sand all around us, the temperature's twenty-seven degrees Celsius, and I can smell the ocean, but I'm locked in this compound."

"Don't forget the women," commented Ridgik as he completed his sit-ups and rolled over for push-ups. "That's all you talked about on the flight."

"Yeah, I know. I'm trying not to think about them."

"Look on the bright side," said the sniper pilot. "We're outside in the middle of January in shorts, and we're about to be part of something big. I can feel it."

"You keep saying that, and I keep thinking about the trip to America Darginsky promised us. You think the two are related?"

"Could be. Here comes our SVR comrade. He has that colonel-walk down pat."

"Good morning, gentlemen," said Prokepenko. "I trust you slept well?"

"Oh, yes, sir," replied Ridgik. "We just couldn't resist sitting in the sun awhile."

"Although we'd rather be at the beach," Bachvaroff chimed in. "A swim in the ocean would be heavenly."

"Yes, I'm sure, but orders are orders. Colonel Darginsky should be arriving shortly from Havana."

The SVR colonel was quiet as they watched the hangar door open. The Su-57 was clearly visible and now fully armed with four R-77M air-to-air missiles hanging from their ejection launchers in the center fuselage armament bays. The two inboard, pylon-mounted fuel tanks had been removed, leaving only the two outboard fuel tanks. The airplane was now in its optimum long-range combat configuration. Colonel Prokepenko noticed the setup as well. "Major, may I ask you a question?" he said, looking directly at Ridgik.

"Of course, sir," Ridgik replied, cutting his eyes toward Bachvaroff, signaling caution.

"The entire base is buzzing about your aircraft. Frankly, I'm in the dark like everyone else. Would you please enlighten me?"

"Sorry, sir, I know little more than you. Even if I did, I wouldn't be at liberty to discuss it without Comrade Darginsky's permission."

"So be it," scowled Prokepenko. "But I can't believe you flew all the way to Cuba without an inkling—"

"That must be Darginsky's chopper," interrupted Bachvaroff as a Russian Mi-17 headed directly for their alert compound. "Now, maybe we'll have some answers."

They watched the helicopter settle for a landing on the far side of the ramp. As the engines whined to a stop, Viktor Darginsky stepped out. Colonel Prokepenko hurried to meet him.

The Sukhoi crewmen watched in amusement as Prokepenko made a big deal of saluting Darginsky, then assisted him with a large picnic basket, several chart cases, and a briefcase. Darginsky carried the maps and briefcase while Prokepenko trailed behind with the basket.

"Valentin! Anton!" greeted Darginsky. "It's great to see you. I trust Colonel Prokepenko has been looking after your needs?"

"Oh, yes, sir! A trip to that little beach would have been nice, of course," Bachvaroff quipped.

"You haven't been to the beach?" Darginsky asked.

They shook their heads. "Orders," Ridgik mumbled.

Frowning, Darginsky said thoughtfully, "Hmm. Well, I hope you haven't had lunch yet. I decided to treat you to some French cuisine. I picked up the items this morning in Montreal. Please lead the way. We have much to discuss."

The two pilots led the SVR agents to the underground quarters. When they were inside the large common room, Darginsky set his items on the dining table and took the picnic basket from Prokepenko. "Thank you for your assistance, Colonel," he said as he withdrew a sealed folder from the briefcase. "This folder needs to be delivered to Major Popovich, the flight lead in the first flight of two tankers that landed last night. They have a scheduled takeoff this evening. Please see that he gets it."

"But, what about—"

"That will be all, Colonel," said Darginsky with a pleasant smile. As Prokepenko started to leave, Darginsky added, "And Colonel, after our briefing here is done, please see that these gentlemen get out to the beach . . . with an armed escort."

When Prokepenko had left the room, Darginsky removed a small electronic box. "Comrades, I think you'll be interested in what I've been doing since I saw you last. Things in Moscow are fine. I had a meeting with the president." He moved slowly around the room, holding the cigarette pack-sized device out in front of him, continuing the small talk. When he passed the wall-mounted public address speaker, the box displayed a red light. Darginsky removed the speaker from the wall, turned it over, then used a small pair of pliers to remove the eavesdropping bug that was mounted inside. He continued his sweep of the room, all the while continuing the small talk. "There," he said. "Only one bug, an early model at that. Now we can get down to business while we have lunch."

They told him everything about the flight, even Ridgik's frustration at trying to relieve himself while wearing the hated anti-exposure suit. Darginsky asked about each of the intercepts. They mentioned that the open hangar door revealed a fully armed Su-57.

"I suppose you would like to know what's going on," said Darginsky. "The two of you are, in fact, going to America. You'll be part of a three-plane strike package that will mount a surprise attack this coming Monday evening. Two bombers, commanded by the pilots you met at the dacha, will launch four nuclear cruise missiles, and you will destroy the American Airborne Command Post. Due to the big speech their president is giving in Washington, it will be airborne."

He paused, seeing their shocked expressions, then summarized the entire mission.

After a few seconds of astonished silence, Ridgik said, "I think I understand the motivation on the part of President Kozlov for such a move, but how does he plan to avoid American retaliation?"

"Excellent question. The answer is dependent on two essential details. First is the terrorist bomb threat. American expectation is that a nuclear explosion will be a terrorist act. It will take them a while to determine that the attack came from us. By then we will have a dagger at their throats. Our command and control will be intact; theirs will be in disarray. Our strategic forces will be ready for immediate launch; theirs will be in normal peacetime readiness. Their submarines will be on routine patrol; ours will be off their coasts in optimum launch positions."

"Viktor," Ridgik asked, "is their airspace monitoring really so inadequate that they won't be able to determine that they are being attacked?"

"Yes it is. The critical component is the launch of our cruise missiles from within American airspace. They won't expect this. Their early warning systems will be looking for threats outside their borders. The cruise missiles launched within their airspace will not be suspected as threats. Their first hint that they're being attacked will be the nuclear flashes of the 'terrorist' bombs."

"Brilliant!" Ridgik said.

"Who came up with such a scheme?" Bachvaroff asked.

Darginsky shrugged and smiled. "Some friends, with a little assistance from yours truly."

TIME TO WEAPONS RELEASE: 54 HR, 48 MIN
THE WHITE HOUSE

Frank Morgan was not looking forward to this meeting with the president and others who had been called in. His FBI staff was stretched thin and grappling with the seeming hopelessness of their search mission. He sensed his people were tired and wary of more workload possibly coming their way and felt pressure mounting on himself by the hour. Who, he wondered, would be held responsible if the truck bombs couldn't be found? But, then, he mused, there might not be anyone left to blame. He sat uneasily, listening to the president chew out one of the CIA officers.

"In summary, Mr. President, we don't see any significance in the movement of Bear bombers to Africa. President Kozlov has some serious problems. Our assessment is that the current Russian government will likely be toppled through infighting and will eventually be replaced. Moving on to Central America—"

"Excuse me, Colonel Avery," said Andrew Phillips, who had

called the Saturday afternoon meeting and requested an in-depth intelligence briefing. "I'm sorry, but right now I don't give a tinker's damn what's happening in Russia. Kozlov has his problems, and I have mine. All I want to hear about is the current situation with those damned Mercedes trucks. Russia verified the weapons passed through Germany, where they were modified to fit inside the truck auxiliary fuel tanks. Is that correct?"

"Yes, sir," replied the red-faced colonel. "I was going to get to that."

"Fine," said the president. "Now, can you tell me what's being done to locate those trucks?"

"Mr. President, FBI Director Morgan will have to answer that question for you."

"What about it, Frank?" asked Phillips, turning toward Morgan.

"We're doing everything we can, Mr. President. Locating four trucks out of thousands is like looking for needles in a haystack. All our agents are working twelve-hour shifts, seven days a week. The same is true for policemen all over the country. We're stopping all Mercedes trucks, searching truck stops, garages, even dealerships. Those trucks could be parked anywhere."

"Do you have any leads?" asked Phillips. "Surely somebody, somewhere, has seen something suspicious. We've been asking the public to help."

"And the public has responded enthusiastically," Morgan confirmed, his frustration showing. "Maybe too enthusiastically. We've gotten thousands of calls and investigated hundreds of Mercedes truck sighting reports."

"Do you need more manpower?" Phillips asked.

"Well, sir, I think the more people we have looking, the better our chances."

"Okay, manpower you shall have. I want to mobilize the National Guard. The Department of Defense can choose which units. In addition, all nonessential federal employees are to be utilized for as long as necessary to assist in the search. Frank, get with your counterparts at the CIA. I want to find those trucks by Monday night. Let's see some results."

"Thank you, Mr. President," said the exasperated FBI director, nodding his head for the good intentions but dreading trying to implement Phillips's plan.

"This meeting's adjourned," said Phillips. "I'll hear about Bear bombers in Angola and what's happening in Venezuela after we locate those damned trucks!"

CHAPTER SIXTEEN

JANUARY 13
TIME TO WEAPONS RELEASE: 46 HR, 7 MIN
LA ORCHILA AIR BASE, VENEZUELA

"Good evening, Luis," said Maria Morales as she entered the cantina. "How are you on this beautiful evening?"

"Ah, Maria," replied the proprietor of The Cock of the Walk, a small bar and casino located just outside the gates of La Orchila Air Base. "I was so-so until you came through the door. Now I'm fantastic. If only I were a little younger . . ."

"Luis, mind your tongue," she said. "If you were a little younger, we could make it a night to remember. So why are you only so-so?"

Luis shrugged. "This should be the busiest night of the week but look around."

The normally bustling establishment was empty. It was rare for a Saturday night, and the absence of the Russian contingent could only mean one thing: something big was happening on the base. It was her business to find out what.

"I see what you mean," she said, allowing her lips to pout in feigned understanding. "And I was ready for a good time. Is there an exercise tonight?"

The man shrugged his shoulders, then leaned toward the woman. "The rumor is that some Russian airplanes are landing tonight. It's all very hush-hush, but I hear they are big airplanes. All Russian advisers are required to remain on base."

"Any idea when that will be?" she asked casually.

"I was told to expect to do a booming business after eleven tonight. How about a drink on the house?"

Her mind was racing so fast she missed the man's offer. Big Russian airplanes. If tonight's rumors were true, her contacts in Washington would want to know with as much detail as possible. That meant photos.

"Will it be your usual, lovely lady?"

"Oh, no, Luis," she said. "I'm sorry, but I'd like a rain check if you don't mind."

"Are you going to leave and ruin an old man's only happiness?"

"Only for a while," she said with a smile. "I'll be back when there's a little more action."

She leaned over and kissed the old man on the forehead. "Who knows, Luis? Maybe one of these nights . . ."

"I'll be waiting," he said softly as she walked out the door.

Maria drove around the winding road that circled the air base to her favorite observation point abeam the end of the runway. She had taken great care in selecting the place. A knot of scrub pine provided cover for the car, and a stretch of tall native grass near the fence allowed her to take pictures of aircraft unobserved. Patrols occasionally passed by, but security was often lax. She'd been successful getting photos of aircraft that had visited the base, and on one occasion, she'd shot pictures of MiG-23s in broad daylight.

The CIA didn't pay her much, but spying on Maduro's thugs and their Russian cronies helped her deal with the terrible memories of the past. Her father was a successful businessman in Caracas, her mother a respected teacher, until Maduro's police came that awful night. Her brother, Juan—

No time for that, she thought as she removed the Nikon from its secret compartment in the car. *Tonight, I'll need the infrared telephoto.*

The tall grass covered her completely as she lay on her stomach. After an hour, the runway lights got brighter, and she heard the far-off rumble of an approaching aircraft. She sat up so she could observe its approach.

Now that's interesting, Maria thought as she used the camera to focus on the distant landing lights. *There's two of them.* She started snapping pictures as soon as she could make out the aircrafts' shape. Using the infrared lens, Maria could tell they were huge turboprop Bear bombers. When the lead aircraft was less than a kilometer from the runway, the aircraft's landing lights washed over her. *Damn!* She flattened herself in the grass and continued snapping pictures.

Maria used the Nikon to catch the arrival of the second aircraft, then she quickly made her way back to the old Chevy. She figured she had an hour to get the SD card to the drop point on the other side of the island and then back to the cantina. Maria placed the film in an envelope using the standard code words for where and when it was shot, then gunned her Chevy toward the main road. She pulled up in front of the old monastery, dropped the envelope in the donation box, and rang the bell so the envelope would be picked up immediately. Minutes later, she was back on the road toward La Orchila village.

TIME TO WEAPONS RELEASE: 45 HR, 20 MIN
NEW HAVEN, CONNECTICUT

"I hope you don't mind my asking," said the flaxen-haired girl, "but this is my favorite group. I was wondering if you'd like to dance." Ilya was jarred from his thoughts by the girl's sudden appearance. He'd been sitting alone at the table for almost two hours keeping an eye on Josh Hawkins—college student, senator's son, and lady's man.

"Uh, not right now," he said. "Maybe later."

"Well, then, would it be okay if I sit at your table?" she asked, smile and freckles blending with green eyes to make a most-pleasant image. "There's not a seat in the whole place, and it's awfully crowded at the bar."

He considered turning the girl down. He was supposed to devote his attention to keeping his subject under constant watch.

"Sure," he finally said, returning her smile. "I'd be delighted. I was about to fight my way to the bar. Can I get you something to drink?"

"A White Russian," said the girl, "and something to munch on if you don't mind."

"Er . . . right," he replied, controlling the desire to laugh. "One White Russian coming up."

It took ten minutes to get the drinks and some popcorn. He'd managed to catch the girl's eye several times while waiting at the bar, and she always flashed a coquettish smile back.

"Sorry it took so long. This place is really busy on a Saturday night."

"It sure is," she replied. "But I love it here. The DJ's a friend of mine. He always plays some of my favorite music. By the way, my name's Donna."

"I'm Charles," he said. "Pleased to meet you, Donna."

"I love your accent," she giggled, "but I'm having a hard time placing it. It almost sounds Scandinavian."

"Oh, it is," Ilya offered. "My parents are from Finland. I learned English there before we emigrated."

"I think it's great," she said.

"Are you from Connecticut?"

"No, I live in New York. I'm going to the University of Bridgeport. I'm just a freshman in general studies right now. I'll decide on a major later. I'd guess you were a grad student."

"Right," said Ilya, enjoying the conversation with this naive girl. "I'm studying foreign relations, and my special interest is Russia."

"Oh, that's neat!" she said. "Hey, this is another of my favorite songs. Don't you want to dance?"

Ilya wasn't much of a dancer. But then he noticed Josh Hawkins on the floor with a girl. He grabbed Donna's hand and pulled her into the gyrating crowd, maneuvering her close to Hawkins and his date.

"Say, you're not a bad dancer," Donna remarked. "Somebody taught you well."

"Thanks!" he replied. The next song was a slow one, the soft music allowing Ilya to hear everything being said between Josh Hawkins and his date.

"Josh, you know I'd love to," the girl said, "but I'd rather come over when I don't have to get up early the next day."

"So, when's a good night for you?" asked the senator's son.

"Monday night would be perfect," replied the girl. "I could come after class in the evening and stay all night."

"Sounds great," the young Hawkins replied. "I'll have dinner waiting for you."

I sincerely doubt that, Ilya thought, delighted that he knew his target's plans for Monday evening. *You and I have a date that night, lover boy.*

SUNDAY, JANUARY 14
TIME TO WEAPONS RELEASE: 33 HR, 45 MIN
LA ORCHILA AIR BASE, VENEZUELA

Viktor Darginsky was pleased with how things were progressing. Yesterday he'd caught an early flight out of Montreal, completed all mission-related work in Cuba, and then caught the last flight from Havana to Caracas. Petrov and Piekarski would arrive later that evening, so there was time to check the status of everything at La Orchila.

"Excuse me," said Darginsky, as he flashed his ID to the Russian soldier guarding the ramp's entrance. "I'm looking for Eduard Bolshov."

"You mean the missile man," replied the guard. "He's in that smaller hangar."

"Thank you," said Darginsky. He heard a low hum, which built in volume and intensity as he approached the building. This engine's sound was different, with more of an ear-splitting whistle. The deafening noise was coming from a Kh-55 missile mounted on a test stand. Eduard Bolshov was observing various readings on a small instrument panel.

"Greetings, sir!" Bolshov yelled. "Put these on!" He handed Darginsky a set of ear protectors.

Darginsky watched as Eduard worked. After testing all the missile's controls, the technician moved the throttle lever to the idle position. Eduard jotted down some readings, lifted a guarded switch on the panel, and punched a button marked "Shutdown." The missile wound down to a stop.

"I trust all is well with the checkout of the missiles?"

"So far, so good," replied the technician. "They're ready to fly, sir."

"Excellent! All of them have been started up and run under their own power?"

"Yes, sir."

"And the terminal guidance package for the missiles arrived as scheduled?"

"I received them two days ago and installed them yesterday afternoon."

"Very good, Eduard," said Darginsky. "When will you load them on the bombers?"

"I want to check out the wiring in each of the Tu-95s first. Then we need to fuel them. We should be ready to load each missile by sunset."

Darginsky nodded as he stared at the Kh-55, amazed again at the destructive power contained in its sleek shape. "Let me know if you run into any problems."

"Of course, sir. Do you mind if I ask you a question?"

"Certainly not," replied Darginsky, "but don't be surprised if I refuse to answer."

"There are rumors going around that President Kozlov may soon be replaced."

"I cannot comment on any rumors," said Darginsky, "but there's one thing I can tell you for sure. If your missiles successfully complete their mission tomorrow night, the rumors won't matter."

TIME TO WEAPONS RELEASE: 30 HR, 5 MIN
THE WHITE HOUSE

"Bobby! Come in," said the president. "You know Frank Morgan from the FBI and John Mims from the CIA?"

"Yes. Good afternoon, gentlemen," said Chatman, noting that the men looked tired. "I hope I'm not intruding, Andrew."

"Not at all. We're all facing this terrorist thing together and you've certainly done your part. We sure would like to locate those nuclear weapons before tomorrow night. Frank and John were just explaining why they've failed in that endeavor."

"Mr. President, it'll take us a number of days to mobilize nonessential federal employees," said John Mims. "Washington must be considered a prime target. I suggest we use the manpower available to sweep the city in circles with the Washington Monument at the center of the circle. I want to be sure one of those Mercedes trucks isn't parked in the city."

"I agree," said the president. "Use every available helicopter and drone. Let's search every possible place where one of those trucks might be parked. I'd like to secure a three-mile radius of the monument."

"Three miles?" Morgan barked, almost jumping to his feet.

"Mr. President," interjected Mims, "if my high school math is still worth anything, you've just told us to search a nearly thirty-square-mile area!"

"That's half of Washington," Morgan added.

Phillips showed them the palms of his hands. "Gentlemen! You'd do the same if you were in my shoes. Now, I don't want any excuses!" After a pause, he continued in a calmer tone. "Let's give the DC mayor a call to enlist her help. We'll keep roadblocks in place until the start of rush hour Tuesday morning. And get in touch with the local television stations. We want to stress our actions are purely a precaution. We can discuss the radius. Keep me posted."

"Mr. President, there's something I wanted to tell you about, personally," said Mims, glancing toward Chatman. "We've noticed something strange among our Russian friends here in town."

"Go on," said the president.

"About a third of the diplomatic contingent left town this weekend. They went to their Glen Cove facility. Everybody that went took family members with them."

"What's so strange about that, John?" asked the president. "Even Russians need to get away and spend time with their families occasionally."

"Yes, sir, but we found the guest list to be interesting. Everybody who left town is an ardent supporter of Nikolai Kozlov. Those who weren't invited, including the ambassador, remained in Washington. Since it's not the recreational season in Glen Cove, we wondered if they know something we don't."

Chatman held his breath while he waited for Phillips to respond. He was surprised the CIA knew which Russian embassy individuals supported Kozlov, and which didn't.

"Oh, John, don't be so spy-like," said the president. "So, the Russian supporters of Kozlov get together for the weekend. It's the same thing as Republican members of Congress getting together and not inviting the Democrats."

"But, sir," Mims countered, "don't you find the timing of that get-together suspicious? I, for one, do not believe in coincidences."

President Phillips seemed to have had enough of this conversation. "John, you may be right, and maybe the Russians are just as afraid of a terrorist nuclear bomb as we are. Now gentlemen, I need some time with the good reverend today, so get out there and find me those trucks!"

"I feel for those guys," said the president when the two directors had left. "They really have their work cut out for them." Chatman nodded his agreement, and Phillips went on. "Bobby, I was hoping you might work with me on my speech for tomorrow night."

"Sure, Andrew. My time is yours."

They were interrupted by an assistant. "Sir, a call is coming in from President Kozlov."

TIME TO WEAPONS RELEASE: 29 HR, 40 MIN
THE COMM CENTER IN THE KREMLIN

"Your call has gone through, sir," said the interpreter. "The president of the United States is on the line."

"Good evening, Mr. President," said Kozlov, staring into the camera of the videophone as the interpreter translated his words. "I bring you greetings from Moscow and my hope that things are well in Washington."

There was a pause as the interpreter listened to Andrew Phillips, then translated.

"Greetings to you, Mr. President. Your call is a surprise as it comes at a time when I'm in the midst of a true crisis."

"I'm aware of your situation. I trust you have received our messages of support?"

"Yes, President Kozlov, we've received information from your embassy. We'd hoped you'd have foreseen this possibility when your nation supported the training of terrorists."

Kozlov resented Phillips's condescending attitude. "Both our nations have made mistakes, Mr. President. I assume you are aware that yours is not the only government embroiled in crisis. We want the sanctions to be lifted. Our people are suffering. Our assistance concerning the terrorist nuclear weapons is our offering of reconciliation."

"We're aware of your difficulties, Mr. President, but it's not the responsibility of the American people to assist you in dealing with those difficulties."

"That's very unfortunate. What will be, will be." He paused to signal a change of subject. "I want to advise you, in accordance with long-standing protocol, of our exercise with our Federation allies. We will initiate a deployment of our strategic submarine fleet beginning at 1400Z tomorrow. In addition, we will launch several transport aircraft from Murmansk to Cuba tomorrow night."

"Thank you for advising us in advance. I'll pass the information to military authorities. Good night, Mr. President."

Nikolai Kozlov sat quietly after his conversation with Andrew Phillips ended. He had tried. There was only one option now. Calmly, Kozlov wrote seven words on a notepad. He then put the proper message code and address sequence on the pad to be sure the seven-word sentence was delivered to Viktor Darginsky in Venezuela.

"General," said Kozlov, "get this message out immediately. Read me the message so you're sure there are no mistakes."

"Certainly, sir," said the general. "The message is 'The lion is king of the jungle.'"

"Good. Send it!"

CHAPTER SEVENTEEN

JANUARY 14
TIME TO WEAPONS RELEASE: 26 HR, 35 MIN
ABOARD REDEX 02

Gregori Petrov wanted to buy something for Olya and Stefan, and for himself. He settled on three American Eagle gold coins he saw in the bank in Raleigh one day. Somehow the gold eagle symbol said just the right thing about America.

"I don't know about you," said Josef Piekarski as he watched the Yucatan Peninsula slide by, "but I'm ready to go home."

"Me too," replied Petrov, as he fingered the coins which he'd sewn into the lining of his coat. "It has been a real learning experience."

"Have you thought about how you're going to write up the feasibility study?" Piekarski asked. "I think there are great possibilities for a new branch of strategic thought. There might even be general's stars in it for both of us."

"Josef, I haven't given it a lot of thought," Petrov replied, showing disdain for his companion's personal ambitions. "I feel honored to have been chosen for this mission, and I've learned much, but it is difficult to get excited about plans to annihilate thousands of Americans."

"I'd be careful who I expressed that opinion to," warned Piekarski. "Remember, the United States is our enemy."

"That's enough, Josef. Let's just be on our way home." He stared out the window to signal the conversation was over.

A short time later, Alex reduced the power for the descent into what Piekarski and Petrov thought would be Caracas.

"We'll be on the ground in a few minutes," Michael told them over his shoulder. Petrov was surprised when the landing gear extended and the view below was nothing but the dark sea.

They touched down on a runway wide enough to handle bombers. They turned off near the southeast end and headed toward the main ramp. Alex taxied to the front door of a huge hangar, spun the Citation around, set the brakes, and shut down the engines.

"There are Spetsnaz soldiers guarding the hangar door!" exclaimed Piekarski.

"You'll need your identification badges," Alex advised as he opened the cabin door.

"Where the hell are we?" Petrov asked.

"Oh! Sorry, comrades. We're at La Orchila Island, one hundred kilometers north of the Venezuelan coast. I wasn't supposed to tell you until we landed."

Surprised, the bomber pilots took a few moments to locate their ID badges. A Jeep's headlights bathed the jet's doorway, and they saw Viktor Darginsky waiting as they stepped onto the tarmac.

"Josef, Gregori, welcome back to Venezuela," said the SVR agent. "I know you were expecting to land at Caracas, but you'll soon know why we brought you here. We have a busy night ahead, so if you will put your bags in the Jeep, you'll be joining your crews in a couple of hours."

"Our crews are here?" Piekarski blurted.

"In due time, gentlemen," Darginsky cautioned as he walked toward the entrance of the main hangar, showing his ID to the guard.

The interior was a maelstrom of activity. The center of all the attention was two Tu-95 bombers. The sight of the hulking warplanes stopped Petrov and Piekarski in their tracks.

"What's going on, Viktor?" asked Petrov. "These birds are a long way from home."

"Those are both Murmansk tail numbers," added Piekarski.

"Right you are, Colonel. To answer your question, Gregori, they are being readied for a mission that the two of you will fly. It will be the most important mission in the history of the Russian Air Force. Let's find a quieter place."

As they headed for a small office, Petrov's anticipation of being on his way home to Olya and Stefan was shattered by an armed Spetsnaz sergeant and the sight of a Kh-55 cruise missile being loaded on the underwing pylon. The only time he'd ever seen such security during a loading operation was when the missiles carried live nuclear warheads.

Darginsky motioned for them to take a seat as he closed the office door. "Comrades, I want to hear what you've been doing the past few weeks. Let's start with you, Josef. Tell me about flying with Bobby Chatman's Red Star Express."

Piekarski excitedly recounted his experiences flying around the eastern and central US along with runs to Latin America. When he finished speaking, Darginsky turned his attention to Petrov. "And what about you, Gregori? Did you also learn a lot about flying in the US and Latin America?"

Petrov had only been listening half-heartedly to Piekarski's narrative. He was bothered by what he had seen in the hangar. He fingered the three gold coins in his coat as he asked himself why Spetsnaz soldiers were guarding the bombers, and what possible mission they could be planning for them. Darginsky's questions brought his attention back to the present.

"Yes, I learned a lot about flying there. It is amazing the freedom Americans have to fly wherever they want and the lack of direct control from air traffic control at lower altitudes."

Darginsky smiled. "Gentlemen, you've been chosen for a very special mission, one that is vital to the survival of the Motherland. You've been training for that mission for the last several weeks. Tomorrow night you and your crews will fly that mission. Yes, that was a Kh-55, and yes, it has a live nuclear warhead. That particular missile is targeted for Washington, DC, and you, Major Petrov, will carry it into the United States. And yes, that lack of control at the lower altitudes will help ensure the success of your mission."

Darginsky's nonchalance informing them of their orders to kill hundreds of thousands of people made Petrov shudder. Shocked, he suddenly realized they'd literally been training for a nuclear attack on the United States of America. *What about a counterattack? And what about Olya and Stefan?* It was all madness!

Darginsky confirmed Petrov's thoughts. "For the last few weeks, you've been training in business jets on Target Routes Alpha and Bravo. Now you'll do it in your bombers."

TIME TO WEAPONS RELEASE: 22 HR, 55 MIN
TACOMA, WASHINGTON

"What's the game plan for tomorrow?" asked Mark Matthews following dinner.

"It's a minimum-manning day," replied Craig Morton. "I'm all caught up with my additional duties, so I can go in at any time. I can take you by base operations and let you do a flight plan and weather briefing. When's the airplane supposed to be ready?"

"The last I heard, I could go first thing in the morning," said Matthews. "I'm planning to refuel at Offutt, and considering the time difference, I'll be pushing darkness when I land at home."

It had been an interesting weekend. They'd made the rounds at McChord, including a few drinks with other F-15 drivers at the officers' club. Today, they'd driven out to the factory in Arlington that produces the Glasair, an all-fiberglass, homebuilt aircraft that both pilots had the itch to own. They'd each taken a test ride and been impressed with the little airplane's performance. Throughout the weekend, though, nothing else had been said about Matthews's impending departure from the service.

"So, Suds, you're sure about the big decision?" Craig asked. "I mean, would I be wasting my time trying to change your mind?"

"Craig, I'm committed," Matthews replied. "I decided it's the right thing to do. It's been fun, but—" They were interrupted by the ringing of Matthews's cell phone. "Well, old buddy," he said, "that was the command post. Maintenance said my bird won't be ready until tomorrow afternoon. One of the alert airplanes broke and they robbed a part off of mine." He shrugged. "Why don't we just sleep in, and plan to go out there sometime after lunch."

Craig nodded.

"Just think," Matthews lamented with a sigh, "my last ride in the F-15 will be a two-legged, nighttime cross-country instead of a rip-roaring air-to-air ride."

TIME TO WEAPONS RELEASE: 22 HR, 30 MIN
LA ORCHILA AIR BASE, VENEZUELA

"So, that's it," said Darginsky. "You have your mission packets. Any questions?"

Piekarski spoke first. "I think it's an excellent plan, Viktor," he said, his eyes big behind his glasses. "I assume the other members of my crew have been briefed?"

"No, they haven't been told anything. The two of you can do that. The mission briefing is scheduled for zero eight hundred hours tomorrow morning. I figured it would take you a couple of hours to go over the motivation as well as the salient points in the mission packets. Then your navigators should have ample time before lunch to work out their calculations."

They were interrupted by a knock on the door. "A message in the comm center for Viktor Darginsky," said the armed soldier. "It's coded 'crypto' for your eyes only, sir."

"Thank you. I'll be right over." He turned to the bomber pilots. "Take a break, but don't let those mission packets out of your sight. I'll be back soon."

They sat in silence, the tension hanging like a fog between them.

"Well, he said it was something big," said Piekarski.

"Shut the fuck up, Josef!" shouted Petrov. "Millions of lives are at stake, not to mention the possibility of an all-out nuclear exchange if the Americans don't buy Kozlov's bluff. And we're the triggermen. How can you be so blasé?"

"I am an officer in the Russian Air Force!" responded Piekarski with conviction. "I learned a long time ago to do what I'm told, and you might be further along the promotion ladder if you had learned to do the same. We've been training for this for years, Gregori, and now it's time to do our duty."

"You're a goddamned fool, Josef. All of you are fools!"

They were interrupted by the reappearance of Darginsky at the door. Petrov wondered if he had heard them shouting.

Darginsky paused for a few moments before speaking. "The message was from President Kozlov," said the SVR agent stoically. "It reads, 'The lion is king of the jungle.' It's the go-code for LUCIFER/INBLUE." He stared straight at Petrov, then asked, "Can I entertain any questions?"

"I think this whole thing is madness," replied Petrov angrily. "I question whether the situation back home justifies the mass murder of hundreds of thousands of Americans. Secondly, I greatly resent the way I've been set up. Two other aircraft commanders had to get those Tu-95s here. You can use one of them in my slot tomorrow."

"I see," said Darginsky. "Is that your final word on the subject?" he asked pointedly.

"Yes, I'd like to forget this entire thing and go home to my family."

Darginsky removed a folder from the briefcase. "Unfortunately, that won't be possible. Josef, as his commanding officer, would you verify that this piece of paper is a copy of the oath of office for a commissioned officer in the Russian Air Force?"

"That's what it appears to be," said an ashen-faced Piekarski, who examined the form Darginsky handed him.

"And will you verify that it is in the name of Gregori Petronovich Petrov."

"It is."

"And will you, Major Petrov, verify that the signature affixed to this document is yours?"

"Listen, Comrade Darginsky—"

"Is it your signature or not, Major?" barked Darginsky.

"It's my signature," replied Petrov quietly.

"Very good. I want to remind you that you swore an oath of loyalty to your Motherland; you swore to obey and carry out any duly constituted order from any official senior to you and qualified to issue such an order. Do you remember swearing such an oath?"

"Yes, I remember," said Petrov meekly.

"Then as the official representative of Nikolai Kozlov, president of Russia, I am ordering you to fly tomorrow's mission. Will you, Colonel Piekarski, attest that I've issued such an order?"

"I will," mumbled Piekarski.

Darginsky stared intently at Petrov. "It would seem, Major, that we have a couple of options. You can do your duty and fly this mission—that's option one. You are the most thoroughly trained and qualified bomber pilot available for the job. One of those other aircraft commanders you mentioned will be flying with you as it is. It's a long way from Venezuela to the interior of the United States, then to the refueling point over the Atlantic, and finally to Africa. You will alternate command of the aircraft once the actual mission is complete. Until the other aircraft commander is needed, he will occupy the zampolit's seat."

The SVR agent picked up the folder and continued. "Now, what about the other options? You said you would like to go home. We can arrange that." He passed the folder to Petrov. "That's your lovely wife, Olya, and your son, Stefan, correct?"

"Yes, that's my wife and son," replied Petrov slowly.

"They appear to be a fine family. They miss you. In fact, they both wrote you a note. The notes are under the photograph. Go ahead. Read them."

As Petrov read a note in Olya's long flowing hand and then a short letter in Stefan's schoolboy script, he felt his emotions welling up. He'd heard about situations like this, where ordinary citizens were forced to do things against their will by the SVR, but he'd never dreamed he'd be in this bind someday. He hated Darginsky, but there was no doubt the notes were authentic. He felt his resolve slipping away.

"I could have you imprisoned for treason in Siberia for the rest of your life, or, if you preferred, I'd have you shot. Colonel Piekarski could do the honors." He picked up a zippered case from the table. "And to show you what a nice guy I am, I'll even offer you some cyanide capsules. Break one open, inhale it, and you're dead in minutes." The agent reached into his coat pocket and withdrew a 9mm Makarov automatic pistol, cocking it. Petrov flinched at the loud snap of the slide slamming into the receiver. Darginsky laid it on the table. "There's this option, too, but I encourage you to use the cyanide. It's less messy."

Tension loomed heavy in the room as Petrov stared at the pistol.

"So, there it is, Gregori," Darginsky concluded. "You can agree to fly the mission and carry it out to the best of your ability, and we will forget what was said here tonight. If you ever want to see Olya and Stefan again . . . there's really only one option. So, what's it going to be? It's getting late, and I'm growing weary."

Despite feeling utterly helpless, Petrov briefly considered picking up the Makarov and putting a bullet between Darginsky's eyes.

"I'll fly the mission," he said.

"Excellent," said Darginsky. "I'll show you to your quarters. You can discuss the mission with your crews tonight, but lights out is in exactly one hour."

The SVR agent drove the bomber pilots to a large Quonset hut where they were admitted by an armed Spetsnaz guard who carefully checked their papers.

"Breakfast is at zero seven hundred, and we brief at eight," said Darginsky. His demeanor changed slightly as he looked directly at Petrov. "I understand why there may be doubts about tomorrow, but I'm convinced it is the only way out for us. Kozlov agrees. We must be successful tomorrow. I'm sure you won't let us down."

They walked into the dormitory, interrupting a spirited card game. The heavy smell of Russian-made Belomor cigarettes filled the air.

"Room . . . *attention!*" somebody yelled. Chair legs squealed and feet shuffled.

"As you were," said Piekarski. "I need to see the members of the crew of tail number 88005 immediately. Over at that table will be fine."

"And I'll see everybody else here at the card table," said Petrov. He was pleasantly surprised to see who was on his crew as bodies went in separate directions. Darginsky had done his homework well. Vladimir Sheptak was the first to shake his hand. He was followed by Itzkoff and Orshansky, while Misha Grotsky brought up the rear. Major Vegard Czinkota, the acting aircraft commander for the trip from Murmansk, hung back until the rest of the crew had greeted their old leader, then shook hands with Petrov. Gregori was glad to see his old friend. The two had flown many missions together.

Questions began to fly before Petrov could say anything.

"What's the word, boss?" asked Sheptak. "The rumor is we're flying tomorrow."

"I heard they're loading up inert cruise missiles," said Itzkoff. "Am I going to get to launch one of those out over the Pacific?"

"Why are they keeping us under lock and key?" asked Orshansky. "I hear the Latin women down here are hot, and so far, all I've gotten to do is listen to Grotsky's bullshit."

Petrov waited for his crew to settle down. It felt good to see them again. The smell of Belomors and the sound of his native tongue made him feel welcome. But he couldn't just walk out the door, start up his Lada, and drive home. It was going to be hard to tell his friends what they had to do tomorrow.

"You're under lock and key because tomorrow we're flying the most important mission in the history of the Motherland. The Kh-55s you saw are not inert. They have live nuclear warheads. Tomorrow, we will be part of a three-ship strike package in an attack on the United States. Our targets are the cities of Norfolk, Virginia, and Washington, DC. You'll get the details at the briefing tomorrow." He paused and studied their stunned faces. "I'm sorry."

As the two informal crew meetings broke up, the crew members moved in silence, lost in their individual thoughts. Petrov found his bunk and collapsed on it. The smell of Belomors was even more pungent than before, and the room was so quiet he could hear the chirping of crickets through the walls.

"Forgive us," he whispered as he thought about all the people living in Norfolk and Washington. "But we have to do our fucking duty!"

LUCIFER/INBLUE: EXECUTION DAY

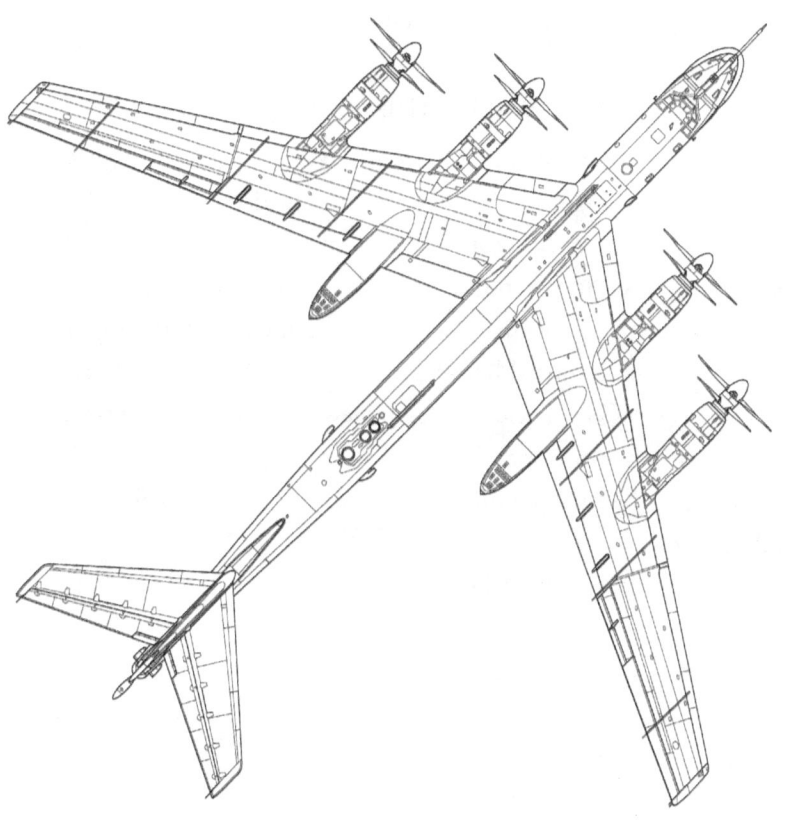

CHAPTER EIGHTEEN

TIME TO WEAPONS RELEASE: 13 HR, 15 MIN
THE FBI BUILDING
WASHINGTON, DC

"That's where we stand," said Frank Morgan, who was briefing the incoming crew of agents. We've sealed off a three-mile radius around the Washington Monument. The Secret Service has asked for our assistance around the White House and the Capitol Building. We can't spare the agents, but the CIA can. There'll be a bus arriving at ten hundred hours with a bunch of spooks. I've asked Agent Darryl McCormick to take charge of them. Does everybody know Darryl? Wave your hand, Darryl."

A reluctant hand went up with an obscene gesture, triggering a round of chuckling.

"Those spooks are all geeks," someone quipped. "You can handle them!"

She flashed a derisive smile and nodded.

Morgan continued, "Darryl will be working directly with me. Okay, any questions?"

"Yeah," said a voice from the back of the room. "Do we have any hard intelligence on the weapons' location?"

"No, but if you were a terrorist with a nuke, what better place than Washington, and what better time than tonight, when everybody in the government is sitting in the Capitol Building?"

"Is a cabinet member out of town?" came another inquiry.

"No," said Morgan resignedly. "The president insisted that everybody be there unless it was a bona fide emergency. He says God is taking care of us. All right, enough. Get out there and find those Mercedes trucks. I want to see Darryl McCormick after the meeting. Good hunting."

As the briefing broke up, several FBI agents stopped to tease McCormick. "I wish I was hanging out at the White House or the Capitol instead of walking the streets searching old garages."

"Yeah, Dare, how 'bout if we swap?" said another. "I'll keep the spooks in line and you go find the nukes."

McCormick smirked. She had sat quietly in the back of the room watching her fellow agents like a reticent chaperone. She was aware that they regarded her as cagey and stoic, and she liked it that way.

McCormick had no illusions about her standing with the current director. She couldn't stand the man, and on numerous occasions, in keeping with her nickname, challenged his various policies and the red tape that wasted so much time. She knew she survived in the bureau solely because she was respected for her competence.

"I have another question for you, chief," said McCormick as she made her way to the front of the room. "Is there any hard intelligence at all confirming the possibility of real nuclear weapons on real Mercedes trucks? I did some research. You know, we have informants embedded in just about every terrorist group in the world. Not one of them has reported anything about Mercedes trucks or nuclear weapons."

"I read your memo," responded Morgan. "I don't have all the answers. The president directed me to secure the city and that's what I'm doing."

"But suppose—"

"I don't have time for suppositions," growled the director. "Those CIA types will be here in a couple of hours. Your job is to tell them what we expect. Remember, these guys are intelligence analysts, not field agents, so they're probably not proficient with weapons, familiar with security procedures, or even in reasonable physical condition." The director smiled in sympathy. "Your job is to be sure they don't screw up. My advice you is to concentrate on that job. Comprende, compadre?"

"I'll take care of the spooks," said McCormick, "but I'll tell you something, chief. I'll bet a month of my pay against a month of yours there's no nukes and no Mercedes trucks."

"I can't afford to take that bet," said Morgan, "and neither can you. Just babysit those CIA people and pray we make it through the next twenty-four hours."

TIME TO WEAPONS RELEASE: 13 HR, 5 MIN
CIA HEADQUARTERS
LANGLEY, VIRGINIA

"C'mon, Hartley. The bus leaves in five minutes," said the supervisor, who stuck his head in the door of the photo lab. "We all have to be on it."

"Listen, boss. These are interesting photos," pleaded Henry "Hank" Hartley, chief intelligence analyst for Latin American affairs. "They came from one of our agents in Venezuela, and they appear to be Russian Bear bombers landing at La Orchila. I'd say they're H-models. We got word a few weeks back there were supposedly inert Kh-55 cruise missiles in La Orchila. I don't like the idea of Russian nuclear-capable cruise missiles and mother ships at the same airfield in South America. I think I ought to stay and check it out. The president's orders specified nonessential personnel."

"They did, indeed. Didn't you get the memo? The Ruskies are having a big exercise. There'll be all sorts of submarine and aircraft movements. So, file the photos and get on that bus!"

"Yes, sir, but it's against my better judgment," Hartley muttered under his breath.

TIME TO WEAPONS RELEASE: 8 HR, 52 MIN
LA ORCHILA AIR BASE, VENEZUELA

"Arming procedures for the warheads will be standard," said Piekarski. "The aircraft commander and missile launch officer must activate their master arming switches within five seconds of each other. The weapons are set for a three-hundred-meter airburst. Launch of all other weapons will be predicated on the successful launch of the weapon targeted for Washington. It is therefore essential that both aircraft communicate via HF radio to coordinate launches. Missile launch officers need to calculate speed settings for twenty minutes of flight time for each missile. Our goal is the destruction of the four targets within ten minutes of each other." He scanned the faces of the two crews. "That concludes the mission briefing. Any questions?"

A solemn silence pervaded the room. Piekarski, at Darginsky's direction, had conducted the entire briefing. The men in the room still seemed stunned. They had trained for this mission for most of their military careers, but they'd never dreamed of having to carry it out.

"Thank you, Colonel," said Darginsky, who took Piekarski's place behind the podium. "Gentlemen, except for the rain showers lying across the early portion of Route Alpha, the weather is good. Your aircraft are ready, and their weapons have been thoroughly tested. The Motherland is counting on you to do your duty. Unless there are any questions, I'll release you now to your aircraft commanders."

Gregori Petrov stood and faced the room. "The Route Alpha crew will meet here on this side of the room. Itzkoff, get with your counterpart on Colonel Piekarski's crew, and let us know about a takeoff time as soon as possible. We need to be in the aircraft by nineteen hundred Zulu. Let's get moving!"

The room filled with the sound of chairs scraping. Petrov saw Sheptak staring at him intently. "There's no other choice, Vladimir. Let's just get it over with."

TIME TO WEAPONS RELEASE: 8 HR, 29 MIN
ALERT BARN
EGLIN AIR FORCE BASE, FLORIDA

"Eglin command post, Tech Sergeant Wilkerson speaking."

"Good morning, Sergeant. This is Major Robertson in the alert barn. I'm up on five-minute alert status in tail number five-zero-five. Call sign is Shark zero-three. I'll be the senior alert pilot for the next twenty-four hours. Captain Rushton in Shark zero-four will be the wingman."

"Okay, sir, I got it."

"Anything going on?"

"Negative, sir. The base is on heightened alert, but that only affects the security police squadron. Almost everybody else is off for the president's Day of Prayer and Unity."

"The weather still holding up?"

"That's affirmative. It's currently ceiling one thousand feet and visibility three miles with light rain. The front isn't supposed to go through until later tonight, and we may get some fog on the back side. The alternate is Jacksonville."

"Got it. Thanks. Keep us posted on any changes."

TIME TO WEAPONS RELEASE: 8 HR, 20 MIN
KANSAS CITY, MISSOURI

Keith Anderson flipped through the channels after a long, restless night, hoping to find something to watch with his breakfast other than the coverage of the goings-on in Washington. His phone's ringtone interrupted his thoughts. He dreaded answering, knowing innately who the unidentified caller was.

"Hello?"

"Hello, Keith. It's Michael. How are you today?"

"Ready to be done with whatever it is you want me to do," he replied, not bothering to hide his hate for the other man.

"Good. You'll be going to work early as we planned?"

"As planned," said Keith. "I learned that both of Tinker's runways are closed for construction, so I'll only check on the Offutt 747 today."

"Excellent!"

Keith hesitated then asked, "I trust you're going to keep your end of the deal? I mean, after tonight you're going to *leave me the fuck alone?*"

"Oh, that," said Michael, unruffled. "You hold up your end and I'll hold up mine. Now, just as a reminder, we want—"

"Yeah, yeah, I know," said Keith impatiently. "Route number five if possible, and you'll call me to verify the actual routing. Keep up with his position because you'll want that later, too. I don't need to be reminded."

"I guess you don't," came the calm reply. "Just relax. It'll all be over soon."

"Goodbye, Michael," he said before breaking the connection. "And fuck you!" he added as he ended the call.

TIME TO WEAPONS RELEASE: 8 HR, 19 MIN
THE CAPITOL BUILDING
WASHINGTON, DC

"You guys all set?" asked Darryl McCormick as she completed her rounds of the Capitol Building.

"Yes, ma'am," replied Hank Hartley. "We checked in with the radio net. What's next?"

"We wait," said McCormick. "If anyone walks in carrying a nuke, let command post know."

"If you don't mind my saying so, you look about as bored as I am," said Hartley, smiling at the FBI agent's irreverent comment. "How did you get stuck babysitting a bunch of CIA bean counters?"

"Let's just say the director and I aren't on the best of terms. By the way, I'm Dare McCormick," she continued, holding out her hand.

"I'm Hank Hartley. Pleased to meet you."

"So, when did you get the word about this little setup?"

"We got the recall late yesterday. They said it would only be nonessential personnel. I figured I'd be doing my usual thing, but the boss had other ideas."

"You didn't have the day off today?"

"Originally I did, but I'm the chief intelligence analyst for Latin American affairs. If we get a package from one of our operatives, I'm on call twenty-four hours a day." He checked that no one else was nearby. "We got a package last night, so I was in the office early this morning. I thought it was more important to figure out why long-range Russian bombers were landing in Venezuela, but my boss thought otherwise."

"Lucky you," said McCormick as she walked off. "I'll check in with you in a couple of hours." Halfway down the hall McCormick stopped. *Russian bombers in Venezuela?* She turned back toward Hartley, but he was already gone.

TIME TO WEAPONS RELEASE: 6 HR, 45 MIN
LA ORCHILA AIR BASE, VENEZUELA

Before-start checks complete," said Orshansky. "I have a yellow standby light on one of the jamming packages, but I think it's because of the heat and humidity."

"Keep working with it," said Petrov. "If this thing goes according to plan, we shouldn't need it. Arkady, how about a navigator/weapons launch officer status check?"

"I'm all set here," Itzkoff replied. "The inertial nav system is set up for the rendezvous with the Sukhoi. Tanker rendezvous over the Atlantic after the mission tonight is also loaded, along with navigation waypoints en route to our airfield in Africa for recovery tomorrow."

"Very well," replied Petrov. "I'll handle the navigation and communication chores once we're working with US controllers."

There was a slight pause as Itzkoff pondered those words. "It's hard for me to believe we're going to pull this off, but you and Colonel Piekarski have been there, so who am I to ask questions?"

"We can pull it off, all right. Now, what's the status of the missiles?"

"All checklist items are complete," said Itzkoff. "I have green lights across the board. Weapons arming system is in standby."

"Standby with a green light here," Petrov confirmed. "Plan on initiating the final arming sequence three minutes prior to launch. Any questions, Arkady?"

"Negative, sir," came the laconic reply.

"If they don't scramble fighters on us, I'm going to be awfully bored," came a comment from the tail gunner's position.

"You can always play with yourself, Grotsky!" Orshansky quipped.

"Let's hope he stays bored," said Petrov. "Arkady, are you all set?"

"Navigator/missile launch officer before start checks are complete," replied Itzkoff, his nonuse of the "missile-man" nickname evidence of the mission's seriousness. "Just as a reminder, takeoff time is twenty hundred Zulu."

"Got it. Colonel Piekarski and I agreed on a start time of forty-five past the hour. I assume you're all set back there, Misha?"

"Tail gunner before start checks complete," replied Grotsky. "My fan blower is out, though, so I'm roasting. If you wanted to go ahead and start an engine so we can get some air-conditioning, it'd be fine with me."

"I don't want to burn the fuel," said Petrov. "Go outside if you want to. Just be back on board by forty past." He looked now at Sheptak and spoke across the cockpit without the interphone. "Vladimir, are we ready to go up here?"

"Before-start checks complete," said Sheptak. "We have an inoperative boost pump pressure light in the number two fuel tank, but the pump is working fine. We also have an inoperative brake pressure gauge here in the cockpit, but it reads normally down in the wheel well."

"How's the fuel load?"

"Full. With only two Kh-55s onboard, we're still a couple of thousand kilograms short of the max allowable gross weight, but she's heavy."

"Sounds like a long takeoff roll."

"The longest I'll ever see. There will only be three hundred meters of runway left. Once we exceed two hundred sixty kilometers per hour, we're committed to fly because we can't stop in the remaining runway."

"Liftoff speed?"

"Three hundred and five."

Petrov preflighted his side of the cockpit. "I'm going to join the guys outside," he said when he was done. "Have you seen Major Czinkota?"

"He said he'd be here at thirty past," replied Sheptak. "He's probably outside trying to stay cool."

"Yeah, I guess so. Are you coming?"

"I suppose," said Sheptak. He grabbed Petrov by the sleeve of his flight suit. "Did you try to get out of this thing, Gregori?"

"With all my might," Petrov answered. "Last night, I told Darginsky he could count me out of the mission."

"And?"

"He offered me some rather unsavory options after reminding me of my oath of office. We have no choice, Vladimir. Maybe as a reward they'll let us move to America. You'd like it there." He nudged the copilot toward the hatch. "Come on, we still have time for a cold drink of water."

TIME TO WEAPONS RELEASE: 6 HR, 30 MIN
KREMLIN COMMAND POST

The colonel who was briefing Nikolai Kozlov on the current status of the ongoing exercise was interrupted by a knock on the door. The major general running the command post stuck his head in. "I'm sorry to bother you, sir, but General Gavrilov is here and insisting that he be admitted to see you."

"Show him in," replied Kozlov.

A moment later Gavrilov burst through the door with a forceful scowl on his face. "Would you mind telling me, Nikolai Ivanovich," Gavrilov demanded without greeting the president, "just what the hell is going on? You've launched the entire submarine fleet, and you have transports standing by with orders to fly troops and supplies as well as a number of strategic missiles to Cuba and Venezuela. The Council of Defense is very concerned about your plans."

"The Council of Defense is dead, General," replied Kozlov dismissively. He opened a folder on his desk and scanned the top sheet of paper. "The Council of Defense was destroyed by a nuclear detonation eighteen hours ago, leaving the president in charge of the war." He closed the folder. "I'm in charge so I can make the decisions I might have to make if this were real. So, what are you doing here?"

"I do not recall launching the submarine fleet or sending missiles to Central America being part of the exercise," growled Gavrilov. "As I recall—"

"As you should recall," interrupted Kozlov, "the forces you mention were on full alert as part of the exercise. If you had read the briefing, General, you would also recall that launching those forces to exercise their real capability was at the commander-in-chief's discretion. I'll discuss my decisions at the debriefing scheduled for zero seven hundred hours tomorrow morning. Until then, I think you should leave."

"But the Americans," protested Gavrilov. "We should notify them of your decision."

"Already done," replied Kozlov. "In the meantime, let's play the game according to the exercise scenario. Also, General, you might want to consider how you enter my presence and address me in the future if you want to continue having such access. Do I make myself clear?"

General Gavrilov hesitated, then nodded his understanding.

Kozlov opened his office door and summoned the armed guard outside. "Show General Gavrilov out of the command post and pass the word that members of the Council of Defense are not to be admitted in accordance with the current exercise game plan. Good night, General."

As Kozlov closed his office door, a wicked smile transformed his face as he considered what kind of 'accident' General Gavrilov was going to suffer. *Maybe a tragic fall out of a high open window.* Whether tonight's mission was a success or failure, the General was a threat that had to be eliminated.

TIME TO WEAPONS RELEASE: 6 HR, 20 MIN
KANSAS CITY AIR ROUTE TRAFFIC CONTROL CENTER

"Hi, Keith. Aren't you a little early?" asked Jud Blackman, the day shift controller of the Omaha sector. "I hear it's gorgeous outside."

"It is a nice day," Keith replied as he dragged up a chair. He studied the controller's scope. "If you're not too busy, I have a question."

"It's been slow all day. What's on your mind?"

"I have a cousin flying copilot on the Airborne Command Post tonight. I was wondering if they'd filed their route yet. If they'll be flying through my sector . . . you know . . . it'd be nice to say hello."

"Sure, I understand. I have a nephew in the Navy. He flies F-18s. He flew through my sector one morning about a month ago. Made my whole day to talk to him. Anyway . . . the Airborne Command Post is filed for route number eight tonight under the call sign Nightwatch zero-one. That route is going to keep them running east and west up close to the Canadian border: from Helena to Buffalo. Looks like you'll miss him."

"I see," said Keith. "Do they ever change the route once they've filed?"

"Occasionally. I sometimes suggest a change if their preferred route has thunderstorms or turbulence. I doubt they'll change it tonight. The weather's pretty good. I guess you'll have to talk to your cousin some other night."

When Blackman turned back to his scope, Keith noted the number for the direct line to Offutt base operations, which was taped to the table under the plexiglass.

"I guess I'd better get going," Keith said. "Thanks for your help."

"No problem," replied Blackman. "Sorry about the routing thing."

Keith decided the best place to make the call was the simulator room. All the direct line phones there worked just as the ones did in the radar room, and he would have privacy. He was relieved to find the room empty. In a matter of seconds, he was listening to the phone ringing at the Omaha air base.

"Offutt base ops, Sergeant Toomey. May I help you?"

"Yes, Sergeant, this is Jud Blackman, Omaha sector controller at Kansas City Center," Keith began, unconsciously shifting into his on-the-job controller voice. "How are you today?"

"Fine, sir. What can I do for you?"

"Reference Nightwatch zero-one, we thought you might like to know that the airline boys are reporting moderate to severe turbulence at all altitudes above flight level 280 along the route he filed," Keith lied. "You might want to consider a more southerly route. We're recommending route number five."

"Okay, sir. Stand by one." The base ops dispatcher was off the line for what seemed an eternity. "Are you still there, Kansas City?"

"Yes, I'm here,"

"The command post said to pass along their thanks. Route number five will be fine for Nightwatch zero-one tonight. I'll refile for that route."

Keith thanked the sergeant, hung up the receiver, and erased the telephone recording data with shaky hands. He couldn't escape the feeling that he'd just condemned a hundred people to death. *I've played it your way so far, Michael,* he thought. *But the night isn't over yet, asshole!*

CHAPTER NINETEEN

TIME TO WEAPONS RELEASE: 6 HR, 10 MIN
THE WHITE HOUSE

"I don't understand it, Frank. We've been at this for forty-eight hours and we haven't found a single weapon. Terrorists are going to make a mockery of me by blowing up four cities right in the middle of my speech!"

"I'm sorry, Mr. President," said an exhausted Frank Morgan, "but we're doing the best we can. We're covering a lot of ground in the major cities. I thought we had our first one in Miami."

"Yes, what's the story in Miami?"

"We located a Mercedes truck in a deserted warehouse. The truck even had one of the auxiliary fuel tanks, but there was no weapon inside."

"Is it true there was a timer attached to the bottom of the fuel tank?"

"Yes, sir," replied Morgan. "We were set up. There was a note inside the fuel tank that said, 'wrong truck, assholes,' signed by a local gang."

"Okay, keep looking. Let's make it through tonight and find those nukes! Once we've done that, Frank, you and John can concentrate again on Russia, Iran, North Korea, and China."

TIME TO WEAPONS RELEASE: 6 HR, 2 MIN
LA ORCHILA AIR BASE, VENEZUELA

"Engine instruments?"

"Checked. Four good engines."

"Fuel panel?"

"Set. Mains on, auxiliaries off, crossfeed valves closed."

"Flaps?"

"Set at one-half for takeoff."

"Airspeed marker bugs?"

"Set over here. Two hundred kilometers per hour acceleration check should come thirty-one seconds after brake release. Refusal speed is 260. Rotation at 300. Initial climb 375."

"Bugs are set over here. Master Jettison?"

"Armed."

"That does it," said Sheptak. "The takeoff briefing will complete the before-takeoff checklist."

"This is going to be the longest takeoff roll any of us has ever seen," said Petrov. "Past 260, we're committed to fly. If we lose an engine between 260 and rotation, Vladimir, jettison those missiles immediately. Any questions about the takeoff? Is everybody set?"

"We're ready back here . . . I guess," said Orshansky.

"Rear gunner position ready," replied Grotsky.

"One minute to go," said Itzkoff.

"Roger, one minute," replied Petrov. "We'll take a minimum of one-minute spacing on Piekarski." He gathered his thoughts before continuing. "I wish I had something comforting to say. I know none of us are happy about this mission, but I am confident each of us is mindful of his duty to the Motherland."

"There's the green light from the tower," said Sheptak. "Piekarski is rolling."

"Roger, heading indicators are good," said Petrov as he maneuvered the bomber into position on the runway. "Attitude indicators are good, brakes are set, power coming up."

"Thirty seconds."

"Roger, full power. Four good engines. Torque meters and all EGTs in the green."

"Ten seconds. Piekarski is airborne. He used almost all of it."

"Roger . . . three, two, one, go!"

"Brakes released."

"Hacking the clock, four good engines."

"Airspeed is alive."

"Alive over here. Two hundred . . . now!"

"Acceleration check is good at twenty-nine seconds."

"Keep me posted on runway remaining."

"Two thousand meters . . . now!"

"There's two hundred sixty. We're committed. Comrade Kuznetsov, do not fail us now," Petrov prayed to the engine manufacturer.

"One thousand meters remaining. Four good engines."

"Airspeed is two-seventy-five."

"Five hundred meters left!"

"Three hundred! Nose is coming up . . . positive rate of climb . . . gear up!"

"Gear up," echoed Sheptak. "We still have four good ones. Shit! I'm glad we're not carrying more cruise missiles!"

"Me too," Petrov uttered. "Let's have the flaps . . . now. Do you still see Piekarski?"

"Yes. He's at three o'clock and rolling out."

"Very good. Let's have the after-takeoff check. Get all your equipment powered up and check for any failures. Arkady, let me have an updated arrival time for the rendezvous with the Su-57."

Viktor Darginsky watched as the Tu-95s departed. He'd heard the crews discussing aircraft takeoff performance, but even he held his breath as the heavily laden bombers trundled down the runway and struggled into the sky. As Petrov's aircraft began its turn to the northwest, the SVR agent headed for the base communications center. Within minutes of Petrov's turn out of traffic, the coded message was transmitted to Moscow, Glen Cove, and Havana. Secure telephones then relayed it to Bay St. Louis, Mississippi, and Chatman's ranch in Kansas. The message said simply, "The polar bear rules the tundra." LUCIFER/INBLUE was a go.

Darginsky wasn't the only one who watched the Bear bombers struggle into the afternoon sky. Maria Morales heard that the airplanes would be departing sometime after lunch. Her CIA contacts in Washington would want to know about this departure, so she moved into her grassy hiding place, camera in hand.

The two Tu-95s taxied out at 1355, and she got several good pictures as they held short of the runway. It was the two cruise missiles each aircraft carried that bothered Maria. She weighed her options. In a secret compartment in the right door of her old Chevy, there was a satellite transmitter to communicate with CIA headquarters. When she was trained in its operation, she was warned to use it only under special circumstances. She decided the sight of the missiles made it special enough. The northwest turn by each bomber also helped Maria make up her mind. They'd arrived from Africa. If they were returning to Africa, they would've turned east.

Decision made, Maria packed her photographic gear, then crawled back to her car through the tall grass. She stowed the camera then peeled away the passenger door's Velcroed panel. Within moments, she unwrapped a plastic bag that held the transmitter. The batteries were packed separately, so it took a few minutes to insert them and unfold the radio's antenna.

They'd told her to make any transmissions as brief as possible. She pushed the transmit button. "Sea Cove, this is Blue Whale. Sea Cove, this is Blue Whale, over?"

At first Maria just heard the satellite tracking signal, but then the steady tone was interrupted by a voice. "Calling Sea Cove, say again?"

Elated, Maria pushed the transmit button again. "Sea Cove, this is Blue Whale. How do you read?"

"Blue Whale, Sea Cove reads you loud and clear. Identification please."

She heard a twig crack and turned to see a young Russian soldier standing a few meters away. She made her decision in a flash. Turning her back to the soldier, she pushed the transmit button and spoke as fast as she could. "Russian Bear bombers with cruise missiles departed to northwest—"

Maria Morales's head exploded in pain. She stared through foggy eyes at figures standing over her. She heard talk in Russian, but the talk faded, and darkness overcame her.

Viktor Darginsky met the truck and examined the woman lying in the pickup's bed. He saw the camera and the radio. He took her pulse. Slowly, he faced the soldiers, his rage building. The woman was dead.

Darginsky gathered the equipment and walked to a desk in the now-empty hangar. He studied the images on his laptop from Maria Morales's SD card. A series of pictures showed the Bears beginning their long takeoff roll. Her camera captured them turning in a wide arc to the northwest.

His eyes shifted to the radio lying alongside the camera. Had she gotten a message off to whomever she was working for? The radio and its antenna were satellite comm equipment. It had to be the CIA. He could have the radio analyzed, but that would take time. He wanted to put a bullet into the head of the one who clubbed her. He might actually do that . . . later.

What if she'd made contact with them? he thought. The message would've been brief. Two Bear bombers heading north toward the US southern border. That's news that would make its way quickly to US command authorities. They would surely order an elevated readiness of their nuclear response forces. He needed to make a quick decision.

He pushed away from the desk, stood, bummed a cigarette off a guard, and lit it. It was his first puff in years. The comm center was a short walk. In five minutes he could have the strike force turned around. Mission aborted.

Stunned, Darginsky watched his hand shake. He dropped the half-smoked cigarette and took a deep breath. He packed away the laptop and picked up his duffel bag. He motioned the guard to pick up the radio with its antenna package and put them aboard the waiting helicopter.

When the chopper cleared the island coastline en route to the Venezuelan mainland, Viktor Darginsky made his decision. He slid the door open and tossed the radio toward the blue Caribbean.

TIME TO WEAPONS RELEASE: 5 HR, 28 MIN
SAN JULIÁN AIR BASE, CUBA

"Radar select switch?"

"Standby."

"Missile master arm switch?"

"Selector switch on rack one, arm switch off."

"That does it," said Ridgik. "Both checklists are complete. Did you get a good look at the missiles?"

"Everything looked fine," replied Bachvaroff. "I found one igniter squib that was loose, so they tightened it up. Other than that, they are all ready to fly."

"I'm going to get out and stretch my legs. I'm showing 2032Z up here. Does that check with you?"

"That checks. We should be hearing something soon."

"Yep. If we're going to be nine hundred kilometers west of here, refueled, and ready to fly Piekarski's wing northbound, they're going to have to let us know within the hour."

"Piekarski's wing. Can you believe that? Now if it were Petrov—"

"I agree, but would you want that little weasel, Piekarski, flying Route Alpha?"

"Speaking of little weasels who wear the rank of colonel, here comes our buddy, Prokepenko."

"Cut it out, Anton," said Ridgik. "We're supposed to be serious today."

The two Su-57 crewmen removed their helmets and took their time getting out of the airplane.

"Good afternoon, comrades," said Prokepenko. "I trust your aircraft is ready to fly your top secret mission." He didn't bother to hide his frustration.

"Oh, yes, sir. We're all set," said Ridgik.

"Very good." Prokepenko studied the Sukhoi. "The tanker pilot is ready to go. He seems to know very little about this mission."

Both pilots remained silent.

Accepting that the two had no intention of enlightening him, the SVR agent said, "This message just came. I am aware of its contents, but it makes little sense to me." He handed the envelope to Ridgik, who read the message, then handed it to Bachvaroff.

"Thank you, Colonel," said Ridgik. "You may advise the tanker aircraft commander and the control tower that we will be making a radio-out takeoff as a flight of two in exactly forty-five minutes at 2120Z. We will see you back here late tonight. Have a nice evening."

Both Sukhoi crewmen popped to attention and effectively dismissed the SVR colonel with perfectly executed salutes. Prokepenko returned the salutes, then stalked off toward the hangar. "I will advise the tanker pilot," he said over his shoulder, "and I am going to want some answers when you two return."

"So, 'the polar bear rules the tundra,'" said Ridgik, when Prokepenko was out of earshot. "Let's go kill a 747."

CHAPTER TWENTY

TIME TO WEAPONS RELEASE: 5 HR, 12 MIN
CIA HEADQUARTERS
LANGLEY, VIRGINIA

"What do you make of it?" the CIA comm center operator asked his supervisor.

"I don't know. We get a garbled radio transmission on a Blue Whale call sign about Bear bombers taking off from somewhere and turning northwest. There's no personal identification, so we have no idea where the transmission originated. It could have been anywhere in Africa or Latin America."

"But since it was in Spanish, it was most probably in Latin America."

"Most probably."

"So, you don't think we ought to move on it?"

"I'd suggest you pass it up the line through normal channels. You might send a special info copy to Hank Hartley, since he specializes in Russian weapons activity in Latin America, but he won't see it until tomorrow morning at the earliest."

"Why's that?"

"Because, unlike you and me, he was deemed nonessential. He's in Washington helping the Secret Service and the FBI. Thank goodness somebody has to monitor message traffic."

TIME TO WEAPONS RELEASE: 5 HR, 4 MIN
THE KREMLIN

"Sir, this message came in for your eyes only almost a half hour ago. I'm sorry it took so long to get it to you."

"Next time I suggest you get it here faster, Major," said Kozlov as he took the folder. "How's the exercise going?"

"Fine, sir. The transports at Murmansk are ready to go."

"Good," grunted Kozlov as he opened the sealed folder and read the message. It was what he'd been expecting, but the actual message took him a moment to assimilate. *The polar bear rules the tundra*, he read silently. "We are committed," he mumbled.

"Sorry, sir?"

The president realized the major had continued talking. "Repeat that, Major."

"Yes, sir. The first of our submarines is approaching the recall point. Shall I have the naval coordinator send the recall message?"

"No, there will be no recall for now. Signal the sub to continue toward its assigned launch point and hold its station when it gets there."

"Yes, sir," replied the major, surprise showing on his face. "Will that be the standing order as other subs approach their recall points?"

"For now," said Kozlov. "Tell them all to stand by for further instructions at 0230Z."

TIME TO WEAPONS RELEASE: 4 HR, 25 MIN
APPROACHING THE NORTHERN GULF COAST

The two Bear bombers were traveling in loose formation at flight level 330, with Piekarski in the lead and Petrov four kilometers behind. Cruising in clear skies, they crossed their navigation checkpoint abeam the Merida VOR on the north coast of the Yucatan Peninsula.

"I'm estimating the rendezvous point with the Su-57 at 2247Z, or a couple of minutes late," Itzkoff announced over the interphone. "We're running slightly behind the projected fuel burn, but that's because we were so heavy in the climb. Kh-55 master panel currently shows green lights across the board on both birds. Navigator status check complete."

"Thank you, Arkady," said Petrov. "What about at your station, Vitalie?"

"I'm getting occasional hits by radars," replied Orshansky, "but they all correspond to air traffic control. I'm looking at an airborne target at twelve o'clock for forty kilometers. It should remain well outside visual range. Jamming package is in standby with green lights across the board. ED status check complete."

"Very good. The fighter will join on Piekarski using his own radar, and we're supposed to do the whole thing radio-out. We will want to have the fighter and the tanker on our scope just in case they need assistance with the rendezvous."

"Understood," said the electronics officer.

"Tail gun status check complete," said Grotsky. "Tracking radar is in standby, green lights everywhere."

"Right seat is good," Sheptak chimed in. "Engines, hydraulics, and electrics are normal. Just a reminder, it's time for the radio frequency change called for in the packet."

"Thank you," said Petrov as he dialed in the new frequency.

"All set back here," said Itzkoff, "and the radio check with Piekarski's airplane is good."

All was quiet again after the status check. It had been that way from the start, thought Petrov. Very professional, in accordance with their training. It was totally unlike any training mission they had ever flown. The thing with Itzkoff bothered him a little. When it came time to turn those keys, would he?

"I'm ready for a cup of coffee," Sheptak said. "Can I get you one?"

"Sounds great," Petrov replied. "Make it black."

Where was I? he thought. *Turning keys. When the time comes, will I? Of course, and Itzkoff will too. It's our goddamned duty!*

TIME TO WEAPONS RELEASE: 3 HR, 55 MIN
THE WHITE HOUSE

"Ladies and gentlemen, the president of the United States, and the first lady, Mrs. Phillips!"

As the band struck up "Hail to the Chief," Bobby Chatman was having a hard time staying calm. As a member of the president's entourage, it had been mandatory that he be seen at the president's side. His phone had vibrated in his pocket an hour ago. The call had come from Alex at the Bay St. Louis farm, but he'd been unable to return the call. Not knowing if the mission was a go was driving him nuts.

"Thank you, my friends," said Andrew Phillips to enthusiastic applause. "God has blessed us richly, and I'm sure each of you are aware of His presence among us tonight. As our Day of National Prayer and Unity continues, I'd ask you to continue praying for our nation as we stand united in the face of international terrorism. Now, my good friend and God's faithful servant, Bobby Chatman, will lead us in prayer."

Shit! thought Chatman, as people bowed their heads. *Of course he calls on me now.*

"Almighty God our Father," he began in his best praying voice, "we thank thee for this day. We thank thee for this gathering, and we pray that you'll bless us as we continue in our efforts to stand strong in the face of our enemies."

"Amen!" said Andrew Phillips forcefully, at the prayer's conclusion.

"Amen!" came the chorus from around the room.

"I don't know about the rest of you, but I'm hungry!" said the president.

As Phillips started toward the buffet line, Bobby Chatman decided he couldn't wait any longer. He had to know the status of LUCIFER/INBLUE. "Excuse me, Andrew. I need to make a phone call. I'll be back soon."

"No problem," Phillips replied. "And thanks for the prayer."

"My pleasure, Andrew," Chatman replied, returning the smile. He moved down the hall to make the call. Alex answered on the first ring.

"Sorry it took so long to get back to you," Chatman said. "But this is the first chance I've had to get away. What's the word?"

"I saw you on the tube, Brother Chatman," said Alex teasingly. "I was really moved by your prayer."

"Cut the bullshit, commie bastard," said Chatman, returning the tease. "What's the damn word?"

"Actually, it's a group of words. The polar bear rules the tundra."

Chatman felt the breath leave him. He hadn't realized he'd been holding it in. "On time?"

"That's affirmative."

"Excellent! Any problems?"

"None that I know of."

"Great! Call me immediately if anything pops up. I'll try to get back to you to confirm they've crossed the coast."

The televangelist was all smiles as he approached the president. Phillips was talking with one of the former first ladies.

"Oh, Bobby. There you are. I think you know Michelle . . ."

TIME TO WEAPONS RELEASE: 3 HR, 35 MIN
THE SU-57
OVER THE GULF OF MEXICO

"Dammit!" said Ridgik. "I know we're trying to maintain radio silence, but if we're going to get any gas, we're going to have to find some smooth air."

"Maybe you could ease up next to the tanker and signal the pilot we need to descend," replied Bachvaroff calmly.

"Fucking heavy airplane drivers," mumbled Ridgik as he nudged the throttles up, passed just under the wingtip of the IL-78, and moved in close to the left cockpit windows. "We need to go down, dumb shit!" he yelled over the interphone—but not over the radio. He moved his left hand from the throttle to the stick and used his right hand to signal the tanker pilot to descend to a lower altitude. "Outstanding!" said Ridgik as the tanker pilot reduced his power and started descending. "How are we doing on time, Anton?"

"Nineteen minutes until the bombers arrive. We have no time for dillydallying, little buddy."

TIME TO WEAPONS RELEASE: 3 HR, 15 MIN
PIEKARSKI'S TU-95
OVER THE GULF OF MEXICO

"Time to the rendezvous?" asked Piekarski.

"Eighteen minutes," replied the navigator.

"And still no contact on the radar," said the EO before the pilot could ask him.

"Can the bastard not read a clock?" whispered the navigator to the EO. "He asks us every five minutes."

"Colonels have lieutenants to read clocks for them," said the EO, also whispering. "He's nervous, comrade. Give him a break."

"We're all nervous," replied the navigator.

"Hold it! There they are. Dead ahead for two hundred thirty-two kilometers. Everyone hold on. It's going to get bumpy!"

The bomber rocked hard as the turbulence jolted it. Pencils and coffee cups hit the floor.

"EO to pilot. I have the tanker and fighter dead ahead for two hundred thirty kilometers. Looks like they're slightly low."

"Roger," said Piekarski.

"I hope it smooths out soon," whispered the EO to the navigator. "I'll be barfing if this continues."

"Hang in there," said the navigator. "We'll be starting down for the run-in to the American coast after we get joined up with the Sukhoi."

TIME TO WEAPONS RELEASE: 3 HR, 0 MIN
THE SU-57

"Steady now, Valentin," Ridgik mumbled to himself as he eased toward the refueling drogue. "Just take it slow."

"Three meters to go," said Bachvaroff. "Height is good, and you're closing on it slowly . . . ten centimeters . . . you're in. You should have a contact light."

"Roger that, and we're taking fuel," replied Ridgik. "How much longer until they get here?"

"My guess is fifteen minutes. I didn't want to disturb you, but I'm getting solid hits from their radar."

PETROV'S TU-95

"They're dead ahead now for 102," said Orshansky. "Looks like they're swinging around southbound in their refueling orbit. Height cut looks like eighteen hundred meters below us."

"Thank you, Vitalie," acknowledged Petrov. "And nobody else is looking at us?"

"That's a negative. Shit, this turbulence is making it difficult to read my scope."

"Sorry about that, but we'll be starting down soon. It's only thirty minutes from the rendezvous point to the edge of the American ADIZ. We want to enter that ADIZ hugging the wave tops. Hopefully the ride will be a little smoother down low."

"Hopefully," replied Orshansky as they were jolted again. He held tightly to the table at his station. "They're dead ahead now for seventy-five."

THE SU-57

"Disconnect . . . now!" said Ridgik. "I show a clean disconnect, full fuel, and the system is pressurizing normally."

"That checks," Bachvaroff replied. "And the tanker is starting his turn for Cuba. The Bears are northbound, dead ahead for thirty kilometers, slightly high, with ten kilometers in-trail spacing. I can lock them up if you like."

"That won't be necessary. I have two contrails in sight. What do you say we say hello to Petrov before joining up on the weasel's wing?"

Ridgik maneuvered the Sukhoi so that the northbound bomber formation was on his right side and away from the setting sun as he approached them. He timed his deceleration so that he would stop abeam the cockpit of Petrov's bomber. "I never would have guessed that day in Kozlov's dacha that we would meet again over the Gulf of Mexico on a strike mission against the United States," muttered Ridgik. He maneuvered in close and waved at Petrov as his comrade waved back. "Look, Anton! Don't those cruise missiles look nasty?"

"Kh-55s and live nuclear warheads," Bachvaroff replied. "Somehow it seems it ought to be dark and nasty outside, and yet here we are, bathed in gold from a setting sun."

"It'll be dark soon enough," Ridgik replied as he shoved the throttles forward and accelerated to join up on the lead bomber.

PETROV'S TU-95

"That's an awesome-looking machine," commented Sheptak, as the Su-57 accelerated ahead.

"It certainly is," replied Petrov. "I never dreamed I would meet up with those two again."

"Looks like Piekarski's starting down," interrupted the copilot.

Petrov reduced the power, nosed the airplane over, and retrimmed for the long descent into the American ADIZ. The descending airplane created the illusion of speeding up the disappearance of the setting sun, and the Russian pilot watched until it had completely disappeared. "Goodbye, sun," he murmured as he unconsciously fingered the three gold coins he now carried in his flight suit pocket.

CHAPTER TWENTY-ONE

TIME TO WEAPONS RELEASE: 3 HR, 0 MIN
KANSAS CITY ARTCC

Keith Anderson was having trouble concentrating. His preoccupation with Michael and the Airborne Command Post, Nightwatch 11, troubled him.

"Are you okay, Keith?" asked Julie Brady with a concerned expression. Julie was working the D-side in Keith's sector for the evening rush out of Denver and Kansas City. "I'll see if someone's available if you'd like to take a breather."

"No, I'm fine," he said impatiently, keeping his eyes on the scope. "Were you able to get that information for me?"

"Of course. I wrote it down," she said as she stuck the note on the edge of Keith's scope. "Nightwatch one-one was over the Denver VOR westbound at 2250Z. You'll be talking to your cousin in about three hours."

"Huh? Oh, yeah," said Keith.

Nightwatch is westbound on route five toward Salt Lake City, Keith thought, *but will be turning eastbound in an hour. He'll be in my sector around 0200Z.*

". . . on American 644?"

Keith realized with a start that Julie was talking to him. "I'm sorry, Julie, would you repeat that?"

"I said, Keith, are you ready for the hand off on American 644? He's coming to you westbound at flight level 360."

"Yeah, I got him," he said, as he noted the American 787 in the upper right corner of the scope.

His phone suddenly vibrated in his pocket, and a bolt of tension charged through him. He tried to ignore it while the American flight checked in. The phone call went to voicemail. As discreetly as possible he pulled the phone out and looked at the call log. It was a strange number with no identification.

"Keith, you look like you've seen a ghost!" He looked up at Julie, his mouth hung open, eyes flashing side to side. "Keith, what on earth is it?"

"I've got to go to the bathroom . . . Julie, cover for me, please."

After his bathroom break, Keith found a quiet corner and punched the voicemail call button.

"Hello, Keith. It's me," said the familiar voice. "Do you have the routing information?"

Keith couldn't help but notice that Michael was all business.

"Yes. Route number five. Position at 2250Z was overhead Denver, westbound," Keith said. "I'm not on break yet. I got someone to cover for me. I need to get back to the console."

"Sure. Just be available for another call around 0130Z. You're doing a great job."

As he returned to the radar room, he felt Julie's eyes on him. "Any big changes on the scope?"

"Nope," she said, watching him. "Tom Miller's on the way over. I think you need more than a bathroom break. Go get a bite to eat."

"Sounds like a good idea. Thanks."

Ten minutes later Keith was in the cafeteria picking at a plate of Salisbury steak and mashed potatoes.

So, he's going to call back at 1930, when Nightwatch one-one may well be in my airspace.

Keith's thoughts were interrupted by the words of Ron Goodman on the television. ". . . in just a little over three hours. The speech will be attended by all the members of Congress, the Cabinet, the

Supreme Court, the Joint Chiefs of Staff . . ."

Keith began to put the puzzle pieces together. *Michael's calling back just thirty minutes before the start of the president's speech. But what does that have to do with the Airborne Command Post?*

TIME TO WEAPONS RELEASE: 2 HR, 55 MIN
MCCHORD AIR FORCE BASE, WASHINGTON

"Good afternoon, sir," said the crew chief. "I guess you thought you'd never get out of here?"

"I was beginning to wonder," commented Mark Matthews, as he climbed up the ladder to place his helmet in the cockpit. "No big deal. What kind of shape is she in, chief?"

"Well, sir, the radar jamming defense system is completely removed, and the radar warning system only gives an aural warning. You do have a good radar, and a good computer, but since you aren't going to war, I guess you can make it to Massachusetts without that other stuff."

"I guess so," agreed Matthews as he perused the maintenance status printout. "So, the gun's empty and safetied also?"

"Yes, sir. I'm going to miss it. I've been the crew chief on this bird for almost a year."

The two of them conducted the preflight together, with the crew chief pulling the landing gear and drop tank safety pins as they went. Neither of them said much. It was the last time the crew chief would see his airplane, and Matthews knew it was the last time he would fly a fighter as an Air National Guard officer, and maybe ever again.

"Thanks for your help, chief."

"Sure, sir. Have a nice trip and take care of my bird."

TIME TO WEAPONS RELEASE: 2 HR, 50 MIN
NEW HAVEN, CONNECTICUT

Ilya was calm as he rang the bell at Josh Hawkins's apartment door. Taking a final look around and then placing the hood over his face, Ilya reached in his pocket for the Glock 9mm automatic.

"I'm in the shower, Michelle," he heard Josh Hawkins yell from inside the apartment. "The door's unlocked. Make yourself at home."

Shit, thought Ilya as he let himself in. *This is going to be too easy.*

"You can come join me if you like," said the senator's son in a seductive tone.

Ilya moved quickly. He locked the door behind him. Then he guaranteed an escape route by unlocking one of the windows at the rear of the apartment, which opened onto an alley. He turned up the volume on the television and pocketed Josh's cell phone. Finally, Ilya headed to the bathroom.

"Come on in, gorgeous," purred the young Hawkins as the SVR agent opened the door to find the boy standing in the shower with the curtain pulled back. "I have . . . what the fuck?"

Ilya slowly raised the pistol until it was even with the young man's nose. "Not another word," he said menacingly. "Turn off the water and step out of the shower."

"Jesus," moaned Hawkins. "Please don't shoot me. Take anything . . ."

"I intend to, asshole," Ilya hissed as he waved the Glock to signal the man to move out of the bathroom. "Hands on top of your head," he said when Josh tried to grab a towel. Ilya herded the senator's son into the bedroom. "Where's your wallet? And there better be money in it."

"On the dresser," replied Hawkins, his voice shaking. "Take it all, only please don't—"

"Shut the fuck up!" Ilya put the wallet in his coat pocket. "Now, how about jewelry?"

"In the dresser bottom drawer. I don't have much."

"Open it!" Ilya barked.

As the young man leaned down, the agent struck swiftly. An open palm chop to the back of the neck sent Hawkins sprawling to the floor, unconscious. Time was of the essence. Ilya dialed 911 on Josh's phone and requested an ambulance.

Fifteen minutes later Ilya was stretched out on the bed in his motel room with his phone in his hand.

He typed a text message to Chatman. *Done. The boy is in the Yale infirmary.* He was amazed to confirm Chatman's receipt of the text on the television. The camera was panning the guests at the head table. It caught Bobby Chatman looking down at his phone. Ilya saw Chatman confide something to the president and then take his leave.

"Mission accomplished," murmured Ilya.

TIME TO WEAPONS RELEASE: 2 HR, 42 MIN
PETROV'S TU-95
OVER THE GULF OF MEXICO

"I show us at fifty meters on the radar altimeter," said Sheptak.

"I wonder if Piekarski sees those oil rigs up ahead," said Petrov. Those things are taller than you think. There are hundreds of them off this coast. Some of them reach as high as one hundred meters. I show us just entering the Coastal Air Defense Identification Zone. Does that check, Arkady?"

"That checks," confirmed the navigator. "Major, we are only two hundred seventy kilometers south of Grand Isle, and three hundred sixty kilometers from New Orleans. Are you sure they can't see us?"

"Not this low. Anybody looking at us, Vitalie?"

"Negative," replied Orshansky. "I'm getting some low-powered signals in the weather radar bands. Could be airliners. No search bands currently."

"Vladimir, confirm all exterior lights are off."

"Confirmed. What a murky night. We can't be more than five hundred meters below the clouds."

"Somehow it seems like the perfect night for this mission," replied Petrov.

"Hold it," said Orshansky. "I just got a solid hit from a search radar! L-band military in the vicinity of Panama City, which is east of us—*shit!* Piekarski just pulled up! He's climbing! Let's hope he doesn't get picked up by the search radar."

"Pull up! Pull up! Pull up!" shouted Sheptak even as Petrov was bringing the control yoke back into his gut.

"Max power!" Petrov yelled. Sheptak shoved the throttles to the forward stop. Petrov glanced to his left and saw a gigantic drilling derrick flash underneath the wing.

"Sorry, Major," Sheptak said. "I filtered out ground clutter while I was looking at the military radar."

"It's okay," said Petrov calmly, getting his breath back. "I'm easing back down. How strong were the hits?"

Orshansky focused on his radar scope. "Three solid hits. Good enough for target verification. I would not be surprised if they scramble fighters on us."

"Shit!" said Petrov worriedly. "We'll know if they've scrambled on us in a few minutes."

TIME TO WEAPONS RELEASE: 2 HR, 40 MIN
TYNDALL AIR FORCE BASE, FLORIDA

"I can't believe we're here on a three-day weekend!" lamented Sergeant Caldwell. "Couldn't they do this damned radar maintenance another time?"

"Yeah," responded Airman Patterson. "Lousy timing for us schmucks. I had planned to go out and do some speckled sea trout fishing."

The Tyndall air defense radar didn't normally operate except during intercept training over the Gulf. But a defect had been reported and the facility commander had ordered it fixed, tonight. The two men were needed to test the equipment after the electronics technician finished.

The technician came into the radar room from the antenna on top of the building and began stowing his tools. "Okay, you guys can fire it up and test it, and maybe we'll get lucky and get out of here."

Patterson powered up the equipment while Caldwell watched. After a few minutes, checking various detection parameters and filters, Caldwell said, "Looking good."

"For now," said the repair technician. "We won't know for sure until they resume intercept training on Monday. I'm outta here. You guys enjoy what's left of your weekend." The two operators were preparing to shut it down when suddenly an intruder detection alarm sounded.

Patterson walked over and looked at the console. "It's working! We're getting returns on something."

Caldwell joined him. "That's in the Gulf, south of Mississippi."

Patterson sat down and typed filter commands into his console. More information appeared on the screen, "Holy shit! Look at this."

Caldwell leaned in for a better look. "Russian? What the hell?"

"It says we're looking at a Bear bomber . . . maybe two!"

"That's a long way over there, Patterson. We've never used it to look that far out. Is it reliable at that distance?"

"I don't know . . . *wait* . . . it's gone . . . just disappeared! What should we do?"

"Patterson, you know it can't be true. It's probably an airliner."

"But it's supposed to filter out civil air traffic."

"I know that, dammit! I think it gave us a false return. Maybe it's an oil platform—they got hundreds of 'em over there. Hell, I don't know. Look, Patterson, tonight there isn't a sober fighter pilot within a hundred miles of this base. This is not our concern. Shut it down. I'm going home."

"Sarge, maybe you're right, but we have procedures for this. I'm gonna call EADS."

"EADS would have gotten an alert from an ARSR unit if this was real. Don't bother."

"I'm calling, Sarge."

"Patterson, if you want to waste your time, then be my guest," Caldwell said as he headed out the door. "Don't forget to lock this place up!"

Patterson looked up the Defense Switched Network number for the duty officer at EADS. The phone rang once before being picked up.

TIME TO WEAPONS RELEASE: 2 HR, 35 MIN
EASTERN AIR DEFENSE SECTOR
GRIFFISS AIR NATIONAL GUARD BASE, NEW YORK

"Eastern sector, Captain Cindy Williams, can I help you?"

"Captain Williams, this is Airman Patterson at Tyndall. We just repaired our search radar that we use for intercept training and were testing it when we got a positive hit on two targets out in the Gulf south of Mississippi. It only lasted about thirty seconds, then disappeared. But the radar identified them as Tu-95 bombers . . . Bears."

"Stand by, Patterson. Let me get Lieutenant Colonel Pearson on the line."

Two minutes later a new voice joined the call.

"This is Lieutenant Colonel Pearson, the director of the eastern sector. Airman Patterson, tell me again what's happening down there."

Patterson went through the whole story one more time. Pearson asked a few questions, confirming the contact only lasted thirty seconds, then disappeared.

"Patterson, there are numerous oil rigs where you got those hits, correct?"

"Yes, sir, and if whoever it is stayed on course to the north, then New Orleans should pick them up very soon."

"All right, son. You did right calling this in. We'll check with New

Orleans and see if they're tracking anything out over the Gulf. Thank you for the call."

Pearson hung up the phone and turned to his weapons director. "Cindy, have we had any alerts from our ARSR radars?"

"No, sir. No alerts at all today, and all sites are reporting as fully operational."

"Okay," Pearson said, as he mulled over his next response. "Have all the units on the northern Gulf Coast run a self-diagnostic routine just as a precaution and give New Orleans a call. Houston Center, too. See if they're tracking anything. It wouldn't surprise me if some drug runner got a little higher than he planned."

Fifteen minutes later Captain Williams walked up to Lieutenant Colonel Pearson. "What'd you find out, Cindy?"

"Sir, all sites tested ops normal. They haven't had any alerts tonight."

"That's what I thought. Remember, the Tyndall training site is a separate facility from the JSS, and it's a dinosaur. It's only used for intercept training. We've had lots of breakdowns and false alerts from it over the last couple of years, but I didn't want to discourage Airman Patterson from calling in a future alert."

"I understand, sir."

"Let's see that this gets entered into the log and continue normal operations. Bear bombers, my ass!"

CHAPTER TWENTY-TWO

TIME TO WEAPONS RELEASE: 2 HR, 29 MIN
THE SU-57
OVER THE GULF OF MEXICO

"Hang on, Valentin. He must be turning to avoid that oil rig ahead," said Bachvaroff. "Just don't skip across the wave tops. I show us at thirty meters exactly."

"That checks," replied Ridgik. "I hope that weasel knows what he's doing. If he turns that bomber too sharply, he'll drag a wingtip."

"Just worry about us. We should be crossing the coast soon."

"Are you all set to talk to Bay St. Louis?"

"All set. I've been monitoring the frequency for the last ten minutes."

"Nothing new on the radar warning receiver?"

"Nothing. Apparently those three hits earlier didn't detect us. Heads up—Piekarski's coming back to the left."

"Shit! Did you see that? A boat just went by off the right wing. Do you think he saw us?"

"A pitch-black night. Blacked out airplanes. The sound of wind, rain, and ocean. He may have heard us, but I think it's highly doubtful he saw us. Heads up. Another oil rig ahead."

PIEKARSKI'S TU-95

Colonel Piekarski was sweating. "How much farther to the coast?" he asked for the fourth time in ten minutes. "I see land off to the left."

"That's the southernmost tip of Louisiana, Colonel," replied the navigator. "The Chandeleur Island chain is dead ahead. We need to pass just west of the main island. We should cross the coast at Bay St. Louis in exactly fourteen minutes."

"Thank you, nav," said Piekarski. "EO, confirm there are still no signs of fighter interceptors?"

"Nothing yet, Colonel," replied the EO. "There's another group of boats, though, dead ahead for ten kilometers, and another oil rig twenty degrees right at seven kilometers."

"Well, give me a heading, dammit!" demanded Piekarski.

"Make it zero-one-seven," said the EO calmly.

The airplane banked sharply to the right.

"I hope he remembers how long those wings are!" the navigator whispered to the EO.

"Easy! Easy!" said the copilot as he purposely bumped the control wheel to remind Piekarski to decrease the bank angle. "Don't drag a wingtip!"

PETROV'S TU-95

"Piekarski's swinging back to the right again, boss," said Orshansky. "Looks like a group of fishing boats slightly left and another oil rig to the right."

"Thank you, Vitalie," said Petrov. We're at 150 meters and able to clear everything. Arkady, confirm the southernmost tip of Louisiana is passing off the left wing."

There was silence on the interphone.

"Arkady, are you there?"

"Huh? Oh, yes, Major. That checks," replied Itzkoff quietly. "We should cross the coast in thirteen minutes. Present heading is good."

"Thank you, Arkady," said Petrov, while casting a concerned glance at Sheptak. "And we're still below the radar coverage, Vitalie?"

"That's affirmative, sir. I'm getting very weak hits from an air traffic control radar, but not strong enough to track us."

"Can you believe it?" Sheptak observed. "We're going to fly unchallenged into the most powerful nation on the face of the planet."

"Yeah, but I wonder if getting out will be as easy as getting in," said Petrov thoughtfully.

TIME TO WEAPONS RELEASE: 2 HR, 19 MIN
BAY ST. LOUIS, MISSISSIPPI

Alex paced nervously. He calculated the strike package should be crossing the coast any minute. He should be hearing from the Su-57 soon. "Where are they?" he muttered as he stepped outside and looked south into the dark sky. "It's time, dammit."

Then he heard something rumbling, buzzing, and growing. The sound built slowly until the ground began to shake, and the windows in the office behind him rattled. There was no doubt in Alex's mind what he was hearing: four massive turbine engines driving a total of thirty-two gigantic contrarotating propeller blades. Holding his hands over his ears, he saw its navigation lights come on as it passed overhead and heard the Kuznetzov engines rev up. Somewhere in the brutal noise he heard the metallic scream of the Su-57's turbine engines. He watched Piekarski's Bear start a sweeping, climbing turn to the northwest into Target Route Bravo. A minute later Petrov's bomber passed overhead and turned northeast onto Target Route Alpha.

"They're here!" shouted Alex. "They're really here!"

The radio speaker inside the office erupted. "This is Redex zero-three calling Redex Ops, how do you read?"

THE SU-57

"Redex zero-three calling Redex Ops. How do you read?" said Bachvaroff. "He's still not talking to me, Valentin. That was the airfield we just passed over, right?"

"Yes, that was it," replied Ridgik as he pushed the power up to move into close formation with Piekarski's climbing bomber.

"Redex zero-three, Redex OPS reads you loud and clear. I was watching you guys fly over. I count three aircraft?"

"That checks," replied Bachvaroff, relieved that the Russian agent was finally answering. "Do you have position information on Redex zero-four?" he continued, using the exact wording for the target information listed in the mission packet.

"That's affirmative. Ready to copy?"

"Zero-three's ready," replied Bachvaroff, his pencil and flashlight in hand.

"Packet page number is seven. Page authentication is Kilo, November. Redex zero-four was at position three-two, routing Papa, time number one-five, last reported westbound."

"Zero-three copies," said Bachvaroff tersely. "Stand by." It took Bachvaroff a minute to work out the coded position report of the Airborne Command Post. "I've got it," he finally said to Ridgik. "At 2250Z he was flying westbound on route number five, over the Denver VOR. Authentication checks. I'm loading it in the computer."

Ridgik nodded. "Sounds good. Thank our comrade and let me know when you have the intercept solution."

PETROV'S TU-95

"Redex zero-two is cleared to the destination airport at Three-Foxtrot-Whiskey-Golf, via present position direct to McComb, Texarkana,

Salina, direct. Climb to flight level 350. Squawk three-one-four-one."

"Excellent," said Petrov as he listened to Piekarski read back the Route Bravo flight plan to Houston Center. "Josef sounds fine. Vladimir, it's your airplane. I'll talk to the controller. Expect to go direct to the Semmes VOR."

"My airplane," confirmed the copilot.

"Good evening, Houston," Petrov said in English. "Redex zero-one is off of Two-Foxtrot-Whiskey-Golf. Standing by for clearance."

"Hello, Redex zero-one. Radar contact. Climb and maintain flight level 330. You're cleared to the One-Foxtrot-Whiskey-Golf airport via direct Semmes, Spartanburg, Raleigh, direct. Squawk three-one-five-four."

"Vladimir, that's the routing in the packet," said Petrov after he'd read back the clearance. "Do you have any questions?"

"Not about the routing," said Sheptak as he banked the bomber slightly to go direct to the Semmes VOR. "But let me get this straight. We're flying in US airspace, going to a cruise missile launch point, and we're doing it with our lights on and under the control of their air traffic controllers?"

"That's right."

"Should we be afraid of detection?"

"Not at this point," said Petrov confidently. "It would take somebody seeing us visually and questioning the controller, and the chances of that happening are slim. Remember, we are just a set of red, green, and white lights."

"Yes, but we're a Russian bomber!" protested the copilot.

"No, we are a Cessna Citation, and we've been flying this route night after night for two months."

"Amazing," said Sheptak.

"Diabolical," commented Orshansky.

"Fucking brilliant," chimed in Grotsky from the tail gun compartment.

"A tragedy," said Itzkoff quietly.

"It is all of that," agreed Petrov, taking note of Itzkoff's tone. "Arkady, keep in HF radio contact with Piekarski's airplane. Vitalie, look at that weather up ahead. Vladimir, keep it at five hundred kilometers per hour. That's the same as two hundred seventy knots. We want to look like a Citation on their air traffic control radar."

TIME TO WEAPONS RELEASE: 2 HR, 10 MIN
MCCHORD AIR FORCE BASE, WASHINGTON

"Suds two-two, I have your clearance."

Finally! thought Mark Matthews. "Go ahead for Suds two-two." He'd crossed out the call sign they'd given him and scribbled in his personal call sign on the flight plan. That could land him in hot water, but what the hell? He was on the way out of the military.

"Suds two-two is cleared to Offutt Air Force Base via direct Yakima, Rapid City, O'Neill, direct. Climb and maintain flight level 390. Squawk two-five-four-five."

Great! thought Matthews as he read back the clearance. *The scenic moonlit route over the Rockies. Then a sandwich at Offutt while they refuel. I should still make it home by midnight.*

"Suds two-two, McChord tower. Winds are calm, change to departure control, cleared for takeoff."

"Cleared to go for Suds two-two. Can you approve an Eagle departure?"

"Eagle departure approved if you can be out of ten thousand feet within five miles of the airport."

"I can handle that," said Matthews as he lined up on the runway and advanced the throttles. He checked the engine gauges prior to releasing the brakes. "Okay. Brakes released. Engines are good. Here come the burners."

There had never been a thrill for Matthews like that of an Eagle departure. A full afterburner takeoff, gear and flaps up, holding the airplane down to the end of the runway, allowing it to accelerate, and then pulling the nose up to the vertical. Eagle pilots rarely got to do it, but it was his last flight, so what the heck!

"Departure, Suds two-two's with you out of three thousand for three-nine-zero on an Eagle departure," Matthews transmitted to the departure controller.

"Roger, Suds two-two," replied the controller. "Call level at 390."

"Will do," answered Matthews as he passed twenty thousand feet inverted, rolled the Eagle upright, and pulled it out of afterburner. *Brake release to twenty thousand in fifty-nine seconds*, he thought. *Not bad.* He felt the big grin under his oxygen mask.

TIME TO WEAPONS RELEASE: 2 HR, 0 MIN
PETROV'S TU-95
OVER THE SEMMES VOR, MOBILE, ALABAMA

"I show us over Semmes," said Sheptak as he started a slow turn to the left. "Outbound course is zero-four-four. Do you want to go around that rain shower to the northeast?"

Petrov studied the weather radar depiction. "It looks like moderate precipitation. We will get a little turbulence and maybe some icing, but I don't see any real problems. Do you concur, Vitalie?"

"That's affirmative, sir," said Orshansky. "We are going to have to cross this cold front somewhere. The zero-four-four course looks as good as any to me."

"Engine inlet and prop anti-ice are coming on," said Sheptak. "And here comes wing heat. Do we need to do anything about the missiles?"

"Hmm—a good thought. Arkady, do we need to be concerned about dragging those missiles through moderate icing conditions?"

"There's little we can do for pylon-mounted missiles," said the navigator quietly. "I would have preferred to carry them on the rotary launcher in the bomb bay, but I know we needed the bomb bay fuel tank on this mission. Let's hope the missile designers foresaw the possibility of dragging them through icing conditions."

"Very well," said Petrov, looking at Sheptak and twisting backward to face Czinkota, the backup aircraft commander who was riding quietly on the zampolit's seat. He made a drinking motion with his hand. "Vitalie, I think we're ready for some coffee." Czinkota flashed a thumbs-up.

"Three black coffees," said the EO a few moments later as he entered the cockpit. He held his unplugged microphone cord in his hand and signaled the occupants of the cockpit to do the same. "I'm worried about Itzkoff," he confided. "He's not himself."

Petrov nodded and turned around in his seat to face the electronics officer. "I'm also concerned."

"He's doing his job properly," said Orshansky, choosing his words carefully, "but . . . he seems so quiet."

"As long as he's performing to standard, there's not much we can do," replied Petrov. "Do you know how to arm and launch those missiles?" he asked the EO.

"Sure, but—"

"Do you have any qualms about doing it if you have to?"

"I guess not."

"Fine. Just keep an eye on him and let me know if you see any real problems." He smiled sympathetically at the young lieutenant.

As everyone plugged back into the intercom, the radio sounded with an instruction from air traffic control. Sheptak asked what the controller said.

"He said, 'Contact Atlanta Center on 132.07. Y'all have a nice night.'"

"Y'all? What the hell does y'all mean?" Sheptak asked.

"Means you all."

"This is too much," uttered Sheptak, shaking his head.

CHAPTER TWENTY-THREE

TIME TO WEAPONS RELEASE: 1 HR, 40 MIN
SENATE OFFICE BUILDING
WASHINGTON, DC

Bobby Chatman had assumed it'd be easy to locate Senator Dan Hawkins to tell him about his son. But after multiple unanswered phone calls, Chatman felt time was running out. He needed time to get to the airport, get airborne, and get clear of the target area.

He was about to cross the street to the Capitol Building when he realized he needed to check in with Alex. *The strike package should have entered US airspace half an hour ago*, he thought as he tapped Alex's contact icon.

"Yes?" Alex said.

"It's me. What's the word?"

"They're here," replied Alex excitedly. "I watched them go over."

"And the Route Charlie position data?"

"Received, coded, and passed to the Sukhoi," Alex confirmed. "Everything here is a go. What's the word at your end?"

"I'm having trouble finding Hawkins."

"You'd better hurry, Bobby."

"I know. I gotta go."

Come on, Senator, thought Chatman as he headed briskly toward the Capitol Building. *Please be here! Petrov is probably approaching Atlanta by now.*

TIME TO WEAPONS RELEASE: 1 HR, 25 MIN
PETROV'S TU-95

"Finally!" said Sheptak as the Tu-95 broke into clear skies passing flight level 290. "Engine, prop, and wing anti-ice are coming off . . . what is that glowing out there?"

"Atlanta, Georgia," Petrov replied.

"X-band radar hits from two o'clock!" Orshansky shouted. "My guess is an older F-16. There are two of them, and they're close enough to get a good return from us."

"Just relax," said Petrov calmly. "Remember, Atlanta has told them we're a Cessna Citation, and it's dark."

"But what if they're able to break our type out?"

"We will deal with that then," Petrov calmly answered.

"Redex zero-one, you have traffic two o'clock, twenty miles. It's a flight of two F-16s."

"Redex zero-one is looking," said Petrov as he scanned the sky. "No joy."

"There they are! I see their lights!" said Sheptak.

"Should I do anything?" asked Orshansky. "Jammers are in standby, green lights across the board."

"Leave them in standby," replied Petrov coolly. "Misha, leave your tail gun radar in standby too. We don't want to do anything to arouse suspicions. Just wave at them as they go by."

"Going by on the right," said Grotsky, "and they're continuing straight ahead."

Septak wiped perspiration from his forehead with his sleeve, sighed, and looked at Petrov. "The moon is coming up at one o'clock," he commented. "If that had been a few minutes earlier . . ."

They were silent as they watched the near full moon climb above the horizon. "I'm glad I can't see outside tonight," commented Itzkoff.

"Why's that, Arkady?" asked Petrov.

"If it's a clear night, you guys will be able to see Washington and Norfolk at launch time. I'd rather not watch."

TIME TO WEAPONS RELEASE: 1 HR, 20 MIN
THE SU-57

"Finally!" said Ridgik as he maneuvered the Su-57 to a loose route formation with Piekarski's bomber. "I thought we'd never break out of those clouds."

"I have the intercept solution, but I didn't want to bother you until we broke out on top," replied Bachvaroff.

"So, what's the solution?"

"Assuming the 747 flies route five by the book, we should intercept him just as he crosses central Nebraska heading eastbound. He'll be about two hundred kilometers west of Omaha at the time over target for the Omaha cruise missile."

"The timing sounds good," said Ridgik thoughtfully. "We should try for a front quadrant shot on a westerly heading so we won't be facing Omaha when Piekarski's missile detonates.."

"Good plan. The eastern horizon is going to get very bright when that warhead detonates. I prefer to go home with my vision intact."

"Agreed."

"By the way, traffic ahead for fifty-two kilometers. Probably an airliner. We're going to meet him head-on. Confirm we're a dark jet?"

"Affirmative," replied Ridgik as he gently moved closer to Piekarski's bomber. "The moon's coming up behind us. They shouldn't get a good look at us."

PIEKARSKI'S TU-95

"Traffic dead ahead for fifty kilometers, sir," advised the EO. "We're going to meet head-on."

"Dammit!" said Piekarski nervously. "And the moon is coming up. Tail gunner, are we contrailing?"

"Negative, sir," replied the gunner. "And the fighter is tucked in with lights out."

"Hopefully they'll only see our nav lights," muttered Piekarski, "and assume we're just another civilian airplane. Is he looking at us with radar?"

"Negative," answered the EO. "He has a weather radar operating but shouldn't get a return from us."

"Redex zero-two, Fort Worth, you have traffic twelve o'clock, twenty-five miles. It's a United 757 at flight level 340."

"Redex zero-two is looking," said Piekarski, his voice shaking slightly.

UNITED 238

"You know those management types," said the captain. "They don't know the pointy end of an airplane from the ass end, and yet they want to tell us how to do our jobs."

"You're right," replied the first officer. "If only the union had its act together."

"United 238, Fort Worth, you have traffic, twelve o'clock, twenty miles, opposite direction, a Citation at three-five-zero."

"Looking," said the captain, as both pilots scanned the night sky.

"There's the traffic," pointed out the first officer. "Did he say that was a Citation?"

"That's what he said."

"Looks big for a Citation."

"Yeah, it does," the captain muttered. "You should talk to the union rep. That's what we pay dues for."

THE SU-57

"Damn, this is right down the tubes!" said Ridgik, who'd maneuvered the Su-57 above Piekarski's airplane and on the opposite side the airliner would pass. "I hope they don't see us."

"Or hear us," mused Bachvaroff. "If we can hear those four monster turboprops, they might hear them too as we go by."

PIEKARSKI'S TU-95

"Shit!" Piekarski exclaimed, as the lights from the Boeing 757 grew larger. "You know they see us, and we're much bigger than a Citation." He reached up and toggled the landing lights on as he'd seen American aircraft routinely do when they were meeting head-on. "Maybe the bright lights will mask us."

UNITED 238

"You're right," said the United captain as he toggled his own landing lights on in response to the approaching aircraft. "That does look big for a Citation. Maybe Kansas City just looked at the wrong strip."

As the brightly lit bomber passed one thousand feet above the Boeing 757, the cockpit of the United jet vibrated slightly with an audible rumble.

"Did you hear that buzzing sound as we passed under that plane?" asked the first officer.

"No, but it's a wonder I can hear anything after twenty years of flying these jets!"

TIME TO WEAPONS RELEASE: 1 HR, 15 MIN
THE CAPITOL BUILDING
WASHINGTON, DC

"McCormick, are you there? This is security checkpoint number two." The FBI agent smiled at the amateurish terminology. The speaker was obviously one of the CIA paper pushers who'd never used a handheld radio.

"Go ahead, checkpoint two," she said. "Ringmaster reads you loud and clear."

"Oh yeah, Ringmaster. We have a problem. There's a guy claiming to be Reverend Bobby Chatman, and he's insisting on being admitted to locate Senator Hawkins. He says it's an emergency, but he doesn't have the proper paperwork to clear the checkpoint. Would you mind coming down?"

Darryl McCormick frowned. Of all the people hanging around Washington, Bobby Chatman's presence peeved her the most. In addition to Chatman's unusual chumminess with the president, she felt that he came across as pompous.

"I'm on my way," radioed McCormick.

Bobby Chatman hadn't anticipated the many new security checkpoints around the Capitol Building, and he hadn't considered that untrained CIA agents would be denying entry to the building without proper credentials. He couldn't believe his ears when the agent consulted his list and informed him his name wasn't there. Entry, they told him, would require the escort of the FBI agent in charge. "Well, get him down here," he'd said testily. "Senator Hawkins's son is in grave condition, and he must be notified!"

"Agent McCormick's on the way, sir."

McCormick? Chatman remembered that name from somewhere. *Dammit, an hour and twenty-four minutes to time over target. It's going* to be really tight getting into the air. Maybe I could request a chopper. No. Too much to coordinate.

"Excuse me, Reverend Chatman," said a voice behind him. "Darryl McCormick, FBI." She didn't offer a handshake. "I understand you need to see me?"

"Miss McCormick, nice to see you again." He smiled confidently. "I had a call an hour ago from a minister acquaintance in Connecticut. He told me Senator Dan Hawkins's son was injured tonight in a mugging, and all his efforts to contact the senator have been fruitless. He asked if I could notify him. In fact, I intend to offer to fly the senator to Connecticut, but I'm running out of time. The curfew on takeoffs out of Reagan goes into effect in an hour, and I still need to locate him, get to the airport, and get in the air before nine o'clock." He smiled as he made eye contact with the FBI agent. "Anything you could do to help would be greatly appreciated."

"Okay, Reverend. Follow me. We'll find Senator Hawkins and I'll arrange for a ride to the airport. We should be able to get you out of town before the curfew."

"Oh, thank you, Miss McCormick, and God bless you."

"Just McCormick will do."

Darryl McCormick smelled a rat. Several things about Chatman's story didn't add up. First, it was odd that one of the most liberal senators in Washington was being sought by one of the most conservative evangelists, "emergency" or not. Considering the importance of the events in Washington, it would seem Hawkins's son would need to be on his deathbed to justify Chatman's actions. Finally, she was certain the Reagan National Airport curfew didn't go into effect until ten o'clock, so why was the reverend in such a hurry? As she led Chatman to the office of the Senate majority leader, she suppressed the urge to confront him.

Suddenly she slowed her pace, remembering the report she had heard of Russian bombers leaving Venezuela northbound.

"Is something wrong?" Chatman asked.

She shook her head without looking back and continued into the building.

"Here we are," she said as they reached the office. See if you can locate Senator Hawkins."

McCormick watched Chatman walk into the majority leader's office. The evangelist's presence was obviously a surprise to everyone. Chatman made his way across the room to Dan Hawkins, and the senator was stunned to hear the news about his son. After a moment of indecision, he nodded and both men started toward the door.

"Mobile five, Ringmaster," said McCormick into the radio as the two men threaded their way through the group of curious senators.

"Roger, Ringmaster, mobile five. Go ahead."

"Mobile five, Ringmaster, meet me at checkpoint two. I need you to make an emergency run to Reagan Airport."

Arriving at the checkpoint, McCormick leaned into the waiting car. "The reverend and Senator Hawkins need to get to Reagan," said McCormick. "It's an emergency, so step on it!"

"Signature Aviation on the south side of the airport," said Chatman to the driver. "And thanks a million, Miss McCormick . . . Oh! Sorry."

McCormick ignored the snub.

"Was that Bobby Chatman with Dan Hawkins?" asked Hank Hartley.

"Oh, hello, Hartley," said McCormick. "Yeah, that was Chatman and Hawkins all right."

"Well, now there's two faces I never expected to see together," laughed Hartley.

"Yeah, I was thinking the same thing," she replied as she watched the car disappear.

TIME TO WEAPONS RELEASE: 0 HR, 50 MIN
PETROV'S TU-95
OVER SPARTANBURG, SOUTH CAROLINA

"There's Spartanburg," said Sheptak. "Coming right to zero-seven-three for Raleigh."

"Zero-seven-three," repeated Petrov. "Arkady, we're overhead Spartanburg. How are we doing on fuel?"

"Still slightly behind the burn and holding," said Itzkoff quietly.

"Why don't you give Piekarski's airplane a call on HF, get a position report on them, and see if they're estimating Launch Point Bravo on time."

"I got it," said Itzkoff. "I'll program the missile based on their progress."

"Let me know when you're done, and we'll do the missile prelaunch checklist up to weapons arm."

"I'll need a few minutes."

"Take your time, Arkady," said Petrov agreeably. "Take your time."

TIME TO WEAPONS RELEASE: 0 HR, 40 MIN
PIEKARSKI'S TU-95
SOUTH OF WICHITA, KANSAS

"Missile prelaunch checklist," ordered Piekarski.

"Go ahead," said the launch officer. "Missile master arm."

"Coming to standby once, and twice. Green lights on both missiles."

"Missile engine monitor."

"Green lights both sides. Both engines are windmilling within start parameters."

"Missile engine fuel system."

"Valves open, positive fuel pressure on both birds. Valves are now in standby for automatic launch sequencer. Tanks indicate full."

"Roger that," confirmed Piekarski. "We'll plan to launch the Offutt bird first. I want us holding at the thirty-second initial point while we wait for confirmation of a successful launch from Petrov."

TIME TO WEAPONS RELEASE: 0 HR, 35 MIN
PETROV'S TU-95
SOUTH OF RALEIGH, NORTH CAROLINA

"Missile speed control."

"Set at eight hundred fifty kilometers per hour on the Alpha one bird and five hundred sixty kilometers per hour on the Alpha two bird. That allows for a twenty-minute flight to both Washington and Norfolk."

"Missile guidance."

"Loaded as briefed. I'm standing by to confirm nav station reception in each bird five minutes prior to launch."

"Missile cruise altitude."

"Set at five thousand meters."

"Missile engine shutdown."

"Set for one minute prior to warhead detonation."

"Warhead burst altitude."

"Set for three hundred meters."

"Arkady, that does it for now," said Petrov. "We'll arm the warheads together three minutes prior to launch and go on autosequencer at thirty seconds. Plan on a launch time of four-zero past the hour."

"Yes, sir. Forty past."

TIME TO WEAPONS RELEASE: 0 HR, 34 MIN
KANSAS CITY ARTCC

"I'm going to take a break," said Julie Brady. "My coffee went straight through me."

"Sure," Keith Anderson answered. "Did you get another check on Nightwatch one-one for me?"

"Yeah, sorry. At 0100Z, Nightwatch one-one was forty west of Denver, eastbound. One other thing. That unit there," she said, pointing at the scope, "is Redex zero-two. He's coming to us at thirty-five."

"And I assume he's going to 3FWG?"

"Yep. The work of the Lord continues. Can I bring you anything?"

"Nope," Keith replied, as he looked Julie in the eyes for the first time all evening. "Do me a favor," he said seriously. "Get back here as soon as you can."

The D-side controller looked perplexed as she met Keith's gaze. "Listen, Keith— something's been bothering you all evening. Don't you want to tell me about it?"

"I can't. Not yet anyway. Just hustle back, okay?"

"There are some things you can't rush, if you know what I mean," Julie replied with a wink, trying to keep things light while taking note of the serious look on her workmate's face.

Nineteen minutes until Michael calls, thought Keith. *Nightwatch will pass through my sector within the next half hour. Fifty minutes until the president's speech. Keep watching.*

"Kansas City Center, Redex zero-two is with you at flight level 350."

"Good evening, Redex zero-two," said Keith. "After Wichita you're cleared direct 3FWG."

TIME TO WEAPONS RELEASE: 0 HR, 30 MIN
WASHINGTON, DC

Bobby Chatman could barely control his anxiety. The FBI car was inching along in heavy traffic, and even though the car had a portable flashing light on the roof, they seemed to be making little headway.

"I can't believe traffic is so heavy tonight," said Chatman.

"It's always like this on a three-day weekend," observed the driver, "and they all want to use Reagan. Dulles is probably a tomb right now. They're all trying to make the last flights out, or they're driving in to pick up someone."

The road opened up slightly, and the agent gunned the Ford along the shoulder. He took the Signature Aviation exit with tires screeching but came to a stop after only a block. A hotel van had broken down and was holding up traffic. Chatman could see the Signature terminal a few blocks ahead.

"We'll get out here and walk," he said. "We're running out of time. Thanks for the ride. Come on, Senator," urged Chatman as he started toward the general aviation terminal.

It took Chatman five minutes to sign the fuel invoice and another ten minutes to get the senator into the airplane, the engines started, and an IFR clearance to New Haven. He released the brakes and prepared to taxi.

"Washington ground, Citation two-two-zero-seven Xray is ready to taxi from Signature with clearance and information Kilo," he radioed.

"Roger, Citation zero-seven Xray, you can get in line to taxi to runway zero-one via the outer and Charlie. Hold short of runway zero-four. You're currently number twelve for departure."

Chatman couldn't believe his ears. *Number twelve! Shit! It's going to be very close.* He knew Reagan National used the same runway for jet departures and arrivals. It could take forty-five minutes to get to the runway!

"Citation zero-seven Xray, Washington."

"Go ahead," said Chatman resignedly.

"We were just wondering why you're not on a Redex call sign tonight?"

"A personal emergency rather than one for the Lord. I appreciate anything you can do to expedite our departure," he said, slipping into the Bobby Chatman role. *And those call signs are all in use*, he thought, wryly. *Wouldn't it be something to come this far and then be sitting here when the balloon goes up? Dammit, it wasn't supposed to work out this way!*

TIME TO WEAPONS RELEASE: 0 HR, 25 MIN
RUSSIAN EMBASSY
HAVANA, CUBA

Viktor Darginsky had taken a helicopter from La Orchila to Simon Bolivar International Airport immediately after transmitting the message announcing the departure of the Tu-95s and had just made the afternoon flight to Havana. Darginsky wasted no time on arrival. He'd called ahead and a driver took him immediately to the Russian embassy. After clearing through several security checkpoints, he was admitted into the embassy's secure command center.

"Good evening, gentlemen," said Darginsky to the two communication specialists as he stood just inside the room's steel door. "In about twenty minutes, I need to listen to a particular HF radio frequency for a coded message. Would it be possible for me to have access to your receiver?"

"Sir, we need to keep our primary HF receiver on listening watch to Moscow for the ongoing exercise, but we have a backup HF transmitter and receiver that you are welcome to use. If you have the frequency, my comrade will get you set up."

"That would be excellent. Thank you."

Three minutes later, Darginsky was sitting in front of the backup HF radio listening to the frequency outlined in the mission packet. *Twenty-one minutes to launch time, if they're on time.*

TIME TO WEAPONS RELEASE: 0 HR, 20 MIN
PETROV'S TU-95
JUST SOUTH OF RALEIGH

"Washington Center, Redex zero-one is with you at flight level 210 with a request," Petrov transmitted.

"Good evening Redex zero-one. Go ahead with your request."

"Washington, Redex zero-one would like to continue the descent below flight level 180. We'll be canceling IFR."

"Stand by on your request, Redex. I have opposite direction traffic at flight level 200. I'll have lower when you're clear."

"Let me get this straight," said Sheptak. "When we get below flight level 180, they won't be controlling us anymore?"

"That's correct," replied Petrov. "We'll be able to go where we want, and we won't be talking to anybody."

"Redex zero-one, Washington. Descend and maintain one-five thousand. Raleigh altimeter is 30.15. Advise when passing flight level 180, and I'll cancel your IFR. Would you like to go direct to 1FWG?"

"Yes, sir," replied Petrov. "Redex zero-one is out of flight level 210 for one-five thousand on altimeter 30.15."

"Roger, Redex. You're cleared direct 1FWG."

Petrov acknowledged the transmission then adjusted the power for the descent. Passing through flight level 180, he canceled their IFR flight plan as Sheptak turned toward Launch Point Alpha.

"Keep the speed up, Vladimir," Petrov commanded. "I want to get there on time. Arkady, does it look like a launch time of forty past the hour is still good?"

"Yes, sir," replied Itzkoff quietly.

"I guess that's Raleigh to the right," observed Sheptak.

"Yes, that's Raleigh at two o'clock, and Richmond is on the horizon at twelve o'clock," replied Petrov. "Transponder and nav lights are off. We are now a blacked-out airplane and a raw radar return."

TIME TO WEAPONS RELEASE: 0 HR, 17 MIN
KANSAS CITY ARTCC

"Kansas City, Redex zero-two."

"Redex zero-two," said Keith Anderson. "Are you ready for a descent below one-eight-zero and a cancelation of your IFR?"

"That's affirmative."

"Roger, Redex zero-two, descend and maintain one-six thousand. Wichita altimeter is 30.05." Keith watched as the Citation started its descent. So far, everything about his shift had been routine. Except for the calls from Michael, of course. And his personal feeling of foreboding. *Nightwatch one-one should be coming on my scope.*

He felt his phone vibrate again in his pocket. "Julie, cover me for a quick bathroom break, would you? Redex is descending. You can cancel his IFR below eighteen thousand." Keith waited until Julie was focused on the scope, then he went back to the dark corner he had used earlier to take Michael's call.

"Keith here," he said, taking a deep breath.

"It's me," said the familiar voice. "What's the word?"

"You're early," Keith replied. "He was forty west of Denver, eastbound, on the hour. Hope it's good enough."

"Everything considered, it should be adequate," Michael said. "And he's still on route five?"

"That's affirmative"

"Thank you, Keith. That should do it. It's been a pleasure doing business with you." The call went dead.

Keith was disappointed. He'd hoped to get in some sort of last word.

"Redex just canceled IFR," said Julie, "and Denver will be ready for a hand off on Nightwatch one-one and Suds two-two in three minutes."

"The former is a USAF 747 and the latter is an F-15," Keith murmured as he studied the scope. "Tell Denver we can take them both." *Now, that's interesting,* he thought. *Redex appears to have turned* his transponder off, a violation at his altitude. And he's headed northwest toward Goodland instead of going direct to 3FWG.

CHAPTER TWENTY-FOUR

TIME TO WEAPONS RELEASE: 0 HR, 23 MIN
THE SU-57
CENTRAL KANSAS

"Piekarski just killed his nav lights," observed Ridgik as the Bear/Sukhoi flight leveled off at 16,500 feet. "Have you tried to call our comrade for a target update?"

"Negative," replied Bachvaroff. "The plan was to wait until thirty past the hour, but it might be good to see if I can raise him."

"My thoughts exactly."

The back seater dialed in the frequency for Bobby Chatman's Kansas ranch on the number two VHF comm radio. "Redex Ops, this is Redex zero-three, how do you read?"

THE KANSAS RANCH

Michael's improvised runway approach lights—basically just outdoor floodlights and extension cords he had bought at Home Depot—were not working on the south end. After unsuccessfully troubleshooting and realizing the winds were out of the south, he decided the north end would do. The distraction with the lights made him forget that he needed to fetch the codes out of the safe to update the Su-57. But the safe was at the main house. As he passed the line shack, he heard a weak call coming over the radio inside. He rushed inside to answer it.

"Redex zero-three, this is Redex Ops, how do you read?"

THE SU-57

"I hear him!" Bachvaroff yelled to his front seater. He pressed his transmit button again. "Redex Ops, this is Redex zero-three. I read you loud and clear."

"I'm transmitting your target information without coding it," responded Michael. "Ready to copy?"

"Valentin, he's giving us the target info. Back me up!"

He immediately heard the information coming in from Michael. "Your target was forty miles west of Denver, eastbound, still on route five, at one hundred Zulu. Redex zero-three, did you copy?"

Bachvaroff's excitement caused him to commit a subtle error. He switched from interphone to Comm 1 instead of returning his selector switch to Comm 2. Comm 1 was set on Kansas City Center's frequency. "Roger, Redex zero-three copies target position forty miles west of Denver, route five, at one hundred Zulu."

"Redex zero-three, Redex OPS. Did you copy target position?" Michael asked.

When Bachvaroff heard Redex OPS's question, he realized his mistake. He quickly selected Comm 2 and confirmed receipt of the target data.

"Roger, Redex zero-three, see you soon."

"What frequency is the number one VHF radio set on, Valentin?" asked Bachvaroff with urgency in his voice. "I think I just fucked up."

"You did. It's still on Kansas City Center," said Ridgik.

"Well, I read back the target routing on that frequency."

"I know, and the controller's been calling us wanting an explanation. I just ignored him. Get the intercept worked up. Those cruise missiles will be flying in ten minutes."

TIME TO WEAPONS RELEASE: 0 HR, 18 MIN
KANSAS CITY ARTCC

"Calling Kansas City Center, say again," transmitted Keith Anderson for the fourth time. *Dammit!* he thought. *Who is Redex zero-three? Why was he reading back the exact route I passed to that bastard Michael? Why did he refer to it as a "target"? And why won't he answer me?*

Keith studied the scope. He was still getting a good primary return on Redex 02. That was unusual because a Cessna Citation rarely showed up so well in primary return. Redex 02 was still headed northwest, rather than toward 3FWG. The Airborne Command Post was just coming on the scope in the north sector, and Suds 22, the F-15, was just entering the southern sector.

It was time to make the decision he'd been putting off for fear of his life. *Fuck Michael. I'm not going to have blood on my hands.* "Julie, call Denver on the landline," he commanded. "Tell them we're unable to accept the hand off on Nightwatch."

"Keith . . . I don't understand."

"Don't ask questions," he ordered. "Just do it! Tell them to reroute him around our northern sector. After that, run a computer search. See if you can find any information on Redex 03. Do it now! Lives are at stake."

"Okay," she replied, frightened.

A call came over the radio. "Kansas City Center, Suds two-two is with you, level 330."

"Suds two-two, Kansas City, copy," said Keith, responding to the F-15's check-in. *How timely*, he thought. *Michael, I just might have a surprise for you, asshole.*

TIME TO WEAPONS RELEASE: 0 HR, 10 MIN
REAGAN WASHINGTON NATIONAL AIRPORT

"How much longer do you think it'll be to get in the air?" asked Dan Hawkins.

"I'm not sure," replied Bobby Chatman. "Soon I hope."

"Tell me, Chatman, what do you know about Josh's condition?"

"My minister friend told me he'd been mugged, and he was in the emergency room at the Yale infirmary. That's all I know. Just relax. I'll have you at his bedside in less than an hour." *If we ever get in the air!* thought Chatman. *This was poor planning on my part. I didn't come this far to end up a casualty.*

"Washington tower, Citation zero-seven Xray, would it speed things up if we requested runway four for departure?"

"That's a negative, zero-seven Xray. We're feeding the IFR departures into the system as fast as we can."

I'm going to wait another five minutes, and then I'm going to take off, clearance or not, thought Chatman.

TIME TO WEAPONS RELEASE: 0 HR, 5 MIN
PETROV'S TU-95

"Five minutes to launch . . . ready . . . mark!" said Petrov. "I have Buggs Island Lake in sight. Our initial point is just ahead. Then we fly up the lake to just before the dam. That's Launch Point Alpha."

"I have a clean radar return on the dam," said the navigator.

They'd been flying in silence for several minutes. Petrov knew everyone was deep in their own thoughts. He chose not to impose on them during these final minutes.

"Both missiles are receiving their respective navigation stations," said Itzkoff. "I'm standing by for the final items on the missile prelaunch checklist."

"Advise Piekarski we're approaching the IP, then continue with the prelaunch checklist," replied Petrov.

PIEKARSKI'S TU-95

"There's the IP," said the missile launch officer. "I'm painting the Cedar Bluff Reservoir on radar."

"Very good," said Piekarski, who seemed to have relaxed since they canceled IFR with Kansas City Center. "I'm going to slow down a little until we hear from Petrov. Have you done the NAVAID reception check on the two missiles?"

"Affirmative, sir. Both missiles are receiving their initial navigation stations. I'm standing by for the final items on the missile prelaunch checklist."

"Roger, we'll hold off until we hear from Petrov." The Russian colonel smiled and looked at his copilot. "So easy, comrade. So easy."

THE SU-57

"I have the intercept solution, Valentin," said Bachvaroff. "The target should currently bear three hundred twenty-five degrees for three hundred seven kilometers."

"Copy that."

"And Petrov's airplane is calling on HF. They are approaching their IP and expect to launch on time. Piekarski should also be launching in just a few minutes. We might as well stay with him until then. I'd like to watch it launch."

"Me too," responded Ridgik.

KANSAS CITY ARTCC

"Denver's taking Nightwatch north," said Julie, "and there's nothing in the computer on Redex zero-three. There was a Redex zero-one on the standard routing toward 1FWG, which is another private airport in North Carolina. It's also a Citation. He canceled IFR and Washington isn't talking to him."

"Okay, thanks," replied Keith, as he wiped sweat from his forehead with his sleeve.

"Keith, what's going on? If I'm going to help, I need to know."

"I don't know the answer yet, but I'm going to find out." He took a deep breath and squeezed the radio transmit button. "Suds two-two, you got your radar up tonight?"

"It's in standby right now," replied Matthews. "Something I can do for you?"

Keith still had a primary contact on Redex 02, and the supposed Citation was still headed well west of its filed destination. He recalled the radio transmission a few minutes earlier from somebody calling himself Redex 03, the pilot who read back "target" information. *Could the "target" have been the Airborne Command Post?* Keith's blood ran cold as he considered what he'd almost allowed to happen.

"That's affirmative, Suds two-two," said Keith. "We're tracking a Cessna Citation in primary only that we'd like to know the altitude on. We're not talking to him. Can your system provide that?"

"Sure, what's the target's position?"

"He's currently at your one o'clock for forty-one miles. Anything you can tell me about him would be greatly appreciated."

"Roger, Kansas City, stand by."

TIME TO WEAPONS RELEASE: 0 HR, 3 MIN
PETROV'S TU-95

"Three minutes to go," said Petrov, emotionless. "Let's do the final steps of the missile prelaunch checklist. Missile nav lock on."

"Confirmed on one . . . and on two," said Itzkoff.

"Missile power packs."

"Set internal on one . . . and on two . . . green lights indicate power transfer complete. Both missiles operating on internal power."

"Missile hydraulic units."

"Coming up . . . stand by . . . green lights indicate normal hydraulic pressure on both birds."

"Missile internal gyro platform."

"Aligned and stable on one . . . and on two."

"Two minutes and thirty seconds to go," advised Sheptak.

Petrov reviewed the next actions. There was nothing left to do but arm the nuclear warheads and release the safety locks on the launch shackles. Then he and Itzkoff would have to activate the master release switch for the first missile at thirty seconds to go, and the autosequencer would take control of the launch. Once the Washington missile was away, they would turn the airplane around in a wide 360-degree turn, line up on the launch point again, and activate the autosequencer for the second missile. They had run this checklist hundreds of times in training. Everyone knew what was next in the sequence.

Slowly, Petrov said, "Missile master arm."

It seemed like an eternity before Itzkoff responded. "Armed back here, green light on one . . . and on two," he finally said, his voice barely audible.

"Warhead master key inserted up here."

"Warhead master key inserted back here."

"Two minutes," said Sheptak.

"Stand by to turn keys on my five-second count . . . mark! Five . . . four . . . three . . . two . . . one . . . mark! Key turned. Green light up here."

They were required to turn keys within five seconds of each other to arm the weapons, but Petrov heard no confirmation from the compartment behind him. He waited a few heartbeats, then turned his key back to standby. "Warhead master key back in standby. Arkady, what's the problem?" he asked.

"I—I can't—I can't do it!" sobbed Itzkoff. For a moment there were the unmistakable sounds of a scuffle. "Nooo!" he moaned. "Please!" Then followed the click of a microphone being disconnected, and another one connecting.

"Warhead master key inserted back here," said Orshansky. "Let's get this over with!"

"Roger. Five seconds . . . mark! Five . . . four . . . three . . . two . . . one . . . mark! Key turned. Green light up here."

"Key turned, green light back here, and . . . there's a confirm light on the system."

"Confirm light up here," said Petrov. "One minute to go."

SUDS 22
THE F-15, OVER NEBRASKA

Mark Matthews welcomed the opportunity to relieve the monotony of the cross-country flight. He powered up the F-15's radar, expecting to see one target at forty miles range. Instead, he was painting two definite targets that appeared to be flying together in formation.

"Kansas City, Suds two-two, I have a radar contact at one o'clock for thirty-nine miles. Did you say it's a Cessna Citation?"

"That's affirmative, Suds two-two, or that's what our information indicates."

"Roger, stand by."

Matthews activated the target-designator control. As the radar achieved a lock-on, the computer evaluated the target ahead. *It can't be. The computer on this thing's screwed up! Let's break lock and take a look at the other guy.*

PIEKARSKI'S TU-95

"Launch shackle safety locks," commanded Piekarski.

"Released on one, and on two," responded the launch officer. "Standing by for master release and autosequencer."

"AI radar!" screamed the EO suddenly. "Definitely an F-15! He's in target-search mode, but he's close!"

"Damn!" swore Piekarski. "What's happening with Petrov?"

"They just called one minute."

"Shit!" shouted the colonel. "Do we have radar contact on the F-15?"

"Yes, sir. He's inside his launch parameters. He has us locked up! No indications of a launch, though. Jammers are in standby with green lights across the board. Do you want me to . . . wait! He just broke lock."

Piekarski wiped sweat from his forehead. *How could the Americans know we're here?* They had to complete the mission but would need to wait for Petrov's launch confirmation. *Or do we?* "Stand by to go full defensive mode on the jamming package," commanded the colonel. "Let me know immediately if he locks us up again and goes into missile-tracking mode."

THE SU-57

"I'm afraid there's some bad news," said Bachvaroff calmly. "We're being looked at by an AI radar. India band, APG-70 type. Has to be an F-15."

"What quadrant?" asked Ridgik.

"One o'clock, and close. It's not us he's looking at. My guess is all hell is breaking loose in our comrade's cockpit. Petrov is one minute to launch."

"I see no reason why we shouldn't power up our own radar," said Ridgik, his voice all business now. "Let's see what's looking at us."

"Radar is on and . . . he's searching again. This time it's us he's lighting up. Stand by . . . I have him on radar, right one o'clock, seventy kilometers. We are inside his missile parameters."

SUDS 22

What the fuck's happening? shouted Matthews's mind as he struggled to process his computer's reading, which showed a Bear bomber and Su-57. He was now also being looked at by Russian radars. *And over the middle of Nebraska!* He decided to select radar missile and go for a lock-on.

Matthews locked up the lead target once again, and the radar scope instantly went black with electronic countermeasures jamming spikes.

He pressed his transmit button. "Kansas City, Suds two-two, confirm this target is a single Cessna Citation."

"That's confirmed," Keith answered. "All I know is that's how we worked him. Then he canceled IFR, descended to sixteen thousand five hundred feet, and turned off his transponder. If he's still at sixteen thousand five hundred, he's violating FAA regulations with his transponder off. Does any of that check?"

"Well," replied Matthews as he worked the radar, trying to beat the ECM, "they are at sixteen-five. I'm breaking them out as a flight of two and I'm getting ECM from the lead aircraft."

PIEKARSKI'S TU-95

"He just went to acquisition mode!" screamed Piekarski's EO. "Could be a launch!"

"Keep jamming him, dammit!" shouted Piekarski. "Nav, time to the launch point?"

"Two minutes and five seconds, assuming confirmation from Petrov," replied the launch officer.

"What's the word, EO?"

"I broke his lock, and he's working to beat the ECM. Range is now sixty kilometers, and he's headed right for us. It's just a matter of time until he gets a burn-through."

"Keep at it," said Piekarski, his voice high from excitement. "Nav, we'll activate the autosequencer the instant we hear from Petrov, and we'll launch both missiles thirty seconds apart. We will see if this American can knock down two cruise missiles."

CHAPTER TWENTY-FIVE

TIME TO WEAPONS RELEASE: 0 HR, 0 MIN, 40 SEC
PETROV'S TU-95

"Master release on my count," said Petrov. "Five seconds . . . mark!" He counted down from five. "Master released up here."

"Released back here," responded Orshansky. "Autosequencer activation . . . ready . . . now and counting! Thirty seconds to launch."

"Roger, thirty seconds," said Petrov. "Confirm all status lights green on missile number one."

"Status lights green. Twenty-five seconds. I'll advise Piekarski we're in the final countdown."

"Roger. Do you have the coded message ready for him when we have confirmation of missile engine start?"

"That's affirmative. Twenty seconds."

Well, it's a done deal, thought Petrov as he watched the autosequencer tick off the seconds to the Washington missile launch.

SUDS 22

Looks like a possible burn-through, thought Matthews as he continued to work with the ECM-emitting target. *On the nose for thirty miles. And once again the computer says Bear bomber.*

"Kansas City, Suds two-two, we should figure out who these guys are. I'm getting heavy ECM from the lead aircraft, and my computer is saying both aircraft are Russian!"

PIEKARSKI'S TU-95

"He has a steady lock-on!" shouted Piekarski's EO.

"Nav, what's the time to launch?" asked Piekarski excitedly. He hated that he had to wait until Petrov dropped his first missile before he could launch his own.

"One minute and thirty-five seconds, sir. Petrov just advised they are on autosequencer for the first missile."

"Dammit!" moaned Piekarski. "Tail gunner, is the Sukhoi still with us?"

"That's affirmative. He's wide to the right and about a kilometer in trail."

The colonel broke radio silence. "Ridgik! There's an F-15 tracking us, on the nose for forty kilometers. We cannot beat him with ECM. Get him off of us!"

THE SU-57

"Valentin, the F-15 is jeopardizing the mission. Petrov is in the final countdown."

"Okay, you convinced me," Ridgik said. "Lock up the F-15. I have missile one selected, master arm is on. Confirm light on missile one."

"Confirm light on missile one back here. There's the lock-up, and we're dead in the center of the launch envelope."

"Roger, I'm coming slightly left. Trigger's going down."

PETROV'S TU-95

Petrov wished the countdown in his ears was a dream.

"Five... four... three... two... one... zero! Missile is away!" called Orshansky. The airplane shuddered slightly as the shackles opened and the Washington-bound Kh-55 dropped away. "I have a confirm light on wing deployment," observed Orshansky. "Standing by for missile engine start."

PIEKARSKI'S TU-95

The flash from the R-77M rocket motor momentarily turned night into day. Piekarski flinched and wondered if he was still holding on to a whole airplane. "What was that?" he screamed over the interphone. "Are we hit?"

"Relax, Colonel," responded the copilot. "That was an air-to-air missile leaving the Su-57."

"Get him!" yelled Piekarski as he watched the missile streak into the night sky "Nav, what's the word from Petrov?"

"They should have launched the first missile ten seconds ago. I'm standing by for confirmation. We are at one minute to launch. Ready... mark!"

Piekarski was barely keeping his fear under control, but he felt he was within seconds of total release. The digital clock clicked off the last minute, guaranteeing his place in history.

SUDS 22

Mark Matthews saw the telltale flash of a missile launch at his twelve o'clock. A couple of seconds into the launch he determined the plume—getting bigger but staying in the same spot on his windscreen—was targeted on him. The Eagle shuttered as he racked it into a hard right turn and jammed the throttles into afterburner.

"OVER-G! OVER-G!" advised Bitchin' Betty, the female computer voice that was part of the F-15's master warning system.

"No shit," murmured Matthews as he strained under the g-load. "*Run, baby, run!*" he shouted as he completed the 180-degree turn and unloaded the Eagle to zero-g for best acceleration. The radar warning tone was still there, steady and incessant. "C'mon," coaxed Matthews. "It's time to go fast! Go, go, *go!*"

The missile's overtake was just enough to catch the accelerating F-15. The last three hundred meters took several seconds, but the proximity fuse in the R-55M sensed the presence of Matthews's Eagle and sent the signal to detonate the warhead.

It came as a slight "whump" in Matthews's cockpit. It felt as though both engines had compressor-stalled.

"WARNING . . . ENGINE FIRE, RIGHT . . . WARNING . . . ENGINE FIRE, RIGHT."

Dammit! thought Matthews as the engine went to zero thrust and the rapid deceleration slammed him into the straps. "Right throttle's coming to cutoff and—"

He saw a flash in the windscreen's bow-mounted rearview mirror. The entire rear of the fighter was a flaming torch.

"WARNING . . . ENGINE FIRE, LEFT . . . WARNING . . ENGINE FIRE, LEFT."

The F-15 began a roll to the right which Matthews was unable to stop, despite full-left aileron and rudder.

"Mayday! Mayday!" yelled Matthews into his mask mic. "They shot a missile! I've been hit! Going down!"

Matthews's eyes began to sting as the cockpit filled with smoke.

"WARNING . . . WARNING."

Matthews could see neither the instruments nor the horizon outside the smoke-filled cockpit, so he assumed the best body position possible, grabbed the yellow arches down by his thighs, and pulled the ejection handles up with all his might. He felt an explosion of air as the canopy departed the aircraft. The last thing he heard before his butt was slammed into the ejection seat by the force of the rocket motor was the voice of Bitchin' Betty.

"WARNING . . . WARNING."

PIEKARSKI'S TU-95

Cheers broke out in Piekarski's bomber as they saw the F-15 explode in the distance. "They got the bastard!" yelled the copilot.

"Fifteen seconds until we go on autosequencer," said the navigator, "but still no word from Petrov."

THE SU-57

"Nice shooting," said Bachvaroff. "I was beginning to wonder if the missile was going to hack his one-hundred-eighty-degree turn."

"Yeah, me too," replied Ridgik. "Well, Anton, I guess we fired the first shot in the big one, huh? Should we press on toward bigger and better things?"

"Sounds good, but I still don't have a launch confirmation from Petrov. Their bird should have been in the air a minute ago."

PETROV'S TU-95

"What's the word, Vitalie?" asked Petrov quietly.

"I have no confirmation of missile engine start," replied the EO. Petrov pondered the words. *No engine start? Then this is over.*

"Then it ought to self-destruct shortly."

"It should have already done that," replied the EO. "The master program allows a minute for engine start, and if it doesn't start, it's supposed to self-destruct."

"It's been in the air a minute and ten seconds. Misha, can you still see it?"

"Affirmative, sir," replied the tail gunner. "It's gliding down toward the lake. Fuel is still streaming like during the engine-start sequence. Looks like a dud to me."

"What happens to the warhead if it doesn't self-destruct?" asked Petrov. His question was met with silence.

"The warhead will break up when the missile hits the ground," answered Itzkoff, now plugged back into the intercom. "The warhead will not detonate without confirmation of engine start. It sounds like a bad master start-relay, which controls both the engine start and detonation sequence."

"Thank you, Arkady," said Petrov, suddenly exhausted. "I guess that's it, gentlemen. We are in abort mode. Vitalie, send the abort code to Piekarski and get confirmation. Be sure you also get a response from the Sukhoi crew. Arkady, if you can handle it, I would like to request your assistance in jettisoning the other missile."

"I can handle it," replied Itzkoff. "I'm sorry about—"

"Forget it, Arkady!" commanded Petrov as he wracked the Tu-95 around to set up the jettison run over Launch Point Alpha.

PIEKARSKI'S TU-95

The clock on Piekarski's overhead panel read forty seconds. As the F-15 spiraled down in a ball of fire, he said, "Master release on my count," trying to make the tone of his voice communicate the honor he felt. "Five seconds . . . mark! Five . . . four—"

"Colonel," interrupted the launch officer, "we just got the abort message from Petrov."

"...three...two...one...mark! Master release depressed up here. Standing by for autosequencer on my count. Five seconds ... mark! Five—"

"*Colonel!*" screamed the copilot as he shook Piekarski's shoulder. "*Stop!* It's an abort! They just got the word from Petrov!"

Something wasn't right. Somebody said something about an abort. "Did you say Petrov transmitted the abort message?"

"That's affirmative, sir," replied the launch officer.

"Read me the message."

"The message is 'the pelican crashed in the sea.'"

"Did you ask for a confirmation?"

"Affirmative. It was confirmed and properly authenticated. We are aborting, sir. I'm standing by to activate the emergency abort switch to deactivate the missiles on your count." Piekarski said nothing. "Colonel Piekarski, sir, I am standing by for the emergency abort switch," repeated the launch officer, his voice steady and authoritative.

The pilot riding in the zampolit seat, obviously alarmed, got to his feet.

"Roger," replied Piekarski with a heavy sigh. "Emergency abort switch on my count. Five seconds ... mark!"

THE SU-57

"Did you say Petrov aborted?" asked Ridgik quietly.

"That's affirmative," replied Bachvaroff. "The word is 'the pelican crashed in the sea.' I confirmed and authenticated it."

"Shit! And we had to shoot down an F-15. We better get some gas and get the hell out of here."

"Would you like me to call our comrade and tell him we'll be there shortly?"

"Yes. Be sure he knows we're going to want the quickest turn possible and pass the abort message to him."

TIME SINCE ABORT: 0 HRS, 3 MIN
CHATMAN'S CITATION

Bobby Chatman's self-imposed five-minute limit had long since passed, but he was still holding short of runway 04 at Reagan Washington National Airport. The tower frequency had been so busy he couldn't get a word in edgewise and almost decided to take off without a clearance. He hesitated just long enough, losing the opportunity as other traffic landed and departed. But it looked like another opening was coming. *Okay,* thought the evangelist. *I'm just going to do it.*

"Citation zero-seven Xray, Washington tower. Taxi into position and hold runway zero-four. Be ready for an immediate takeoff."

"Outstanding!" Chatman blurted as he maneuvered the jet onto the runway. *Now, to hell with noise and speed restrictions. It's time to get the hell out of here!*

RUSSIAN EMBASSY
HAVANA, CUBA

Viktor Darginsky couldn't believe his ears. The HF radio transmissions had been slightly garbled, but he distinctly heard the coded message for an abort on the Washington weapon. He also heard an authentication, which he was able to verify from his copy of the mission packet. The Russian agent's mind raced as he considered what steps needed to be accomplished immediately. Notifying Nikolai Kozlov of the abort was of primary importance, and he needed to advise Lucifer and his cohorts to cover their tracks.

"Excuse me," said Darginsky to the senior communication specialist. "I was wondering if you could send a coded message to Moscow for me."

"Certainly, sir. If you write it out, I'll transmit it immediately."

As Darginsky scribbled down the coded message, his mind kept returning to Petrov and the abort. "You had better not be responsible for this, Gregori," he muttered under his breath, "or I'll see to your execution."

BUGGS ISLAND, VIRGINIA

"Come on," coaxed the young man as he urged his female companion toward the steps of his parents' Buggs Island Lake cabin. "We'll get a fire going, then we'll open the wine."

"I don't know," said the girl. "Are you sure your parents won't mind?"

"They can't mind what they don't know."

"Well, let's go look at the lake first. It's so pretty in the moonlight. Listen. Hear that whistle?"

They both turned to face the source of the strange sound. "Look, it's a small airplane," said the teenage boy. "And it's going to land in the water."

The young man watched the approaching aircraft touch the surface of the lake, bounce once, then impact the water just off the end of his parents' pier.

The couple fell to the ground as the craft crashed into the pier, disappearing under the wooden structure with a huge splash.

"Jesus!" said the young man. "Are you okay?"

"Yes," replied the girl as she stood up. "Do you think there were people in it?"

"I don't know, but we'd better call the police . . . what's that?"

"What?" asked the girl as she looked up in the direction her boyfriend was pointing. "Wow! It looks like fireworks."

"Or something blowing up."

SUDS 22

Mark Matthews had no idea it would be so quiet. After the explosive ejection from the aircraft, and the tumbling free fall to fifteen thousand feet where his parachute opened, the letdown seemed peaceful by comparison. He saw the fireball where the F-15 impacted several miles away.

As he looked over snow-covered fields below, he hoped his locator beacon was at that moment transmitting its eerie tone over the emergency frequency. Then he looked up. He saw black silhouettes against the full moon, running without navigation lights. There was no mistaking the shape of the one, and the deep rumble of its turboprop engines. As he hung in the sky, he saw twin afterburner plumes on the other as it accelerated. The computer was right. A Bear and a Su-57—here. In the middle of Nebraska. *I have to tell somebody!*

Matthews returned his focus to the ground rushing up to meet him. He realized the terrain wasn't nearly as flat as it appeared initially. He was coming down into a steep ravine. The audible "crack" that came the instant he landed signaled a broken leg. As he lay on the frozen ground, the last thing he heard before lapsing into unconsciousness was the faraway sound of turboprop engines.

CHAPTER TWENTY-SIX

TIME SINCE MISSION ABORT: 0 HR, 4 MIN
KANSAS CITY ARTCC

"Suds two-two, Kansas City."

No answer.

Keith Anderson sat stunned. He had watched as the Eagle's radar altitude rapidly decreased until he stopped receiving data. His attempts to contact Suds 22 and Redex 02 had been fruitless. He noticed one of the two Redex contacts was now heading southeast instead of toward 3FWG.

"Still no contact with Suds two-two?" asked Julie, who'd watched the entire sequence.

"Negative," replied Keith. "Did you call Jenko?"

"Yeah. He had to get some relief before he could come over. Is there anything you want me to do?"

"Yes," Keith said. "Go to the area desk and tell the area manager to call air rescue. Tell them we probably have an F-15 down. Tell them its location."

Jenko arrived as Julie left. "What's up, Keith?" he asked as he dragged up a chair. "Julie said y'all might have an aircraft down."

"That's affirmative," said Keith. "I believe an F-15 is down. Do you see that weak primary return there? We worked him earlier as Redex zero-two. It was the usual routing to 3FWG. Supposedly a Citation. Jenko, I know you'll think I've slipped off the edge, but I believe that is a Russian aircraft."

"You're kidding," said the supervisor, smiling.

"No, dammit, I'm not kidding!" Keith replied heatedly. "Pull the radio tapes in my sector from the past ten minutes. You'll hear me ask Suds two-two to check out a target, then you'll hear him respond that the target is jamming him electronically, and then he'll say they look like Russian aircraft. Moments later you'll hear his distress call, and I'm certain he said they fired a missile at him. I'd like someone to take over my sector, and your permission to stay at this console with this primary return until you can listen to the tapes. Trust me! We need to let the military know!"

CHATMAN'S CITATION

"Citation zero-seven Xray, Washington tower, cleared for takeoff, runway zero-four. Wind is calm."

Bobby Chatman slammed the throttles to the wall. *Come on*, he thought, as he willed the jet to go faster. His fear began to ebb upon liftoff. *How far away do I need to be? GO!* he almost said out loud as the airspeed increased.

"Citation zero-seven Xray, Washington departure, turn right heading one-eight-zero, and maintain two hundred ten knots."

"Hell no!" Chatman mumbled as he pointed the jet due east and kept the airspeed on redline.

"Citation zero-seven Xray, Washington. How do you read?"

Chatman ignored the repeated calls. When he was ten miles from Reagan Airport, he began to breathe easier. *We're going to make it!* he shouted in his mind.

PIEKARSKI'S TU-95

"Nav, give me the heading for the jettison site over that lake," said a dejected Josef Piekarski. "We'll jettison the Kh-55s, then get the hell out of US airspace. EO, watch for military radars. There are going to be fighters swarming."

"Roger, Colonel," acknowledged the EO. "All defensive systems are operating normally."

"It was *also* working normally when the F-15 locked us up at forty kilometers," snapped Piekarski. "Nav, can we do the exit run at low-level?"

"Negative, sir. We would run out of fuel before we reached the tanker over the Atlantic. We're going to have to climb. My suggestion is to stay down here until we reach the jettison point, then climb."

"Very well," muttered Piekarski. "But I'm going to take it down as low as we can until we reach the jettison point. We'll make it difficult for search radars until the jettison, then we'll climb as high as possible."

PETROV'S TU-95

"Jettison checklist complete."

"Thank you," acknowledged Petrov. "Let's start a slow climb to conserve fuel. Vitalie, we're climbing back into the high-altitude route structure. Traffic in this area is high. Watch that radar so we can avoid a midair."

"Roger, Major. I have several hits in front of us," said Orshansky, "but they're well clear."

Petrov felt very tired. He hadn't realized the level of stress he'd been under. Mentally, he felt relieved. Thank God he wouldn't have to carry that burden for the rest of his life.

"Arkady," said Petrov quietly, "what was that you said about the master start-relay on the missile?"

"Failure to achieve engine start followed by failure to self-destruct could only be caused by a faulty master start-relay," replied Itzkoff. "They sent out an advisory notice about a similar failure just before we left. Apparently, some uninsulated relays found their way into the Kh-55 assembly line. And remember, sir, the master start-relay controls both the engine start and self-detonation sequence. So that thing was in one piece when it hit the water."

"I remember," Petrov said.

"We were told our missiles were thoroughly tested prior to the mission, but perhaps they were not," Itzkoff added. "It must have been our climb through icing conditions that caused the failure."

"Thank you, Arkady. We'll go home and let the investigators sort it out." Petrov turned to Sheptak. "Vladimir, let's go direct to the Raleigh VOR."

"Raleigh is on the nose for sixty kilometers," said Sheptak after he had completed the turn. "Why Raleigh, Major? Why not avoid large metropolitan cities and the air traffic control radars located there?"

"Because Raleigh is an airline hub, Vladimir. Our first priority is to find a southbound airliner. We're going to hitch a ride."

THE SU-57

"Our comrade is ready for us at the ranch," advised Bachvaroff. "He said to keep the drag chute until we're parked and leave the engines running."

"Excellent," said Ridgik. "How's the weather?"

"Clear skies with light winds from the south. He said to plan an approach from the north, because that's the only end with operational approach lighting."

"Got it. We'll go to the Salina VOR and fly a long straight-in approach." Ridgik voiced the thought that was on both their minds. "Do you suppose he got out okay?"

"I don't know. He had time to eject."

"I hope so. Should we jettison these missiles to lighten our load and fly southbound as high and fast as possible?"

"Not a good idea. The Americans are not going to be pleased

about the loss of the F-15. We may have to fight our way out. I vote for keeping the missiles."

"That makes it unanimous," agreed Ridgik. "Did you advise our comrade at the ranch of the demise of the pelican?"

"Affirmative."

"Good. I show Salina on the nose for thirty-two kilometers. I'm starting down."

"Are you disappointed, Valentin?"

"I'm disappointed our stay in America is going to be so short. Darginsky promised us Texas-style steak, but that's not going to happen."

"Stop—you're making me hungry!" Bachvaroff laughed.

TIME SINCE MISSION ABORT: 0 HR, 5 MIN
WASHINGTON, DC

"Ringmaster, checkpoint two. The building is secure."

"Thank you, checkpoint two," said Darryl McCormick on the FM radio.

Hank Hartley looked around the quiet grounds of the Capitol Building. "What happens now?"

"We're supposed to hold our breath while Phillips delivers his speech," uttered McCormick. "And pray they don't detonate one of those supposed nukes in one of those supposed Mercedes trucks."

"You think the whole thing's a hoax?"

"I don't know, but it stinks to high heaven. That asshole Ron Goodman is responsible for creating this panic, and all he knows is he got a phone call from one of the terrorists."

Hartley shook his head. "How the hell did we get into this mess?"

McCormick snapped her head around to him. "Because we're dumb shits. We don't learn from history. We don't change the way we react. We're too damn complacent!"

McCormick saw the stunned look on his face.

"You talking about the bureau?"

"I'm talking about everything, from the president on down." She paused. "You told me they know that Bear bombers landed in Venezuela last night. Don't you think that's something we should be concerned about? Nobody gives a shit."

TIME SINCE MISSION ABORT: 0 HR, 10 MIN
KREMLIN COMMAND POST

Nikolai Kozlov had been watching the American broadcast for the past twenty minutes. He wanted to know the exact second the fool, Andrew Phillips, ceased to exist. By his watch, the broadcast should have been terminating any second.

"Mr. Speaker, honorable colleagues of the House and Senate, distinguished members of the Supreme Court, and honored guests. It is my distinct pleasure to give you the president of the United States."

"Any second," murmured Kozlov as he watched Phillips enter the chamber of the US House of Representatives to tumultuous applause.

"Excuse me, sir," said the major who was acting as his secretary. "This just came in, for your eyes only. It is immediate action from an agent code named Gabriel."

Kozlov took the sealed envelope. He read while continuously cutting his eyes back to the television. The second sentence stunned him.

> *Greetings from Havana. The news is bad. 'The pelican crashed in the sea' for reasons unknown. I personally heard it transmitted and authenticated. Sincere regrets. Gabriel.*

Kozlov couldn't believe they'd come this far to fail. His survival instincts took over and he began planning. Covering their tracks was important for everybody involved in LUCIFER/INBLUE. The president of the United States was delivering his State of the Union address, so how serious could things be?

He scribbled two orders and passed them to the general in charge of the command post. One ordered the recall of the submarine fleet, while the other ordered the return to Russia of the transport aircraft bound for Cuba and Venezuela. He then coded a personal message for Darginsky. Consisting of only five words, it read: *We must cover our tracks.*

TIME SINCE MISSION ABORT: 0 HR, 15 MIN
CHATMAN'S CITATION

Something's wrong, Chatman thought. *Unless they're really running late, I should have already seen the detonation.*

"Where are we, Chatman?" asked Dan Hawkins, who was leaning into the cockpit. "Is that Philadelphia?"

"Yes, Senator. We should be in New Haven in a half hour."

"I thought we'd never get out of Washington."

"I was beginning to wonder too," agreed Chatman.

He kept the Citation running on the airspeed redline. *I've got to get on the ground and find out what happened.*

TIME SINCE MISSION ABORT: 0 HR, 17 MIN
KANSAS CITY ARTCC

"Shit! He's fading again," swore Keith Anderson. "Still heading one-one-zero. He's down low. He's pretty much following the reverse of the route up. Get Wichita Approach on the landline."

"Roger," replied Julie Brady.

"If he follows the original route, it'll be Tulsa next."

"Wichita's got him," said Julie. "He's not going to Tulsa, though. He's holding that one-one-zero heading. He's boring right through the final approach course for Wichita Dwight D. Eisenhower National Airport. They asked an A-320 on final approach if they saw him when he was just two miles away, but the crew saw nothing. He must be running lights out. Hold it . . . Wichita says he's fifteen southeast of them."

"I got him!" shouted Keith. "Tell Wichita to stay with him. Give Memphis Center a call. Tell them what's coming. We're going to lose him in another hundred and fifty miles."

"You were right, Keith," confided Jenko quietly as he bent down to study Keith's radar scope. "The F-15 pilot distinctly said his computer indicated Russian aircraft, and he said they fired a missile at him. Search and rescue is on the way."

"What do we do about this bastard?" Keith asked, pointing at the blip on the scope.

"I don't know. We've always planned for the military to tell *us* what to do. The area manager is talking to FAA headquarters in Washington. Just try to keep him in radar contact."

Jenko shook his head. "We have always pointed our radars offshore to see any bad guys coming. September 11, 2001 made us start looking inward, but we haven't done enough. By the way," continued the supervisor, "Tom Miller is on your original sector, and he reported that something landed at 3FWG. Primary contact only. He's going to let us know if there's any more activity up there."

TIME SINCE MISSION ABORT: 0 HR, 30 MIN
3FWG, THE KANSAS RANCH AIRFIELD

"Greetings, comrades!" yelled Michael into the headset he'd plugged into the belly jack of the Su-57. The fighter was taller than he remembered as he had strained to reach the exterior intercom plug. The scream of the fighter's engines flowed with Michael's voice into the crew's helmets. "Welcome to America!"

"Nice to be here," replied Ridgik. "Just wish we had better news."

"Me too," agreed the SVR agent. "I'm all set to fuel you. I'll have you out of here in no time."

"Can you believe this setup?" asked Bachvaroff after the SVR agent disconnected his headset. "Your own private runway and . . . look at that jet over there. I'd say we're in the wrong business."

"He must be having a problem," Ridgik said. "We're not taking fuel."

They were interrupted by the click of the SVR agent's microphone being plugged in again. "I'm sorry, but I need help. I didn't realize the refueling compartment was so far off the ground, and I'm not strong enough to lift the hose up and twist it to make the connection. There's nobody else here, so one of you is going to have to come down."

"That's going to be difficult with the engines running," replied Ridgik.

"How about if your back seater steps onto the wing and drops down onto the hood of the truck?"

"What do you think, Anton?" Ridgik yelled over the engine noise.

"I'll give it a shot," Bachvaroff replied as he started to unstrap. "I need to go outside, stretch my legs, and take a leak anyway."

"You bastard," laughed Ridgik. "How did you know that was on my mind?"

"I know you. Why don't you just stand up and hang it over the side? Think about how much better you'll feel."

"You're right. Be careful going over that wing."

As Bachvaroff helped Michael with the hose, he saw Ridgik standing in his cockpit, relieving himself over the side. He stayed on the ground until the refueling was complete, then climbed back up the hood of the truck and onto the left wing. Bending low for balance, he walked across the Su-57's wing and slid into the back cockpit.

"Okay, I'm all done," Michael yelled over the interphone, "but I need to ask you guys a question so we can plan our immediate actions. Did you knock down the Airborne Command Post?"

"Negative. Piekarski's bomber was being threatened by an F-15, so we eliminated the threat."

"You destroyed an F-15?"

"The last time we saw it, it was a big fireball," said Ridgik.

"Shit . . . there are going to be some pissed off Americans," said Michael. "You need to get going. I'll tell you one thing, though. I never figured I'd see a Su-57 parked on this ramp."

"Well, I never thought I'd land in the middle of the USA for fuel, either," laughed Ridgik. "Is a departure to the south okay?"

"Yes. Just come out of burner as soon as you break ground. The locals are used to jets here, but they've never heard afterburners."

Minutes later Ridgik locked the brakes for the engine run-up. "Cuba here we come," he said as he released the brakes and went into full afterburner.

Michael stood, with his fingers in his ears, at the edge of the runway to watch the Sukhoi's departure. The fighter roared by, accelerating quickly. As it broke ground, the landing gear retracted, and the afterburners winked out.

TIME SINCE MISSION ABORT: 0 HR, 45 MIN
PETROV'S TU-95
50 MILES SOUTH OF RALEIGH

"He's still dead-on the Q87 airway and climbing," said Orshansky. "We're out of flight level 310, tracking direct to the Florence VOR."

"What's his range?" asked Petrov.

"Five kilometers and we're gaining slowly," replied the EO. "If he doesn't pull away when he levels off, this may be our man."

"And if we don't start contrailing," muttered Petrov. "Vladimir, I have the aircraft. Give me everything you can on the power. I'm going to try to close it up to close-trail formation. We'll get right in there like we do to refuel. To anybody's radar, we'll be a single contact. We'll follow him all the way to Florida. When he starts down, we'll turn out over the Atlantic."

"You don't think the Americans suspect anything yet?" asked Sheptak as he adjusted the power levers.

"Why should they? We haven't done anything to arouse suspicions. I think we could just fly out of the country since we're an intermittent primary return that nobody cares about. Just in case, though, we'll use this airliner to cover our exit."

TIME SINCE MISSION ABORT: 1 HR, 22 MIN
KANSAS CITY ARTCC

"Tom Miller just got a primary return on something departing 3FWG," reported Julie excitedly. "It's a fast mover. Looks like he's going direct to Wichita. Tom will keep you posted."

"Excellent," said Keith. "I just lost my target. There he is again. He's been fading in and out for the last few minutes. He's got to be pretty low. Did you get Memphis on the line?"

"Yeah, they're standing by. Here comes Jenko."

"There's not much progress to report," advised the supervisor. "Nobody with real decision-making capability is working in Washington, but the duty controller finally gave us the number for the Eastern Air Defense Sector at Griffiss Air Force Base in New York. Nobody's ready to believe we're dealing with Russian aircraft, and nobody's willing to take responsibility for declaring an emergency. Jesus, it feels like 9/11 all over again." Keith and Julie looked at him with questioning expressions. "The information," he continued, "went from bottom to top, and the top didn't know what to do with it." He pointed at the scope. "Do you still have radar contact with the target in question?"

"Yeah, that's him there," said Keith as he pointed to the scope. "He's just approaching the Lake of the Cherokees near Tulsa. He'll be entering

Memphis Center's airspace shortly. Tom had a fast mover out of 3FWG a few minutes ago. I think we ought to try to track him, too."

The supervisor studied the scope. "I'm with you, Keith. I think it's time the military helped us identify those tracks. Let me see what's happening at the area desk."

TIME SINCE MISSION ABORT: 1 HR, 27 MIN
PIEKARSKI'S TU-95
LAKE OF THE CHEROKEES, OKLAHOMA

"Missile jettison master arm."

"Safety wire broken, cover up . . . armed on one and on two . . . two green lights back here."

"And up here. Launch shackle safety locks."

"Released on one and on two. Standing by for autosequenced jettison of both birds, ten seconds apart. I have a green light on both detonation packages."

"Roger, autosequencer in five seconds . . . mark! Five . . . four . . . three . . . two . . . one . . . mark! Autosequencer activated."

"Tail gun, I would like a visual confirmation of detonation," requested Piekarski.

"Tail gun copies."

"As soon as we dump the missiles, we'll be climbing to flight level 410," said Piekarski to the copilot. "It's time to start conserving fuel."

"I have them both in sight," confirmed the tail gunner after both missiles were jettisoned. "They're both dropping toward the lake."

"Here comes climb power," said Piekarski.

They were passing 3,800 meters when the first Kh-55M self-destructed below them. Ten seconds later, the second missile destroyed itself with an audible "whump."

"Both missiles detonated and destroyed, right in the middle of the lake," advised the tail gunner.

"Good," uttered Piekarski. "Confirm no acquisition radars working us?"

"That's affirmative, sir."

"Very strange," mused Piekarski. "I figured the sky would be full of fighters by now."

TIME SINCE MISSION ABORT: 1 HR, 30 MIN
KANSAS CITY ARTCC

"I've lost the target just east of Tulsa by Lake of the Cherokees," said Keith dejectedly. "What's the word from Memphis?"

"I'm talking to them now," said Julie. "The controller says he has a weak primary target just south of Razorback VOR. They're going to try to stay with him. Have you had any luck with that departure out of 3FWG?"

"Just occasional weak primary hits," Keith replied. "This target's a much smaller aircraft than the first one, and he's moving fast. Ground speed is almost six hundred knots. Citations don't go that fast. He's backtracking the original route. He must be up high because they can't find him on their approach radars."

"You're not going to believe this," said Jenko, walking up. "The area manager is now talking to the director of operations at Griffiss. They're sending us up their chain of command, one level at a time, making us repeat the entire story about the F-15."

TIME SINCE MISSION ABORT: 1 HR, 35 MIN
TWEED-NEW HAVEN AIRPORT, CONNECTICUT

"Senator, watch your step," said Bobby Chatman as he opened the door of the Citation. "If it's all right, I'm not going to accompany you to the hospital. I have some pressing matters to take care of."

"Sure, Chatman, I understand," replied Dan Hawkins as he walked toward the general aviation terminal. "I'll get an Uber to the hospital. Thanks a lot for the ride. Your offer took me by surprise, seeing as we don't see eye to eye on a lot of things. I appreciate it more than you know."

"Senator, you're very welcome. My prayers will be with your son."

"Yeah, right," smiled the senator awkwardly as they entered the lobby. "Looks like your brother in the faith is doing fine." He nodded at the television where Andrew Phillips filled the screen. "I was concerned that Washington might be vaporized tonight," said Hawkins with a wink, "but I guess God's watching over it after all."

Chatman thought about Hawkins's last remark as he pulled out his phone and dialed the number for the Bay St. Louis farm.

"Yes?" Alex answered tersely.

"It's me," Chatman began. "I'm in New Haven, looking at a television with Andrew Phillips's smiling face and trying to figure out why he isn't dead. What happened?"

"Beats me, Bobby. The word is 'the pelican crashed in the sea' for unknown reasons. The Sukhoi crew passed that word to Michael shortly after the scheduled launch time."

Chatman pondered the impact of Alex's words. "Well, damn!" he finally exclaimed. "There's been no other word from the bombers?"

"That's correct . . . as far as I know. Michael just called a few minutes ago with some interesting news, though."

"I'm listening."

"The Su-57 landed at the Kansas ranch as planned. He refueled it and they blasted off almost twenty minutes ago. Michael questioned the crew and they confirmed they shot down an F-15 that threatened Piekarski's bomber."

Chatman's mind raced as he evaluated all he had just learned. Finally, he responded. "Here's what we do. For now, we lie low and see if they're successful getting out of the country. In the meantime, we need to start covering our tracks. You stay put for now. I'll call

Michael and get him started on a few projects."

Chatman broke the connection and started to dial the number for the Kansas ranch but changed his mind and hung up the phone. There was no reason for haste. Phillips would take time to assimilate the information that's coming to him.

Bobby Chatman walked into the deserted crew lounge, poured himself a cup of coffee, and settled down in front of the television. He looked at his watch. In another hour and a half they would be out of the country. For now, he'd just watch and wait. *An F-15?* he thought, as he watched Andrew Phillips raise his hands to quiet the applause. *What the hell went wrong?*

CHAPTER TWENTY-SEVEN

TIME SINCE MISSION ABORT: 1 HR, 35 MIN
JOINT RESERVE BASE NEW ORLEANS

"Houston departure, Jazz zero-two is a flight of two F-15s with you out of five thousand feet for ten thousand on an active air scramble."

"Roger, Jazz zero-two, fly heading zero-one-zero. Climb and maintain flight level 250, and I need your maximum rate of climb."

"Cleared flight level 250, Jazz zero-two. Do you have any info on this scramble? The air defense people didn't have any other information except to get into your airspace and help you identify something."

"We're working on that. For now, I need a maximum climb to get you over inbound traffic."

"Roger," replied the F-15 flight lead. "Jazz zero-two flight, burners . . . now!"

TIME SINCE MISSION ABORT: 1 HR, 40 MIN
KANSAS CITY ARTCC

"Fort Worth's on the line," said Julie. "They're tracking that fast mover. He's weak and intermittent, but still backtracking along the original route."

"Good," uttered a weary Keith Anderson. "I guess we've done all we can. Here comes Jenko again."

"Okay, kids," said the supervisor excitedly. "The F-15 pilot is lucky he ejected about a hundred and fifty miles from Warren Air Force Base in Cheyenne, Wyoming. They got a helicopter out to him pretty quick. He broke his leg on landing, but other than that, he's okay. As soon as he got off the chopper, he called the air defense people. Based on his story, they're finally scrambling some fighters to identify those tracks."

"Outstanding!" Julie cheered.

"It's about time," grumbled Keith.

"The word was they're going to scramble a pair of F-15s out of New Orleans, and another pair out of Eglin, on the assumption that he's heading for Cuba."

"So, what happens next?" Keith asked.

"We wait," replied Jenko. "It's out of our hands now. My compliments to the two of you for an outstanding job tonight."

"You might not think so when you hear the entire story," said Keith dejectedly. "I think it's time I told it. Is there somewhere we can talk privately?"

"Sure. We'll go to the facility manager's office. Don't worry, Keith. It can't be that serious."

"Oh, yes it can. If you don't mind, I'd like Julie to be a witness."

Jenko studied Keith's face. "Keith, if that's the case, you don't need a witness, you need a lawyer."

TIME SINCE MISSION ABORT: 1 HR, 45 MIN
EGLIN AIR FORCE BASE, FLORIDA

"Shark zero-three and zero-four, scramble! Initial heading three-three-zero, climb flight level 360."

"Shark zero-three, check," said Major Robertson.

"Two!" replied Rushton, as the pair of Eagles taxied quickly toward the runway.

"Eglin tower, Shark zero-three flight's with you, active air scramble."

"Roger, Shark zero-three. Winds are calm, change to departure. Runway twelve cleared for takeoff."

"Cleared for takeoff, zero-three flight, channel four, go!"

"Two!"

The two F-15s spooled up to takeoff power. Both Robertson and Rushton had been totally surprised when the Klaxon went off. They were even more surprised at their instructions. One thought kept running through Robertson's mind: *Why are we being sent northwest over the US mainland instead of out over the Gulf?*

"Shark zero-three, check!"

"Two!"

"Eglin departure, Shark zero-three is requesting confirmation that initial scramble heading is three-three-zero degrees. We're going *north?*"

"You're loud and clear, Shark zero-three. We asked Jacksonville Center the same question and they confirmed the heading."

"Roger," replied Robertson. "Two, take twenty seconds spacing. Releasing brakes, now!"

TIME SINCE MISSION ABORT: 1 HR, 47 MIN
THE SU-57
THIRTY MILES SOUTHEAST OF TULSA

"I just got the empty lights on the drop tanks," said Ridgik. "We're doing well on fuel."

"I was surprised we could lug these drop tanks up to flight level 370," replied Bachvaroff. "We might even be able to make it to flight level 410 now."

"Sounds good," said the Su-57 pilot as he started the climb. "We need to make it as difficult as possible for anyone looking for us. If we drop the tanks, it will be much harder to see us on radar."

"But, Anton, we're still over land. If we drop them now, they'll be found, and the Americans will know for sure a Russian fighter was deep in their airspace."

"I know," Ridgik agreed. "Let's wait until we're over water."

"I think we're fat enough on fuel to take an indirect route back to Cuba to confuse them. Direct Dallas, then Houston, and out over the Gulf of Mexico to San Julián. Dallas and Houston are large airline hubs. That means lots of traffic to mingle with."

"Multiple radar contacts are going to make it difficult for any interceptor crew to identify us. Sounds like a good idea. I'm turning direct Dallas," said Ridgik, as he banked the fighter to the right while continuing to nurse the climb.

"Anton, the Aeroflot captain told us all aircraft, including scrambled interceptors, would be controlled by civilian air traffic controllers, who had little to no training in working military fighters in combat conditions. So, would it make sense for us to monitor the appropriate radio frequency?"

"Maybe. The US fighters will probably be on the ultra-high frequencies. We don't know what those frequencies are, but we might be able to hear one side of the conversation on the civilian very-high frequencies. Should I set that up? I have a list of VHF frequencies by location."

"Please do."

TIME SINCE MISSION ABORT: 1 HR, 50 MIN
PIEKARSKI'S TU-95
FORTY MILES SOUTHEAST OF LITTLE ROCK

"You need to come right to one-two-zero for direct to the refueling point," said the navigator. "As a reminder, sir, we will exit the United States just south of Jacksonville. My recommendation is to stay high as long as possible, then exit the Atlantic Coastal ADIZ at low-level. If the Americans are looking for us, it's the best plan to avoid detection and conserve fuel."

"Sounds good," said Piekarski. "We have to cross that cold front again. I would prefer to fly above all that weather if possible. "EO, any sign of American fighters?"

"Negative, sir. We're only being looked at by air traffic control radars."

"Thanks. Keep me posted."

TIME SINCE MISSION ABORT: 1 HR, 51 MIN
JAZZ FLIGHT
SOUTHEAST OF DALLAS

"Fort Worth Center, Jazz zero-two is with you, flight level 280, assigned heading three-four-zero."

"Roger, Jazz zero-two. Heading three-four-zero is still good."

"Fort Worth, can you confirm we're to identify an unknown target?"

"That's affirmative. We've been tracking this target in primary return only for almost an hour. I don't know why the military is interested in him. He currently bears three-five-zero for one hundred fourteen nautical miles. Ground speed is five hundred fifty knots, so we're assuming he's up high. He appears to be going direct to the Maverick VOR, and we expect you'll meet him head-on in the vicinity of Dallas."

"Jazz zero-two copies."

"Jesus!" moaned the F-15D back seater. "Talk about a needle in a haystack! My scope's covered with targets between us and Dallas. How do we know which one?"

"Shit if I know," replied the front seater. "And after that burner climb, we aren't going to be able to stay up here very long."

TIME SINCE MISSION ABORT: 1 HR, 52 MIN
SHARK FLIGHT
SOUTH OF MONTGOMERY, ALABAMA

"Atlanta Center, Shark zero-three. Do you know anything about the scramble we're on?"

"Very little, Shark zero-three. There's a target up around Greenwood, Mississippi, that the military's interested in. Memphis is trying to track the target in primary return only. He's about a hundred and twenty miles at your twelve o'clock."

"What's his altitude?"

"Unknown. His ground speed is four hundred five knots, and he's been holding a steady one-two-zero heading for the past several minutes."

"Roger, Atlanta, Shark zero-three copies. Two, I'll search twenty-five thousand feet and below. You search twenty-five thousand feet and above."

"Two."

TIME SINCE MISSION ABORT: 1 HR, 54 MIN
JAZZ FLIGHT
THE DALLAS VICINITY

"Jazz zero-two, Fort Worth. How do you guys want to do this?" the controller asked the lead interceptor that had launched out of New Orleans.

"We're going to need radar vectors to roll out three miles behind him."

"Roger, Jazz zero-two. I'll do my best. He's at your two o'clock for thirty-five miles right now."

"Do you have any radar contacts there?" the lead pilot asked.

"That's affirmative. We have numerous contacts at various altitudes. I'll put you behind the one I think is the target."

TIME SINCE MISSION ABORT: 1 HR, 55 MIN
THE SU-57

"That's interesting, isn't it?" said Bachvaroff, having heard half of the conversation. "I think 'Jazz' is a flight of two F-15s. I'm getting hits from both their radars."

"F-15s, huh? We can assume he's carrying a bunch of missiles, and a drop tank or two. What are the chances of him dragging all that shit up to flight level 410?"

"Not good. It will take afterburner, and that'll run him out of fuel quickly."

"Want to have some fun?"

"Sure."

"Let's see if they manage to get close first."

PIEKARSKI'S TU-95
NEAR MERIDIAN, MISSISSIPPI

"AI radars are getting closer," said the EO nervously. "I'm painting two targets, one o'clock for seventy kilometers. They're heading for us and appear to be running in trail formation with eight-kilometer spacing. Definitely F-15s."

"Dammit to hell!" swore Piekarski. "Can you tell their altitude?"

"Not for sure, but they're up high."

"Electronic countermeasures status?"

"All in standby with green lights," replied the EO. "Do you want me to start jamming now?"

"Negative!" shouted Piekarski. "We'll make them find us first. Tail gunner, what's your system status?"

"Everything in standby with green lights, sir."

"If they get too close, we'll make them pay."

"I would be careful about that option, sir," said the copilot calmly.

SHARK FLIGHT

"Shark zero-three, Memphis. I've lost the target completely. He's masked on my scope by all that weather ahead of you. His last known position was at your one o'clock, forty miles. He was tracking a steady one-two-zero heading."

"Roger," replied Robertson, his voice shaking slightly. "I have a couple of contacts on the nose. One appears to be eastbound at flight level 290, and the other is westbound at flight level 280."

"Those are both known targets, Shark. Is that all you see?"

"Lead, I'm just getting a contact on the left edge of the scope . . . *Jesus!*" Tom Rushton couldn't believe what the mission computer was telling him. "Stand by." He purposely broke radar lock, placed the acquisition symbol squarely over the contact once again, and commanded a lock-on. "This must be our guy, Memphis," said Rushton. "He's left ten o'clock for thirty-five. Computer says he's at flight level 410, and you won't believe what else it says."

When Robertson said nothing, Rushton took the initiative. "Memphis, Shark zero-four. If our equipment is correct, we're going to need to talk to somebody at Eastern Air Defense. Do you have them on the line?"

"That's affirmative, Shark. They want a positive visual identification of the target. What does your computer say?"

"Mine says Tu-95 bomber," replied Ruston. "Lead, do you want to do the ID?"

Robertson's radio was silent.

THE SU-57
OVER DALLAS, TEXAS

"I got them both!" said Bachvaroff. "Two-thirty, low. They're trying to come around the corner in afterburner."

"Tallyho," replied Ridgik. "They look like they're at least three thousand meters below us. They'll never get up here."

JAZZ FLIGHT

"Do you see anything out there, Jazz?"

"That's affirmative, Fort Worth. Jazz zero-two has multiple contacts at various bearings and ranges. What's his position relative to us right now?"

"I show blips merged, but my resolution capability with a primary target isn't too good. Do you see any lights in your vicinity?"

"That's affirmative. We have one aircraft in sight, two o'clock low, another at ten o'clock and way low, and one on the nose, for at least five miles, westbound and slightly low."

"Jazz zero-two, all of those are known targets. I don't know what else to do. We have airplanes holding as far as two hundred miles away."

"*Two's got a visual!*" shouted the Jazz wingman. "On the nose for four, and way up high! He's directly above you, lead, and he's running lights out!"

"Roger," said the Jazz leader. "No joy. Can you get up to him for an ID? Fort Worth, can you approve a climb for my wingman?"

"That's affirmative. Jazz zero-two, you're cleared to climb. Altitude your discretion."

THE SU-57

"Looks like the leader is directly below us," noted Ridgik as he rolled the Sukhoi briefly to a ninety-degree angle of bank to be able to see below him.

"And the wingman is behind us with a lock-on," said Bachvaroff calmly.

"They'll never get up here. Just for fun, though, here comes minimum burner. Let's ease up to fifty thousand and see if they can stagger up there."

JAZZ FLIGHT

"Holy shit," said the pilot of the second F-15. "The fucker's got afterburners!"

"Yeah, and he's climbing!" exclaimed his back seater. "There's no way we're getting up there."

"Lead, do you see those afterburners?"

"Affirmative. Can you get up to him?"

"No way, unless we drop the tanks and get a running start, and then we'd never make it back to New Orleans."

"Yeah, dropping tanks isn't an option. We're only two thousand pounds above bingo. Fort Worth, Jazz zero-two. You can tell them we're looking at an afterburning target. He's above flight level 410 and climbing, and there's no way we're going to get up to him without running out of gas."

"Copy that. Jazz zero-two, you're cleared back to New Orleans. Fly heading one-seven-zero."

"One-seven-zero for Jazz zero-two, and we need to stay up high for fuel conservation."

THE SU-57

"Sounds like they're calling it off," laughed Ridgik, as he eased his engines out of afterburner.

"Yeah, but we might get some more visitors before this is over."

"You could be right, Anton. I have a plan. Can you see the one behind us?"

"Stand by," replied Bachvaroff as he strained to look behind the Su-57. "Uh . . . that's a negative. You're going to have to maneuver some."

"Okay, I'm coming left now . . . that ought to do it . . . and rolling back right . . . there. Do you see them?"

"Yeah. The trailer is just drawing abeam us."

"I got them too," said Ridgik. "Throttles are coming to idle and here come the speed brakes."

The Felon pilot slowed the Sukhoi almost to a stall. Then, with the airframe buffeting slightly, he turned ninety degrees toward the F-15 flight. When the trailing Eagle was almost three kilometers out in front, Ridgik retracted the speed brakes and started a descent. In a matter of seconds, he was coaltitude with the F-15s. A hard left turn put him on the same heading they were flying.

"Are you doing what I think you're doing, you sly bastard?"

"They're going to New Orleans, right?" responded Ridgik. "Well, why not make this a three-ship? I'll hold a kilometer in trail and we'll just cruise to New Orleans with them. It's close to our route to Cuba, correct?"

"Damn near right on it."

"And if they do scramble more F-15s, we're flying in a known formation, so they won't bother looking at us." Ridgik snickered. "Then when these guys start their descent, we'll just stay up here and head out to sea."

"Fucking brilliant!"

CHAPTER TWENTY-EIGHT

SHARK FLIGHT
NEAR MERIDIAN, MISSISSIPPI

"We'll do a standard stern attack for a visual ID," said Robertson to his wingman. "I have him locked up, holding at two o'clock and ten miles."

"Roger," said Rushton. "Be careful, Major. If it's a Bear, don't forget that tail gun."

TIME SINCE MISSION ABORT: 2 HR, 5 MIN
PIEKARSKI'S TU-95

"They both have solid lock-on!" called the EO. "Eight o'clock for ten kilometers . . . Wait! They're setting up for a stern attack!"

"I see them," said Piekarski, his voice shaky.

"Do you want me to jam them?" asked the EO excitedly.

"I don't know . . ."

"I have them in sight!" shouted the tail gunner. "They're coming around the corner. I'm tracking the leader with the radar! Do you want me to fire if they get in range?"

"I'm not sure . . ."

Josef Piekarski's mouth had become so dry that he could hardly form his words. He saw the two shapes moving toward his six o'clock, then bending around and becoming larger, growing vestiges of wings, stabilizers, and missiles. He was suddenly aware of all the fears flying had evoked in him over the years. He was certain the tail gunner would scream out a missile launch warning. *Any second now . . . any second.*

"Colonel, the crew is standing by for your orders," advised the copilot. Piekarski didn't respond. "*Colonel!*" Obviously frustrated, the copilot took matters into his own hands. "EO, do not jam at this time. Tail gun, do not shoot! Acknowledge!"

"But we can't just sit here, sir, and—"

"No!" repeated the copilot. "Everybody stand down!"

The copilot jammed the control wheel forward, sending coffee cups, pencils, and maps floating around the cockpit. The huge bomber was soon in a steep dive, headed for the clouds below. As they entered the clouds, the copilot began a right turn due south as he eased the aircraft back to level flight.

Piekarski continued to sit silently. He had always been very vocal about "doing one's duty" and "service to the Motherland," but now that their lives were at risk, he realized it was just his own bravado.

The EO advised, "Sir, there's heavy precipitation dead ahead for ten kilometers."

"Good," replied the copilot. "Everybody strap in tight. We're going to see how serious these F-15 pilots are."

SHARK FLIGHT

A feeling of inadequacy slammed into Richard Robertson's awareness. He realized he'd never envisioned himself in this position. It was as if all the training, the drills, and the tests had just been games. He wanted urgently to be back in the alert barn, in his comfort zone.

He felt confident in performing the pass until the target dove into the clouds. Now he was being tracked by a radar of some sort. Holding the target straight ahead at three miles, he had no intention of trying to complete the ID pass in the clouds. To make matters worse, his Eagle was being buffeted by turbulence and rain.

"Shark zero-three is stabilized at three miles," said Robertson, finally. "The target's now at flight level 230, and—"

Robertson suddenly and violently slammed the F-15 upward as he followed the target into a thunderstorm. As he fought to keep control, lightning flashed around the Eagle and the fighter was deluged by heavy freezing rain. Robertson could barely control his fear. The thunder that accompanied the discharge sounded like a shotgun had been fired right behind his ear.

Robertson screamed over the radio, "Knock it off! Knock it off! I've been struck by lightning! Shark zero-three declaring an emergency and returning to Eglin. Two, if you want to stay with the target, that's approved."

"Roger," replied Tom Rushton. "I'm at flight level 350, in the clear. The target has to come out of the clouds sooner or later, and when he does, I'll be there."

PETROV'S TU-95
OVER THE KENNEDY SPACE CENTER

"Looks like he's starting down," observed Sheptak.

"Arkady, how are we doing on fuel?" Petrov asked.

"We're fat," replied Itzkoff. "We should arrive at the refueling point with two hours and thirty-five minutes of fuel remaining. That assumes that we stay up here."

"I was just mulling that over. We could stay up here, but as soon as we separate from this airliner they will start tracking us. Then F-15s in Jacksonville will scramble."

"While Arkady was working with the fuel figures, I talked to Piekarski's airplane on HF," said Sheptak. "They're over southern Mississippi with two F-15s sitting behind them in firing position.

They descended into the weather along that front. They're in and out of thunderstorms and hoping to make the coast in the weather."

"Very well," said Petrov calmly, as he reduced the power levers to maintain position on the descending 737. "That makes our decision easy. We'll descend with him, turn southeast, and clear the ADIZ on the wave tops."

Petrov was pensive for a moment while he fingered the three gold coins in his flight suit pocket. "We'll stay with the 737 as long as we can," he finally said. Once we are well clear of the ADIZ, we will climb back up to conserve fuel. Arkady, I'm going to need some airspeed numbers for maximum endurance."

"I'll have that shortly, sir."

"Vitalie, keep talking to Piekarski's crew and keep me posted." *Poor Josef,* thought Petrov. *I hope the little weasel gets out okay.*

PIEKARSKI'S TU-95
JUST NORTH OF MOBILE

"We're coming up on Mobile," said the navigator. "We'll be over the Gulf of Mexico in another three minutes."

"Another big cell ahead," advised the EO.

The Tu-95 rocked violently as it entered another storm cell. Heavy frozen rain pelted the airframe while St. Elmo's fire crawled along the outside of the windscreens like miniature lightning strobes. "The F-15 is still with us," continued the EO, who had to yell to be heard over the din of the storm. "He's in search mode but still close. My guess is he's trailing us and hoping we'll come out of the weather."

"Thanks," said the copilot, who was still directing the crew's actions as Piekarski sat silently as if in a catatonic state. "He obviously requires a visual identification before he can take any further action. EO, what does the weather look like once we cross the coast?"

"Not good," replied the EO. "The heavy precipitation ends about twenty kilometers out to sea. After forty kilometers, I'm not painting any precipitation at all."

"Nav, I'm going to need a heading for the refueling point that will take us around the western end of Cuba," said the copilot finally. "Plan to penetrate no further than the outer Cuban ADIZ."

"The fuel is going to be really tight if we go that way," said the navigator. "You don't want to go between Key West and Cuba?"

"Negative. That routing means dealing with additional US fighters. I want to stay clear of US airspace. If we encounter Cuban MiGs, so be it."

"Roger," said the navigator as the Bear was jolted by more turbulence. "It's probably all academic, anyway. As soon as that F-15 pilot can visually identify us he's going to—"

"Just work out the numbers!" interrupted the copilot angrily.

SHARK 04

"Oak Grove, Shark zero-four's with you at flight level 350."

"Roger, Shark zero-four. Confirm you're still trailing the target."

"That's affirmative. I'm in the clear and the bomber should exit the clouds shortly. Shark zero-four requests clearance to maneuver for a beam identification pass."

"That's approved."

Rushton felt his adrenaline ramp up. He had trailed the target through Memphis and Houston Center's airspace, and now they were with Oak Grove control. Military controllers were now directing the operation. He was certain he was going to positively identify a Russian airplane that had been deep in US airspace. If it was a Bear, there was a tail gun. He also needed to keep an eye on the fuel. The afterburner climb out of Eglin had used up fuel he wished he had now. But he knew there were several close bases he could drop into for fuel if necessary.

It's time, thought Rushton, as he pushed up the throttles of his

F-15 to draw line abreast of the target three miles away. *You should be coming out of the clouds any second . . . there!*

Even though he expected it, Rushton was still shocked when he saw the silhouette of a Russian Tu-95 emerge from the cloud bank. There was no mistaking the shape of the four turboprop engines and the swept wings. The Bear bomber, though still running lights-out, was clearly visible in the moonlight.

"Oak Grove, Shark zero-four. ID is one Tu-95 Bear bomber."

"Roger, Shark zero-four. Stand by."

JAZZ FLIGHT
APPROACHING NEW ORLEANS

"Jazz zero-two flight, Houston Center, descend and maintain twelve thousand feet, altimeter is three-zero-zero-one."

"Out of flight level 330 for twelve thousand."

"Roger, and Jazz zero-two, we haven't had any further contact with that unknown target. Any suggestions?"

"Negative, Houston. We only saw his afterburner plumes as he was heading southbound above forty-one thousand feet."

"Okay, zero-two, I'll pass that on. Call approach now on 257.2."

"Copy 257.2. Jazz zero-two flight, button four, go!"

THE SU-57

"Looks like they're descending," said Bachvaroff. "I wonder what they told the controller about us."

"I don't know, but it's obvious they have no idea who we are," said Ridgik. "How's the fuel?"

"We're good. Once we cross the coast, it's about thirteen hundred kilometers to San Julián."

"And we'll get there with our reserve?"

"Just barely, but I'm good with it."

"Any other F-15s looking at us?"

"No."

"What say we dip into that reserve fuel just a little?"

"Do I sense something sinister in that question?"

Ridgik pushed the throttles up and drew alongside the F-15 flight, displaced a half mile to the left. He hesitated, plugged in the afterburners, rolled hard to the left, and started a climb toward Cuba.

"I just couldn't resist."

JAZZ FLIGHT

"Did you see that, lead?" shouted the F-15 wingman. "The son of a bitch has been shadowing us."

"We saw him, but it could be an F-15 or even an F-22. May have been an F-18. The Navy assholes will do anything to screw with us."

"How about a MiG-31 or a Su-57?"

"Yeah, those too. You'd better go back to the center frequency and tell them he's climbing away from us to the southeast. Maybe somebody with some fuel can identify him. We're minimum fuel."

THE SU-57

"Well, Anton, say goodbye to the USA. We're crossing the coast."

"Roger. The F-15 is looking at us. But too far away now."

"Master jettison is armed up here. Drop tanks selected."

"Armed back here."

"Trigger's down."

"They're gone. We're a clean airplane."

"Roger. Here comes minimum burner. We'll accelerate to Mach 1.3 and coast up to flight level 550. Cuba, here we come."

SHARK 04
SOUTH OF MOBILE
TIME SINCE MISSION ABORT: 2 HR, 25 MIN

"Shark zero-four, confirm the target's still southbound?"

"That's confirmed."

"And confirm you haven't received any electronic countermeasures?"

"That's also confirmed."

"Roger, Shark zero-four. The director of operations has decided that no further action is required. You are to continue to shadow the target as long as your fuel allows, and then we'll take you back to Eglin."

Tom Rushton couldn't believe his ears. A Bear bomber had been inside US airspace, committing some number of hostile acts, and they were just going to let him fly away?

"Shark zero-four copies," said Rushton, "and I need an authentication on those instructions. Authenticate Alpha-Zulu, please."

"Roger, Shark zero-four. Authentication is Tango."

That did it. There was nothing else he could do. "Roger, Oak Grove," said Rushton, not hiding his disappointment. "Shark zero-four is ready for direct Eglin."

"Shark zero-four, come off target heading zero-four-five. Direct Eglin when able."

Rushton couldn't resist it. He closed to within a hundred feet of the Bear's left side—the side he knew the aircraft commander sat on. He paused for a moment, then nudged his throttles into afterburner. He saw the Bear's left side become bathed in an orange sheen as the burners lit. The Eagle sprang ahead of the Bear, and Rushton pulled up and rolled across the Bear's nose. He pressed his pickle button and filled the Bear's windshields with blinding phosphorus flares.

Today's your lucky day, Ivan, he thought, *but next time . . .*

PIEKARSKI'S TU-95

All the men in the bomber looked left, trying to see the closing Eagle. "Holy shit. He's right there off our left wing," called the copilot.

Colonel Piekarski's mouth fell agape just as the F-15's afterburners lit. The Bear's crew felt and heard the thunder of the burners, and its cockpit crew shielded their eyes from the flares.

"Tail gunner, can you still see him?" shouted the copilot.

"That's affirmative, sir. He's headed northeast away from us. I think he's returning to his base."

"But his point is well taken," said the copilot. "Let's get the hell out of here and head for home ourselves. EO, are there any other airborne radars looking at us?"

"Negative, sir."

"Good. Nav, do you have that heading?"

"Heading one-six-five for now."

The copilot rolled the bomber to pick up the new heading. "Colonel Piekarski, sir. It's all over. We're going home."

"Home? Good," Piekarski uttered meekly, looking down at his lap. "You take us home."

The copilot's nose crinkled as he looked at the colonel's lap. "Colonel Piekarski, sir. Please go to the lavatory and clean yourself up."

The backup aircraft commander rose from the zampolit's seat. "Sir, the crew and I can handle it from here. Go get some rest."

"Rest . . . yes, that sounds good," muttered Piekarski, his voice trembling as he unstrapped from his seat and stood on shaky legs to walk to the rear compartment. While the new aircraft commander evaluated the cleanliness of the seat he was about to settle into, the copilot laid his head back against his headrest, closed his eyes, and let out a huge sigh.

CHAPTER TWENTY-NINE

TIME SINCE MISSION ABORT: 2 HR, 10 MIN
TWEED-NEW HAVEN AIRPORT, CONNECTICUT

Bobby Chatman felt an apprehension he had never known, nor imagined could grip him so powerfully, as he called Michael.

"Bobby! Thank God! I've been waiting for your instructions. Where the hell are you?"

"I'm still in New Haven. It's too bad the rest of the night didn't go as planned."

"I know," Michael agreed. "So, what happens now?"

"We need to cover our tracks. There are only a few people who could positively connect us with events this evening. Keith Anderson is the first that comes to mind."

"But he couldn't make a positive identification. He never saw either of us."

"Yes, but he's heard your voice a number of times."

"That's true, but the FBI will protect him. It would be very difficult to eliminate him. There are two other people who can tie me to Anderson. The clerk at the hotel in Kansas City thought it odd that I paid cash for three rooms."

"Was there a written record?"

"Sure, but it was under a false name."

"To be on the safe side, we ought to eliminate the clerk and the records at the same time."

"It's risky. We might have to wait a couple of days to catch that clerk at work . . . and to get the computer files. I think we're talking about a fire."

"Well, you had better beat the FBI to it. Who else can connect us with Anderson?"

"The hustler," Michael said quietly. "Shawn Cochran can tie us directly to Keith Anderson."

"Then he'll have to be eliminated," said Chatman decisively.

"I'd rather not have that particular job, Bobby."

"I understand. I'll advise Darginsky. I can get him to eliminate both the hotel clerk and the hustler quicker than you can anyway. First priority is to get you and Alex out of the country. Did you use the burner phones for calls to Anderson?"

"Of course."

"Good. Can you think of anything else?"

"We don't know what the Americans know yet, right? Maybe our aircraft entered and left completely undetected."

"Except for the downing of the F-15."

"True. If you don't mind my saying so, we have a desperate need to know what information the Americans have, and you, Bobby, are the one to get it."

"You're right," said the evangelist. "I'll see what I can find out."

Dammit! thought Chatman as he pondered calling the president of the United States at 11:05 p.m. *I was planning on Andrew Phillips being dead right now.*

TIME SINCE MISSION ABORT: 2 HR, 17 MIN

THE CAPITOL BUILDING, WASHINGTON

"Ringmaster, Falcon's Nest."

Darryl McCormick frowned as she reached for the radio. "Falcon's Nest, Ringmaster. Go ahead."

"Frank Morgan here. Has that bus carrying the CIA contingent left for Langley yet?"

"That's a negative, sir," replied McCormick.

"Good. Now listen to me carefully, McCormick. There's a man in the CIA group named Hank Hartley. I want you to have Mr. Hartley call us, then accompany him to the White House helipad. There'll be a helicopter waiting for him. Did you get that?"

"Affirmative, sir. As a matter of fact, Hartley is standing next to me." She hung up the phone and turned to Hartley. "Now what do you suppose that's all about?"

"I think I know why," Hartley replied. "But I wish they'd chosen somebody else."

"Oh? Why's that?"

"I hate riding in helicopters."

Eight minutes later Hartley slid through the open door of McCormick's car. "So, what's up?" she asked as she put the car in gear.

"I don't know yet. The Washington command post had a call from a deputy sheriff in Mecklenburg County, Virginia. It seems that an aircraft of some sort crashed right at the edge of Buggs Island Lake. It appeared to be too small to carry people. So, considering the terrorist threat of the past few weeks, he decided on a hunch to get out his Geiger counter."

"I'm afraid to ask what happened."

"The thing went crazy. The wreck is radioactive. So we're going down to check it out."

"We?"

"Yes, we," replied Hartley with a smile. "I personally requested that you be assigned to the investigation. The director was reluctant, but I insisted."

"Thanks a lot," moaned McCormick. "I hate riding in helicopters, too."

TWEED-NEW HAVEN AIRPORT, CONNECTICUT

Bobby Chatman tried to call Andrew Phillips, but the president didn't answer. He left a voice message, apologizing for the late call. In his finely honed, charismatic way that often resulted in useful feedback, he offered prayer support and assistance to the president. As he pondered how he would frame his questions for Phillips, his phone snapped him out of his thoughts.

"Chatman here."

"Hi, Bobby, it's me," said Viktor Darginsky.

"Viktor, I'm glad you called. I'm concerned about what our immediate actions should be."

"First, we must do everything in our power to save your ministry. It's too valuable to us."

"I agree. Can you take care of the New York hustler? And I'll send you the name of the hotel and clerk who Michael dealt with. I think a fire would eliminate any threat from Kansas City."

"I'll handle it. Have Michael board a commercial flight to Montreal and send Alex to New Orleans for a flight to Caracas. If any investigation points to you, the plan is for you to plead ignorance. Agreed?"

"Yes. My friendship with Andrew Phillips will help."

"It most definitely will. Have you talked to him yet?"

"No. I called, but he didn't answer. He's probably in the Situation Room."

"Talk to him as soon as you can. It's important to find out what the Americans know. If it gets too hot, I'll pull you out." Darginsky paused. "Bobby, it was a good plan. I'll try and let you know why it failed."

"Please do. My curiosity is killing me."

KANSAS CITY ARTCC

"So what happens now?" Keith asked.

"I honestly don't know," said Jenko. "I'm going back to the radar room to see if they identified those unknown tracks. Stay here at the Center. The FBI's going to want to talk to you."

"Thanks, Jenko," said Keith gratefully. "You believe they may come down hard on me?"

"They're going to be looking for somebody to blame. They'll want a written statement, but make sure they don't have the only copy. You need to get a good lawyer to represent you when they come and interview you. I'll be back in half an hour."

TIME SINCE MISSION ABORT: 2 HR, 58 MIN
BUGGS ISLAND LAKE, VIRGINIA

"Can you get any closer?" asked Hank Hartley over the intercom of the Marine helicopter. "We can't quite see it from up here. Come right a little. We need to see the part that's underwater. Just a touch more . . . hold it right there. Jesus! That's what I was afraid of. Okay, you can get us out of here now."

"So, what's the word?" asked McCormick over the interphone. "What is it?"

The CIA agent looked at the FBI operative and made a writing sign with his hand. McCormick handed him a pen and pad of paper. Hartley spent a few seconds writing on the pad before he handed it back to McCormick. The FBI agent couldn't believe what her colleague had written.

"Are you positive?" asked McCormick. The CIA intelligence expert merely nodded his head.

"Okay," McCormick told the pilot. "We've seen enough. We need to land and make a call."

Five minutes later the two federal agents were at the Mecklenburg County sheriff's helipad. The sheriff was waiting for them.

"You did the right thing, Sheriff," said McCormick. "For now, we want you to continue to maintain the no entry zone, and we want your people to be absolutely certain that no one gets near the thing."

"Do you know what it is?" he asked.

"Yeah . . . we know what it is," replied McCormick as she stole a glance at Hank Hartley, "but we can't discuss it."

"This is a matter of national security," agreed Hartley. "You'll get more detailed instructions later, but for now, this entire area is to be sealed off. No one, and I mean no one, is to be allowed within a quarter-mile radius of the site. Pass the word that none of your people are to discuss that business about the Geiger counter either. The government will issue a statement to the press. Now, we need a private place to make some phone calls."

TIME SINCE MISSION ABORT: 3 HR, 15 MIN

A half hour later Hank Hartley emerged from the sheriff's office. "Well, we have our marching orders," he said to McCormick with a grim smile. "For now, we both head back to Washington. The chopper is to drop me off at Langley where I've been tasked with trying to figure out how that thing got here. You, ma'am, are heading for Andrews. A Learjet is standing by to take you to the great states of Kansas and Wyoming."

"Kansas! Wyoming!" said a surprised Dare McCormick. "Why am I going to Kansas and Wyoming?"

"Because an F-15 crashed in western Nebraska tonight. You've been directed to talk to the pilot and the ATC controllers involved."

McCormick's eyes widened as her jaw dropped.

"A helicopter rescued the pilot and took him to Warren Air Force Base in Cheyenne. The pilot is convinced he was shot down by a Russian air-to-air missile . . . Why are you looking at me like that?"

"Remember earlier I was telling you about the F-15 pilot I've been seeing? Well, Mark was flying tonight. He was ferrying a plane from

Washington to Massachusetts. God, I hope that wasn't him. Is the pilot okay?"

"All I know is he's alive."

McCormick jumped up and started for the helicopter.

"Wait! There's more. The FAA tracked some radar contacts that were in the vicinity of the F-15 when it went down. After almost an hour, the Air Force finally scrambled some fighters to identify the contacts. They only positively identified one of the aircraft, and it was already over the Gulf of Mexico headed south—but guess what kind of airplane it was."

"A Russian of some sort?"

"A Tu-95 Bear bomber."

"*I knew it!*" she shouted, poking the air with her forefinger. "Goddammit, I knew it!"

"I know, I know. You told me. Remember? Now just get out there and get the facts!"

CHAPTER THIRTY

TIME SINCE MISSION ABORT: 6 HR, 15 MIN
HENDERSON, NORTH CAROLINA

Bobby Chatman groaned as he sat up in bed, getting his bearings while his "Onward Christian Soldiers" ringtone chimed insistently.

"Hello?" said the groggy evangelist.

"Reverend Chatman, this is Colonel Webster at the White House Situation Room," said a very efficient voice. "Please hold for the president of the United States."

Chatman snapped awake.

"Bobby, are you there?" said a tired Andrew Phillips.

"Yes, Andrew, what's up?"

"We have a crisis here. I need you at the White House as soon as possible."

Chatman instantly became suspicious. Being called to the White House after last night's debacle smacked of a trap. He decided to get as much information as possible before committing to the trip.

"Gee, Andrew, I have some rather pressing ministry business first thing in the morning. What's going on?"

"I can't talk about it on the phone . . . wait just a minute."

While Phillips went offline, Chatman again felt the unaccustomed nervousness that had beset him the last few hours. He wondered if the president was consulting someone about how to ensnare him.

"Bobby? Sorry about that," said an obviously harried Phillips. "I know it's the middle of the night, but turn on your television, and catch the lead story on Headline News. I'll tell you more when you get here. I feel like I'm up to my neck in alligators."

"Oh, Andrew, it can't be that bad," counseled Chatman while he reached for the television remote. "You delivered a marvelous speech last night and there's been no nuclear terrorist attacks, correct?"

"I don't know the answer to that question," said Phillips. "Could you be here by nine a.m.?"

"Well, sure, but I've had some interesting problems of my own."

"What do you mean?"

"I seem to have lost the services of both my pilots," Chatman replied. "They aren't answering my calls. I'll have to fly myself, but I'll be there."

"Great!" said the president. "Trust me, your problems are minor in comparison to mine. I'll meet you in the chapel. See you then."

Chatman had to wait a few minutes for the lead story to come up on the half hour.

> "... with our lead story from Buggs Island Lake, Virginia. Go ahead, John."
>
> "David, a small plane, or a missile, crashed into a pier on the northern edge of Buggs Island Lake at about 8:45 last night. Initial reports were that radioactivity levels around the crash site were high, indicating the vehicle might have been carrying some sort of nuclear device.
>
> "US military officials moved rapidly to secure the crash site, and they've imposed a total news blackout. All attempts to talk to government officials are being met with 'no comment.' The site commander told us the government would have a statement once its preliminary investigation was complete. This is John Parker for Headline News."

Jesus! Could it be one of our Kh-55s? He forced himself to remain calm. The president hadn't sounded suspicious, so they hadn't linked it to him—yet. But they were bound to when they discovered the use of the Redex call signs.

I'm going to take my chances with Andrew Phillips, he thought, as he got out of bed and headed for the shower. *If worse comes to worse, they'll delay any action against me, thanks to him, and I'll use that to make myself scarce.*

TIME SINCE MISSION ABORT: 10 HR, 0 MIN
WASHINGTON, DC

Chatman parked the Citation and opened the entry door. He was surprised to see a man waiting for him.

"Good morning. Are you Bobby Chatman?"

"Yes, I am. Is there something I can do for you?"

"I'm Special Agent George Richardson, FBI." He presented his badge. "The president has requested that I escort you to the White House. If you'll follow me, the helicopter is waiting."

Chatman had the distinct feeling during the short hop to the White House helipad that the FBI escort was more than just a courtesy extended by Andrew Phillips. He momentarily regretted not flying the Citation out of the country. Richardson treated him with respect, which calmed him a bit. The agent escorted him to the White House chapel.

When the door opened to the chapel, Andrew Phillips came in, followed by FBI Director Frank Morgan and Darryl McCormick, the agent from the Capitol Building the night before. Chatman knew his suspicions were correct and that he would need to be very careful. With his best pastoral smile, he extended his hand. "Andrew, how are you? My prayers have been with you since your phone call. I trust all is well."

"I don't know yet," said the president. "Bobby, we have a serious crisis on our hands. These people need to ask you some questions."

"Of course," replied Chatman as he held out his hand to Morgan and nodded his greeting to McCormick. "Frank, it's good to see you."

It was obvious to Chatman that Morgan was unsure how to handle the situation. McCormick took the lead. "Reverend Chatman, is it true that your ministry has been operating some aircraft using Redex call signs?"

"Sure," said Chatman. "As the president can verify, God has been leading us to minister to the citizens of Latin America through our own airline of sorts. We call it Red Star Express. The call sign was a play on words."

"I see," said McCormick. "Were any of your aircraft flying last night?"

"No. I spent the day here in Washington. One of my other pilots was at my farm in Bay St. Louis, Mississippi, and the other was at my ranch in Kansas. As supporters of the National Day of Prayer and Unity, we didn't fly any Redex flights last night."

"Are you sure your other two pilots weren't in the air last night?" McCormick asked while studying Chatman's face intently.

"As far as I know, they were on the ground. I didn't order any flights. What's going on here, anyway?"

The two FBI agents exchanged glances. "Just a couple more questions, Reverend," said McCormick. "Why'd you leave the state dinner and fly out of town last night?"

"As you'll remember, I received a call regarding the mugging of Senator Dan Hawkins's son up in New Haven, Connecticut. I told Andrew what was going on." The president nodded his head in confirmation. "I left the dinner to find Hawkins, then rode in the FBI car *you* arranged to Reagan Airport. From there I flew Hawkins to be with his son." Chatman smiled proudly. "I'm a qualified Citation pilot—oh, just for clarity, we have *three* Citations. I had flown the third one up for the speech. But I decided doing the work of the Lord was more important, even though I wanted to be here."

The two FBI agents were quiet for a few moments. Finally, Morgan spoke. "About these two pilots of yours, where are they now?"

"It's funny you should ask," said Chatman, feigning confusion. "I honestly don't know. As I told the president when he called this morning, I've been unable to reach either of them since last night."

"Can you provide us with information on them?" asked McCormick.

"Sure," Chatman replied, outwardly cooperative, but inwardly thinking that he must allow Michael and Alex time to exit the country. "I have employee information at my headquarters in Raleigh."

"Could somebody there give it to us?"

"No," Chatman replied, stalling. "All that information is locked up in my personal safe." He smiled cooperatively. "I'll be glad to give it to you as soon as I'm back there." Chatman decided it was time to seize the offensive. Addressing the president as his authoritarian equal, he said, "Andrew, what's going on here? Why all these questions?"

The president hesitated a moment before asking, "Bobby, last night some very strange things happened. Did you watch that news story I told you about?"

"Yes, I did, but what does that have to do with me?"

Phillips hesitated again, looked at Frank Morgan, and continued. "The aircraft that landed in Buggs Island Lake appears to have been a Russian Kh-55 cruise missile. Apparently three Russian aircraft entered our airspace. One of our aircraft positively identified one of theirs as a Tu-95 Bear bomber. We aren't sure why they were here, but we believe the Airborne Command Post was a target, we know one of our F-15s was shot down, and we think a nuclear-armed cruise missile was dropped into Buggs Island Lake. That's down near Roanoke, isn't it Frank?"

"Closer to Raleigh," Morgan said.

"We also know they worked with US air traffic controllers . . . and the call signs they used were Redex zero-one and Redex zero-two."

Chatman adopted a look of horror. "You've got to be kidding!"

"It had to be a setup," the president soothed. "Don't worry—we'll get to the bottom of it."

Chatman sank into a chair. "I don't understand! Why me?"

"Probably to get even for your defection," said Phillips. "The more important question is what was the overall game plan? Your two pilots might have the answers." Phillips turned to his FBI director. "Frank, we need to find them."

"Yes, Mr. President, I agree."

Chatman couldn't tell from the FBI director's answer if his performance had been convincing. McCormick's poker face was totally unreadable, adding to his discomfort. The door to the chapel opened and Agent Richardson stuck his head inside.

"Bad news," he said, eyeing Chatman. Morgan nodded for him to continue. "The Kansas City hotel clerk and the hustler in New York that Agent McCormick wanted us to pick up? They're both dead. The clerk was blown away in a firebombing just two hours ago, and the hustler was found dead in his Manhattan apartment."

The other two FBI agents simultaneously turned toward Chatman.

Morgan frowned as he addressed the pastor. "That's all we have right now, Reverend. You won't need to fly your plane back to North Carolina. We'll have a government plane spare you of that expense, and Agent Richardson here will go along to assist."

Chatman felt his innards coil. He was trapped.

"Now, now!" the president counseled, holding his hands up. "I trust my brother completely. Reverend Chatman will fly his own plane back to his home." He turned to Chatman, smiling. "Bobby, it would help if you could return here as soon as possible with those documents."

"Sure, Andrew. I don't know what to say."

"I know. Just pray for us."

"I will," Chatman replied warmly.

CHAPTER THIRTY-ONE

JANUARY 16: DAY AFTER LUCIFER/INBLUE
ANDREWS AIR FORCE BASE, WASHINGTON, DC

An exhausted Darryl McCormick got off the government Learjet and was met by Agent George Richardson. "Nothing personal, but you look like shit," Richardson remarked as he took her bag.

"Nothing personal, Richardson, but fuck you," she retorted, as she walked to the waiting car.

As they made their way through traffic toward the White House, McCormick thought about the early morning interview with Bobby Chatman. She had stood quietly and considered all that Chatman had said. She didn't buy one ounce of his hogwash. As far as she was concerned, Chatman was up to his eyeballs in this debacle, and she was going to nail him if it was the last thing she ever did!

"Did you find out anything?" Richardson asked, interrupting her reverie.

McCormick ran her fingers through her hair and sighed. "No. It seemed like the air traffic controller wanted to talk, but his coworkers urged him to lawyer up. Something's going on there. I got some basic information, but not much else. I'm going to ask Morgan to put him under protective custody until we can get back out there. One of the others, a young lady air traffic controller, told me some things that I think we can use."

"I heard you tried to persuade that Lear crew to take you to Cheyenne to see the F-15 pilot"—He paused and smirked—"whom I think you are acquainted with?"

She turned to him with an unbelieving look. "How the hell did you know that?"

He shrugged. "It's my job to know everything, ma'am."

"Well, then you know they were supposed to fly me to Warren Air Force Base after my stop in Kansas City. Instead, they were ordered to bring me back here for a briefing with the president. But I called Mark and got some information that you haven't heard about."

"What?"

"Wait till the briefing."

THE WHITE HOUSE

"Do you need to hit the head before we go to the Cabinet Room?" asked Richardson. "It's probably going to be a long briefing."

"Nah, but I wish I had time to freshen up. This will be the first time I've briefed the president."

Richardson smiled. "Well, you look as good as anybody else who'll be there. There's a lot of sagging eyelids and crumpled suits. By the way, the Joint Chiefs of Staff, the secretaries of state and defense, the director of the CIA, and our own boss will all be in attendance." Richardson opened the door of the Cabinet Room for his fellow agent. "Knock 'em dead, Dare."

The two FBI agents entered the Cabinet Room as a briefing was being conducted by a three-star Air Force general. The general paused to allow them to take their seats.

"So, that's where we stand, Mr. President. Our strategic units are all at DEFCON 2. Our tactical units are still mobilizing and should be up to DEFCON 2 status within a couple of hours. The same goes for our air defense units."

"Are you sure we *even have* air defense units, General?" asked a sarcastic Andrew Phillips. "Where were they last night?"

"Well, sir, they were on peacetime alert like they were supposed to be. They did manage to identify one of the intruders."

"According to your own briefing, they identified only one of three intruders. And that was after those intruders had operated within US airspace for at least two hours!" barked the president. "It was also after they apparently shot down one of our own airplanes, over the middle of Nebraska, for Christ's sake, and after they had launched, dropped, or otherwise released some sort of nuclear-tipped cruise missile!"

McCormick surmised, from the stunned looks around the room, that no one had ever seen Andrew Phillips so disturbed.

After an awkward silence, a more composed Phillips resumed his questioning. "I'm sorry I took the Lord's name in vain. Now, General, one more time. The Russians are standing down?"

"Yes, Mr. President," replied the general, visibly relieved to discuss questions he knew the answers to. "All their submarines are returning to their home waters. All aircraft are at their home bases. The only aircraft launches from the beginning were transports out of Murmansk that were preannounced as part of their exercise. If it *was* a surprise attack, we don't know if it was done under the direction of Kozlov or another faction. We do know their strategic rocket forces never came up to full-alert status."

"Is it possible that this nuclear terrorist situation was a hoax on their part?" asked Phillips. "If that cruise missile in Virginia had gone off over its target, the American people probably would have thought it was one of those Mercedes trucks we've been looking for."

"Many of us have been discussing that possibility."

"Thank you, General. Mr. Hartley?"

The president's question to the general quickened Dare McCormick's tired mind. Suppose the Russians had engineered the entire nuclear terrorist threat scenario? Suppose they'd used it to cover up a limited surprise attack? She knew from her interview with the air traffic controller named Julie that Redex call signs had been used by the intruders. Chatman had two airplanes that flew under Redex call signs, and his two pilots named Alex and Michael had disappeared. Chatman was the key. McCormick had sensed it when they initially questioned Chatman, but now she was certain.

Hank Hartley began to speak. "I want to keep this as brief as possible," he said as he began the PowerPoint presentation. A picture of a damaged flying machine appeared on the screen. "Last night this vehicle landed on the north shore of Buggs Island Lake in Virginia. We retrieved it and transported it to our lab for identification. The vehicle is a Russian-built Kh-55M cruise missile, NATO reporting name 'Kent.' It was carrying an armed nuclear warhead." Hartley paused to allow the implications of his comments to register. "The guidance package was severely damaged in the crash, but we've been able to determine some interesting facts."

The slide changed to show a few damaged black boxes. "The guidance system on this missile was designed specifically for a surprise peacetime attack because they knew if we had advance warning, we would shut down our ground navigation stations and possibly our GPS satellites as well. We were able to determine the route of flight and target for the missile." Hartley paused. "Gentlemen, the target for this missile was Washington, DC."

The room erupted into a frenzy of chatter. Finally, the president shouted a question. "Mr. Hartley, are you absolutely sure that Washington was the target?"

"Absolutely," replied the CIA agent. He waited for the room to quiet down. "Much of the electronic guidance package was destroyed on impact. But the actual memory section was electromechanical. Once we figured out what we were dealing with, it was easy. There's absolutely no doubt."

"Why did the missile crash?" asked Phillips quietly.

"Its engine failed to start," Hartley replied. "We haven't figured out why yet. It had a self-destruct package that failed to detonate also. My technicians say it's too coincidental that both functions would fail simultaneously, so they are obviously interdependent.

The nuclear device only needed one more confirmation signal to complete its arming sequence. And, if that wasn't bad enough, one of the eyewitnesses saw what looked like fireworks, high in the sky above the lake, shortly after the missile crashed. My theory is that a second missile was jettisoned and blown up above the lake. I had a call just before the beginning of the briefing in which one of my agents verified higher-than-normal levels of radioactivity in the middle of the lake. Apparently, the Russians chose the lake as the launch point in case of an abort so they could hide the evidence. If the self-destruct package had functioned properly on the first missile, they probably would've been successful."

"Do we know where they came from?" asked the president.

"We can't answer that question with certainty," Hartley responded. "We know that some supposedly inert Kh-55s were shipped to Venezuela. We know two Tu-95 Bear bombers, equipped to launch the Kh-55M, landed at the new Russian base on La Orchila Island just offshore Venezuela late Saturday evening. We also know the Russians moved some aircraft, including IL-78 Midas tankers and possibly a Su-57 fighter, to Cuba under some rather suspicious circumstances Friday night. And I know that my agent on La Orchila is probably dead."

"So, your feeling is that the attack came from Venezuela?"

"Yes, Mr. President. My own guess is the two bombers picked up the cruise missiles in Venezuela. They started for the US midafternoon yesterday and were joined by a fighter over the Gulf of Mexico, which we think came out of Cuba because of its shorter range. All the aircraft entered US airspace undetected by flying under the radar cover. Miss McCormick from the FBI just got in from Kansas City with fresh information on that part of the story."

"Fine, Hartley," said the president. "But before you go, let me ask you one more question. If we had all these tidbits of information, why didn't we see this coming?"

"Three reasons," said Hartley. "First of all, the Russians told us not to worry about seemingly unusual aircraft movements because of the ongoing exercise. That's standard practice for both countries. So, we took them at their word. Secondly, there was no obvious pattern of what was happening. Several different agencies had pieces of the puzzle, but no individual piece pointed toward such a dastardly whole. Finally, we were so concerned about locating those Mercedes trucks that we weren't thinking about this. I was personally pulled away from my desk to help with security at the Capitol Building even though I told my supervisor we had photographs of Bear bombers landing in Venezuela. We didn't see it coming because we weren't looking, sir."

"Thank you, Mr. Hartley."

The president leaned over in whispered conversation with the secretary of defense. Hank Hartley leaned closer to McCormick and whispered. "I'm willing to bet a month's pay that the entire nuclear terrorist scare was an SVR setup."

McCormick nodded pensively.

"Miss McCormick!"

She sprang to her feet. "Sorry, sir," said the FBI agent when she realized the president had said something. "I was just trying to figure this thing out."

"You're next," replied the president with a patient smile. "Why don't you tell us what you've learned, and we'll see if we can help you figure it out."

"Yes, sir. My investigation has been focused on the F-15 pilot who was shot down over western Nebraska, and the FAA personnel who dealt with the intruders last night."

McCormick outlined the sequence of events up through the time the intruders exited the country. She mentioned that recorded data tracks were still being analyzed in conjunction with voice tapes of radio transmissions, but it appeared that two target tracks in the vicinity of Bay St. Louis, Mississippi, had picked up IFR clearances from prefiled flight plans. They operated as Redex zero-one and zero-two and were supposed to be Cessna Citations.

After recapping for the president her preliminary findings, she said, "The big question is how this entire operation was mounted, right under our noses, without any of our agencies picking up on it. It seems to me the SVR was involved in a successful inside job. The Redex flight plans and call signs were the key to success. Since those call signs are used by Reverend Bobby Chatman, it seems that an investigation of Reverend Chatman and his ministry is called for, and—"

"No, Miss McCormick," interrupted the president. "I will not allow any investigation of my brother, whose faith and character I know is impeccable."

"But, sir," protested McCormick, "the evidence—"

"His personal commitment to this country is beyond question. As you know, two of his pilots are missing, but he's as baffled as any of us. It was a setup, Miss McCormick. You may very well find that the missing pilots are SVR agents. I suspect they decided to single out Bobby as retaliation for his defection twenty-plus years ago. Frank Morgan and I decided there will be no investigation of Bobby or his ministry. It would also be a waste of time. Bobby should be back sometime this afternoon with the personnel files of the two missing pilots. My advice to you and the bureau is to concentrate on locating those two."

McCormick couldn't believe her ears. "Mr. President, if you don't mind," she began, despite looks of warning from Frank Morgan and George Richardson.

"But I do mind, Miss McCormick!" Phillips pressed with a final wave of his hand. "Now, I have some questions. Where's the F-15 pilot, Captain Matthews, right now?"

"He's at the base hospital at Warren Air Force Base in Cheyenne, sir."

"Very good. Keep him isolated until we sort this out. How about Mr. Anderson, the air traffic controller?"

"I'm recommending we place him under surveillance, if not put him in protective custody, sir," replied McCormick. "I feel his life might be in danger."

"Why is that?"

"Sir, he refused to submit to some of my questions until he gets a lawyer. I feel he's hiding something."

"I see," said the president. "Okay, we'll deal with him later. And all the other FAA personnel involved understand that the events of last evening are not to be discussed with the press?"

"Yes, sir."

The Cabinet Room door opened to reveal a Navy admiral being escorted by an armed guard. "Mr. President, sorry to interrupt, but I thought you would want to see this immediately." The admiral stepped to the podium and laid an envelope in front of the president.

Phillips put on his reading glasses and opened the envelope. "I want everybody to stand by." He flashed the paper as he headed for the door. "We'll reconvene this meeting as soon as I'm done talking to Kozlov on the hotline."

As Phillips stepped out into the hall, McCormick could see Bobby Chatman waiting. The two friends greeted each other warmly. As the president hurried off, she noticed Chatman looking into the room. The television evangelist broke eye contact with her to scan the room for other known faces. Then, in a move that surprised McCormick, Chatman started in her direction.

"Nice to meet you again, Miss McCormick," Chatman said as he held out his hand, a pompous smile on his face. "My thanks, again, for last night. Andrew told me that Kozlov is calling, so he suggested I give these folders to one of you."

"Are those the personnel folders of the pilots, Reverend Chatman?" asked George Richardson.

"Yes, and I hope you get to the bottom of all this. Excuse me. I told Andrew I would wait for him in the chapel."

Richardson stood watching Chatman make his way down the hall, arms folded, shaking his head. "Every time I see that character, I can't help thinking what a slippery fish he is."

"For the record, George," said McCormick, "that's no fish. That's a snake, and I intend to catch it, cage it, or kill it."

"You got to be careful with snakes, Dare," Richardson advised. "If you don't handle them just right, they'll bite you and make you wish you were dead."

THE KREMLIN COMMAND POST

Nikolai Kozlov sat in the commander's cab studying the situation map and watching officers, NCOs, and various civilians moving about on the floor. He noticed there was no sense of urgency among them, which was good; word had not leaked out about the events going on in the US. He had decided to talk privately with Andrew Phillips and try for a deal before General Gavrilov learned the truth about the failed mission.

Kozlov hoped a mutual resolution with Phillips over what amounted to dual embarrassing failures would be to his advantage. But he couldn't be sure of the extent of Andrew Phillips's knowledge regarding the whole affair, and that was the weak link in his hoped-for survival plan.

"Sir, your video call has gone through," announced an aide.

"Everyone except my interpreter, out of the room, NOW!" barked Kozlov.

"President Phillips is on the line," said the interpreter.

"Good evening. Mr. President," said Kozlov, as he stared into the television camera. "I trust your interpreter is the only other person in the room with you?"

"Yes, Mr. Kozlov. What's this about?"

"I'm calling because my government is very concerned about the ongoing American military mobilization." He allowed himself to sigh. "I fear there has been a misunderstanding, and I think it is essential for us to discuss and resolve it."

"Misunderstanding, Mr. President? Now, there's an understatement," said Phillips. "We're on elevated alert because we have irrefutable proof that at least three of your aircraft entered our airspace last evening and flew to points deep inside our sovereign territory. Judging from the calling card they left, their intent was unmistakable. Your nation, sir, attempted to mount a surprise nuclear attack on mine. The only reason we're not responding with a massive retaliation is that our intelligence indicates your military is standing down."

"Mr. President, I won't deny that it was our aircraft that entered your airspace," said Kozlov, "but I categorically deny they were there on my orders. Unfortunately, a faction of our military decided to take matters into their own hands. They felt the Motherland was better off focusing on a common outside enemy than trying to survive the internal turmoil. We have arrested those responsible. They *will* be dealt with most harshly. We are indeed lucky to be even having this conversation. Let us use this opportunity to get past this crisis."

"Mr. President," Phillips said, "I have no choice but to accept your explanation of events in your country. The only other option is nuclear war. What do you have in mind?"

"You and I have the same problem. If word gets out in my country that a renegade military faction mounted a failed surprise attack on your country, our government would collapse, creating even more instability. And, if word got out in your media that our aircraft managed to penetrate your air defense system and fly deep into your sovereign territory, leaving the 'calling card' you mentioned, the consequences would be similarly unacceptable. Therefore, I propose a mutually beneficial accommodation."

President Andrews remained silent for a full minute before responding. "I would agree with your assessment, President Kozlov. Just what would be the terms of this 'mutually beneficial accommodation'?"

"I propose we both take measures to guarantee that no information regarding last evening makes its way into our respective news media."

"That sounds simple on the surface," said Phillips, "and it's easier for you to do than me. But just what do you propose I do about that 'calling card'? Representatives of our news media are already pounding on my door for answers."

"Could you not simply say that one of your bombers accidentally dropped the missile? One thing we learned long ago is that in a crisis, the truth is a relative thing. As a matter of fact—" He picked up a piece of paper, purposefully making a show of it, and continued. "It seems your aircraft have experienced numerous accidents involving live nuclear weapons. They dropped a nuclear bomb over North Carolina and another one in the Mediterranean."

"Those were more than seventy-five years ago," Andrews said pointedly.

Kozlov chuckled. "Indeed, Mr. President? As if 2007 was so long ago. It seems one of your B-52 crews mistakenly carried live nuclear-tipped cruise missiles between your Minot and Barksdale Air Force bases. I'm not making this up. It was reported in your own media. Could they not have accidentally dropped them?" Kozlov paused. "You see, our little cover story is not so far-fetched. And if you choose such a story," he continued, "I will protest the accident in the strongest terms, saying that carriage of live nuclear weapons in peacetime is an unnecessary risk and an accident waiting to happen, citing the incidents I just mentioned. The 2007 accident will make the present one more believable, and Russian push-back will do the same."

Phillips took his time considering Kozlov's proposal. The Russian president watched with fascination as the American president bowed his head to pray. Finally, he opened his eyes. "President Kozlov, I can't begin to express how angry the events of last night have made me. I also don't mind telling you, it's not in my best judgment to make deals with you considering last night as well as your government's aggressive and deceitful long-term track record. However, these would seem to be extraordinary circumstances. I'm going to need more details before accepting your proposal."

At first Kozlov glared at the monitor, then he offered a smug smile. "Of course, Mr. President. I propose mutual acts of goodwill. I remain committed to purchasing grain at most-favored-nation prices, and we need freedom from your sanctions to sell our petroleum products. My hope is that you will now see the benefits of helping me solve this problem."

"Supposing I can now see the benefits you mentioned," said Phillips, "what gesture of goodwill can I expect in return?"

"Mr. President, my intelligence operatives have positively located the missing 'suitcase' nuclear devices. You will be pleased to know they never left the Middle East. As a gesture of goodwill, I will see that they never again become the source of a nuclear terrorist threat. For obvious reasons, I am not disposed to allowing them back in Chechen hands, but I will see to it that the West never has to worry about them again."

"Am I to understand, Mr. President," asked Phillips, "that your operatives will transport the bombs to Russia?"

"That is what I am proposing, Mr. President."

"And we can send a team to verify their acquisition?"

"Certainly," said Kozlov. "We will notify you as soon as they are safely on Russian soil."

"I think you have a deal, Mr. President," said Phillips. "I trust you will see to the implementation of this exclusively verbal agreement immediately?"

"Absolutely, and I am confident you will do the same. Thank you for talking with me tonight. As you Americans are fond of saying, it seems every cloud has a silver lining. Good night, Mr. President."

THE WHITE HOUSE

Everyone in the briefing room was standing except Darryl McCormick, who sat quietly in the back of the room, sipping coffee and trying not to nod off. When the door opened, the president's chief of staff came in first, followed by the president, who swept to the podium. He nodded to his chief of staff, and she left the room, closing the door behind her. McCormick thought the dismissing of the president's chief of staff was odd.

Andrew Phillips cleared his throat. "Ladies and gentlemen, I'm sorry to keep you waiting. I've been on the phone with Nikolai Kozlov. He maintains a renegade faction planned and executed the mission—"

"Bullshit!" someone blurted.

Phillips put up his hand. "Perhaps, but right now that's a secondary concern. Our problem is *we* failed last night. We failed to defend this nation against a nuclear attack!" He paused to let his audience grasp that statement. "So, what do we do about it?"

The secretary of defense began to offer a solution, but the president cut him off. "That was a rhetorical question. For now, anyway, Mr. Kozlov has a solution which, after some thought—and, yes, prayer—I decided to accept. He's in a pickle too. If word gets out in Russia about the failure it will be pinned on him, and he'll get canned. Literally. And who do you think will replace him? A Gorbachev type? A Yeltsin?" He paused. "Those days are gone. At least we know what we've got with Kozlov.

"And if the voters here found out what happened last night, we'd all get canned. But there's something at stake here that is much higher than our damn jobs. We stand to lose the public's confidence in our government's and our military's ability to protect them. This, people, is the basic reason we even have a damn government—to protect the people!"

He paused to take a sip of water. "Kozlov proposes we install a cover story. We issue a press release that one of our bombers accidentally jettisoned a cruise missile with a live warhead."

"But, sir," the SecDef interrupted, "our policy for decades has been *not* to fly nukes except in transport aircraft and defused, so who is going to believe this story?"

Phillips stared at the man. "Apparently you don't know what

happened not many years ago. One of our B-52 crews flew two live cruise missiles. There was no accident, but they got caught doing it. It was all a mistake, but it broke out in the press. I was just a rookie lawyer in Wichita at the time. I didn't know anything about this. But Nikolai Kozlov told me about it! He proposes the Russians use that incident as an excuse to lodge a protest against our *accident* last night. Says that'll give the story more credibility. I have to agree. What happened last night was an unfortunate accident by an unauthorized flight. We'll take heat for it, but hopefully, the press's interest in it will burn out."

"And the F-15?" the Air Force chief of staff asked.

"A mechanical problem," Phillips responded. "Happens all the time, doesn't it, General?"

"Did Mr. Kozlov provide any details regarding the attack plan?" continued the Air Force chief of staff. "I mean, did he give away anything of a specific nature that we might use to prevent such an attack in the future?"

"No," replied Phillips, "but I'm glad it was you who asked that question. I want to see, on my desk and in less than forty-eight hours, your personal explanation for why such an attack could take place and nearly succeed. I also want to see, in that same report, a master plan to guarantee that such an attack scenario in the future will be doomed to failure. Our basic assumptions regarding the ability to detect low-flying aircraft approaching our borders—especially our southern border—have been in error. Would you agree with that assessment, General?"

The general's head dipped. "Absolutely, sir."

"Nobody else has a question?" asked Phillips as he looked around the room. "Good. Now, here's what I'm ordering. We'll stand down to DEFCON 3 immediately. Kozlov was nervous about it, and I suspect he's having a hard time controlling his own military. The press is going to want to know why we started mobilizing. We'll tie it to the big Russian exercise. Tell them we didn't get the customary advanced notice, so our reaction was normal based on the lack of communication.

"Furthermore, tell them the crashed missile in Virginia was ours," he said, looking straight at the SecDef, "and that the decision to fly it was made by junior officers and is under review. No one is to be punished for this. I'm not going to make anyone a scapegoat.

"Since there are no representatives from the Department of Agriculture here, I'm charging the State Department with seeing to it that President Kozlov gets first priority on grain shipments. I also want the State Department to submit a resolution to the UN to remove the embargo against the sale of Russian oil worldwide." Phillips faced the secretary of state. "Any questions, Ward?"

The secretary shook his head.

"I have one, sir," said the secretary of defense. "What about the terrorist bomb threat? Did Kozlov talk about that?"

The president studied the SecDef's facial expression. "Are you thinking that was all part of Kozlov's scheme to distract us?"

The man nodded, as did several others.

"So do I," Phillips said. "And we took the bait. We had no choice. Kozlov admitted the devices never left the Middle East. I doubt they were ever there in the first place. But we will tell our press that the Russians found them. We have to give Kozlov his cover. Quite possibly everyone will be so relieved they won't pay much attention to the crashed missile. Let's hope."

Phillips paused to take another sip of water. "Now, many of our citizens have direct knowledge of the events of last evening. There are several FAA controllers, including our traitorous friend, Mr. Anderson, who knew that strange things were going on. I want a written pledge of silence from each of them. Regarding Mr. Anderson, in return for his silence, he'll be allowed to keep his job since he did, after all, act rather heroically." The president faced Darryl McCormick. "Miss McCormick, you'll see to it that our FAA friends at the Kansas City facility each pledge their cooperation."

"What about the military people involved?" the Naval chief asked.

"Yes. Thank you, Admiral. I'll want written pledges of silence from each of them. As for the pilots involved, I'll want written pledges of silence, but since they were there, and know for certain what they were dealing with, I'm willing to okay early promotions, choice of assignments, etc. Miss McCormick, I want you to be my direct representative to the F-15 pilot."

"Yes, sir!" McCormick was barely able to hold back a smile. She planned on having some fun with her new role as the president's personal representative to the world's greatest fighter pilot.

"Of course, I'll want written pledges of secrecy from each of you. Folks," the president continued, "I don't mind telling you that I've had the shit scared out of me. I'm convinced that it's only by the grace of God Almighty that we're sitting here now. It was His will that the Russian mission failed, and I believe it's His will that we now do what we've been discussing. Last night never happened."

Twenty minutes later, Frank Morgan walked out of the restroom, where Darryl McCormick waited for him in the hallway. The FBI director looked around, as if to verify they had the hallway to themselves. Then he leaned toward McCormick and began to talk in low tones.

"What do you think about the president's cover plan?"

"It's bullshit. It'll never hold up. Too many people know."

Morgan nodded in agreement. "So, I guess you'll be needing a plane?"

"Yes, sir. That's why I was waiting for you. I figure I'll go to Cheyenne tonight, and then go to Kansas City first thing in the morning."

"I'll arrange it." The director was silent a few moments. "On the record, do everything you can to support the president. Off the record, remember that Andrew Phillips won't always be president. With that in mind, I think you ought to make it, shall we say, your personal project to keep an eye on a certain . . . television evangelist."

Without another word, the FBI director turned and walked away. Dare McCormick stood where she was, shaking her head in amazement.

CHAPTER THIRTY-TWO

JANUARY 17: TWO DAYS AFTER LUCIFER/INBLUE
THE KREMLIN

Viktor Darginsky had been waiting to see the Russian president for more than twenty-four hours. The early morning flight from Havana to Moscow the previous day had left him dragging from jet lag, and the delay to see Kozlov made him so nervous that he got little sleep that night. The SVR agent expected Kozlov to be upset over the failure of LUCIFER/INBLUE, and he hadn't forgotten Kozlov's initial threat. Consequently, he could hardly believe his eyes when the leader of the Russian Federation walked into the outer office, saw him sitting there, and smiled.

"Viktor! Perfect timing! Come in. Sorry to keep you waiting a day, but the exercise debrief and defense council kept me busy until late yesterday."

Darginsky followed him into the inner office and watched as Kozlov poured them both a glass of vodka. "To success, at last," toasted the president.

"To success!" replied a confused Darginsky.

Kozlov started laughing. "Ah, Viktor, your loyalty is admirable, but aren't you curious what I'm celebrating?"

"I didn't know how to pose the question, sir. Considering the events of the last forty-eight hours, I hardly expected you to be happy. What's happened?"

"A phone call, Viktor. A simple phone call to that pompous Andrew

Phillips. A phone call, a mental chess game, and a victory that is more pleasing to me than the success of LUCIFER/INBLUE would have been."

Kozlov relayed the previous day's conversation with the American president. "I am confident we can make it through the winter and my government can survive. But our immediate actions during the next few days are critical. We must successfully cover up all vestiges of the LUCIFER/INBLUE failure if we are to guarantee our own survival."

"Absolutely, sir. I have already taken some steps. In addition, I have a plan of action that will require your approval."

"I'm listening."

"I talked to the two Sukhoi pilots. Everything on Route Bravo went according to plan until two minutes prior to launch. An F-15 appeared and threatened the mission. Apparently, it was a chance encounter. So, Ridgik and Bachvaroff destroyed the American fighter."

"Hmm. Phillips didn't mention that," mused Kozlov.

"Probably because they haven't figured it out yet. The Americans now have a surveillance aircraft watching every aircraft movement in Cuba and Central America. I directed Ridgik and Bachvaroff to return home by Aeroflot in a few days. I also directed that the Su-57 be disassembled and shipped back some weeks from now, when things have quieted down." Kozlov nodded his approval. "The bombers left their refueling base in Africa this morning. They should be arriving at Murmansk sometime this evening. I thought I would meet them and take whatever actions are necessary to ensure the crews don't talk."

"If they did their duty properly, consider some inducements to guarantee their silence. Early promotions and choice assignments should be sufficient." Kozlov paused as he remembered something. "I might have something special for the Su-57 crew. I'll have the Air Force chief call you today."

Both men were silent for a few moments. Finally, Kozlov asked the question Darginsky knew was coming. "What happened, Viktor? Why did LUCIFER/INBLUE fail?"

"Eduard Bolshov, my expert on the Kh-55M missile, will arrive from Caracas later this morning. I hope after I talk to him and Petrov's crew, I will know the answer to that question."

F.E. WARREN AIR FORCE BASE, WYOMING

A security policeman opened the door and a disheveled Darryl McCormick shuffled in. Mark Matthews couldn't help but chuckle.

She looked around the hospital room. "They told me the world's greatest fighter pilot was in here."

"If you don't mind my saying so, McCormick," said Matthews with a smirk, "you look like warmed-over shit."

McCormick made a pretense of searching her coat pocket. "I brought you something." She withdrew her hand with her middle finger sticking up. After checking her six she leaned over and kissed him. "For the record, I *feel* like warmed over shit."

Matthews laughed despite the pain in his sore ribs.

As she moved around the room checking for cameras and bugs, she asked, "So, how was *your* day?" not bothering to hide the sarcasm inherent in the question.

"Oh, as good as a battered and banged-up man can be, and who seems to be under arrest, and maybe under surveillance, but can't figure out what crime he's committed. How was yours?"

"Very interesting." McCormick pointed to the button near the pilot's pillow. "I'll tell you as much as I can, but first, I must have some coffee . . . and a sandwich, if you can get it."

Matthews punched the call button and ordered some food for both of them. Then he folded his arms behind his head and looked at McCormick expectantly. "Well? What's the story?"

McCormick couldn't resist a grin. "Do you want to hear the truth? Or do you want to hear 'the story'?"

Matthews returned the smile. "Everything considered, I'd like to hear both."

"I was afraid you were going to say that." The FBI agent dragged a chair over to the edge of Matthews's bed and sat down. She began to talk in low tones. "We've pieced together a rough picture of what happened, based on what you told me on the phone and what the air traffic controllers in Kansas City told me. The United States was attacked by Russia. It appears that three aircraft were involved, two bombers and the fighter that nailed you. We think the bombers departed from Venezuela and joined up with the fighter, which had departed from Cuba, over the Gulf of Mexico. They flew under the radar cover and entered US airspace around Bay St. Louis, Mississippi. One bomber flew northeast. We know one of its targets was Washington, DC. It apparently launched a cruise missile that was a dud."

"That's the missile they found in Virginia?" asked Matthews. "I saw it on the news."

"That's the one," confirmed McCormick. "Anyway, the other bomber came up this way. We're not certain what its targets were, but my guess is one of them was Offutt Air Force Base. The fighter apparently accompanied the Offutt-bound bomber. We know for a fact its target was the Airborne Command Post."

"How do you know that?"

"I can't answer that question, but I've paid a visit to the Kansas City Air Route Traffic Control Center." She leaned closer and whispered, "Trust me when I say we know that for a fact. So, you happened on the scene prior to the fighter leaving the bomber to attack the Airborne Command Post, which was only a hundred and fifty miles away. You were obviously a threat to the mission, so the Russian fighter eliminated you. My guess is when the missile targeted for Washington ended up a dud, the entire mission was aborted. Nobody did anything for almost an hour. It took your phone call to get some action, but by then it was too late to do much. The eastern bomber escaped unscathed. The western bomber was finally intercepted by an F-15 out of Eglin and—"

"Out of Eglin!" blurted Matthews. "That had to be my deployed squadron buddies. Do you remember who they were?" McCormick shook her head. "Where did the Russian fighter go after it splashed me?"

"We're not sure, but it appears it refueled at a Kansas private airstrip, took off, was tracked over Dallas, and then exited the country just south of New Orleans. More of our planes were scrambled but they didn't get an ID."

"On the one hand that's an unbelievable story. On the other, it's just too believable."

They were interrupted by the nurse bringing in the snacks. McCormick took her tray and gobbled down the food while Matthews sipped a soft drink.

"You said the Russian fighter refueled in Kansas?" asked Matthews. "That means there had to be inside help in the US. Have you pursued that?"

McCormick rolled her eyes. "I'm certain I know who's the main man, but I've been forbidden to pursue it."

"Bobby Chatman?"

She smiled. "No more talk about that. Now, to the main reason for my visit." McCormick reached for her briefcase. "President Phillips and President Kozlov talked on the hotline and have mutually agreed that public knowledge of the events two days ago could result in severe damage that might—are you ready for this?—threaten 'international stability and world peace.' They agreed that no knowledge of those events should ever leak out."

McCormick withdrew a piece of paper from the briefcase and continued. "The story is that the missile in Virginia was accidentally dropped by one of our bombers. Your F-15 experienced mechanical difficulties that resulted in an uncontrollable fire. The two events are unrelated. The proper agencies will release the story soon, but to guarantee its success, the president is 'requesting'"—she held up quote marks with her fingers—"that all parties involved sign a personal pledge, guaranteeing they'll never discuss what happened. In the president's own words, 'Last night never happened.' I need to get your signature, Mark."

Matthews took the piece of paper and studied it carefully. He then laid it down and folded his arms in defiance. "I'm not going to sign that. The American people have a right to know what happened. Otherwise, how do we guarantee it never happens again?"

"I agree with you in principle. Listen, Mark, the president is mad as hell. I'm authorized to offer you an immediate promotion to major, and your choice of assignments for the rest of your military career, including going back to active duty."

"Dare, you know I've put in my papers to get out. Going back now would be a sellout."

"How many times have I heard you talking about that? Of course, but this is a golden opportunity to—"

"To compromise my integrity!" interrupted Matthews. "Have you signed one of these yet?"

She sighed audibly. "Not yet."

"Why the hell not?"

McCormick grinned. "Principles."

"Well, here, here!" mocked Matthews as he clapped his hands.

The two stared silently at each other. "Mark, it's too big, and we're too small." She reached over the fighter pilot and grabbed the sheet of paper he had cast aside, then took out her pen and scribbled her signature on the appropriate line. "I have no choice but to sign, and you don't either," said the tired FBI agent as her eyes met his. "So don't give me any shit, okay?"

Matthews took one of the forms, hesitated, then signed his name. "This is against my better judgment, but I guess you're right."

"So, do you want that promotion to major?" asked McCormick as she took the pilot's hand in hers and gave it a gentle squeeze.

"Let me sleep on it. What about you? Are you in the FBI to stay?"

"Yeah, I like it too much to leave," admitted McCormick. "Besides, you know that 'main man' I mentioned? I'm going to nail him. It may take me the rest of my life, but somehow, I'm going to get him."

Matthews smiled. "You still look like shit. Go get some sleep and you'll look like your usual gorgeous self."

MURMANSK AIR BASE COMPLEX, RUSSIA

Gregori Petrov awoke from a troubled nap to the howl of the cold arctic wind outside the window of the minimum-security barracks. He was almost home. Olya and Stefan were only a few kilometers away in their apartment, and he hoped he'd be reunited with them today.

The Russian pilot felt totally exhausted. They had flown to Angola, rested for little more than a day, and then continued to Murmansk with only a single refueling stop at Sevastopol on the shores of the Black Sea.

Petrov felt he'd spent an entire month in an airplane during the last seventy-two hours. His body didn't know if it was time to eat or sleep. He nursed a persistent headache and had the first signs of a head cold.

However, Viktor Darginsky was the real source of the pilot's misery. The SVR agent had been waiting with armed guards and a crew bus when their Tu-95 arrived in Murmansk. The entire crew was ordered onto the bus, transported to the barracks, and locked in separate rooms. Petrov was growing impatient. He wanted to go home.

The sound of a key unlocking his barrack door interrupted his thoughts. The door swung open, and he saw Darginsky framed in the dim hallway light.

"Greetings, Gregori," said the SVR agent affably. "I'm sorry to have kept you waiting. I trust you're doing well?"

"I'm tired, hungry, and pissed," said the Russian pilot. "But other than that, I'm doing well."

"Hungry too? You mean they haven't given you anything to eat?"

"You forget, Viktor, the food I've been enjoying the last few weeks."

Darginsky chuckled sympathetically. "I completely understand. I suppose you have a right to feel all those things. You didn't ask how I'm doing, but I'm going to tell you anyway. I'm disappointed. We came too far to fail in the last seconds. I want to know exactly what happened. That's the reason for the . . . detention."

As Petrov slumped into the only chair in the room, Darginsky paced. The metallic clicking of his heels reminded Petrov of that night when the SVR bastard left him no choice but to fly the mission.

"Gregori, I think you understand that my initial reaction was to come after you. I don't mind telling you that, if you had sabotaged this mission, I would have personally seen to your execution. But, alas, it seems that you performed admirably. At least that's the report from everybody on your aircraft, including Major Czinkota, whom I charged with keeping an eye on you."

"Itzkoff says the cruise missile was a dud," Petrov interjected. "Something about the master start-relay. He said they had been notified of the potential problem just before they left for Venezuela."

"That would, indeed, seem to be the reason for the failure," agreed Darginsky. "Unfortunately, the missile expert who was working for me left for Venezuela before the advisory bulletin was distributed." The SVR agent shrugged. "What can I say? The war in Ukraine proved our weapons were unreliable. We build poor-quality refrigerators and televisions, and cannot even produce a decent ballpoint pen! Gregori, in your time in the US, did you ever see a product that was stamped 'Made in Russia'?" Petrov considered this.

Darginsky threw up his hands. "So, why should we be surprised that we build 'dud' cruise missiles? That's why Kozlov wanted to merge the two mightiest nations on the planet. Gregori, you've been to America. You know the truth when it comes to their system versus ours. We're talking a new world order!"

"We're talking the loss of many thousands of innocent people, dammit!" Petrov shouted angrily. "If you want to know the truth, I'm glad I don't have to bear the burden of being the triggerman on such devastation the rest of my life!" Darginsky stopped his pacing and glared at the pilot. "So, what happens now?" Petrov asked dejectedly.

"Without going into details, let's just say Kozlov and the American president have made a deal—a deal which should ensure that both governments are not affected by these events."

"It has to be an enormous effort to cover the entire thing up."

"Correct," nodded Darginsky. "But in order for that to happen—"

"You need agreements from everybody involved to remain silent. As Kozlov said at the dacha, 'the mission never happened.'"

"Precisely," confirmed the SVR agent. "We could, of course, use some of the older methods to guarantee the silence of the parties involved."

"Executions."

"Well . . . yes. But since we're talking about a rather large number of people, who did perform as expected, we prefer to use—"

"Bribery."

Darginsky couldn't help but smile. "Such strong words, Gregori, with such negative implications. I prefer to think in terms of, let's say, inducements. I'm willing to offer you certain inducements to remain silent."

"Since I'm the last, I assume, to be interrogated—"

"Interviewed!"

"Whatever. Since I'm the last to be 'interviewed,' tell me about some of the inducements you've offered the other members of the mission."

"Fair enough," said Darginsky agreeably, as he opened his briefcase. "Let's see. Captain Sheptak requested an upgrade to the left seat of the Tu-95 without having to go back to the alert pad. He will also be promoted to major. Major Czinkota requested a transfer as an instructor to Dyagilevo Air Base. He says he wants to live closer to Moscow where there's some nightlife. Lieutenant Orshansky wants an assignment near either Moscow or St. Petersburg." The SVR agent smiled. "He says he wants a greater number of 'tatas' to choose from. Misha Grotsky has requested further education leading to Officer Training School and a commission." Darginsky closed the briefcase and folded his arms. "So, Gregori, it's your turn."

"What about Arkady?" asked the bomber pilot.

"Lieutenant Itzkoff will never be allowed to fly in the Russian Air Force again," replied the SVR agent seriously. "He has asked to be discharged. I'm willing to allow his discharge under honorable conditions."

"You can mark that down as my first 'inducement,'" said Petrov.

Darginsky shrugged. "What else?"

The pilot wasn't sure what price the government was willing to pay for his silence. He'd been thinking about it during the entire trip back.

"I want to go back to America with my family to stay permanently."

Astounded, Darginsky responded, "You have to be kidding!"

"You asked me what I wanted, and I've told you. Can you deliver?"

"Deliver, Gregori?" mocked the agent. "I could 'deliver' you and your family to virtually any spot in the world within the next twenty-four hours." He shrugged, then shook his head. "But it would only defeat the purpose."

"I don't understand."

"Gregori, to be absolutely certain everyone involved remains silent for the rest of their lives, we have to be sure we retain some degree of control."

The SVR agent tore a scrap of paper from a notepad in his briefcase. He scribbled some numbers. "You know, Gregori. I like you. So, you went to America and fell in love with it and now you want to go back. I've spent a lot of time there, so I can certainly understand. Therefore, I'm willing to make you a deal." He handed the paper scrap to the pilot. "That's a phone number and a code you can use to reach me anytime. Give it a month or two, and if you still want to go to America, call me. I can have you out of the Motherland within twenty-four hours of the call."

Petrov couldn't believe his ears. "You mean just like that? My family and I can leave?"

"I didn't say anything about your family, Gregori. No, I'm afraid taking them would be out of the question. With you in America, and the two of them here—"

"You'd still have control," interrupted the dejected pilot.

Darginsky shrugged. "I know it'll be a tough decision. Speaking of decisions, I need to know whether you really intend to leave the Russian Air Force."

"Yes, I would like to resign my commission as soon as possible."

"No problem," said Darginsky. "Anything else?"

"Yes. Flying is my life. I would like to continue to do that in some capacity."

"Would a position with Aeroflot suit you?"

"Could you guarantee a captain's billet in heavy jet equipment and a home base in a city with a warmer climate?"

"Sure," replied Darginsky. "Is that it?"

"Yes," said Petrov glumly.

The SVR agent closed his briefcase and started for the door. "Gregori, it's been a pleasure working with you. It was a good plan."

"May I ask about Ridgik and Bachvaroff before you go?"

Darginsky smiled. "It seems our fighter crew is in high demand. I got a call today from the Air Force chief. The Chinese are just starting to ramp up production of their J-20S two-seat 'Mighty Dragon,' which bears some similar characteristics to our Su-57. Since Ridgik and Bachvaroff are the only experienced pilots in two-seat stealth operations, they've been asked to go to Chengdu for an airshow flight display. We are hoping they will be asked to stay for flight testing and crew training of their new J-20S. Think about how much we will learn."

"They are the best. The Chinese would be lucky to get them. And what about Piekarski?" asked Petrov.

"Why, he gets a promotion, of course," replied Darginsky. "It'll soon be Major General Piekarski. What is it the Americans say? Fuck up and move up? The main benefit is that he'll never fly again. I think you'll agree that's a positive accomplishment . . . Oh! Did you hear he shit his pants when that F-15 hot-nosed him?"

Petrov's face broke into a grin. "No! You're kidding!"

Darginsky nodded vigorously, grinning back. Then they both broke into wild cackles.

When Darginsky regained his breath, he offered his hand to the bomber pilot. "See you, Gregori. Call me if you decide you want to leave the Motherland."

The door opened, Darginsky nodded, then was gone.

As the cold arctic wind blew new snowflakes against the frost-covered windowpanes of their on-base apartment, Gregori Petrov, with Olya now asleep beside him, watched the shadows dance across the walls and ceiling as the candle on the nightstand burned low. It had been a fantastic homecoming. Someone had called to let his wife know he'd soon be home, and Olya had prepared all her husband's favorite dishes for supper. Stefan, who had grown at least four centimeters in the ten weeks he had been gone, whooped with delight when his father walked in the door. Petrov couldn't help but smile when the boy-becoming-a-man awkwardly held out his hand for a handshake and then, with tears in his eyes, came into his arms. "I missed you so much, Papa," the boy said, his voice cracking.

"Not as much as I missed you," Petrov replied.

Supper was a nonstop talkathon with Olya and Stefan constantly interrupting each other to bring him up on the latest happenings in their lives.

Petrov waited until supper was done and the talk had slowed to a trickle before he told them he had traveled to several new countries, and that he'd learned a lot during his travels. Finally, he unwrapped the three gold coins and presented one each to his wife and son. There were questions about how he had gotten his hands on US coins, but Petrov merely commented about bargains in some underdeveloped country. The coins were an instant hit with Olya and Stefan. They left the table to put them with their most prized possessions.

Petrov decided to wait until his orders came down to tell Olya about his decision to leave the Air Force. He didn't want her to associate that decision with his recent activities. He knew that would only lead to more questions, and he was determined to protect his family by living up to his agreement to remain silent.

Stefan fell asleep with his head on his father's shoulder. After escorting him to his own bedroom, Petrov and Olya celebrated his homecoming in their own private way. Now, Olya was asleep, but Petrov kept thinking about the events of the past several weeks.

He had known all along what his decision would eventually be, and once he had made it, he knew it was important to do something symbolic to commit himself to it. He eased quietly out of bed, then padded to the closet and rummaged through his flight suit pockets until he found what he was looking for.

He held the scrap of paper with the phone number and code on it to the candle, where it flared briefly in flame, and, in a matter of seconds, disintegrated into a small pile of ashes. Petrov let out a long sigh, then blew out the candle and slipped under the covers. *It's really good to be home*, he thought as he cuddled up next to his wife. In a matter of seconds, the exhausted Russian pilot was fast asleep.

OLATHE, KANSAS

Agent Darryl McCormick greeted Keith Anderson and his lawyer. "Nice to see you both again," she began. "Much has happened since we talked last. Mr. Anderson, it's the president's desire to operate as if none of the events of January 15 ever occurred. In return for your silence, he has agreed not to charge you with espionage, and you can keep your job. Furthermore, the state of Missouri will never find out that you had sex with an underage person." She paused, added, "If they do, we'll take care of it."

Keith felt enormously relieved as he closed his eyes and let out a deep breath.

"Do you accept these terms?" McCormick pressed. Keith looked at the lawyer. "I'll leave the room so you two can talk," McCormick continued, rising from her chair.

"Wait!" Keith said, looking again at the lawyer.

"It's far better than I expected, Keith," the man offered.

"Stay, please," Keith said. "Yes, I accept those terms. So, what happens now?"

"You're free to go. You need to sign this nondisclosure, then I need to talk to your boss and Miss Brady next. Mr. Jenkins told me if I could make you available, he could really use you today."

After leaving Keith Anderson's workplace, McCormick hurried to her hotel room. "Move your ass or you'll miss it," she muttered as she hung up her coat, then grabbed the remote control for the television. She focused on Ron Goodman as the reporter began to speak.

> "In news from Washington tonight, the Phillips administration finally cleared up the mystery surrounding the crash of a missile-like vehicle on the shores of Buggs Island Lake, Virginia. In a brief statement, Air Combat Command admitted that the vehicle was an Air Force AGM-86B cruise missile that had fallen from a B-52 bomber during a routine training flight involving the simulated launch of actual nuclear-loaded aircraft. Both the administration and the Air Force refused further comment on the incident, but they admitted the warhead had cracked open on impact, resulting in the release of a small amount of radioactivity.
>
> The Russian government, in a tersely worded statement, blasted the Buggs Island Lake incident. According to the Russian News Agency, 'carriage of live nuclear weapons during peacetime is an accident waiting for a time and place to happen.'
>
> Also, from Russia comes welcome words regarding the missing 'suitcase' bombs. According to the Russian News Agency, Russian

intelligence operatives have located and removed the missing devices from the Middle East. The US immediately called off the search for the weapons here in the States, and an elated Andrew Phillips announced that, in the spirit of cooperation, he has decided to change his previous position and is now willing to sell Russia as much American grain as they'd like to buy. Furthermore, the president pledged to lift all sanctions and embargoes on Russian oil and gas."

As McCormick finished some paperwork and placed it in her briefcase, she happened to glance up in time to catch the image of Bobby Chatman on the television. The FBI agent sat mesmerized as the television evangelist spoke with tears rolling down his cheeks.

"I was startled by what I learned in Washington today. It seems that agents of a foreign power have been using my ministry, and our Red Star Express project in particular, to further their own goals. Needless to say, I am shocked and saddened. We will still be coming to you here on the Free World Gospel Hour Network, and we will still be standing behind our brother, Andrew Phillips, but our primary focus going forward will be on our people, here in Raleigh. As we make these changes, we solicit your prayers for God's guidance . . . that His will be done. Thank you, and good night."

As Chatman's face faded from view, he was wearing that pompous smirk of self-righteousness that Darryl McCormick so intensely hated. Ron Goodman's face appeared in its place.

"That announcement aired just moments ago on the Free World Gospel Hour Network. No comment yet from the Phillips administration. That's it from Washington. This is Ron Goodman reporting."

Keith Anderson felt as if he'd been granted a new life as he drove home after his shift. His smile faded when he saw lights on in his house. Entering through the door in the kitchen, he was startled by the sound of feet sliding on vinyl as a medium-sized black and white ball of fur scrambled up to him and slid to a stop at his feet, tail wagging and big eyes sizing Keith up. Both stunned and delighted, Keith stooped and smoothed the puppy's ears back, just as he had done Lucy's a thousand times. He stood, looking around the room, and spotted an envelope on the counter. He looked around, then opened it.

> *In my country the Siberian husky is known for his strength and endurance. He is also praised for his loyalty. A man is considered privileged to own one. I figured I owed you this. In case you're worried about hearing from me again, don't be. I'm on my way home. I envy you, American!*
> *Michael*

CHAPTER THIRTY-THREE

SIX MONTHS AFTER LUCIFER/INBLUE
NEW YORK CITY

Katarina Feskanich was worried. Ever since the LUCIFER/INBLUE failure six months ago, her life at the SVR in New York City had been turned upside down. She hadn't been a part of the plan except to find a compromisable person. But she hadn't survived this long in the brutal world of Russian intelligence by ignoring the signals surrounding her.

She knew from the American news media that something of a subversive nature had happened. But her worry began when she found out about the death of the young New York hustler, Shawn Cochran, whom she had recruited two years ago. That, and the firebombing of the hotel in Kansas City, convinced Feskanich that her boss, Viktor Darginsky, was getting rid of anyone who could tie the SVR or the Russian government to what happened the night of President Phillips's speech.

She knew it was only a matter of time before someone came for her. Immediately after January 15, she was moved to a small internal cubicle within the New York SVR complex and given relatively unimportant assignments. She also began to suspect that she was being followed when not at work. That didn't bother her at first, but when one of her young lovers told her about being followed to and from her apartment, she started to pay more attention.

Feskanich was scheduled to return to Russia in the new year.

That's not what she wanted, as she had grown fond of the freedom she enjoyed in America. So, she began to seriously ponder how to survive and stay in the US.

Recently, she'd overheard Darginsky talking on the phone to someone, and her spyful curiosity drew her attention when she heard the words "Bobby," "ministry," and "Redex." It was obvious who the boss was talking to. The Good Reverend Bobby Chatman was something more than just a television evangelist. She began finding out more about Chatman's relationship with the SVR, even though it was risky to snoop. When she came across some documents that referenced Chatman, she knew she had found the winning lottery ticket. That's why she was now standing on the curb in front of the FBI office at 26 Federal Plaza in Manhattan. Katarina Feskanich had something to trade.

FBI HEADQUARTERS
WASHINGTON, DC

Darryl McCormick approached the office of the FBI director. She didn't have to wait long before the secretary's intercom buzzed and Dare was escorted into Frank Morgan's inner sanctum. The director greeted McCormick with a poker face and offered her a seat.

"Good morning, sir. I wasn't expecting the call from your office. What's going on?"

"Darryl, I got a call this week from our New York office. It seems an SVR agent, one Katarina Feskanich, waltzed in two days ago and offered some very interesting information in exchange for asylum."

Something in Morgan's expression excited McCormick. "What did Miss Feskanich offer?"

"Remember our good friend Bobby Chatman? It seems he's been working for the SVR for the last twenty years. Agent Feskanich made copies of some documents she found, and we verified the movements of Chatman and the SVR chief, Viktor Darginsky. Seems they had several clandestine meetings, especially during the months leading up to the president's State of the Union address."

"Well, I'll be damned," McCormick said with a grin of satisfaction. "You know I always suspected him of being a phony."

"Yes, I know you did. We did some fact-checking before I approached the president with the evidence this morning. That's what it took to finally convince him. We've been given permission to pick up Chatman and bring him back to DC. I figured you'd like to do the honors."

"Director, it would please me immensely to invite the reverend to join me on a trip. Thank you. Do we know where he is today?"

"We do. He's at his North Carolina ranch. I have a jet and several agents, including Agent Richardson, standing by at Andrews. I'd like you to go straight to the airport and snatch that slippery fish before he swims away."

"With pleasure, sir!"

HENDERSON, NORTH CAROLINA

Bobby Chatman had just finished breakfast and was reviewing his schedule for the day. Ever since the failure of LUCIFER/INBLUE, he'd been focused on his ministry, except for occasional trips to Washington, DC, when Andrew Phillips requested his presence. He was confident his cover was secure, as there'd been no further questioning about his former pilots or his Redex operation.

His cell phone rang. "Hello?"

"Bobby, do you recognize my voice?" asked Darginsky.

"Yes, of course. It's been a while. What's going on?" Chatman asked.

"Bobby, we had an agent give herself up to the FBI a couple of days ago. She somehow got hold of some documents with your name mentioned. The FBI did some cross-checking and they're going to arrest you today. I have a mole in FBI headquarters. It's time for you to return to the Motherland."

It took a minute for Chatman to respond as a hundred thoughts raced through his brain. "Viktor, thank you for letting me know. I'd better get out of here quick. I'll call you from Venezuela tonight."

Chatman didn't need to take much with him. He always had a small suitcase packed for last-minute trips. He opened his safe, removing his passport and the cash he kept there for just such an eventuality. Then he left the house and walked briskly to the hangar.

A Gulfstream G550 in plain white paint bobbed to a halt at Bobby Chatman's airfield near Henderson, North Carolina. Its engines were still winding down when the entrance door opened and half a dozen men and women in plain clothes hurried down the steps and fanned out.

Agents McCormick and Richardson trotted to the airport office and found the door locked. An elderly man appeared from around back and startled the agents. His eyes grew big as they reached for their side arms. The frightened man said he worked for the ranch and had come to fetch the reverend's car and take it back to the house.

"Where's the reverend?" McCormick commanded.

"Ma'am, I don't know. He comes and goes in that little jet of his all the time. He just left about an hour and a half ago."

The man gave her the keys to the house and hangar. While the team searched the structures, McCormick had a sudden thought. She immediately called Hank Hartley at the CIA. "Hank, we came down to North Carolina to arrest Bobby Chatman, but he's not here. An employee said he took off ninety minutes ago. He doesn't know where Chatman's going." She saw Richardson emerging from the hangar shaking his head. "His Citation is gone. Dammit! He's been tipped off. Can you track him for me?"

"No problem," Hartley responded. "Give me a minute."

In a few minutes Hartley called back. "Dare, he's headed south. His flight plan lists Caracas as the destination."

McCormick's mind raced. "He'll go over or near Cuba, right?"

"I'll have to ask the FAA, but I think so." Hartley waited for a response. "Dare, are you there?"

"Yeah, yeah. I've got an idea. Why don't you contact your counterparts in Havana and make a deal? Tell them to intercept him and take him into custody. Say he's a fugitive from justice—which he is—and offer them something in return."

"Dare, I have to go through Director Mims, and he'll go to POTUS, and he'll give it to State, and Chatman will be passing the tip of Cuba in an hour."

"*Do it now, Hank!*" she shouted. "I don't care how you do it. You're the CIA, for Christ's sake! You must have contacts down there. Maybe if you tell them this is one of the guys responsible for the nuclear terrorist threat, they'll be motivated to force him to land in Havana. Work out an extradition or prisoner swap. Lie to them. Whatever. And if he refuses to land, tell them to shoot the bastard down!"

"Goddammit, McCormick. You're gonna get us both fired!" Hartley groused. "Okay, let me see if I can cash in some favors."

N2207 XRAY
OVER EASTERN CUBA

Bobby Chatman was alone in the cockpit of November 2207 Xray, at thirty-nine thousand feet, just passing the VOR station at Santiago de Cuba in eastern Cuba. He'd been extremely nervous until he was airborne from the Henderson farm, and he didn't truly relax until he'd left US airspace.

His thoughts were interrupted by the radio. "Citation zero-seven Xray, Havana."

"Havana, zero-seven Xray, go ahead," responded Chatman.

"Zero-seven Xray, you are being intercepted by two Cuban Air Force fighter aircraft. They are approaching you from your five o'clock position, one mile. You are to comply with their instructions. They will escort you to Havana, where you will land."

"Havana! No. My destination is Caracas. I filed the proper Cuban overflight and paid the fee. What seems to be the problem?"

"Zero-seven Xray, Havana. I've been directed to coordinate your intercept and landing at José Martí International Airport. That's all I know. The fighters should be coming up beside you now."

Chatman was stunned. Had the Americans called Havana? Were the Cubans going to hand him over?

As the minister looked out his left cockpit window, a MiG-29 in Cuban Air Force markings slid up abeam him and held position just a few hundred feet away. Then the fighter started a slow, level turn to the left. Chatman knew that was the signal for him to follow. *No way I'm going to land in Havana and get extradited!* Instead, Chatman disconnected the autopilot. *If I can get down to the wave tops, maybe they won't be able to follow me.*

As the lead fighter broke away, Chatman rolled, dropped his nose, closed his throttles, and opened the speed brakes. The high descent rate and noise of the rushing wind made him think he just might pull off his escape.

But he forgot about the wingman.

Chatman's hope of escape was instantly shattered as a swarm of 30mm rounds slammed into his rear fuselage. The cabin filled with smoke and vapor as it rapidly depressurized. Both engines suddenly disintegrated. Chatman tried to regain level flight, but with the elevator jammed in the forward position, he was helpless. His life didn't flash before him like in the movies, but he cursed himself for not leaving the US when he'd had the chance months ago. Before the ocean brought oblivion, Bobby Chatman's final thoughts flashed through his mind. *So this is how it ends. I'm sorry, Papa. I'm sorry, brother. I tried to avenge you. I really tried!*

THE WHITE HOUSE

An exhausted President Phillips walked into his bedroom suite and began unbuttoning his shirt. He heard his wife crying in the sitting room. "Oh, Andrew! Come look!"

As he stepped into the sitting room, he recognized Ron Goodman's voice on the TV. He put his arm around his wife's shoulder. "I'm sorry, Ann. I should have come up sooner. I didn't want you to hear about it this way."

> "... *The crash reportedly happened in the eastern Gulf of Mexico. Cuban naval authorities have found some floating debris that included a cushion with Mr. Chatman's ministry logo embroidered on it. There is no indication yet as to the cause of the crash, but Cuban authorities reported a Mayday call from Mr. Chatman and a mention from him of mechanical difficulties. President Phillips is expected to address the nation tomorrow morning lamenting the loss of his dear friend and spiritual adviser. And that's all for tonight. Ron Goodman reporting from Washington.*"

EPILOGUE

ONE YEAR AFTER LUCIFER/INBLUE
ALONG THE FLORIDA PANHANDLE

Mark Matthews was thoroughly enjoying himself. A cold front had pushed through the day before, leaving crystal-blue skies dotted with scattered cumulus clouds, and the Glasair "mini fighter," as he called it, was responding to his every whim.

"Okay, nose coming up, rolling now to ninety degrees of bank, and nose is coming down," said the fighter pilot. "Wings nice and level. We're lined up on the beach. There's one hundred eighty knots . . . one hundred ninety . . . two hundred . . . ready. And nose is coming up. Hold it, now pull hard, and . . . hold it, hard again, and . . . hold it . . . one more time . . . and there it is, a square loop!"

"Easy does it, big boy! You do that again and you'll be cleaning it up!" said Darryl McCormick from the right seat.

Matthews winked at his passenger.

Between maneuvers Matthews gazed down at the Florida coastline and marveled over how well things had turned out. His leg had healed with no complications. And he was seeing a lot more of Dare since she was promoted to assistant director in charge of the New Orleans Field Office, a reward for her handling of the bomb scare a year ago.

He smiled, remembering the day he hobbled into the squadron on crutches for the first time since returning from Wyoming. All his friends were waiting for him, including Tom Rushton.

Everyone had wanted to hear his story that day, but he knew

he couldn't tell them what really happened. Rushton finally pulled Matthews into one of the empty briefing rooms.

"Suds, did you happen to notice who wasn't here to greet you today?" he'd said.

"No, unless you're talking about my *good* friend Major Robertson."

"Do I detect a note of sarcasm?" Ruston asked, grinning. Matthews shrugged and nodded. "You know about Robertson bugging out on the intercept of that Bear? He was leading me in the two-ship that intercepted the bomber when he aborted after supposedly being struck by lightning. Maintenance couldn't find anything wrong with the aircraft when he returned to base."

Matthews grinned. "Are you kidding me? Robertson led that scramble? Well, that doesn't surprise me, and it is poetic justice."

"That didn't surprise us either, but it didn't go over well with Air National Guard headquarters. He's being transferred to a desk at state headquarters."

"So, who actually completed the intercept?"

Rush had given Matthews a wolfish grin. "Well, it was yours truly!"

Mark Matthews smiled and slowly shook his head, remembering that conversation as he performed a clearing turn prior to his next maneuver.

"Okay, the entry speed's there, nose is coming up, and . . . hold it. Now roll until the wings parallel the beach . . . right there! One hundred forty knots . . . one hundred twenty . . . one hundred. Let's make the hammerhead look good. Ready . . . now!"

Darryl laughed on the intercom, "Oh shit. Here we go again!"

Matthews had really lucked out on the Glasair. The three-quarters completed kit was advertised as a "must sell due to divorce" item, the workmanship was superb, and the price was right.

Shortly after his encounter over Nebraska, he'd been asked to report to his unit's headquarters. The wing commander was puzzled about the letter he'd received from the Department of the Air Force, but he knew better than to ask questions. Matthews had received an invitation to return to active duty with the 33rd Fighter Wing at Eglin Air Force Base in the Florida panhandle. If he was willing to accept the assignment, the Air Force would promote him to major immediately and give him a slot in the next F-35 Lightning II training class.

As if things couldn't get any more exciting, Matthews had been told he would be placed on a short list for an instructor pilot exchange tour with Singapore and other Asian partner nations that were scheduled to get F-35s.

He forced his mind back to the present as the Glasair accelerated for the next maneuver. "Out the bottom of the hammerhead and we're paralleling the beach again with the speed coming up. A hundred eighty knots . . . one hundred ninety . . . and what's this? An unsuspecting enemy Navy T-6 trainer twelve o'clock high. He obviously doesn't see me. Let him go over, and ready . . . pull. Keep him in sight in the canopy, gun selected on the thumb switch, coming through the horizon, put the imaginary pipper square on him . . . hold it . . . trigger's down, and GUNS, GUNS, GUNS on the Navy T-6 headed west along the beach. An inverted gunshot!"

"Nice shooting, cowboy!" exclaimed Dare.

The T-6 continued on its merry way, its occupants unaware they had been chalked up as a "kill." As Matthews rolled the Glasair upright and headed toward his home airport in Destin, Florida, he grinned at the thought of putting a T-6 profile decal on the side of Glasair N5713L, his magnificent little personal fighter.

That evening, as Dare was choosing a movie to watch, he brought drinks and popcorn in and set them on the coffee table. He snuggled in beside her and asked, "Can the world's greatest fighter pilot sit here?"

She looked around the room, then gave him a devilish smile. "When is he arriving?"

As the movie played, his thoughts returned to his pending instructor assignment in Asia. Since getting his new job, Matthews had been studying up on the coming challenges. He knew he was about to become part of a complex and volatile theater of operation.

The threats to Taiwan, the Philippines, and others had only gotten bigger with China acting like a schoolyard bully in the South China Sea. Matthews promised himself that, next time, he would be flying a bird armed and ready for whatever may come.

END

www.ingramcontent.com/pod-product-compliance
Lightning Source LLC
LaVergne TN
LVHW091702070526
838199LV00050B/2258